Sexual Hunger

Books by Melissa MacNeal

ALL NIGHT LONG

HOT FOR IT

SEXUAL SECRETS

SEXUAL HUNGER

THE HAREM
(with Celia May Hart, Emma Leigh, and Noelle Mack)

NAUGHTY, NAUGHTY
(with P. J. Mellor and Valerie Martinez)

UNWRAP ME
(with Susan Lyons and Melissa Randall)

TEMPTED BY A COWBOY
(with Delilah Devlin and Vonna Harper)

THE PLEASURE OF HIS BED
(with Donna Grant and Annalise Russell)

ONLY WITH A COWBOY
(with P. J. Mellor and Vonna Harper)

Published by Kensington Publishing Corporation

Sexual Hunger

MELISSA MacNEAL

APHRODISIA

KENSINGTON BOOKS

http://www.kensingtonbooks.com

APHRODISIA BOOKS are published by

Kensington Publishing Corp.
119 West 40th Street
New York, NY 10018

ISBN-13: 978-0-7582-3450-6
ISBN-10: 0-7582-3450-3

First Kensington Trade Paperback Printing: November 2010

10 9 8 7 6 5 4 3 2 1

Printed in the United States of America

1

London, 1899

"I foresee sexual ecstasy and joy juxtaposed with excruciating pain," Rubio whispered as he studied the tarot cards on the table. "Deception, yet revelation . . . a journey into the unknown. Loss of love and life as you now know it, dear sister."

As her younger brother tightened his hold on her hands, Maria Palladino turned away with a puzzled frown. "How can you predict such nonsense? Jason Darington's the man of my dreams, and tomorrow when I marry him—"

"Have I ever deceived you, Maria? Knowingly led you astray with my abilities?"

Maria paused, unconvinced. "If you made such grim predictions for members of Queen Victoria's court, you'd not remain London's most celebrated medium for long!" She widened her eyes at Rubio. "Mama didn't tell you to say that, did she? While we loved her dearly, she never drew a happy breath her whole life. I refuse to believe in gloom and doom, the way she did!"

Her brother shook his head poignantly. "I received her gift of second sight, yes, but not her eternal sense of darkness or damnation." His shoulder-length hair fell in artful disarray around his striking face, framing the relentless brown eyes that had captured many a lady's fancy at his séance table. The reds and purples in his flowing paisley shirt seemed to glow with his rising agitation. "While I agree that the future Lord Darington is indeed the perfect match for you, I sense trouble . . . a separation that will tear at your sweet, loving soul. Disparaging remarks and damage to your reputation, through no fault of your own."

"And what do you mean by *that*?" she demanded. "I see nothing of the sort in these cards! I have better things to do than—"

"I only reveal what my guides tell me, and for your benefit, Maria. Forewarned is forearmed, you know." His eyebrows rose expressively as another idea occurred to him. "And what happens with Jude when you become his brother's wife? You can't turn the poor man's affections off as though he had a spigot."

Maria's cheeks prickled with heat. "And why is that *your* business, little brother?"

"Because no matter whom you marry, you will always be my sister. I will always watch out for you, even though—"

"I hate it when you use your powers to spy on me!" She rose from her chair and swept her brother's tarot spread from the table. The rest of his well-worn deck scattered on the floor, save one card that fluttered to the toe of her kid slipper.

Rubio's dark brows peaked. "The Tower. Harbinger of sudden surprises. Bolts out of the blue." He stood beside her, entreating her with his troubled gaze. "I meant no harm, Maria, and you know it! I shall escort you home, in case—"

"You'll do no such thing!"

"—evil lurks between my door and yours."

Maria grabbed his head between her hands, gazing pointedly into his hot-coffee eyes. "The only *evil* here lurks in your imagination, Rubio! Your dire predictions will *not* spoil my wedding tomorrow!" She left his studio with a swish of her skirts, driven by a sudden urge to be on her way—away from the brother whose pronouncements often struck too close to the truth.

And that's what bothers you, isn't it?

As Maria stepped from Rubio's dim reception parlor into the light of the early summer day, she regretted her brusque tone, the way she'd mocked his efforts to protect her. Damn it all, he was too often accurate in what he foresaw, and on this day before her glorious wedding she wanted *nothing* to come between her and the happiness she'd awaited so long. She was nearly thirty. It was high time she walked down the aisle. And Rubio's talk of excruciating pain—loss of love, and deception— well, she could not allow such predictions to block her path to happiness!

As she approached the post office, Maria glanced about at the passersby. She entered the building with a secretive smile and walked to the back of the stuffy lobby area, toward the larger commercial boxes along the wall. Seeing no one, she stood in front of number 111 and then twisted the knob to the right . . . the left . . . the right. Without stopping to read the ad-dresses, Maria slipped the week's letters into pockets secreted in the side seams of her belled skirt. Moments later she strode down the sidewalk again, her mission nearly accomplished.

And how will you keep your sideline a secret, once you be-come Mrs. Darington? What if those blasted servants snoop in your trunks and armoire drawers before you can dispose of—

"Miss Palladino! How fortunate that I happened by!"

Maria nearly ran into the slender fellow who had stepped into her path while she was lost in thought. And why was the butler from the Daringtons' town house gazing at her as though he could see through her clothing? Just at the moment she'd been thinking about servants? "Ah, yes—Quentin!" she stammered. "I was attending to a few last details before the wedding!"

"A lovely day for it, too. At your service, dear lady." He bowed before offering her an elbow. Although he looked excruciatingly proper in his dark frock coat and fresh white shirt, McCallum's hooded eyes gave him a furtive air. "If you're returning home, it would be my pleasure to escort you."

She'd met him just two days ago, when she'd moved her belongings from her apartment, and she was *not* fond of answering to anyone about her comings and goings! Experience told her this man could not possibly detect the stash of letters beneath her worsted skirt, yet he seemed so *intent* on accompanying her. "Thank you, Quentin, but that won't be necessary! I would hate to detain you from—"

"Not at all, Miss Palladino. Were your groom to learn I'd let his beloved walk these streets alone, I'd be out of a job! And rightly so, don't you think?"

How could she answer that? He was correct, damn it, but she was tired of the men in her life always being right! "Your secret would be safe with me."

Wrong thing to say!

Quentin's sideburns shifted with his smile, suggesting he knew too much already. "Very kind of you, Miss Palladino, but please! It would be my pleasure to walk with you. A nice alternative to spending time at Mrs. Booth's beck and call."

Maria chuckled. The imperious housekeeper found every excuse to order Quentin around, on the pretext he was much younger and more agile than she. "Please excuse me if I seem impertinent," she replied more politely. "I'm not accustomed to servants—"

"And we in the Daringtons' employ will be most happy to indulge your every whim. It's good to have you and your Jason living in town, giving the two of us something useful to *do*."

Quentin squeezed her hand in the crook of his elbow as they started down the street. "You've no idea how Ruthie baits me with her innuendo and improper advances when it's just her and me! And frankly"—the butler shook his head dolefully—"she's beyond that sort of thing, you know? All the pity and politeness in the world won't compensate for slack thighs and saggy—"

"Quentin!" Maria stopped to stare at him, yet couldn't keep from laughing.

"I've gone and done it now," he said with a sigh. Then he fixed his stricken gaze on her. "Please excuse my indiscretion, Miss Palladino! I had no call to carry on about—"

"Mrs. Booth—*Ruthie?*—propositions you?"

"Yes, miss, and I'm running out of excuses, too! She fancies herself as my personal goddess—the one to instruct me in the ways of ladies, you see. It's downright embarrassing!"

While the mental image of the matronly Mrs. Booth shaking a wrinkled thigh at Quentin astounded her, Maria wondered why the butler was revealing his plight to *her*. Wouldn't he be better off to air his grievance to Jason? Or to Jason's father, Phillip, Lord Darington, who owned the town house?

"I can't tell just anyone, you see, because they won't believe me. And Mrs. Booth would deny it all, of course."

"Of course," Maria murmured. She looked at him more closely: while his teeth shone in white contrast to his tawny skin and dark, silky hair, his facial shape reminded her of Jemma Darington's pet ferret. Even so, she could foresee the distinguished features Quentin McCallum would acquire with age—if Mrs. Booth let him live that long. The old biddy was prone to fits of temper, which might explain why so many butlers had come and gone at the Daringtons' London address. It was a joke among members of the family, but this beleaguered young man didn't find it funny.

"Thank you for your kind indulgence, Miss Palladino. I promise to never insult you with my own petty problems again," he murmured. "A bride's got better things on her mind."

"And I hope one of those things would be her groom!"

At the sound of that resonating bass voice, Maria turned to smile at Jason Darington. At last, a man to chase away the perplexing words of her brother and this butler! "And what brings you home in the middle of the day, Jason?"

"Why, *you*, sweet Maria," he crooned with a suggestive grin. The sun burst out from behind the clouds as though to announce his arrival, and in his natty double-breasted suit of deep blue he seemed the handsomest, most dashing man on earth. Jason tugged his red print bow tie from beneath his collar, and as it dangled provocatively in his hand, he unfastened his top two shirt buttons. "What else could I possibly be thinking of?"

2

"Aarrrrrgh! Naughty wench! There's no help fer yer wicked soul save to tie yer pretty arse to the mast and spank it! Like *so!*"

The *smack!* of Jason's hand on her bare bottom made Maria squeal and clutch the bedpost. Blindfolded, with her wrists bound to the bed by his red bow tie, she laughed and then cried out again as he playfully slapped each half of her backside.

"Do ye repent of yer lewd and lascivious ways?" he teased near her ear.

"And what fun would *that* be?"

"Are ye sorry fer baitin' poor Quentin? Leadin' him astray with yer feminine wiles?"

"No! Never!" Maria squirmed with need as his warm breath tickled her neck. How she loved it when he took her captive! Jason kissed her relentlessly, until her knees went weak. As he wrapped his hot, bare body around her from behind, his erection throbbed between her thighs, preparing for entry.

"I thought as much. Ye've had yer eye on me young butler ever since ye met him!" He claimed a breast in each hand and held her firmly against his chest. "There's no help fer ye then, save to let Blackbeard have his way with ye. Plunder and pillage, it is! Assume the position, lass. I'm comin' in!"

Her moan joined his in a lusty duet as Jason entered her, bending her forward over the bed to find the best angle. He thrust into her fully, until she thought she might die from the exquisite pressure when his long cock found that sensitive spot deep inside her; held her absolutely still, with her eyes squeezed shut beneath the blindfold. Her jaw dropped in a silent scream. This man knew precisely how to control her, how to bend her to his will with his skilled finesse.

When Maria thought she might faint from the mounting suspense, the sharp sensation of feeling nailed to the bedpost, Jason eased his cock out until its tip tickled her rim. Then he began to rock, slowly and rhythmically . . . in and then out . . . in and then out, until they breathed and pulsed as one. The pace between them quickened as *need* overtook the urge to play.

"You drive me mad with hunger, woman," Jason rasped against her neck. "I swear it was all I could think of from the time I arose: your hot, sweet cunt swallowing my cock. Poor Blackbeard finally stayed so hard for so long, he nearly got severed by the seam of my trousers. I had to leave the office because I could sit no longer! Were it not for my suit coat, everyone would've seen I was a man about to shoot like a cannon."

Maria held her breath to keep from crying out. All the while he talked, Jason was stroking her wet passageway, quickening the pace. "I—I hope we're not agitating poor Quentin with our noise," she rasped. "And Mrs. Booth! She looked appalled when you grabbed my hand and we went flying up the stairs—"

"They'll have to live with it, my love," Jason purred. His lecherous laugh reverberated all the way down her spine. "It's why Mother insisted we live here rather than at Wildwood, you know. Our amorous outcries would be the undoing of her prim and proper sensibilities—not to mention an education for young Jemma. But why are we talking about *them*?"

He leaned her farther down, slapping his thighs against the backs of hers in his urgency. Gasping her name in a frenzied whisper, Jason stiffened—and then cut loose in a series of shudders and moans.

Maria clutched the bedpost. Like a whip her climax snapped inside her, surging into a cataclysm of clenching muscles and inner spasms. On and on it continued, until her lover had spent himself inside her. She was vaguely aware that Jason untied her wrists. The two of them landed in a sweaty, heaving heap on the bed, still a-tingle from nerve endings teased beyond tolerance . . . laughing and kissing and sucking in air until they could breathe normally again.

"God above, but I love you, woman!" he whispered reverently. He removed her blindfold so she could see the adoration in his smile. "Who else would play my pirate games? Who else *excites* me so much that I feel sorry for the chaps coming tonight to bemoan the last of my bachelorhood?"

Maria yanked off his eye patch and then coyly widened her eyes at him. "I don't know. *Who?*"

Jason held her in a long, glorious hug. What a man he was, all taut body and smooth skin, large enough to wrap himself completely around her like a cocoon. With a bandanna still tied rakishly on his head and a slender mustache that shimmered whenever he grinned, Jason looked the part of the pirate he often played when they made love: randy and powerful in a way that always made her pulse skitter, even after he'd sated her.

"You're incorrigible!" he muttered into her hair. He inhaled deeply, sighing his appreciation. "And in my haste to plunder your fine body, I nearly forgot something! Check the pocket inside my suit coat."

Prickling with curiosity, Maria slipped off the tall bed to

find Jason's jacket among the garments strewn around the room. When she fumbled beneath its lapel, her fingers felt a fine mesh chain . . . a flat, shaped piece of metal, cool and smooth on one side . . . pronged and bumpy on the other. As she pulled it out, its brilliance made her gasp. "Oh, Jason! Jason, it's—it's so beautiful! And you know how I love butterflies!"

Her fiancé rolled to his side to watch her with a lazy grin. "A gift for you on the day before we wed, sweet Maria. I told Jude to spare no expense when it came to the stones. Did he choose well?"

Holding the pendant up to catch the light, Maria could only gaze in disbelief: if Jason's twin had fashioned this exquisite piece, these colorful gems were genuine. Never in her wildest dreams had she hoped to own such stunning jewelry. "What have I done to deserve such—"

"Deserve?" Her beloved bent his arm to rest his head on his hand. "You've shared your heart and soul with a man whose only thought was of his next adventure; a man who spent his days avoiding matrimony. Until I met *you*."

Fully stretched out, naked, with his dark chestnut hair in disarray beneath his bandanna, Jason Darington was the picture of a rakish aristocrat whose ambition burned behind his shining brown eyes. Or was that a love like she'd never hoped to know, glowing like the stones his brother had so expertly arranged for her? "Thank you, Jason, but this piece must've cost you—"

"*Nothing*, compared to what you have given *me*, Maria." He smiled sweetly. "In the years to come, I hope you'll realize my family's wealth and possessions are merely . . . decoration. Window dressing." Jason rose from the rumpled bed to take the pendant from her. With utmost care, he fastened it around her neck and then steered her toward the cheval mirror. "Now *here's* a picture worthy of Matisse or Renoir! True wealth of spirit and affection, without a stitch of clothing or pretense to hide behind! *You*, Maria. Simple, yet simply *everything* to me."

She swallowed hard. Fixed her eyes on his in the glass, praying the devotion she saw there would never waver. "You could have chosen any woman you fancied. Certainly a more socially acceptable—"

"*Acceptable?*" His finger drifted along the column of her neck before following the pendant's chain to rest directly above her heart. "Pay no attention to my mother's blather about one's station in life, or what passes as acceptable in her circles, Maria. You're like this butterfly: free and uniquely beautiful, because you follow no one else's preconceived ideas about love and marriage. You came to me—gave yourself to me—expecting nothing in return. Have you any idea how *refreshing* you are?"

She smiled shyly, only now allowing herself to relish the gemstones that shimmered in the hollow of her collarbone. The butterfly's body curved slightly, in beads of onyx. Lustrous sapphires and rubies formed the lower wings and then swirled into spiral antennae. Diamonds and blue topaz made the upper wings seem to flutter when they caught the afternoon light. "I—I don't know what to say."

"Then I've performed a miracle! I've left you speechless!" He brushed his lips against her temple. "I hope you'll accept this pendant as a token of the love I intend to rejoice in every day, for the rest of my life."

Jason grinned wickedly, cupping her breasts. "And to think I could have been sailing off on one of Father's ships to once again lose myself in Jamaican rum, island women, and gambling! No, thank you!"

Maria's lips curved wryly as she thrust into his caress. "That *is* a miracle."

"That's what Father said. Jude is just damn thankful I haven't gotten myself killed during some of my wilder forays," he added with a chuckle. "Nothing he fears more than bearing up under the mantle of family responsibility, you know. In his way, he's every bit the vagabond I am. Just indulges in more artistic pursuits."

"And he's very, very good at it, too." She teased her fingertip along the prongs of the butterfly's jeweled wings. "I'll wear this tomorrow, instead of the pearls Jemma loaned me. Your mother will fuss, but—"

"My mother has a chest of jewelry that rarely catches the light of day. So many exquisite pieces she's demanded over the years, as payment for Father's perceived shortcomings."

"What a shame! And what a sad commentary on their marriage." Maria's hand flew to her mouth. "I'm sorry! It's not my place to judge or—"

"You hit the nail on the head. And your outspoken honesty is one more reason I love you," he murmured. "It's also another means of defying their authority when they insisted I marry on *their* terms. So you're perfect. Absolutely perfect for me."

Once again her throat tightened with emotion. While Jason Darington often showered her with compliments and encouragement, this afternoon was a rare treat: his words shone as brightly as the jewels he'd just given her. Maria watched him dress in a fresh shirt and suit then, openly admiring his fine body, his casual donning of the Darington wealth and its trappings. Would she ever forget her meager years of scraping by, looking after her younger brother, when their mother's untimely death had left them alone on foreign soil?

Or was this a dream? A vision that would disappear like morning mist in the bright light of day?

"Have a good time tonight," she offered.

"Oh, my friends will see to that." He deftly tied a fresh necktie and then folded his shirt collar over it. "I'm only succumbing to tradition, spending this evening at the club to avoid loving the night away with my bride. Not that I give a damn about tradition."

Maria smiled. She smoothed the broad shoulders of his serge suit, a houndstooth check in shades of umber and cinnamon. "You look very handsomely put together—"

"Jude chose the fabric. Says it complements my eyes."

"—except your hair looks like, well—a pirate's, after he's romped with a wayward lady."

Jason laughed and checked his reflection. "I should leave it this way. Give the boys something to speculate about, eh?" He swept a comb through his chestnut hair as though good grooming was the farthest thing from his mind. "There. Better?"

"Until I get my fingers in it again, it'll have to do."

"Can't happen soon enough." Jason bent to kiss her, quickly taking her beyond a going-away peck into those realms of passion that once again had her succumbing . . . surrendering. With a sigh, he released her. "Damn. Better get going before Blackbeard overrules my better judgment."

He strode briskly toward the bedroom door and then turned to gaze at her. "By this time tomorrow, I'll be the happiest man alive because you'll finally be mine, sweet Maria. Pleasant dreams tonight, love."

As his boots beat a rapid tattoo on the stairs, Maria's body prickled with a premonition. *Ecstasy and joy juxtaposed with excruciating pain. Loss of love and life as you now know it.*

"Oh, stifle yourself, Rubio!" she muttered. While she had a glimmer of second sight now and again, Maria preferred to let her renowned brother be the medium—and sometimes *one* bearer of future tidings was too many. She watched out the window until Jason's horse-drawn carriage rolled smartly into the street. And then she listened.

Stillness. A hint of baking beef wafted up from the kitchen, but otherwise the town house felt deliciously peaceful.

Maria gathered up the skirt she'd stepped out of before Jason could feel how heavy it was, to pluck the letters from the deep pockets she'd sewn into its sides. Quickly she crossed the bathroom that adjoined their separate bedchambers, grateful this house had been built with a master and a lady's needs in mind. Jason intended to sleep with her every night, but having her own room made it easier to keep the one secret no one but her brother knew. Still, it would be a challenge to carry on her career in the presence of a husband, not to mention the servants—

Was that the swish of skirts in the hall?

Maria yanked open the bottom drawer of the armoire, cringing when it creaked. She dropped her mail into it. Was shoving it shut with her foot when someone tapped lightly on her door.

3

Mrs. Booth poked her head in. "Will you be dining downstairs to—Lord A'mighty, Miss Palladino! You're quite nude!"

Something in her rose to the old biddy's challenge, despite the way she'd pay for it later. Maria turned to give the housekeeper a full frontal view of her body. "Not really! Would you *look* at this pendant Jason gave me? Isn't it the most exquisite—?" She swayed toward the door as she spoke, until Mrs. Booth stepped into the hallway and shut it briskly behind her.

"Lady Darington has graciously provided you with dressing gowns and all manner of nice attire!" the housekeeper's voice sliced through the door. "While it's *apparent* you are ignorant of proper conduct, Quentin and I have been ordered to *humor* you until the family can instruct you in—"

"Yes, I find this quite *humorous*," Maria mocked under her breath.

"—deportment expected of titled society! So when you've made yourself decent, you may come downstairs for your evening meal!" Mrs. Booth railed. "And by the powers, I'll inform Lady Darington she should hire you a maid immediately!"

To preserve the propriety and decency associated with the family's fine name!"

So tempting it was, to fire back with Quentin's tales of Ruthie Booth and her improper propositions! But while she was the outsider here, she was no fool: Dora Darington and her adolescent daughter, Jemma, had repeatedly warned her against such *common* behavior, reminding her of her *lower* station at every opportunity. "Thank you, Mrs. Booth, but I prefer to spend the evening before my wedding in silent meditation."

The housekeeper coughed pointedly.

"Praying for the grace and fortitude to rise into the upper crust from such a humble upbringing," Maria continued wryly. "It's probably prenuptial jitters. Every bride gets them, they say."

"Prenuptial jitters, my arse! You won't be getting away with such talk—and such carousing in bed—after tomorrow, Miss Palladino!"

"And neither will you be eavesdropping and tattling, Mrs. Booth. Not to mention using such a *tone*. Thank you for thinking of my needs. Good evening."

Ear to the door, Maria waited until the housekeeper's footsteps descended the stairs. Had she overstepped? Perhaps baited the sanctimonious old biddy beyond her tolerance? She understood now why Jason insisted on ruling his roost! Asserting his rights as the heir to the Darington title and estates! Once they lived here as man and wife, no housekeeper would be telling *her* what was proper or acceptable!

The thought warmed her. She opened the tall doors of the armoire to gaze at the billowing ivory gown she would wear tomorrow, when she would become Jason's wife—acknowledged by all as *his*, and therefore a Darington, with all the privileges that came with such prestige. After tomorrow, stodgy Phillip, Lord Darington, and his socialite wife could do nothing further about her *deportment* . . . her lower rung on the ladder of life. Although they'd say anything they pleased when guests weren't present.

But for now, in the privacy of this chamber overdecorated in candy pink and sunshine yellow—at Jemma's insistence—she could finally read her mail in peace. It might be days before she had the chance to answer these letters, to pen the paragraphs her editor—her readers!—eagerly awaited.

Maria opened the drawer more carefully this time, and then rubbed its edges with a bar of soap to silence its squeal. She carried a fat handful of letters to the window seat and then reclined on its plump pillows to rip open the envelopes. Her eyes raced across the handwritten lines of one missive after another: *so hoping you can respond personally to my plight . . . have enclosed an envelope for a reply that must remain absolutely private . . . would be most pleased to provide the unbelievable details of my sister's sordid affair . . . as I live and breathe, you are the woman my heart yearns for. . . .*

She sighed. While her position as social observer and advisor to the lovelorn had its rewards, it wore her thin at times. So many lonely, needy people vying for her time and attention. So many readers of elevated social circumstances wishing to see their gossip in print, and therefore considered gospel by thousands of subscribers. She settled more deeply into the cushions, absently fingering the butterfly pendant and wondering how she'd juggle the inner life she shared with so many readers, now that she was about to marry a man with whom she'd spend her *apparent* life. Would there come a time when she could reveal her occupation to her husband? Didn't wives share every little dream and secret with the one they loved?

Jason will feel slighted. He intends to be the center of my world.

True enough. Jason Darington, heir to his father's title, estate, and shipyards, was a fine, feisty lover. A man to be seen with and adored. But he did *not* understand taking second place to *anything*.

Maria sighed. A movement caught her eye on the driveway below and she gazed intently through the lacy curtains: the man approaching the town house could have been Jason, except he wore a flowing poet's shirt tucked into his fitted trousers. He kept to the shadows of the nearest buildings, using the dusk to his advantage. And damned if he didn't gaze up at her window, as though he knew she'd be watching for him!

Jude! Her body prickled. Logic told her no one could distinguish her naked form through the camouflage of the curtains, yet his sly smile suggested otherwise.

How would he enter the house without alerting Mrs. Booth to his presence? Unlike his brother, this Darington—younger than Jason by mere minutes—felt no compulsion to make an entrance or otherwise attract anyone's attention. He moved through life in total contentment as long as he was free to pursue his artistic projects. Those who speculated about Jude's inclinations toward men obviously didn't know him the way *she* did, but he allowed such rumors to be his social smokescreen.

Why wasn't he attending the bachelor party?

Maria gathered the letters from the floor and stuffed them back into the armoire drawer. She padded into the bathroom to twist the spigots of the tub and then liberally sprinkled the water with her favorite lime-scented bath salts . . . the ones Jude had given her upon hearing she found floral scents overpowering. Stepping into the frothy water, she listened for his footsteps on the stairs.

Moments after she turned off the water and relaxed in the high porcelain tub, her bedroom door opened. Her visitor could've been a cat slipping in on velvet paws—at least until his low chuckle gave him away.

"So you *were* in the window. Dare I believe you were waiting for *me*, Maria?"

She glanced up languidly, immersed in the soothing, scented water. "Believe what you will, Jude," she teased, "but *I* believed you'd be at the club with your brother, toasting the demise of his freedom."

Jude sat on the rounded rim, letting his fingers drift through the iridescent froth. "Why would any man choose a stuffy old club that reeks of his forebears' cigars, when he could be drinking in such a sight, such alluring scents, here with you?"

Maria smiled slyly. "Because he was expected to be there?"

"Because he's more a slave to *you* than to any convention or tradition. May I wash your hair, darling? You know how I love to lose myself in it."

Just that quickly Jude had shifted from the world of his privileged upbringing into the intimate realm that centered around *her*. Like his twin, Jude wore his hair carelessly raked away from his slender face, reminiscent of a windblown angel's wings. And when he grinned, his close-clipped mustache glimmered in the low light. But there the likeness ended. As night differed from day, Jude Darington ruled an earthier universe where his love of sensory indulgences—his joy in creating pleasure—filled his every waking hour.

"Yes. Please do." Although she lounged against the back of the tub, concealed by the dense, scented soapsuds, Maria's bare body tingled beneath this man's avid gaze, anticipating what he'd do to her as the hours of the night flew by.

"Good of him to give you the butterfly before he left. It looks as lovely against your bare skin as I envisioned while I was making it."

His voice had dipped into that lower register that made her even more aware of his scrutiny, his intentions, on this night before she married his brother. "Thank you so much, Jude!"

she murmured as her fingers found the jeweled pendant. "Never have I seen such a combination of colors and stones! I'm wearing it tomorrow, instead of Jemma's pearls!"

"Thank you." His whisper was a grateful prayer that wrapped around her heart. "May I interpret that as a declaration of your affections? As your unspoken vow to . . . continue our relations after tomorrow?"

Was that wistful desperation in his plea? Did he wish *he* had proposed to her before his twin had? It wasn't a question she would ask aloud, for the glow in his tawny eyes told of a love deeper and truer, in its way, than the declarations Jason made at the drop of a hat. "*I* certainly want to continue," she murmured. "Has your brother said anything to the contrary?"

Jude shook his head, smiling as he lifted the pendant from her chest. He shifted it, watching light from its jewels play against the wall. "As long as Mum remains unaware of our arrangement—and as long as Jason produces an heir—all requirements shall be satisfied. But not nearly as satisfied as *you* shall feel by the time I leave here tonight."

His quiet promise rang in the small bathroom and in every fiber of her being, for Jude Darington did indeed know how to please her. She shifted beneath the warm water: Jason would've been squeezing her breasts, squirming as he freed his erection, yet this man lingered over the details. Made her wonder. And wait. And anticipate. He cupped her chin with his damp hand, to gaze at her with adoring eyes, and she melted. While her mind told her this triangular relationship might be their undoing if—when—someone caught them at it, her heart sang the words to the sensual song Jude inspired every time he came to her. By unspoken agreement, one twin was never present when his brother made love to her or accompanied her in public. It seemed a convenient way to make people believe she spent her time only with Jason, the man she would marry tomorrow.

Right now, however, Jude Darington was reaching around her head to let down her hair. Pins pinged to the floor and her raven waves fell around her shoulders, section by slow section. He smelled of old cognac, not because he drank it but because he patted it on his face after he shaved. His silk shirt whispered seductively as he scratched her scalp with his fingernails, easing the tension at her temples . . . taking his sweet time and thoroughly mussing her hair with his tender massage.

Her head fell forward in submission. "I love what you do to me, Jude," she whispered.

"And I love the way you let me do it." He cradled her head in one hand and gently pinched her nostrils shut. "Ready?"

Maria curled her legs against her body so he could submerse her completely. He brought her back up then, stroking the wet, heavy waves of hair out of her eyes. With practiced ease, Jude poured her shampoo into his palm and rubbed his hands together. She felt warm and limp and submissive as he massaged the rich lather from her scalp to the ends of her hair. Her head again lolled forward as he cast his spell, caressed and manipulated the muscles of her upper back with slow, knowing strokes.

A sigh escaped her. She felt so completely pampered and spoiled. Cherished.

"Shall we rinse and move on to other delights?" he murmured. "I brought you a surprise."

And how had he done that? When she'd seen him in the driveway, his hands were empty—

"Magic," he answered. Again he held her head and nostrils, grinning at her. "It's my mission to keep you guessing. Down you go."

As Maria allowed him to dunk her head beneath the water, she realized how much she trusted this man. Even as he held her under for a few seconds longer than usual, she felt the playful vibration of his chuckle: Jude didn't have a mean bone in his body. She surged to the surface then, sputtering and gasping, laughing with him as she filled her lungs—and then became breathless again, in a different way.

Jude framed her wet face between his hands and kissed her, tenderly at first, nibbling at her lips to make her giggle. With a low moan, he settled in for the longest, most relentless kiss she could remember . . . as though he wanted her to wish she'd be *his*, come tomorrow. With only the power of his affection, he held her captive against the back of the tub. His mouth plied hers eagerly, restlessly, and then retreated to the point she thought he'd allow her to stand and dry herself.

But no! Jude launched into another lovely, languid kiss that nearly made her cry with its exquisite pressure . . . the dance of their tongues as though he might pleasure her all night . . . the melding of their sensibilities and their souls.

He at last broke away, to gaze raptly at her. "If I can't be your husband, I want to be your port in a storm: the man who listens to your complaints and whims and brings you resolution."

Maria blinked. He appeared so serious, sounded almost ominous. "I—"

"Life amongst us Daringtons won't be a rose garden, darling," he continued quietly. Still he held her head, his eyes afire with a golden flame, as though he burned for her on this night before her wedding. "And at times when Jason must carry on in the name of duty and honor, as the firstborn, I hope you'll allow me to be the comic relief, or the sexual release, or the answer to whatever you pray for. May I aspire to such things, at least?"

Again he'd left her speechless. This man, so talented with gemstones and camera, paintbrush and piano—any artistic endeavor he undertook—was asking to be her *fool*. A slave to her desires. Maria nuzzled his palm, hoping to find words as lovely as his. "I would like that, yes," she whispered. For a moment, only the soft lapping of the bathwater filled the little bathroom. "While I love Jason with all my heart, I would grieve deeply if something happened to you and if we were forbidden to spend time together. Does that make me a whore? A wife without conscience or scruples?"

"I think not. But then, I'm biased." Jude laughed softly. "Jason and I have agreed that a woman like you—a lover with such diverse and intense passions—is probably best satisfied by having *two* admirers. We know damn well that if you chose, you could exhaust us both and move on to the next man. So we've agreed to please you at every turn, in every way. A challenge, but we shall *rise* to it."

Maria's gaze dropped. Yes, indeed, this man's trousers were tented, yet he made no overt move to satisfy his need. "What if I got out of the tub, and you got out of your clothes—"

"All in good time, dear lady. First we shall dry you, so your skin doesn't crinkle like Mrs. Booth's."

Her grimace made him laugh as he reached for a towel. "Hard to believe, but Quentin claims she drops her drawers. Invites him in."

"See there? We should never judge a book by its cover—even if it looks like it's been left out in the rain." Jude stood beside the tub, offering his hands to help her stand. "You'll be the same way when you're her age, darling. Insatiable. A vixen on the prowl."

"Is that a *bad* thing?"

"Certainly not. I intend to be there, too, watching you in your glory." Jude tossed the towel around her shoulders. As he tugged it side to side, inhaling, he gazed at the sway of her bare, wet breasts. "Lime. Not using these bath salts just because I'm here, are you?"

Maria shook her head, relishing the way he caressed her body. "I am, however, wondering how I'll ever repay you for all the ways you've spoiled me."

He smiled slyly. "Now that you mention it . . ." He raised her leg so her foot rested on the tub's rim, to dry it—but then he sat down and ran his tongue along her inner thigh. When she sighed, Jude tossed the towel. Parted her nether lips and kissed her there.

Maria's head fell back. She grabbed his shoulders and closed her eyes as the sensations made her need surge to a new peak. To this point, Jude had toyed with her, but now he was determined to make her respond—to make her *his*. As he lapped the dampness from her sensitive folds, she swayed with the force of his intimate kiss . . . braced herself for the crack of lightning that made her pulse thunder in her head.

"God, Jude . . . Jude," she whimpered as the jolts of pleasure became almost unbearable.

He thrust his tongue inside her, rubbing the nub he knew so well . . . exploring the depths of her desire as only Jude knew how. Just as the spasms began in earnest he grabbed her backside to steady her. He licked and tickled her rim, driving her to a frenzy before pressing his mouth against her, *hard*.

Maria cried out. Their moans mingled as Jude kept thrusting, until she felt she might collapse in a boneless heap. Her hips took on their own rhythm until all her spasms were spent. She eased him away then, to regain her sanity, her balance, before stepping out of the tub. "It's my turn to please *you* now, but I must catch my breath—"

"Not so. This is my night to give and yours to receive."

"That makes no sense! Why should I be the only one to—"

"Because I said so!" Jude grabbed her hand, his grin wet with her juices. "On to the next course! Champagne to toast the lady's wedding day, and fine chocolate to sweeten the deal."

As Maria followed him to her bedroom, she could only wonder how he'd smuggled such treats upstairs past the ever-vigilant Mrs. Booth. "I could've sworn you were empty-handed when I saw you slipping in."

"Father stocks a fine cellar here at the town house. And since his ships' captains know better than to sail home without the candy Mum craves . . ." Jude shrugged boyishly, which made his silk shirt shimmy around his shoulders. "Lean low, my queen. We'll wrap your hair in this towel and then you may recline on your bed. Your serving boy shall fulfill your every desire."

Maria chuckled to herself: Jason would *never* declare himself her servant, nor would he lead her through these circuitous little games to arrive at his own satisfaction. But sprawling on plumped pillows, propped against the headboard naked while a handsome lover poured fizzy champagne into two flutes on a tray? She could grow accustomed to such indulgence!

Jude broke off the end of the dark chocolate bar he'd smuggled in. "Sweets for the sweet," he murmured. He laid the confection on her tongue, much like a priest would administer communion, and then he placed a piece in his own mouth.

As the intense cocoa melted in their mouths, they gazed at each other. Anticipating. Savoring. Again she was struck by the way this twin appreciated such subtle nuances—and her! When the candy was a coating of thick richness on her tongue, the first sip of the liquor sent a rush of electricity straight to her head. Giggling, she downed the rest of it and held out her flute for more.

Jude chuckled. "Let the festivities begin! A toast to your marriage tomorrow, Maria!"

"And to you, dear man. If I roast in hell for this wickedness, at least I won't be alone!"

The slender man seated on the bed's edge began to shed his clothing. While he wasn't as athletic as his twin, Jude's whipcord muscles rippled as he dropped his shirt and then escaped his pants. His eyes shone brightly, focused on *her* . . . full of his yearning for *her*. He took the towel from her hair, and from there it was a sensual collage of images: Jude slipping into bed alongside her, caressing her with his velvety skin . . . chocolate kisses that elevated her pulse, her awareness of how she craved him . . . how he inspired her playful response even more than their candy and champagne had. Sighs drifted between them as they languidly rolled . . . as Jude entered her with an expression of exquisite joy she'd never forget.

Maria let her body follow his whims: all rational thought was gone. Their lovemaking took on a special poignancy on this eve of her wedding. He refused to be rushed, so Maria followed his lead in this intimate dance . . . lingered in each kiss and reveled in the way his golden brown eyes reflected her—and held her spellbound when his climax led to hers.

"Maria . . . Maria," he prayed as his body convulsed. When he was spent, he enfolded her in his arms. Rested with his lips in her damp hair until his breathing once again matched hers. "I must go now. Before the urge to carry you off and marry you myself overrides propriety."

Propriety? She grinned wickedly yet held her tongue. Jude looked so solemn as he dressed, gazing at her in the dimness. Somehow the evening had flown and the candles had gone out without their awareness. With a final kiss, he left her sprawled on the rumpled sheets.

"Sleep sweetly, Maria," he murmured as he reached her door. "I look forward to making your portrait tomorrow, before your groom sees you in your bridal finery."

Silently Jude slipped from her room and down the stairs. Her mantel clock tinkled delicately and then struck two.

Maria smiled. It was her long-awaited wedding day.

4

"Not even married yet, and already henpecked, are we?"

"Come on, Darington! Last chance for a wild ride before the noose tightens!"

"And we wouldn't want to disappoint Miss Beddow, would we? She's sizing you up, mate, and it's not just because we're paying handsomely for this trick! Do the deed, man!"

Jason drew a deep breath to steady his swirling head. While he'd often passed Amelia Beddow's brothel on the harbor, carrying out business for his father's shipping empire—and while he was no stranger to ladies of the type she employed—he'd given up sporting women once Maria had claimed him. Who needed whores, when his own woman sated his sexual hunger so exuberantly? With sincere affection for *him* rather than his money or position. "It's two o'clock. I really should—"

"Lame! Limp!"

"Never thought *you'd* refuse a lady. Dare!"

"C'mon, now! It's early yet! We brought you here to show us how it's done!"

He blinked to clear his vision, blurry from too many toasts.

His three best friends egged him on with their lopsided grins: Daniel Hackett, Nicholas Northwood, and Clive McCaslin, who held the keys to their fathers' kingdoms in textiles, mining, and banking, had outlasted the others. They'd escorted him to this finale of his bachelorhood with fistfuls of money donated by their cohorts at the gentlemen's club. There was no denying Amelia Beddow's intentions, either. The fiery-haired madam sized him up with a knowing smile, letting her lush, loose bosom speak for itself in an indecent gown of emerald silk. A gold tooth winked at him when her ruby lips parted. The tip of her tongue came out to play.

"Well, well, well," she crooned, advancing with a slow sway of her hips. She remained focused on him as she coyly extended her open palm. Her expression waxed triumphantly feral as Clive handed over his cash. "Why don't we retire to my quarters while my girls entertain your friends, sir? Your tide's about to rise, and I wouldn't *miss* such an exciting voyage."

It was so blatant an invitation Jason almost laughed—except he suddenly regretted coming here. What if this little episode got reported to Maria, or—God forbid!—appeared in Miss Crimson's gossip column in the *Inquirer*, right alongside the account of the wedding? But when Amelia grabbed his hand there was no backing out.

"Polly! Cynthia—and Violet!" she called into the parlor behind her. "You've guests to entertain! Treat them like the fine, upstanding gents they are while I provide the bridegroom his last wave of pleasure as an unattached man!"

He glanced toward the rear of this room, noting a sailor—or were there two?—seated at the shadowy bar. They nodded, seemingly unconcerned, when the madam waved as though she'd return after she'd wrung him dry. The furnishings of scarlet chintz and black lacquer blurred as he followed her down the hall. Jason tried desperately to think of an escape, a story that would satisfy Miss Beddow's proposition, as far as his friends were concerned. To their delight, three voluptuous sirens had appeared in the hall.

So, once behind the madam's door, perhaps he could buy his way out of this predicament . . . offer the sloe-eyed madam more to let him go home than his chums had paid her to seduce him. It was a coward's way out; a ploy that would disgust his father, who'd been a legend with the ladies. But his body prickled with unsettling little signs that he shouldn't stay here. Some predatory women inspired the playful rake in him, but this vixen felt too sure of herself. Too smug by half.

Did she know who he was? As her door shut behind him, Jason nearly blurted out his father's name and pedigree—yet something silenced him. While he'd paid a few sporting girls for the occasional in-and-out, he'd remained anonymous and that seemed the better idea here: Mother would die, mortified, if he returned to Wildwood with telltale bruises and his clothes reeking of cheap perfume. She'd already announced that this wedding must outdo the matrimonial events her friends had engineered—especially since he'd chosen a bride none of them knew. A foreigner whose only virtue was her beauty, the way they saw it.

Maria's lovely face flashed before him and Jason faltered. Amelia poured him a drink he had no desire for. Why the hell didn't he just walk away? *Now.* She'd been well paid for her time, after all.

The madam assessed him coolly. She looked older from this proximity, and the lines around her world-weary eyes appeared deeper in the shadows of her dim room. "Methinks the gentleman might benefit more from a tonic than a fumbling match," she offered. "Something to steady your stomach before the wedding." The crystal decanters on her tea cart whispered as she chose one.

"That's very kind of you. I—"

"I'm not partial to cleaning up your dinner after it splatters my floor—or my sheets. And besides" she dribbled the potion into the brandy she'd poured—"I've already been paid. Your friends were quite generous, so it's the least I can do." The snifter she offered beckoned him. "I'll have my driver take you home while your friends have their fun. Easier on everyone, should they pass out. Don't you agree?"

It seemed so unexpectedly practical. Amelia went to her window, so he stepped up beside her, more grateful than he could say. The harbor stretched before them, a sea of deep blue punctuated by the skeletal black masts of ships bobbing near-by . . . a picture of tranquility few lanterns interrupted. The stench of dead fish drifted in with the breeze to poke him in the stomach, so he quickly quaffed his tonic. "How kind of you to realize needs my . . . friends don't understand. They . . . envy me my . . . bride, I . . . think."

Amelia's face blurred. He felt the sudden urge to retch, nearly opened the window to lean out, but he couldn't grip the handle on the windowsill. The room swung sideways and he lost his balance. The snifter fell from his hand to shatter on the floor, a crash that echoed mercilessly inside his head. He tried to focus on her, tried to right himself and demand—

She pulled a lever camouflaged by the curtain and the floor dropped out from under him. Jason flailed—had the sensation of falling like a rock—and then landed with an impact that knocked the wind out of him as it racked his entire body. His head struck the hard surface and he saw shooting stars like fireworks before he passed out.

"Thank you, Captain. This is most generous . . . but considering who he is, my fee is double."

The seaman scowled. "I didn't get a good look at 'im, so—"

"Were I you, Terrence, I'd set sail immediately. Lady Darington doesn't take it well when her plans go awry."

His bloodshot eyes widened, and he fished more money from his pocket.

"Pleasure doin' business with you, Amelia. Here—let me deposit that for you." He chortled, slipping his hands down the front of her dress. Took his sweet time fondling her breasts, and then pressed them together to kiss the crevice. His money remained in the cups of her corset as he reverently placed her assets back inside her gown. "Looked like a solid enough sort, for peerage. Might have to beat some obedience into him, though."

"Never met a man who didn't require training."

Captain Dunner and his first mate laughed as they slid from their stools. "Might I bring you anything from the Americas, my dear? Trinkets, perhaps? Least I can do, for the way you supply me with crewmen."

Amelia shook her head. Captain Dunner and his sailors lavished a lot of their pay on her and the girls, but it was best not to accept any gifts that might leave her beholden. Terrence wasn't the sort she fancied. Had a mean streak as deep and wide as the sea when he got provoked: she couldn't recall how many smashed lamps and chairs she'd replaced after his rampages. "Smooth sailing, gents. Come back and see us when you return."

As the two seamen lumbered out her back door to fetch the fellow who'd fallen to the deck of the *Sea Witch*, she finished her drink . . . listened for signs of activity in the rooms above. None of those girls kept their passion quiet, so the absence of creaking and moaning told her their three guests had probably passed out.

As Amelia quietly opened the doors to their upstairs compartments, she was greeted with knowing female smiles as well as soft snores. The young man who'd handled the money snorted and turned restlessly, so she grabbed his shoulders. "You must go now!" she ordered as she shook him. "And take your friends with you!"

He sat up with a start, glancing around the unfamiliar room as he raked his blond hair out of his bloodshot eyes. When he spotted Violet beside him, he flushed. "I—could be I was so tired from—and what of Jason? Our groom?"

"He was magnificent. I sent him home in my personal carriage."

"Ah. Right kind of you."

"The least I could do. You've been most generous, but other guests await my girls." She gazed at the disoriented young man and raised her voice. "I suggest you take your friends down the back stairs, as the four stevedores in my parlor are becoming . . . *impatient*. And, as I have only these three girls tonight . . ." She shrugged, allowing him to figure the odds.

He struggled to the edge of the bed. "Don't reckon we're in any shape to tangle with stevedores."

"My thoughts precisely." Amelia stood with her arms crossed; exchanged a glance with Violet as the young man bent to pull on his boots. Hastily dressed and ready to keel over, he swayed out the door, cursed loudly at his cohort in Cynthia's room, and stumbled across the hall to hail the friend who was dead asleep in Polly's bed.

As their boots clumped unevenly down the narrow wooden stairs that exited into the alley, Amelia emptied her corset of the captain's commission and then pulled the entire evening's take from her skirt pocket. Not a bad night's wages, considering she and her doves had done so little work for most of it. Violet, Polly, and Cynthia were dressed and proceeding down the main stairway so she followed them into the empty front parlor. She smiled at their quizzical expressions as they looked for those stevedores.

"Seems an opportune time to visit my house in Brighton. I

recall rumors of conventions there this week—lay pastors and undertakers, I believe." Amelia opened the safe hidden beneath the carved bar. She counted out the three girls' wages and added an extra twenty pounds to each pile. Then she smiled as her daughter, Millicent, came from the back room where she kept their accounts. "If anyone inquires, dear, you have no idea where we've gone or when we'll return. And if you see Phillip, Lord Darington, approaching tomorrow, *lock up*."

Millicent smiled slyly. Had she not been born as plain as paste, with a clubfoot, she could've done well for herself upstairs. "Yes, Mum, of course. The usual song and dance."

Polly grinned knowingly as she counted her pay. "We'll be dancing indeed, what with servicing those funeral directors. They've got their quirks, they do!"

"We'll be teaching those pastors a bit about *laying*, too!" Violet added with a snicker. "Let's pack, girls! Nothing like a trip to the shore to lift a girl's spirits. And her skirts."

5

"Never, *never* have you looked so lovely, Maria! Even more beautiful than last time I saw you—"

"Mere hours ago," she quipped quietly.

"—which is nothing short of a miracle! My brother will be stunned." Jude fluttered her voluminous ivory skirts to display their layers of beaded lace to full advantage, and then stepped back for a final assessment. At his request, she wore her veil draped back over her shoulders, to better reveal her exquisite smile, the face he could gaze at forever. He adjusted the butterfly pendant for the excuse it gave him to touch her warm skin. "Relax, now, and hold those happy thoughts. No bride has ever been captured for posterity with such poise, such grace—"

"Better get your shots taken. Lady Darington is spinning like a crazed top." Rubio Palladino entered the small parlor and then stopped in his tracks, visibly affected by the sight of his sister. "But then, it's Maria's day, is it not?"

"So true. Mum will just have to adjust." Grinning, Jude ducked beneath the black cape of his camera and took hold of the shutter bulb. "Steady now . . . tilt your chin up just a bit, love, as though you're telling Jason who's really in charge—perfect!" He squeezed the bulb, confident he'd captured Maria at her charming, challenging best. "And while you're here, Rubio, perhaps you'd like to pose with your sister? We so seldom have these occasions in our lives—"

"What a fine idea! I feel so—so *obvious*—standing here all alone!" Maria replied. Then she smiled wistfully at her younger brother. "You're all I have left for family, Rubio. And although I adore Jason, I'll treasure this likeness of us . . . my last moments before I take on the Darington name."

"And all the *privilege* that entails," Jude remarked with a chuckle. He watched brother and sister position themselves. No mistaking their Italian heritage: the planes of their faces beneath well-placed cheekbones, the coquettish angle of their eyes, and their luxurious hair. Maria's waves were swept up into a high Psyche knot beneath her veil, with two flirtatious tendrils curling on either side of her face, while her brother's mane swelled out around his temples and brushed his shoulders in a way that defied the current trend. Together, the two of them made a timeless statement: the lovely bride and the proud brother who would escort her up the aisle to her new husband.

Jude sighed to himself. What he wouldn't give to trade places with Rubio . . . to stand in as the groom, just this once—

But he didn't dare. While most people couldn't distinguish between him and his twin, such behavior would be tempting fate: his mother had been able to tell them apart since the day they were born.

"All right, you two, we're not at a wake!" he teased. And as the sparkle leaped into their dark eyes, as they instinctively leaned in toward each other, he snapped the shot.

"And now *me*, Jude! Make my portrait, too! Please? *Please?*"

Jude closed his eyes, pausing, so he wouldn't tell Jemma what a royal pain in the arse she was. Into the parlor she flounced, her blond curls a-flutter around her flushed face. At sixteen, his sister fancied herself the belle of every ball—and she *was* a bud developing into an exquisite rose, if one could avoid the thorns of her tongue and her temperament. Her gown of cerise silk faille complemented her pale complexion, *almost* to the point where she looked like a young woman rather than the brat he knew her to be.

"Mummy wants to see you," she informed Maria pertly. She lifted a speculative eyebrow. "And where are the pearls I loaned you? When Mummy sees that—that vulgar piece of *paste*, she'll—"

"What *will* she do?" a voice demanded from the doorway. And to make the scene complete, their mother entered the parlor with a decisive swish of her taffeta gown. A stunning, one-of-a-kind gown from LeChaud Soeurs, it shimmered in ever-changing shades of periwinkle and aubergine. Although its cut was more form fitted and sophisticated than most women's gowns, Dora's presence made the parlor feel even smaller and more confining.

Jude stood taller, waiting. His mother, Lady Darington, would spare no one as she spoke her mind about the butterfly pendant.

She stepped in front of Maria, taking the jeweled piece between her fingers to study it: because she was too vain to wear spectacles, only close family knew how poor her vision had become. "Hmmmm . . ."

Why was he holding his breath? It wasn't as if his mother's opinion would change anything—except perhaps poor Maria's high hopes for a perfect wedding day.

"Highly unusual," she remarked. "We agreed upon Jemma's pearls, however. In keeping with the bridal tradition of—"

"Jude made it! As a wedding gift, which Jason gave me to wear today!" Maria blurted. Bless her, she stood her ground, her eyes aglow with dark fire. "And now that it's in my bridal portrait, we can hardly remove it, can we?"

Clever girl! Invoking Jason's name had helped, but she'd also acknowledged his contribution to her wedding day. Jude exchanged a quick glance with Rubio, who stood poised next to Maria to prevent Jemma and his overbearing mother from injecting any more venom.

His mother's breath escaped with a hiss. "Far be it from me to criticize Jude's talent or *taste*. But if Jason approves—"

"Oh, he was proud to give it to me! Even Mrs. Booth remarked on its unusual beauty!" Maria pressed on. "And don't *you* look lovely, too? Camille and Colette outdid themselves, flattering you with such an exquisite fit and color, Dora!"

His mother took the bait, focusing on this flowery praise rather than her disdain for Maria's habit of using first names. "Well, I—thank you, Maria. And for what I paid them, the LeChaud sisters should well have transformed me into a goddess!"

"And they made *my* gown, too!" Jemma chimed in. She plucked her skirt between her fingertips and twirled like a little girl—until she grabbed her bodice under the gown's short cape, which seemed to be . . . squirming. "Willie! Willie, stop it!" she whispered tersely.

"You did *not* bring that damn ferret—"

"He's my best boy, Mummy. Queen Elizabeth's ferret was an albino, too!"

"—to *church*? To a wedding?" Dora gasped. "My God, Jemma, what were you thinking? If that infernal pest gets loose—"

"I have him perfectly trained! Wilbert has impeccable manners!" the girl replied shrilly. She coaxed the slender white creature out through her scalloped neckline, to cradle him against her chest. "And I *will* have my portrait made with him! Jude has already agreed!"

Jude stood rooted beside his camera. Pitting mother against daughter was a losing proposition, but at least the ferret had re-

lieved poor Maria of being the target for the negative attention
his pendant had created. She, too, stood absolutely still; remained outside the running tantrum that erupted between the
Darington females several times each day.

"This is not the time nor the place for such foolishness,
Jemma." Their mother squared her shoulders and lifted her
chin, silently announcing that the matter was settled. "Enough
distractions! I came here looking for Jason, as it seems no one
has *seen* him today. We've a mere twenty minutes before the
wedding is to begin!"

The bottom dropped out of Jude's stomach. As his brother's
best man, he was ultimately responsible for the groom . . . and
he could *not* confess where he'd been during Jason's bachelor
party last night. His gaze met Maria's. She, too, was forcing an
expression that camouflaged their secret, but she couldn't keep
quiet.

"He was fine when I saw him yesterday! When he gave me
this pendant!" The words rushed from her mouth as she fingered the jeweled butterfly. "He left the town house dressed for
his party, so—"

All eyes found Jude, and he prayed for a convincing cover
story. "Last I knew, he was at the gentlemen's club near the harbor, fulfilling all those male rituals one observes at a bachelor
gathering," he added with an apologetic glance toward Maria.
"I insisted he come home with me, but—as always—he and his
friends ridiculed me for wanting to leave early. For acting *re-
sponsibly*, considering today's wedding."

His mother's face tightened. "Are you not your brother's
keeper, Jude? You should have—"

"Jude! Jude, where the hell's your brother?" Into the airless
parlor stalked his father, whose expression said the devil had
come to collect his due. "I've just quizzed McCaslin and Hackett—who look like Death itself dragged their arses out of bed.
They have no idea of Jason's whereabouts." Lord Darington's

hair had gone white at the temples and his skin had assumed the patina of his advancing years, but he was still a battle cannon who fired first and asked questions later. "And here *you* are, looking as fresh as a daisy! As oblivious—or deceitful—as your brother's fine-feathered friends!" he blustered. "What the hell's going on here?"

Jude gripped his tripod, knowing three extra legs still didn't give him a good one to stand on: in his white tie and tails, Phillip, Lord Darington, cut a formidable figure. Not a man to be trifled with, even when his wealth and standing weren't being showcased at his heir's wedding. "As I was telling Mum," Jude rasped, hoping his story matched what Clive and Daniel had said, "when I informed Jason it was time to head home, he and his friends laughed at me!"

"As well they might," his father replied stiffly.

Jude bit back insults he'd wanted to hurl at this pompous old goat for years. "Jason believes he can do no wrong. Who am I to imply otherwise?"

"That's a dodge and you know it!" Lord Darington—for he had assumed his role as guardian of the family name and reputation—drilled Jude with his steely gray gaze. "McCaslin and that nutless wonder, Hackett, claim they last saw your brother at—" He glanced at his wife and daughter, then gripped Jude's shoulder. "No more hiding under that camera's cape. You can only *imagine* the consequences if we have no groom for today's wedding!"

"But the ceremony *must* go on!" Jemma cried. "I've been preparing myself for *weeks*—"

"I shall *not* abide such an insult to our reputation! Not even the suggestion of it!" his mother said. She pointed toward the door. "Go! And don't come back without my son!"

With a last apologetic glance at Maria, who stood like a porcelain statue, Jude followed his father. His temples pounded as though he'd imbibed as much brandy as his brother and those cohorts who'd led him on last night's misadventures. And indeed, Clive McCaslin and Daniel Hackett appeared green around the gills outside the church doors, weaving and bleary-eyed. At the sight of Lord Darington, they tried in vain to square themselves up.

"Now tell me again! We have no ladies present, so where did you sots leave Jason?"

Clive swallowed as though trying not to retch. He looked to Jude for support, but Jude kept his mouth clamped shut, hoping McCaslin didn't ask where he'd been last night. "Best I can remember, Miss Amelia—" He blinked and pointed at Dan. "*You're* the man who suggested we take up a collection for—"

"Amelia Beddow? The madam who runs a house on the harbor?"

Jude flinched. Their father had escorted them to the madam's establishment for their sixteenth birthday and paid the lady to make men of them—or of *him*, anyway. Jason had already dipped his stick when the daughters of their parents' peers succumbed to his persuasive ways. And while her sporting girls had come and gone over the years, the enterprising Miss Beddow knew a gold mine for its worth, there amongst the sailors and ship captains and captains of London's shipping industry. Surely she'd known better than to detain Jason on the eve of his much-publicized wedding. . . .

Dan's vomit splattered the foundation, a doleful sound that brought Jude out of his musings. His father's face resembled a raw beefsteak, and had the vicar not stepped through the door, he might've shoved Dan and Clive against the church's stone facade.

"Have we still not located the groom?" Father Stoutham tugged at his white collar, not daring to ask any further questions.

Lord Darington cursed. "Do you think we'd all be standing here, trying to nail down the truth, if—oh, here!" He pulled a thick wad of pound notes from his pocket. "I'm leaving *you* to maintain order until we get back! My wife and daughter are working themselves into a frenzy, and the gossip's going to fly among the guests. Handle it for me!"

His father's expression brooked no argument: Jude followed closely as they strode toward the carriage. Pearson, the driver, looked startled when he learned of their destination, but moments later they were clattering down the street and toward the harbor.

Across from him, his father looked suddenly older, despite his rage. "Why do I suspect you ducked out of the festivities as soon as Amelia Beddow came into the picture?" he demanded in a low voice. "You could've waited in the front parlor—"

"I had no idea!" Jude protested. "I left before there was any mention of visiting Miss Beddow's!"

And it was true. Almost. Damn his brother for messing up everyone's day—and not telling him! In a pinch, he could've stood in for his more adventurous twin—and God knows he'd wanted to, plenty of times—so the wedding could've proceeded. They could've claimed *he*, Jude, was the missing twin! To avoid scandal, his mother would've gone along with the ruse, and would throttle Jason the next time she saw him.

The look on Maria's face as he'd left the parlor haunted him. She'd stood still and silent during the fuss his sister had kicked up, but she had to be hurt . . . concerned . . . heartsick. What awful thoughts must be racing through her mind, these minutes before her wedding? While Maria loved him dearly, she loved his brother in a deeper, different way. And what bride wanted to be crying in the parlor, worried about her man's whereabouts, when she'd spent the past months dreaming of this moment—this biggest promise and celebration of her life?

And we left her to fend for herself while Mum and Jemma whirl like dervishes, he thought as the masts and piers of the harbor came into view. At least Rubio was there to help

Stoutham control the gathering crowd. Things were bound to get ugly—or very interesting, depending on how their guests speculated about their long wait. And when all was said and done, Jason would have to learn to apologize, wouldn't he? He owed all of them—his bride, most of all—a major explanation.

As the carriage clattered through the traffic toward the modest two-story building near the pier, however, the air of desolation around the place didn't bode well. His father peered intently out his window, as though to see through the bordello's drawn draperies. "Why the hell, on a Saturday afternoon, does Amelia's place of business look deserted?"

"It's early yet?" Jude offered, knowing it was the wrong thing to say.

His father nearly knocked the footman backward as he threw open the carriage door and strode toward the whorehouse. Lord Darington grabbed the handle, but the place was locked tight. "Open up, damn it! I know you're in there!" he called out. He pounded continuously on the door as Jude peeked through a front parlor curtain.

Was that a movement, near the bar? The room looked dim and empty, yet someone stirred . . . shuffled unevenly toward them without making a reply.

"Amelia, we must talk! And you know why!" his father continued in an ominous voice. Heedless of the curious passersby, the iron-haired man in formal attire banged the heavy door with his fist—

Until the lock clicked and it flew open! His father nearly punched the young woman who stood scowling at them, jaded and unafraid. "And what might this mindless racket be about?" she demanded. "Can't ya see the place ain't open?"

"Why the hell not? I must talk to Amelia about—"

"Gone, she is. To Brighton, to work a convention. Not that it's any of *your* business."

"Cheeky *chit*! Have you any idea to whom you're speaking?" he demanded. "When Miss Amelia returns—"

"Father, please! We haven't time for such confrontations." Jude grabbed the arm that was poised to slap the young woman, giving the girl an apologetic smile. "If Jason Darington is passed out in one of your rooms, we'd be pleased to relieve you of him, miss."

She was thick in the middle and rather homely; not one of the madam's working girls. Her freckled face and prim gray dress bespoke a maid, perhaps—yet she stood fast as the establishment's gatekeeper. Jude had no doubt she'd back them off the doorstep, if she chose.

"I'm tellin' ya, nobody's here."

"Then who are *you*?" his father cut in. "My son, Jason Darington, was *here* with friends last night, and he's past due at his wedding! Do *not* waste my valuable time with these silly games of hide-and-seek!"

As she opened the door wider so they could see the deserted premises for themselves, Jude noticed an enlarged foot that pointed off to one side, beneath her skirts. A clubfoot. "As you can see," she replied in a haughty tone, "no ladies are present, nor is Miss Amelia. But the police shall arrive *moments* after I hit the alarm button, if you don't leave immediately."

His father's eyes widened in a face that grew ruddier. "Call the police, if you *please*," he jeered. "Since you're obviously covering for Miss Beddow, the law does indeed need to be notified!"

"So notify them yourself, sir!" The door shut with a loud *whump*.

"Well, of all the—have you ever seen such insolence? When I catch Amelia—"

"We'd best be getting back, Father," Jude insisted. "Our guests are in a state of pandemonium by now, unless the vicar has uncorked the wine. Can't expect Rubio to keep the peace as the only sane male on the premises."

His father's body vibrated with pent-up wrath. "Yes, well, if I don't get to the bottom of this—get a confirmation of McCaslin's story, or the *truth* from the police—who will?"

As Lord Darington pivoted on his heel, Jude wanted to stay behind and investigate on his own: he and Jason might be polar opposites in temperament, but they shared a bond that kept them connected even when one didn't know the other's location. He resented the way his father berated him, but resentment wouldn't get his twin brother to the church to marry Maria. With a sigh, Jude returned to the carriage to find his father inside, engaged in a window conversation with a uniformed officer.

"—weren't no different hereabouts last night than usual," the policeman claimed, talking around a fat cigar. "Didn't hear no reports of foul play, nor bodies bein' throwed off—"

Jude winced.

"—but for *you*, Lord Darington," he offered in a more gracious tone, "I'll dig deeper. See if anybody reported anything amiss last night, or recalls seein' your Jason."

His father didn't look any happier, but at least he accepted the lawman's story. "Be quick about it, too, while I go back to this fiasco of a wedding. Even if I have nothing to tell our friends—not to mention my wife—you can be sure the illustrious Miss Crimson will get wind of this scandal and publish her own ludicrous version of it!"

"Yes, milord, she keeps the *Inquirer* in print—not that I condone such gossip, you understand!" The officer, a stubby man with short, thick fingers, flicked the ash of his cigar. "If I learn anything, where might I find you, milord?"

"Saint Paul's Knightsbridge. You'll be handsomely rewarded if you show up with my son."

The ride back to the church did nothing to settle Jude's nerves. His father sat across from him, legs outstretched and twitching, arms crossed so tightly he appeared to be squeezing the air from his lungs. Even so, it wasn't love or concern etching themselves into Lord Darington's commanding countenance: he appeared more angry and inconvenienced than worried.

"Christ Almighty, if Jason doesn't show up, there'll be no living with your mother. The two of you nearly killed her during your birthing, but *this*!" he muttered. "She's poured every ounce of her energy into making today's wedding the year's social high point! You've no idea how much pride it's cost her, because her firstborn has chosen to marry beneath him when so many of our friends have lovely, eligible daughters *throwing* themselves at him!"

Jude smiled wryly. His father's remarks only added to his dismay at how horrible—how betrayed—Maria must be feeling by now. What would happen to *her*, if his twin had found trouble he couldn't get out of? And if everyone knew the Darington heir was missing, there'd be no more rendezvous about town with Maria—no more passing himself off as his brother.

But it was too soon to assume his brother was in dire straits. No doubt Jason would awaken from his drunken stupor to find he'd wandered onto a ship moored at the pier, or that he'd slept off his brandy while curled up in a doorway—or in some willing woman's bed.

The thought made Jude smile. Most likely, *this* was his brother's fate rather than the more odious ideas that came to mind. Jason was deeply, madly in love with Maria, but the whole point of a bachelor party was to have one last fling with the boys, wasn't it? And those *boys* were paying dearly today for all they'd imbibed. . . . So his brother was, too. Had to be.

"And what are *you* so happy about?" his father snapped. "Already setting yourself up as the Darington heir? And your brother not gone but a few hours?"

Jude stood up before the carriage came to a complete halt at the church. "That remark doesn't even deserve an answer, Father! And why do you believe he's *gone*, in that way?" he demanded. "Lord knows you've always applauded—encouraged!—his escapades, so who can say what sort of fix he's in? Or, for all we know, Jason has appeared and the ceremony is being delayed because *we* are not present."

As he stepped into the vestibule, however, the strident tone of the organ and the chatter of the congregation told him nothing had improved in their absence. Jude slipped into the parlor and wished he hadn't: his mother and sister were weeping, carrying on as though their lives had been ruined, while Maria sat glumly in the corner. Her ivory skirts billowed over the arms of her chair. Her hands lay tightly clasped in her lap, and her expression told him she was trying to believe the best—trying to be brave despite the horrible scenarios Mum and Jemma conjured up.

"Those worthless friends of his were the last to see him!" Jemma twittered between sniffles. "We should be holding *them* responsible for—"

"My God, what shall I tell the cook? We've prepared for three hundred people—"

"—the fact that my reputation is now *ruined!*" the younger blonde wailed. She was holding her ferret against her shoulder as though Willie were the last friend she had. "Who will want *me*, now that Jason has disgraced the entire family? I cannot believe he'd be so cruel as to—what did I ever do to *him* to deserve—"

Jude smiled apologetically at Maria and then stepped from the room. "Nothing's to be accomplished in *there*," he murmured to his father. "I'll find Clive and Daniel. Quiz them more closely about last night's activities."

"As though they'll recall anything. Or admit to it." Lord Darington followed him down the narrow hallway, muttering.

"Already four o'clock. If Jason doesn't show in the next twenty minutes, we must make the only logical decision."

Blinking his eyes against a wave of regret, Jude rounded the corner to find Rubio Palladino standing before Jason's three motley-looking friends, whose backs were to the wall. "What are you not telling us?" the medium demanded in a low voice. "You may either volunteer what you know, or I can simply lay my hands on you and listen to your innermost secrets."

Jude's eyes widened. Did Maria's brother truly have such powers? Had they consulted this medium first, perhaps he and his father wouldn't have wasted time driving to Miss Amelia's.

"I'm telling you, Jason was *fine* when Amelia took him to her room!" Clive rasped. His skin still resembled that of a dead fish, but he seemed sincerely concerned for Jason's welfare.

"And the rest of us, we each had our own—diversions!" Daniel Hackett sputtered. "And the fact that I can't even recall her face, much less what she did to me, should tell you how drunk we were!"

"All I remember is McCaslin beating on the door, telling us to go down the back stairs because there were stevedores awaiting their turn in the parlor." Nicholas Northwood had apparently overslept, but he looked no more recovered than his two friends. As he brushed his hair from his haggard face, his hand shook. "I have no idea how I ended up at home in my own bed, but before we left, someone assured us Miss Beddow's driver had taken Jason home. We would *never* have left him behind!" he insisted. "What sort of louts do you take us for?"

Rubio's gaze didn't waver. His disdain filled the narrow hallway. "My opinions don't matter," he replied in an ominous tone. "What you recall about last night not only determines what happens here in the next few minutes, but it may well set my sister's future. *Details*, man! At what time did you last see Jason?"

The three hungover friends glanced helplessly at each other. "Was it midnight? Or closer to—"

"Two, it was!" Nicholas piped up. "The bell tolled the hour when we got to the door and Jason tried to beg off. Remember?"

Rubio crossed his arms. "So it might have been, what? Three, or half past, when you staggered out of those rooms? Why do I suspect this impressive pack of Romeos paid to *sleep* in those ladies' beds?"

As their stricken faces betrayed this very possibility, Jude listened closely. If Jason had arrived at the whorehouse in the wee hours, how likely was it that Miss Amelia had *planned* to go to Brighton today? His father's expression said he, too, had heard this glaring discrepancy—and that he was fed up with the entire situation.

"This yammering gets us nowhere," Lord Darington snapped. "We have waited half an hour and still have no idea where the groom is. Meanwhile our friends are making up their own stories in the sanctuary. If the organist plays that song one more time I'll bloody well knock her off the bench!"

Jude grabbed his father's arm. "We must first inform Maria and Mum! Consider *their* wishes—"

"All the wishing in the world won't get Jason to the altar! If something has happened to my son, this church is the *last* place we need to be, damn it!" His face grew mottled as he took one last look down the corridor in either direction. "I shall inform our friends of this unfortunate situation and ask them to assist in our manhunt! *You* may tell your mother and sister. And Maria, of course."

Jude's insides constricted. But when his father strode toward the sanctuary, there was nothing else to do but carry out his orders . . . and bear the brunt of three females' dismay. He prayed for the right words, damn glad Rubio Palladino walked with him. Maria's younger brother believed Jason's fate had gone beyond the revelry of a bachelor party and that Maria would be the one who suffered most, even if she wasn't showing it.

When Jude stepped into the overheated parlor, the room seemed to hold its breath: two shrill voices stilled and three sets of eyes drilled him. "Father is in the sanctuary announcing that we must cancel—"

"No! He *cannot* do this to—*no*, I say!" Jemma screamed. When she rushed forward as though to strangle him, Willie jumped to the floor. The ferret raced between him and Rubio and out the parlor door. "Father has no right to—"

"Intolerable!" his mother snapped. "Once again that insufferable man has taken it upon himself to wreak havoc! It's *my* place to—"

Despite the increase of their volume and pitch—and the way Maria's face crumpled—Jude smiled to himself. It *was* his mother's mission to create a stir wherever she went. As Jemma chased after Willie and Mum followed her, vengeance against Father on her mind, he stepped over to take Maria's hands. "I'm so sorry this is all whirling like a hurricane—"

"Do we know what might have happened to Jason?" She stood up, blinking bravely, gripping Jude's fingers as she looked at her brother. "Yesterday afternoon, he was his usual playful self! Declaring his love—fastening this pendant about my neck and proclaiming himself the happiest man on earth. I will not believe he backed out of our wedding!"

"Nor will I, Maria. Father and I encountered . . . a suspicious story at the parlor house where Jason last went with his friends."

A bloodcurdling shriek from the sanctuary made them look toward the door.

"My God, there's a white *rat* running down the aisle!" someone yelled.

"He's jumped up my skirts! Sweet Jesus, save me! Save me—ooohhhh!!"

More shrieks and screams followed. Whatever his father had been saying to their assembled guests, Jemma's ferret had called a halt to his announcement and all hope of having a ceremony. Not even Jason's appearance would convince the women to stay now. Jude sighed, torn between duty to his family and affection for Maria. "Since Jason's absent, I should try to catch that infernal little rodent," he muttered. "If you'll wait here, Maria, I'll see you home—"

"I'll take her." Rubio slipped a protective arm around his sister's shoulders, his eyes shining with concern. "We'll leave now, while the uproar is diverting the guests' attention. Saves you a lot of explaining, dear sister. Shall we go out the side door?"

She nodded mutely. Her midnight eyes looked huge with unshed tears as she gazed at Jude, and his heart ached for her. "It's probably best," he agreed. "I'll talk with you later—and meanwhile, please believe we *will* find Jason! This is all a horrible twist of fate, and he is not to blame! He loves you, Maria!" *And so do I. More than I can say.*

Maria sighed and turned to go, making the exquisite choker wink in the late afternoon light. As he noted her shaking shoulders, and the way even her gown had lost its luster, Jude hoped he'd said the right thing. And he prayed the bejeweled butterfly wouldn't become a memento of the nightmare this wedding day had become.

6

Maria slumped in the carriage seat, invisible to the crowd departing the church in such haste. At last she allowed the tears to fall, grateful that Rubio held her. She'd heard enough complaints and insinuations from the Darington family to last her a lifetime, yet it was Jason's voice she needed to hear. Where could he be? What could have happened to him? Never mind that his mother and sister were so wrapped up in their dramas they didn't care about him. If only she had a way to know her beloved fiancé was all right. . . .

She raised her head. Studied her brother, who looked so handsome today despite the suit that constrained his usual flamboyant style. "What are you not telling me, Rubio? You talked with Jason's friends! You heard them, and felt their vibrations, yet—"

"Something doesn't add up. If I speak too soon, I'll only upset you more."

"Nonsense! *What do you know?*" Her voice sounded high and shrill, as though she'd spent too much time around Dora and Jemma. But her brother's expressive face belied a concern, a puzzlement, that went beyond any pranks pulled at a bachelor party.

Rubio shifted on the seat. Held her hands and closed his eyes . . . relaxed until his shallow breathing and slow pulse told her he was in a trance state, plumbing the depths of the unseen worlds around them. "Secrets," he whispered. Then he was still a long time. "I feel the presence of untold stories . . . of emotions that hide from the light of day. And they involve *you*, sister."

She cried more earnestly then. First Jason went missing and now her dear brother accused her of withholding valuable evidence! "If you're saying I had something to do with Jason's disappearing, I saw him just yesterday! As I've told you, he gave me this pendant as a wedding gift—"

"He was in your bed, was he not?"

Maria's mouth clapped shut. "We've watched over each other since Mama died, Rubio, but that gives you no right to—"

"I am not judging or accusing, Maria. I can feel Jason's imprint . . . on your heart and soul, as well as your body," he said in a faraway voice. "But he is not the only one."

The breath rushed from her lungs. Did her powerful brother intend to betray her triangular relationship? "You must not breathe a word about—"

"That's not my purpose. But if I am to differentiate between your fiancé's . . . emotional energy and another's . . . Identical twins present a challenge for me, dear sister. I don't encounter them often." He opened his eyes, trying not to laugh at her while she was mired in such a dicey situation. "Why are you afraid to tell me what I already know?"

Playfully she slapped his face. "This is so unfair, damn it! Why don't you tell *me*?"

Rubio glanced away, smiling. Ever the elusive younger brother, baiting his hook.

"All right, so Jude was in my room as well!" she confessed.

"He came to admire this glorious pendant he made, and to spend time with me while Jason was cavorting with his friends last night."

Her brother kept his eyes averted, as though he knew more. Maria released his hands, exasperated. "You already know Jude loves me, too. And that this triangle has existed for quite some time—and that Jason favors its continuation. How does this *intimate* knowledge of my love life affect the fact that he hasn't shown up today?"

Rubio flashed her a sympathetic grin as he thumbed a tear from her cheek. "Again, it helps me to differentiate between the brothers' bonds with you. If I held that lovely pendant, I would run into the same situation because Jason's energy is on it, as is Jude's, because he created it. Even without my sixth sense, I know Jude is in love with you, Maria. Anyone with eyes can see it. Be very careful."

Her throat constricted. Were she and Jude that *obvious* when they were together in public? "I—*please* don't let on about this to—"

"Of course I won't. Give me your hands again, Maria," he murmured. "We're nearing the town house and I want to ascertain whatever I can about Jason, now that I feel the differences between him and Jude."

Cautiously she offered her hands, and as he clasped them his pulse surged. Maria felt a concentration, a funneling of his mind and soul that made her entire body shimmer with inner electricity. She watched his chestnut mane of hair shimmy around his collar as his eyebrows peaked and his nostrils flared. What was taking so long? Usually, he knew within moments what was happening.

" A vast body of water," he murmured, so softly she had to lean forward to hear him. "Water all around . . . a rocking, and—" His hand flew to his head and he grimaced with pain. "Foul play. Raised voices! A loss of control over—" Rubio convulsed, even as his thoughts remained in the netherworld. His eyes flew open, fearful, and he released her hands as though they were scorching his. Fought for breath until he could settle himself.

"What's happening? What do you mean, *foul play?*" Her heart was pounding so hard she could barely get the words out. Never had she seen her brother look so frightened while he was in trance, as though horrible, painful things were being done to him in that other plane. He'd explained astral travel and how his soul left his body during these psychical forays, yet Maria had never fully understood how it worked, how he could *slip inside* the soul and body he connected with.

Rubio stared at the opposite seat. This was the time he allowed his soul to reenter his body, so Maria sat still, pressing her lips together to keep from blurting out her questions. They were only a block from the town house. No doubt the Daringtons would arrive soon, after they'd dealt with the cancellations: the food and cake no one had eaten, the bills that must be paid as though she and Jason had actually married.

Maria hugged herself. She was in no mood to endure Mrs. Booth's opinions or Lord Darington's temper, let alone the weeping and wailing Lady Darington and Jemma would delight in. She detested being their whipping girl: they would construe Jason's disappearance as a sign that he didn't want to marry her.

And then it struck her, hard: what if his family insisted she move out of the town house? Where would she go?

Rubio's hand closed around hers. His long, soft fingers bespoke an artiste or a philosopher, but they gave her comfort; provided something to cling to, now that serious doubts would arise about Jason's motives and methods.

"Jason's motives never changed, dear sister," he murmured. "I sense he is injured. Most likely incoherent, so he has no idea he missed his wedding. His sole objective right now is to survive."

Maria's jaw dropped. What could possibly have happened that—who could've overwhelmed him, physically and mentally, to the point he might *die*? "Oh, Rubio," she breathed. "We must find him! We must do *something*! But how do we reach him?"

Her brother stroked her hand between his. Never had she seen him look sadder as he gazed at her, as though she wore mourning rather than bridal white. "The pieces will fall into place, Maria—if we believe they will. You must keep your faith and hope *strong* and send them out to Jason in your prayers. Right now, it's all he has to hang on to."

"Please, Mrs. Booth! I assure you this plate of bread and cheese is all I want, along with a pot of tea," Maria insisted. The nosy old cook and Quentin had been hovering since Rubio left an hour ago, and she was reaching her wit's end. Why was it more work to live with servants than to do without such insistent *assistance*? "My concern is for Jason's well-being. The fact that he didn't show up at the church—nor has he come *here*— tells me something is gravely amiss."

"We're concerned for *your* well-being, as well, Miss Palladino," Quentin remarked with a worried scowl. "The last thing we expected was to see you coming back here with your brother! You must be devastated, now that the biggest day of your life has turned into such a fiasco!"

"And what of Lord and Lady Darington?" Mrs. Booth queried in a rising voice. "One might suppose they would come here to discuss plans for your future—"

"Or for locating their son," the butler cut in.

Maria gasped, exasperated. "I suspect the Daringtons are indeed discussing their plans, and they won't inform me until they've made their decisions. I'm only the bride, after all!" The words tumbled out before she could catch them: while she'd been holding up rather well, this nattering with the help would be her undoing. "I'm sorry," she murmured. "I wish to spend the rest of evening in my room, undisturbed. You're dismissed. Thank you both."

Was that how the lady of the house received time alone? Maria was too upset to care. She, too, had expected Phillip, Dora, Jude, and Jemma to roll up in their carriage at any moment—and the last thing she needed was *their* yammering in addition to what the servants had heaped upon her. No amount of concern would compensate for Jason's absence, so she was damn tired of hearing about how she *surely* must feel or what Lord Darington and his family *might* decide. All the words in the world wouldn't bring Jason back to her!

She climbed the stairs with her tray, sighing tiredly. Once behind her closed door, she gazed around the too-cheerful yellow and pink room, the chamber where she'd expected to be celebrating with Jason before they left for an extended holiday in Spain. Her wedding gown hung outside the armoire, a sad testament to this difficult day.

Maria gazed out her window, wrapping her dressing gown more tightly around her. Twilight always brought a sense of serenity to London, as the time between a bustling, busy day and the evening, when business was done and family matters held sway. *Serene* hardly described her mood, however: Rubio's visions had scared her more than any decisions the Daringtons might make about her future . . . for if Jason was injured and incoherent, how would they find him? Help him? Sending out prayers seemed so trivial and ineffective. . . .

Yet she was in a unique position to call out for help of a more tangible sort, wasn't she?

Maria smiled, her pulse thrumming. She moved her vanity bench beside the window seat, set her tea tray on it, and then took up pen and paper. Ensconced in this little niche, overlooking the lamplit streets, she closed her eyes . . . assumed the persona of Miss Crimson, society columnist . . . smiled as a grand idea came to her, fully developed yet so simple. She would write as though she'd been a wedding guest—for she could *not* reveal herself as Jason Darington's intended bride! Perhaps this point of view would give her a fresh perspective on the day's events. Stir her to action. Place her above the debilitating pity others would heap upon her.

Dear Readers, Miss Crimson entered Saint Paul's Knightsbridge with high hopes for having her faith in love and marriage—her delight in a happily ever after—reaffirmed, she wrote. The words flowed from her pen, a sure sign of divine inspiration. *Yet—as you may have heard—the wedding of Miss Maria Palladino to the dashing Jason Darington, heir apparent to Phillip, Lord Darington's title and estates, left the guests gaping.*

It began as any wedding, with the gathering of family around the beautiful bride. Miss Palladino's gown, an original design from the house of LeChaud Soeurs, befitted a queen with its layers of elegant lace and seed pearl embellishments. When I caught sight of her posing for a bridal portrait being made by Jude Darington, twin brother of the groom, she glowed with a rosy anticipation—not to mention the glimmer of an exquisite jeweled butterfly pendant unlike any I have ever beheld. Maria Palladino was the picture of bright-eyed anticipation, a dusky rose opening to the life of privilege and sophistication her dashing groom would surely provide. Her brother, Rubio Palladino, London's esteemed trance medium, waited to escort her up the aisle.

Maria paused, smiling as she nibbled the end of her pen. It was a treat to sketch her own wedding from a columnist's viewpoint.

Lady Darington and Jemma, her daughter, were exquisitely arrayed, as well, she scribbled. *But as the minutes ticked by, the assembly of friends murmured beneath the organ prelude: where WAS the groom? What reason could he possibly have for not taking this lovely woman as his wife? Upon questioning Jason's groomsmen, Lord Darington and his younger son set out to locate Jason while Father Stoutham assured the guests all would be well.*

WELL, indeed! The guests erupted in disbelief when Lord Darington canceled the ceremony! Then, an albino ferret scampered down the aisle and up a guest's skirts, causing the crowd to disperse in hasty, shrieking dismay. One can only imagine the bride's devastation, her concerns about her groom and her future. Yet her dignified grace under such scrutiny and pressure impressed this columnist so deeply that I am moved to depart from my usual juicy fare to lend my assistance.

Maria paused, her pulse pounding with the sheer *nerve* of what she was about to do. But damn it all, if Miss Crimson couldn't come to the distraught Miss Palladino's aid, who could? Who *would*?

I implore you, Dear Readers: anyone knowing details of Jason Darington's disappearance would be performing an act of tremendous generosity by informing me of his whereabouts! It's quite plausible he's ill or injured, unable to get word to his beloved Maria. Please submit any information to me in care of the Inquirer, *as soon as possible, and I will see that this beleaguered bride and the Darington family receive your assistance. Something is gravely amiss, and we must use the power of the press to hasten Jason's return. Thank you so very much for your understanding and cooperation!*

There, she'd done it! Maria stepped into the plain dark skirt she wore while delivering her columns, and then paused. The town house was silent, except for the delicate ticking of her mantel clock, but what if Mrs. Booth and Quentin were hovering in the hallway, peering through the keyhole? If she allowed the servants to stop her now, what did that say about her devotion to Jason? To the life she'd hoped to share with him?

Maria slipped into her charcoal cloak and pulled the hood up over her hair. She paused outside her door to listen, chose the main stairway as the most direct route to the door, and within moments she was hurrying along the side streets. As she avoided the light from the gas lamps, she again realized how much more difficult her secret occupation would become once she became Jason's wife.

We'll worry about that when the time comes, a voice much like Miss Crimson's echoed in her head. And who knew when that would be? All she could do was move along this path she had chosen, hoping it would lead her to the man she intended to marry. She blinked away Rubio's visions of dark, boundless water and Jason's disoriented expression, slipped the envelope containing tomorrow's column into the mail slot of the *Inquirer*'s door, and then hurried along the buildings' shadows again, back to the town house.

Had she done the right thing? Or had she asked for more trouble?

Too late to worry about that! The wheels are set in motion . . . and please know I've done this for YOU, my dear Jason. I love you! So please, please come home to me!

7

"Never in my life have I felt so—exposed! Hung out to dry, like so much dirty laundry!" Lady Darington spewed. Then she grasped Jemma's hands and peered into her daughter's red-rimmed eyes. "Mark my words, darling! We *shall* hold the *Inquirer* responsible for such—such irresponsible gossip! And when I learn the identity of that vile, hateful Miss Crimson, I intend to tear her limb from limb! And you may watch!"

"Oh, I intend to *help* you, Mumsy!" Jemma gushed. "Such slander—such a *slight*!—shall not go unanswered, so help me God!"

Maria perched on her chair in the parlor, holding her face expressionless. While she was not surprised at this outburst, she again wondered if she'd done the right thing last night and if other readers would share Dora Darington's outrage. Had she inadvertently endangered Jason by publishing her plea for help? Would she find an irate note from the editor in her postal box, informing her Miss Crimson's column would be cut? This visit was a grim reminder of her vulnerability—and of how she might be depending upon her journalistic income soon, if Jason's family booted her out.

Across from her, on the striped ottoman, Jude pored over the morning's newspaper. He, too, refrained from showing emotion, although his reasons were different from hers. What did *he* think about Miss Crimson's bold request?

He glanced up at her, clearing his throat. The rings beneath his eyes told of a sleepless night, either because his mother and sister had kept him awake with their tirade or because he was becoming more worried about his twin. "We had hoped to arrive this morning to *protect* you from Miss Crimson's news, Maria. Or at least to warn you of it, before you were quizzed about the column's contents," he remarked wryly. "But being a man, I must plead ignorance, I'm afraid. Why are you so offended, Mum? Miss Crimson has called upon all of London to help us find Jason! What a gracious, generous thing to—"

"Gracious?" his mother cried.

"Generous?" Jemma echoed as she popped up from the settee. She glared at her brother as though he were a pile of horse manure on the parlor carpet. "How *dare* that mean-spirited gossipmonger rave about *poor* Miss Palladino and not even *comment* about *our* gowns? *They* came from LeChaud Soeurs as well, you know!"

"And indeed I paid far more for my attire—and for Jemma's—than I did for that wedding dress!" Dora Darington joined her daughter. The two of them paced around the perimeter of the room like caged tigers at a circus.

"Even *Willie* received more coverage than Mum and me! And in the worst way!"

Jude rolled his eyes. "Call her mean-spirited if you must, but she merely reported the facts about your runaway ferret, Jem. Do you think I wanted to spend the rest of the evening trying to trap him, in that enormous sanctuary?"

Maria shifted, trying not to laugh. That explained why the

Daringtons hadn't descended upon her last night, and the vapid attitudes of mother and daughter justified the way she'd given them short shrift in print, didn't it? What *lady* would speak, in front of an abandoned bride, as though a simple wedding dress represented the supreme act of charity rather than a gift from a family that could well afford it? A family that was using this wedding to flaunt their affluence.

"Actually, I applaud Miss Crimson for taking our part," Jude stated. He glanced at the column again, as though inspired by it. "Rather than stirring up doubt and speculation about why Jason didn't show up, she has enlisted *thousands* of readers to watch for him. Anyone with information will be *far* more likely to slip her a note than to approach the police. No one wants to be subjected to an inquisition."

"The police!" Dora jeered. "Your father has already reported Jason's disappearance to Scotland Yard. They know nothing!"

"Probably miffed because a mere columnist upstaged them, too." Jude's gaze at Maria apologized for the ordeal these two were causing. He appeared eager to spend time alone with her—as though *that* would happen anytime soon.

"And what does this matter, *really*?" Fresh tears dribbled down Jemma's face as she wrung her handkerchief in her hands. "I wanted to meet the unattached men in attendance, a preview to my coming out. And now my hopes are dashed!"

"You could've asked those unattached men to help me corner that ferret," her brother muttered. "Not that your request would've endeared you to any of them."

"Jude! That's quite enough!" Dora whacked his shoulder with her fan. "*Must* you always bait your poor sister?"

He bit back a grin. "I'm making up for Jason. In case Jemma misses him more than she can say."

"If you'll pardon my intrusion," came a voice from the door. "I've come with your tea."

Maria could've kissed Quentin McCallum at that moment. They were in dire need of fresh air, and the butler's bright smile cut through the gloom that was closing in around her. "Thank you, Quentin. Please set the tray on the table and I shall pour."

Nodding, he approached, but was intercepted by an indignant Dora Darington. "You'll do well to remember who signs your check, Quentin," she said in a low voice. "You shall place the tray on the sideboard, where I shall serve when I *feel* like it!"

"Yes, milady. Of course." With an obsequious bow, he paused beside Jemma. "Mrs. Booth sends her condolences and these lovely lemon tarts, knowing how you favor them, Miss Darington. Might I inquire if you've heard news about Jason this morning?"

"If you call this *news*!" Lady Darington pointed at the newspaper her son was folding.

"Ah, yes. That."

"Miss Crimson's identity should be revealed, as much as my son's whereabouts! I suppose you and Mrs. Booth shared a laugh at our expense upon reading about the wedding?"

Quentin folded his hands before him. He was the picture of cautious diplomacy in his dove gray coat and pin-striped trousers. "A most unfortunate turn of events," he hedged, glancing around to see whom his allies might be. "And Miss Crimson's request for assistance may well lead to her unveiling—for if your son is found because of her column, all of London will want to know whom to thank."

Dora's smile suddenly shone like the sun come from behind a cloud. "Why, Quentin, I believe you're on to something!" As she poured their tea, her face took on a feline delight. "When Jason is located—for I believe he will be—I shall personally request an introduction to Miss Crimson! To thank her for bringing my son home, of course!"

As she accepted her tea, Maria's knees quivered. This was an angle she hadn't anticipated! And the butler seemed awfully proud of himself for mentioning it. She chose a tart, although she had no appetite for the beautifully crafted confection, which resembled a yellow rosebud. "I'm sure she must be someone perfectly ordinary, someone we've all seen at social events," she speculated. "How else would she know what to write about, after all?"

"How else could she harass so many of London's finest families?" Dora countered. "I've always figured her for a vindictive biddy with nothing better to do. Perhaps a jilted mistress or a dumped debutante, now unable to catch a man. It'll be fascinating to find out, will it not?"

"Oh yes, Mumsy. We'll have to have these incredible tarts when we celebrate *that* occasion, as well!" Jemma forked the last bite into her mouth, grinning at Quentin. "Please pass along my gratitude to Mrs. Booth. Her consideration has delivered this day from total ruination!"

The butler fumbled with his tie. "Indeed I shall, Miss Darington! So happy to play a part in your recovery."

As though Jemma ever has anything from which to recover! Maria didn't miss the butler's between-the-lines efforts to gain the young lady's favor, but as Dora and Jemma plotted the unveiling of Miss Crimson, she withdrew into her own thoughts.

Perhaps she's a jilted mistress . . . or a dumped debutante . . . now unable to catch a man. Maria concentrated on the final bite of her tart, burning hotter than she cared to admit. Yesterday at this time, such remarks wouldn't have cut so close to the bone. What a difference a day made—and *this* day, without Jason, was already feeling endless.

8

Lord Fenwick's manor was brightly lit the following Saturday evening, with fine carriages lining the semicircular drive, yet Maria felt anything but festive. She lingered inside her brother's carriage, watching those who approached the door. "I should be in Spain, enjoying my honeymoon with Jason," she murmured. "While it was kind of you to escort me, Rubio, I'm not sure I want to face everyone's . . . pity. Or their morbid curiosity."

Rubio slung an arm around her shoulders. "I'll not leave your side, dear sister, unless you ask me to. I only accepted Fenwick's invitation because his dear, departed wife was a client—and because he hinted the evening's guest of honor might be of special interest. We can leave whenever you please."

Maria chuckled ruefully. "We're a fine, feisty pair tonight, aren't we?"

"The evening might provide you relief from brooding in your room. Fodder for a column, too, no doubt."

"There's that," she agreed. "My readers would wonder at my silence if I didn't report this evening's gossip."

She smiled at her brother in the dimness of the carriage: wearing a purple cape with an Egyptian-print scarf draped dramatically around his neck, he would cut a brazen figure in this fusty crowd of old money with older ideas about decorum. The gold ring in his nose glimmered as he grinned at her, mentally preparing to make his entrance. Fenwick was a peevish old wasp who stung whenever anyone challenged his opinions: Rubio had often been his victim when Fenwick's much-younger wife had sought advice from her spiritual guides.

"Shall we go, my dear?"

Sighing, Maria nodded. She preceded him from the carriage and paid close attention to the other guests, noting a gaggle of older ladies whose jewels twinkled in the lights as they approached the door. Many of them wiggled their fingers at her brother, and one of them broke away to greet him with a spry smile.

"Mr. Palladino, what a pleasure to see you here!" she chirped. "And don't you look dashing, as always?"

Rubio grinned, bowing over her hands. "Meriweather, it's a particular joy to see your face this evening," he crooned. "I feared tonight's event might be a crashing bore if Fenwick's old-guard cronies started talking politics, or—God forbid—religion!"

The old dear twittered, her gaze lingering on Maria then. "And have we heard any news about your Jason, dear? What a worrisome situation for you."

"No news from the Yard or anywhere else, I'm afraid." Maria forced her lips to remain curved upward. This was only the first of such remarks she'd endure this evening, and already she'd tired of playing the abandoned bride.

"I have all faith he'll return to you." Meriweather Golding nodded as though she had inside information. "Your brother will be instrumental in locating him. Rubio never misses a prediction!"

"Thank you," Maria murmured, relieved when the little woman rejoined her friends at the entrance. "See what you've let yourself in for, bringing me here tonight? Gloom and doom. Not to mention questions about why *you* haven't led the police to Jason."

"I'd do that in a heartbeat if I could connect to his vibrations. You know that, don't you?"

"Of course. But don't tell anyone that, or they'll hound you about losing your power," she replied in a thoughtful tone. "No need to put your reputation—your work—in the same unfortunate spotlight *my* life is in right now. My real concern is *why* you sense no vibrations, no sign of him on your otherworldly planes."

He held her gaze with his bottomless black eyes. With his hair a-flutter in the evening breeze and the earnest expression on his flawless face, he resembled an ancient god: potent and all-powerful, yet benevolent. "Set aside your worries, Maria. Let's have a good time observing Fenwick's odd assortment of friends, shall we? Always good for a chuckle over a brandy later."

"I'll drink to that!"

Situated on an estate outside the city, the Fenwick mansion loomed like a Gothic cathedral, with its arched windows and scowling gargoyles. The vestibule seemed shadowy and cluttered with odd furnishings: a pile of newspapers had toppled in one corner, and calling cards, pens, and even hat pins littered the credenza. Maria wondered if the gasolier had been cleaned within recent memory.

"Nothing says *widower* like an untidy home," Rubio murmured after he'd handed the butler his cape.

"Or *reprobate*," Maria remarked. "They say Fenwick's disagreeable nature sends housekeepers scurrying away without their pay."

"Convenient, if one's also a miser." Rubio followed the others up the stairway, nodding at those who greeted him. "I hear no music. Smell no food. Odd, don't you think?"

Maria smiled at the Bentley twins, Camille and Colette, who had designed her wedding gown—and who now defied societal niceties by appearing in public pregnant, bulging with their first babies. They waved back and trundled up the stairs behind the other guests. "Did the invitation specify the evening's entertainment?"

"No, but Lord Darington looks none too happy about being here."

Maria topped the stairs and quickly scanned the faces: guests were seated in rows, on either side of the wide second-floor hallway. It was an area sometimes used for receptions and wakes, and indeed the low lighting suggested something more somber than a Saturday evening's entertainment. Or had Fenwick turned the gas down to save a few shillings? She nodded at Jason's father, and then acknowledged Dora's acerbic scowl—as though Lady Darington believed a bride left in the lurch ought not show herself in public.

Something inside her snapped. Maria stood straighter, inspired now: if Jason's mother disapproved of her presence here, well, she felt more determined to *enjoy* whatever this occasion brought her way. And then Miss Crimson would write a column about it, of course—not bothering to note Dora's presence. Maria grinned wickedly. Took the last vacant seat on the front row, beside her brother, who was acknowledging greetings from around the crowd.

Lord Fenwick then ushered the last guest up the stairs and stood before them, awaiting their attention. His hair framed his face like unkempt chicken feathers, white and wispy, and while it was true men's fashions didn't change much from season to season, this old goat might've been attired in clothing from his larger father's trunks. Perhaps the legendary Fenwick fortune was on the wane. . . .

"Without further ado, I present Yosef Polinsky," he announced in a raspy voice. Then he stepped to the back of the crowd to lean against the wall.

Maria blinked. That was all the welcome they got? No background on the gentleman who walked alone to the center area between the rows of chairs?

"Good evening to you. I am Yosef Polinsky, celebrated medium and magician from Old Country." He bowed, a courtly gesture that made everyone sit up: his resonant voice and guttural accent filled the hall with an air of mystery and ancient intrigue. Fans flapped open. Skirts rustled as the ladies craned their necks for a better view of the man clothed in muted tweeds.

And Yosef Polinsky looked at *them*, too. The breathless silence accentuated an electrical element in the air as he met every woman's eyes: his steel gray hair and thick eyebrows gave him a rakish, Continental air while the cleft in his chin and his prominent nose played up thin lips pressed together in concentration . . . as though he were reading each of their minds, their secrets, from the pages of a titillating novel. When his gaze lingered on her, Maria held her breath, compelled to return his brazen, assessing gaze. Polinsky's nostrils flared. Then he focused on the butterfly pendant.

Beside her, Rubio stiffened. "You may stop ogling my sister now, and get on with whatever you're trying to prove."

A rumble of male approval filled the airless chamber. Polinsky smirked. "Rubio Palladino. At last we meet," he stated in his heavy accent. "Your cousin Eusapia sends her greetings from Milan."

Maria knew a challenge when she heard one: this man, probably from Russia, was challenging Rubio to defend his territory, his reputation as England's renowned medium and tarot reader. They snarled like two male dogs, circling and sniffing, yet as far as she knew, Rubio had never met this man.

"Au contraire, Mr. Polinsky. My cousin and I haven't been on speaking terms since Eusapia stole the ring from Mama's finger as she lay in her casket."

The sudden intake of breath made the crowded space feel even more claustrophobic. Everyone's gaze bounced from the newcomer to Rubio and back again, as they silently speculated about how this exchange might escalate.

"She's a sly one, your cousin. Earthy. Quite . . . free with her passions."

"You are one of many who would know." Rubio vibrated in his seat, controlling his urge to throttle this man. "If you are such a celebrated medium, Mr. Polinsky, why have I never heard of you? You know of *my* work, however—most likely because you've seen my flyers since you arrived, rather than through any psychical ability."

The man stepped closer. His nostrils flared as he inhaled loudly, and he seemed to grow taller—or at least he made his presence felt on a larger level. Maria peered quickly at the faces around her: every female in the room perched on the edge of her seat, following Yosef with avid eyes. Even Meriweather Golding and Rubio's other longtime clients seemed enthralled by this fellow's rakish behavior.

Why was Yosef Polinsky here, in Fenwick's home? And what did he want from her brother?

"I come at Lord Fenwick's invitation," he replied, as though Maria had asked her question aloud. "My spirit guides call me here, to London. To begin next phase of my sacred journey. My journey of soul."

Maria sensed it immediately: this man was hedging. Hiding something, perhaps? Yet again, the women followed his every word, his subtle changes of expression, and the inflection of his rough-hewn, accented English. Here was a man who took the low road yet alluded to a higher way—and invited them to follow along. And what an alluring invitation they saw in his glimmering blue eyes!

Beside her, Rubio shifted. "Does this mean you've been run out of your country? Perhaps declared a fraud by the Society for Psychical Research?"

Polinsky coughed harshly. "You English perceive yourselves as so superior. Is nothing but snobbery! I will overlook, however, as I am guest here." With that, the man reached forward, but rather than shaking her brother's hand, Yosef cupped Rubio's ear and pulled a red silk scarf out of it!

Maria gasped, as did everyone in the room. Rubio sprang from his seat to snatch at the prop. "That's nothing but parlor magic—a trick children perform on street corners for tips!" he blurted. "It has nothing to do with your ability to channel messages from the spirit realm!"

As the audience twittered, Polinsky focused intently on Maria, on a point just above her eyes. "You have . . . lost one dear to you. A lover, yes?" he murmured.

The crowd sucked in its collective breath as Maria's jaw dropped. "Yes, but—but you could have read that in the newspapers!" she challenged. "Or you could've learned it as you discussed tonight's guests with Lord Fenwick."

"I see . . . vast body of water. Ship is sailing . . . westward. With the one you are missing."

Silence. Everyone around her strained to catch Polinsky's prediction while Maria's stomach knotted. She was accustomed to her brother's mystical musings, but this foreigner—a man they'd not seen before—had repeated what Rubio told her earlier! Her brother froze in his spot, clenching his jaw rather than responding to this pronouncement. A sudden movement in the back row made heads swivel.

"Is—is that my *son* you're talking about?" Lady Darington cried. "The police have given us no help whatsoever! Nor has Mr. Palladino—"

Polinsky pivoted to focus on her. All eyes followed his. All bodies strained forward, anticipating drama like they hadn't seen since the aborted Darington wedding! When Maria saw the flush of her brother's face, she grabbed his hand.

"Don't let him bait you!" she whispered. "You're losing your perspective!"

"How dare he imply—"

"You're inferring the worst, Rubio! And now he's provoked Dora into spilling the story and discrediting you! Back away!"

"You wish to come forward, madame?" Polinsky extended his hands, gazing over the audience's heads at Jason's distraught mother. "You and I . . . perhaps we reach out together? Send our prayers—our pleas—to your son, yes?"

"Yes! Oh yes, please!" Dora squeezed awkwardly between those in front of her, unaware of how she unseated them in her haste to contact Jason. Around her, the guests' whispering rose to an excited hiss, as though the hall were filled with gossiping snakes.

Marie felt as though this medium—or magician, or whoever he was—was physically tugging on her hands to lure her into this demonstration as well. But somehow she kept her seat. She gripped Rubio's arm as Yosef Polinsky took Lady Darington's dainty hands in his.

Was it her imagination, or did Dora seem . . . enthralled beyond the lure of contacting her son? *And if they contact Jason's spirit, does it mean he's . . . dead?*

"Listen closely," her brother murmured against her ear. "We will discuss this later."

Nodding, she watched the foreigner clasp Lady Darington's hands and then close his uplifted eyes. Long moments passed while Polinsky appeared to summon the unseen . . . to pull predictions out of the ether, as it were. Or did he truly possess psychical powers, as Rubio did?

"I sense he is . . . floating. At sea, perhaps. He is very confused."

Dora gasped. "Confused about what? How could he be floating on the—"

"In unconscious state. Cannot reach us." Polinsky's eyes flew open as though he'd been very far away while his physical body remained here among them. As he gazed at the sleek blonde before him, a smile eased over his features. "His body, it rests. His mind, it has gone . . . deeper. Seeking refuge. Your son, he is . . . adrift. Healing."

"From what?" Dora cried. Still clasping his hands, she gazed up at Polinsky as though he held the secret to her salvation— and Jason's as well. "We must find him! If he's injured—"

Again a gasp flew around the crowded room.

"—we must send a ship, or—the whole damn Royal Navy! Or—"

"Dora. That's quite enough." Lord Darington stepped between the guests who'd moved for his wife, his features growing ruddier. "This man is a huckster and a heartless fraud, playing upon your emotions! We're going home."

"But I—how can you *think* of leaving?" she cried. "Neither Scotland Yard nor that gossipmonger Miss Crimson has produced a shred of evidence about Jason's circumstances! We've learned more tonight from Mr. Polinsky than—"

"Claptrap. None of your sass, woman!" Lord Darington clamped his arm around his wife's shoulders and, without glancing at anyone, marched her down the stairway. The hall grew so quiet, Dora's whimpers haunted them until the front door closed heavily.

"I've seen enough, too. Come along, Rowena." The portly Lord Galsworthy stood up, clasping his young, redheaded wife's hand. "Whatever Fenwick had in mind for tonight's entertainment, this Polinsky character has only inflamed the ladies' imaginations and incensed the gentlemen's sensibilities. Good night, all."

Maria blinked. And before she could sift through the implications of Galsworthy's pithy remark—one she might paraphrase in her column—two other men excused themselves, wives in tow. Yosef Polinsky stood out of their way. He didn't protest these exits, nor did he call anyone back with the promise of proving himself legitimate.

She felt Rubio's gaze. His hot-coffee eyes insisted they leave as well, now that it wouldn't appear Polinsky had intimidated him. As Maria stood, it occurred to her that those who remained had all consulted regularly with Rubio . . . all of them ladies who'd come without male escorts: Meriweather Golding and her bejeweled widow friends, as well as Camille and Colette Bentley.

And wasn't *that* interesting?

9

I predict, Dear Reader, that London is in for an awakening. We have in our midst a force unlike any we've encountered before.

Maria studied the playbill she'd found fluttering outside Lord Fenwick's home—not by accident or coincidence, she believed. It featured a sketched likeness of Yosef Polinsky with one hand raised dramatically above his head as though he were summoning a spirit. But the medium's expression drew her beyond the hyperbole written below him, about his astounding feats of a "fantastical, phantasmagorical nature." Although his face was raised slightly toward the heavens, his eyes still looked directly at her no matter where she moved the paper or moved around the room.

Was it this medium's eyes, often an outstanding feature seers were born with? Or was it the way his nose and lips and brow ridge showcased those orbs to form a face so compelling, so charismatic, that she couldn't stop gazing at it. He wasn't a blatantly handsome man, yet he had a presence that defied description.

It was his voice, her memory prodded.

Ah, most certainly that played a major part in Polinky's presentation. What woman could resist a resonant baritone, thick with the intrigue of a foreign accent? Yosef Polinsky could have read from a legal textbook and still held his audience spellbound. Or at least the females. Men apparently saw right through his arrogance—

Or does he truly have the power? The ability to communicate with those not present?

Maria contemplated this. She needed to complete her column and deliver it soon, before the servants saw the light beneath her door. Yet she pondered Polinsky's face on the page as she recalled his brief presentation this evening. She had grown up in a family of prophets and soothsayers, and living with Rubio since their mother's death had accustomed her to his startling mannerisms and manifestations. She knew all about charisma, because her brother, too, had the power to wield influence over women . . . to shape their expectations and their beliefs.

Polinsky was different. Unsettlingly so.

Yes, my friends, she continued to write, *the arrival of one Yosef Polinsky, most likely of Russian descent, will shake our society to the core. Or he will at least startle and enlighten those who seek his counsel.*

She paused again. Was she making too much of this man, to the detriment of her brother's livelihood? Or would her column bring Lord Fenwick's guest so much notoriety—so many clients—he'd be too busy to challenge Rubio Palladino? Rubio, of course, would continue to enlighten those who came to him, but his behavior tonight, the wrath that had so quickly consumed him, warned her he might become his own worst enemy. Such anger was an announcement of a fear so primal few men dared admit to it, or to see it for what it was.

Fear did not suit Rubio Palladino. Nor did it serve him.

Mark my words! I predict—for, like our beloved Palladino, I possess an uncommon intuition—that very soon, prominent citi-

*zens will either benefit or suffer immensely from the appearance
of this star on our horizon.*

Had she overestimated him? Overstated an arrogance that
masqueraded as ability, until Polinsky proved himself? Or did
the fear radiating from Rubio echo in her own soul?

Something about Polinsky struck a discord. Maria hoped
her own prejudices—her love for her brother—didn't determine how she would deal with this new player on London's social stage. The way Yosef had gazed into her eyes, had studied
the butterfly pendant, and had then announced Jason's predicament to a desperate Dora Darington. It seemed too uncanny to
be true.

Was she becoming as overly dramatic as her future mother-
in-law? She *did* believe Jason was alive and that he would return to her. She was afraid *not* to believe those things.

Maria quickly folded her pages, aware of the late hour. All
this pondering of the credibility beneath Polinsky's showman-
ship had kept her awake far into the night.

As always, she donned a cloak the color of midnight, listened at her door, and then slipped away from the town house.
Her active imagination brought the shadows to life, even
though she'd walked this same path many times on her mission
as Miss Crimson. Maria laughed harshly at herself. She was letting her imagination run away with her, much as those ladies at
Lord Fenwick's gathering had fancied themselves in Polinsky's
inner circle. Poor dears, their lives seemed limited without their
men. Yosef Polinsky offered new opportunities for contact not
only with other realms but with flesh and blood manhood.
Manhood that reveled in its effect on their shining eyes and
fluttering hearts. And their purse strings, no doubt.

What else would they surrender to this man? And what advantage would he take of them?

Maria paused in the shadow of the building across the street
from the *Inquirer* office. Everything looked the same in the

dimness, yet she sensed something different. Something afoot. Perhaps someone watching her every move.

It's your runaway imagination, she chided herself. *You're wound so tightly that if you were a clock, your spring would snap.*

It was true: her breath came in short, quick bursts and the tattoo of her pulse warned her of Polinsky's power. Power *she* was allowing him by letting her mind dwell on him. Better to deliver her column and get back to the town house before anyone discovered her absence.

Maria quickly crossed the narrow street, the hairs at her nape prickling. She'd been aware of the potential danger of walking these back ways at night yet had never experienced this extreme uneasiness, which tensed her entire body.

Seeing no one, she slipped her column through the mail slot of the *Inquirer's* door, and then strode toward the dim light of the next streetlamp. If someone were going to accost her, she wanted to see his face—

"Miss Crimson, you should not be out alone at this hour."

Her pulse galloped crazily and every fiber of her body froze despite her urge to run the other way. Miss Crimson, he'd called her! If this interloper knew who she was, and he killed her here in the street, what a story *that* would make! Had Yosef Polinsky gazed into her eyes and known her secret, and realized she would then write about him, so he was stopping her before—

"Miss Palladino, I did not intend to frighten you," the man behind her stated. "But my appearance here is a case in point. I've been following you, and I could have been *anyone*. And you could be lying lifeless in an alley now, if I'd had any such inclinations."

That voice . . . vaguely familiar. She turned as Quentin Mc-Callum stepped from the deepest shadow alongside the building.

"Quentin! You scared the living daylights out of me!"

"Better to be living in daylight than lying cold as a cobble-stone in the darkness, is it not?" He crooked his arm, offering it to her. Smiling smugly.

He knew.

She'd lived at the town house only days before her unfortu-nate wedding day, and a week since, and the butler had discov-ered her secret occupation. Knew when she stayed up late to write, and knew, from her schedule of late, that Miss Crimson's column reflected it. "I should have you fired! For—"

"For what, Miss Palladino? Doing the gallant, proper thing by following you into the night? To protect you?"

"You have no right—it is *not* your place to—"

"Your beloved Jason gave me strict orders to watch over you," Quentin replied smoothly. "He warned me that you were an independent, rather . . . headstrong woman." His fea-tures sharpened. He appeared craftier in the midnight mist, yet he'd made no threatening moves. Had merely performed what he considered the proper service, supposedly at Jason's com-mand.

Maria glared at him anyway. "So you've eavesdropped on me? Watched the light under my door and listened for my foot-steps late at night?"

"The house has ears, Miss—"

"So you and—and *Ruthie* are the Daringtons' *spies*? I sup-pose you entertained yourselves *royally* on the eve of my wed-ding!"

Quentin's lips quirked. He glanced around them and steered her forward. "We shouldn't tarry here, milady. I've wondered, since the first time I observed your nocturnal journeys, how you've remained unharmed for all the years you've written your column. At the very least you could've been smuggled into one of the nearby opium dens or brothels. Forced into slavery of a sort we don't want to contemplate. *Do* we?"

Was that a veiled threat? How did he know of such base establishments along this street, unless he frequented them himself?

Stop it! There go your thoughts, running amok again!

When they reached the next block, her escort slowed his pace. Maria jerked free. She whirled around to block his path, glaring at him. "How long have you known? And what do you intend to do about it?"

With the mist swirling about his angular face, Quentin reminded her more than ever of Jemma's pet ferret. He stood head and shoulders above her; possessed a corded strength his uniform camouflaged—yet he seemed more amused than menacing. He smiled like a boy who'd discovered the truth behind Saint Nicholas yet still believed the old elf would bring him gifts, if he behaved himself.

This insight pierced Maria's suspicions: he didn't seem the type who would shout out Miss Crimson's real identity from the rooftops. But she couldn't let down her guard. Couldn't assume he was more a young, enamored swain intrigued by her dual identity than a threat to her veiled occupation. For if Miss Crimson quit publishing, it would be all his fault that London had lost one of its most celebrated secrets, and that readers could no longer depend on the *Inquirer* for juicy tidbits about their friends.

She crossed her arms, looking him square in the eye. "Again," she insisted. "How long have you known about Miss Crimson?"

The tightness around his eyes relaxed. They were within sight of the town house now, and he wanted to chat before they reentered Mrs. Booth's domain. "Oh, all right," he said with a half laugh. "While I wasn't so surprised that your betrothed came for a conjugal visit before his bachelor party—"

"We made enough noise that anyone would know what we were doing," she recalled with a sad sigh.

"—I was a bit, shall we say . . . astounded? Amazed?" he continued in a hushed voice. "I had no idea Jude had the—the—"

"Balls?"

"Yes, I—my stars, Miss Palladino!" the butler murmured. Yet he was clearly more fascinated than offended by what he'd witnessed. "To think that you not only write London's most popular column in the *Inquirer*, but you have *two* men in love with you! I stand in awe of—of your sheer allure! Your *power* over the male gender, and over the Darington twins in particular! Those lucky dogs!"

Maria maintained her stern expression, chuckling inside. "I could have you fired for insinuating such a—"

"Your secrets would be in far worse hands than mine, dear lady."

The little weasel had her there. Maria could no more tattle to Lord or Lady Darington about this presumptuous butler than she could admit she was bedding both their sons.

Best to remain businesslike; to use that *allure* to her advantage. She softened her voice. Lowered her hood so her face would be clearly visible. "So what do you *want*, Quentin?"

Recognizing a shift—an opportunity—McCallum stood tall. "We are in a similar situation, you and I."

"How do you mean?" She raised an eyebrow, waiting for him to spell it out.

"We both retain our positions at the whim of the Daringtons, which depends upon Jason's homecoming. He put old Hettrick out to pasture so a younger man—myself—might be his personal servant when he took up residence at the town house," Quentin explained. "If he doesn't come home, God love us, both you and I could be"—he gestured at the shadowed streets around them—"out on our backsides. Not a leg to stand on."

"We pray for Jason's return," Maria agreed. "But when he

does come home, your occupation remains a great deal more *secure* than mine if Jason learns I write as Miss Crimson. You've heard how Dora and Jemma would have me dismembered!"

He smiled slyly. Waiting for her reaction, damn him.

"Does Jason know about Miss Crimson?" she blurted.

"No, milady. Nor does Mrs. Booth, specifically." He glanced toward the town house, contemplating what he would reveal. "She thinks you write in your diary at nights, heartsick after a wedding gone wrong. A social pariah. Alone and without . . . a family."

Maria considered this, relieved that the busybody housekeeper wouldn't betray her to Lord or Lady Darington—unless this crafty man decided to share his secret. "Then what do you *really* want?"

Quentin McCallum was no idiot: they'd reached the place in the conversation he'd been awaiting. Yet again, she sensed no cruel intent, for his smile waxed almost adolescent. "It's more a question of *whom*, Miss Palladino. You see, to Jemma Darington I'm quite invisible: as functional as window glass, yet no one really notices until I make a misstep or—"

"Or until the glass needs washing."

"Precisely. People of their ilk curse the dirt rather than appreciating how a window lets in the sun while keeping out foul weather. As long as I perform as expected, I remain unseen—"

"But you want Jemma to notice you?"

"Oh, Miss Palladino, I worship the ground she treads!" he gushed. "Isn't she the most beautiful—the most spirited—young woman you've ever met?"

Well, *there* was a revelation! The *ground* was far more stable and reliable than the girl herself, but of course she couldn't say that while bargaining for her own security. "There's no one quite like Jemma," Maria affirmed carefully.

"But she's so far above me, I don't stand a chance unless—

unless *you* might provide opportunities to be of assistance to her. I would do *anything* to be near—"

"You would keep my secrets. *All* of them."

"Yes! Yes! I *adore* your secrets, Miss Palladino!" The butler clasped her hands between his, beseeching her with his shining eyes. "I feel quite honored to serve in your household! And I sincerely pray it will *remain* your household even if—"

"Then *you* must look after *my* welfare as well, Quentin! Promise me you'll do everything in your power to keep a roof over my head!" Maria stood taller, pressing every advantage she could think of. Deadly serious now, she lowered her voice. "If the Daringtons see me for my dirt—my soiled literary reputation, or the triangular arrangement I have with their sons—I'll not only be out of a home, I'll be out of an income. More at the mercy of their whims than you are! A woman left alone at the altar has nothing but loneliness and destitution in her future, Quentin."

"Oh, I would never forgive myself—or Lord and Lady Darington—if you were left destitute, Miss Palladino! Miss Crimson is my idol!"

"Excellent! We have an understanding!"

They stood nearly nose to nose. Then Quentin coughed to cover his chuckle. "I should tell you something about the house that will ensure your privacy. Or at least delay Mrs. Booth's discovery of your other identity."

Maria raised her eyebrows. "She knows of Jude's physical affections for—"

"When I saw him slipping in through the service entrance, and then coming from the wine cellar, I . . . I distracted Ruthie with, well—sex," he confessed. "So she wouldn't notice any unseemly noises coming from your room. She makes plenty of her own."

Maria blinked. It was still inconceivable that *Ruthie* and this young man would—but what could she say? Quentin had just covered her bare ass!

"I doubt you're aware of the whispering tubes."

Whispering tubes? Many large homes had been constructed with a system for communicating with the help, wherever they happened to be. But in her room, she'd never noticed . . .

Quentin cleared his throat, smiling. "Knowing you were to occupy that chamber, Jemma and Lady Darington cleverly concealed those holes in the walls with a decorative piece that hangs beside your door. Therefore, anyone who cares to can—theoretically—eavesdrop on the activities in your room."

"Which means the holes have been open since I moved in?" she demanded. The *nerve* of those meddling women! "And Dora and Jemma informed Mrs. Booth of this?"

"Of course. Because they cannot always be present themselves. Jason was most insistent that his mother and sister not intrude upon his newlywed state."

She exhaled slowly, considering her options. "But if I cover those holes, Mrs. Booth will know I've discovered their little ploy to—"

He grinned engagingly. "Miss Crimson is resourceful enough to use such knowledge when it's in her best interest."

Maria snickered. Wasn't it *fine* to be privy to a Darington secret, thanks to this confederate? He'd done her a huge favor—and oddly enough, she trusted him. She slipped her arm through Quentin's again and they walked toward the house that was their home, yet wasn't, really. "Thank you," she murmured.

"My pleasure, milady. Nothing I want more than to see Jason return for you. And to see more of Jemma, of course. Much, much more."

Ah, puppy love. She had to smile at his eagerness. "Miss Crimson *can* be very resourceful. I won't guarantee Miss Darington's devotion, but I can certainly . . . arrange things."

10

A few days later, Maria stepped inside the door and listened, as she always did. Except for the ticking of the grandfather clock in the vestibule, the town house seemed unusually quiet for the middle of the afternoon.

Perfect. She hurried up the stairs as the clock began the sonorous chiming that announced the hour, letting the stately *bong . . . bong . . . bong* mask her arrival. The muslin pockets hidden beneath her skirt bulged with Miss Crimson's mail, and she hoped to spend the afternoon answering correspondence— composing future columns. Closing the door to her room, she smirked at the biblical needlepoint sampler hanging beside it: A GOOD WIFE WHO CAN FIND? SHE IS FAR MORE PRECIOUS THAN JEWELS, it declared in pink satin stitches. Maria lifted its bottom edge and stuck out her tongue at the three holes: whispering tubes that would carry any messages to the kitchen, the laundry area, or to Mrs. Booth's quarters on the third floor.

"Oh, Quentin, you mustn't lick me there! You *mustn't!* What if His Grace returns and catches us in the throes of our passion?"

Maria blinked. *Quentin? His Grace?*

"Ah, but you know how I cannot resist you, sweetling! Your nectar drives me wild for more! His Grace be damned!"

She covered her mouth to keep from laughing out loud. That was indeed Quentin's voice, although he sounded like a bit player reading from a badly written script. Where might he and Ruthie be playing out their little melodrama? And why had she never heard their voices before?

Maria considered this while impassioned moans drifted into her room. Had Quentin turned the tables on Mrs. Booth? Had he opened the speaking tubes on their end, so Maria could eavesdrop? While the idea of the housekeeper seducing the young butler still seemed ludicrous, something about their game intrigued her. And who knew how *useful* such information might be in the future?

She slipped out of the cumbersome inner skirt containing her mail, removed her shoes, and then crept noiselessly up the service stairway. She paused to study the third-floor hallway, where she'd never ventured: Mrs. Booth could *not* catch her spying! Maria crept carefully past the two closed doors of the servants' quarters, thinking it quite *convenient* that all the help was housed on this level. When she entered the small ballroom, the balustrade of another stairway assured her she had an escape route, if she needed one.

Tingling with curiosity—for wasn't it Miss Crimson's mission to seek out newsworthy behavior?—Maria tiptoed toward the hallway again. The shifting of furniture on a plank floor told her their little charade was being played out in the room nearest the service stairs. Holding her breath, she leaned down to peer through the keyhole.

She would not have believed it, had she not seen it herself: was that the venerable Mrs. Booth wearing a bridal gown? Veiled in white lace—probably so poor Quentin wouldn't look upon her withered face—she sprawled on the narrow bed with her legs spread as her lover knelt on the floor beside her.

"Oh! Oh, my darling, you've ruined me for any other man!" the housekeeper moaned. She writhed and opened herself farther, clutching the gown's voluminous skirts to keep them out of Quentin's way. "Please, we have so little time before the duke returns to—"

The butler stuck out his tongue and teased the rim of Ruthie's portal. She cried out, pleading incoherently as he rubbed and licked her into a frenzy. His hands splayed over the tops of her white stockings, plump thighs that shimmied with her excitement.

Maria clenched, shamelessly aware that she was getting wet. Jason had been gone for too long! Jude had stayed away because it would be too obvious if he stayed the night. As she felt the inner tremors intensifying, she focused on Quentin's busy tongue. What a lucky girl Jemma would be if she encouraged this young swain's attentions, for he knew how to satisfy a woman . . . in ways that would keep her chastity intact.

Not that she herself would encourage Quentin's attention. He already knew too much.

But the little play went on—another exchange of heated endearments—until the housekeeper screamed and grasped her lover's head. The narrow bed knocked against the wall, faster and faster, until Mrs. Booth let out a primal cry. As she lay panting, still spread-eagle with her gown thrown up over her head, Quentin rose to his full height. He wiped his mouth on a small towel and tossed it back to the nightstand.

Then he looked right at her. As if he *knew* she was watching through the keyhole.

Maria covered her mouth to keep from gasping. How could he possibly have sensed—?

But he was grinning. As though the joke was on Mrs. Booth. Maria relaxed, yet the ache between her legs had become an itch needing to be scratched. She should retreat now, return to her room before the Daringtons' housekeeper suspected her presence—

Except Quentin was unfastening his pants. Quite nonchalantly, as though he *wanted* to display himself to her, the young butler let his trousers drop.

He wasn't wearing anything under them.

Maria's eyes widened as he stroked himself to an impressive length. Slyly he turned toward the bed again, giving her a profile view, and then he loudly cleared his throat. "You know the rules, Ruthie," he announced imperiously. "What's good for the goose is good for the gander. Assume the position—and be quick about it! If His Grace returns, I'll swear you provoked me, you wicked thing!"

With a short laugh, the housekeeper rolled to her knees. White garters stretched down her thighs as she spread her legs so her backside protruded lewdly. While her attributes didn't interest Maria in the least, it *did* fascinate her that these two had developed such a ritual . . . which implied a longtime arrangement. Quentin entered her without ado and began pumping, eager to relieve his pent-up energy. Ruthie had come first, after all.

Maria watched, chiding herself for spying, and yet . . . hadn't Quentin set this up? Wasn't he baring himself to *her* as much as finishing the script with Mrs. Booth? His dark hair swayed around his collar as his head fell back; his lean hips thrust and thrust and thrust—until he grimaced and gripped his partner's hips. His entire body shook as he released his seed. A deep breath steadied him, and then he withdrew, almost businesslike.

"I can't think Miss Palladino shall be gone much longer," he announced. "We'd best freshen ourselves and resume our duties downstairs. And while you enjoy her veil, you'd best find another prop. Only a matter of time before we tear the delicate lace or leave an . . . unseemly stain on it."

Maria's eyes widened. That *was* her veil! She'd been so intent on watching the servants' little game, she hadn't noticed how the familiar headpiece shimmered when its seed pearls caught the light from the window. Mrs. Booth wiped herself with the towel and then dropped her white skirts over her legs: at least she was too short and stout to fit into Maria's bridal gown!

Maria rushed down the hall on light feet and descended to her second-floor bedroom. She closed the door quietly and locked it. Checked her armoire: yes, the gown she'd worn for Jason still hung there, behind the dresses she'd worn since his mysterious disappearance. Should she follow Quentin's cue by slipping outside to make her official entrance, after the two lovers had time to return to their posts?

She thought better of it. Still felt needy . . . with images of Quentin's quivering hips and Mrs. Booth's spread, white thighs flitting through her mind. And then it was Jason she imagined, just as he'd been in this very room, the last time she saw him. Jason, playing the pirate . . . growling lustily in her ear, telling her what he intended to do to her as she remained his captive, tied to the bed in her blindfold.

Aarrrrrgh! Naughty wench! There's no help fer yer wicked soul save to tie yer pretty arse to the mast and spank it!

She suddenly had to have him back, if only in her mind. Maria reached into her nightstand, behind her lace handkerchiefs and the prayer book she'd had since her childhood . . . back to her fiancé's favorite toy, wrapped in another of his bandannas. When she beheld the dildo of sleek ivory, she felt a jolt of passionate need. He'd brought her this oversize, rather lurid gift after one of his journeys to southern islands where Darington ships took on their cargo of cacao beans. While she loved the chocolate he provided her after such trips, she craved the handsome voyager's touch even more.

And she needed it *now*. Placing a knee on the cushion of the window seat, she slipped the phallic toy, so suggestive of Jason's bold, brazen cock, up her skirts.

There's no help fer ye then, save to let Blackbeard have his way with ye. Plunder and pillage, it is! Assume the position, lass. I'm comin' in!

Maria inhaled his masculine scent from the bandanna, working the ivory column against her inflamed folds, scratching an intimate itch. Her hips wiggled, fueling the flames she'd ignited while peeking through Mrs. Booth's keyhole. She surged toward release, rubbing the nub that cried out for attention. Finally she plunged the thick phallus inside herself.

"Jason . . . Jason . . ." In her mind, he was pumping her from behind, moving his body against hers with the decisive power that swept her away with his fiery-bright passion. She hadn't been able to see him that afternoon, wearing his eye patch and bandanna, but she hadn't needed to: the pressure of his hands was forever emblazoned on her body, her memory. And the thunder of his low voice still rumbled in her ears.

You drive me mad with the hunger, woman. . . . It was all I could think of from the time I arose: your hot, sweet cunt swallowing my cock.

His intimate language, hot and crude, drove her over the top. Maria clenched and strained toward satisfaction, in perfect rhythm and harmony with her absent lover. As he moaned those love words again in her imagination and shot his warm honey inside her, Maria muffled her cries with his pirate scarf. She writhed against the dildo until the spasms ceased and her sexual hunger felt sated—for now.

My God, it felt so real. His hands had pressed into her flesh and the coarse curls on his chest had tickled her back. She suddenly wanted him so badly, missed him so much . . . *needed* him. Maria rested her forehead against the wall as tears slithered down her cheeks.

There was no way around it. She had to find Jason Darington.

Her resolve rising, Maria freshened herself in the bathroom and put away her toy, one of the last things Jason had given her—

But this is not his final gift! He WILL return! We WILL be together!

Relieved and recommitted to him, she reached into the pockets of the muslin underskirt she'd worn to the post office. More than a dozen envelopes addressed to Miss Crimson . . . from readers asking to be noticed or advised, most likely. An unembellished script drew her attention to one of them, so she slipped her fingernail beneath its seal, which was a blob of red wax without any initial or insignia. The paper was coarse, and she saw no return address. *Having seen your plea in behalf of Jason Darington, Miss Crimson, I can no longer withhold what I know.*

Maria's breath caught. She skimmed the page of plain penmanship, sensing the answer to her prayers.

I cannot reveal my name or how I came upon this information, but I suspect the handsome, intrepid Jason Darington met with a twist of fate during his bachelor party on the pier. He is most likely aboard a ship. Most likely in the unwilling employ of its captain. I pray for his return, and for Miss Palladino as she awaits him.

Maria swiped at her eyes. Who could have written this? How did this reader *know* about Jason being aboard a ship against his will—and how had he gotten there? It fit with Rubio's visions of endless water and a rocking sensation, didn't it? And it coincided with what Yosef Polinsky had uttered, as well.

Frantic yet hopeful, Maria pawed through the remaining notes and instinctively plucked another one. It only made her pulse pound faster:

Miss Crimson: please inform Miss Palladino that her beloved,
Jason Darington, was most likely shanghaied—

Shanghaied! Maria sucked in her breath. Who had done this
to him? Had he been knocked unconscious? Taken hostage?
How had this happened while he was among his friends—the
very cohorts who'd come to his wedding the next day unaware
of his fate?

Or had those three been covering their lack of vigilance?
Covering a truth so horrible they hadn't dared reveal it to her,
or—more likely—to Jason's temperamental father, Lord Darington?

Maria exhaled, trying to control her wild thoughts. Whom
could she ask about this? It was a minor miracle that she'd received two responses to that impulsive plea she'd published in
her column, but she'd written herself into a corner: if she asked
just *anyone* about this matter, her identity as Miss Crimson
would be revealed.

She folded the notes back into their envelopes. She stashed
the muslin skirt and the rest of the letters in the bottom of her
armoire and shut its doors. Down the stairs and out the front
door she went, praying Quentin and Mrs. Booth were still
putting themselves to rights. So intent on her purpose she was,
Maria strode quickly between the passersby thronging the side
streets—past the flower girls and street vendors—until she
turned onto Regent Street. She entered the side door of the tall
building that housed the LeChaud Soeurs couturier.

From the small waiting area, she heard her brother's voice as
he gave a reading in the back room. But she could restrain herself no longer.

"Rubio!" she cried. "Rubio, we must talk! Something quite
urgent has occurred!"

11

"Yes . . . yes, this affirms my original visions. I sense that your Jason is far out to sea. Sailing west across the Atlantic . . . perhaps toward the Caribbean."

Maria grabbed her brother's arm, rattling the letter he held, in her excitement. "What else do you see?" she cried. "Is he all right? Does he realize what's happened to him?"

Rubio closed his eyes again . . . raised his face in utter concentration. For what seemed like forever, he remained absolutely silent. Then his eyelids vibrated. His respiration slowed. "The Americas," he murmured as his hand fluttered to his crown. "He is alive but—"

Maria gazed at his face, so striking in his trancelike state: his lustrous hair fluttered back over his shoulders and the tiny ring in his nose caught a ray of light from the window. He smelled of sandalwood and exotic cologne, and his silk poet's shirt shimmered in shifting shades of red and purple as he searched inwardly—searched the universe—for signs of Jason. "But *what*?" she finally rasped.

Rubio's eyes fluttered open. It took a moment for his gaze to stabilize. "I get no sense of *him*, but all around Jason I feel great . . . resentment. Desperation."

Maria frowned. After begging for information in her column, waiting endlessly, and then receiving two responses, she did *not* want to hear bad news! "What do you mean, no sense of him? Either you have contacted Jason's spirit, or—" She stopped there, afraid to think the unthinkable.

Her brother held her hand between his. He inhaled deeply to clear away whatever he'd seen—or wherever he'd gone—on a different plane. "While I sense he is present aboard the ship, I cannot feel his unique vibration," he explained patiently. His dilated eyes looked huge in a face paler than usual: his astral journey had required a surge of sheer determination and psychic energy. "I have not established contact, meaning Jason has not responded, but I believe he is alive. Possibly injured or perhaps . . . unconscious."

Her throat tightened around a scream. "Why do these little forays into your spiritual realm always leave me with more questions than answers, Rubio? This is so—damn—" Maria exhaled forcefully, fighting a fit of self-pity. All the tears in the world wouldn't float Jason home, after all.

"Frustrating," Rubio completed her complaint. "Frightful. *Annoying*. Do you think I enjoy leading you partway to the answers we seek, dear sister?" He sighed, pondering. "I would rather not involve other parties in our search for Jason, but time is of the essence. So we must."

Maria's eyes widened as she considered the possibilities. "You're not going to consult with Yosef Polinsky to—"

"Why would I have anything to do with *that* impostor?"

Maria smiled meekly. "I'm sorry, Rubio. I didn't mean to imply you aren't powerful enough to—"

"Considering Lord Darington's shipping interests on the eastern shore of North America, I believe we can best expedite this search by informing him of this latest—"

"You can't tell him Miss Crimson received these two replies to her column! They'll string me up and hang me by my toes!"

Rubio's expression mellowed, yet he obviously wished she was more astute. "No, but *you* can tell him your brother, London's most celebrated medium, has seen visions of Jason on a ship bound for America."

"As though he'll believe *that*!" Maria sprang from her chair to pace the small room where he performed his readings. "Jason's family already considers me beyond the fringes of acceptability, so I can't very well tout my brother's predictions about—you'll have to go to Wildwood with me!" she declared. "That doesn't mean Jason's father will believe either of us, but perhaps if Dora clutches these most recent straws—"

Maria paused, irritated, when she took in his catlike smile. "Why do I suspect that's what you had in mind all along?"

"I don't know, Maria. Why *do* you?"

Maria waited anxiously in the manor's vestibule with Rubio while Thomas, the butler, announced them. It seemed they had arrived while a tempest raged among the Daringtons, for voices rang in a room down the hallway.

"It is only proper to declare ourselves in a state of mourning!" Dora cried. "My son—the heir apparent to the Darington title and estate—has been absent for an *unseemly* amount of time, and he's sent us no word! People are beginning to *talk*!"

"Mother, that's absurd!" Jemma replied just as vehemently. "Why should I forgo *my* social engagements, just because my brother got so stewed at his bachelor party—"

"Jemma! You will *not* speak ill of your dear, departed brother!"

"And besides that, I refuse to shroud myself head to toe!" the girl retorted. "The way black drains the color from my face, I might as well be dead myself! You're just wanting a whole new wardrobe, even if it *is* weeds!"

"If you insist on this infernal bickering," Lord Darington interrupted, "you shall take it to another wing of the house! I'm reading my newspaper, for God's sake!"

Maria cleared her throat nervously. "I don't like the sound of this," she murmured. "Perhaps we should return another—"

"Nonsense." Rubio draped his arm around her shoulders. "Perfect time to present them with a preferable alternative. No one *wants* Jason dead, after all."

A movement in the hall caught their attention—the butler, muttering as he stalked toward the back of the house. But when Jude came out of the parlor, Maria's hopes rose. "Jude!" she called. "Jude, what's happening? What's the fuss about?"

Jason's twin brother brightened immediately and strode toward them. With a cautious look at Rubio, he grasped Maria's hands and bussed her temple. "Just another day of drama here at Wildwood. Do you see why my brother insisted on living in town?"

"Perhaps we can help," Rubio suggested. "We've received new information that might lead us to him!"

Jude's eyebrows rose. "You should have come back to the—"

"I'm waiting to be announced . . . like the outsider I am," Maria remarked quietly. "And I doubt Thomas could get a word in edgewise, with all that squawking in the parlor."

"Damn manners anyway." Jude led her by the hand, past impressive gilt-framed mirrors and marble statuary. Then he stopped short of the doorway, his voice covered by the rising tide of female voices in the parlor. "It is positive news, I trust? Mum's in a peevish way today, I'm afraid."

"It is. And *you* may be a part of our revelation, Jude." Rubio winced when Jemma shrieked in defiance. "And it should quiet your darling sister, as well."

"I'm for that!" Jude straightened to his full height, as though the past days had been difficult: the onus was on him for not knowing how his brother had disappeared on the eve of the wedding. "Mother and Father! Jemma! Look who's here—with news about Jason!"

The three in the parlor turned, looking doubtful. Dora appeared thinner and her red-rimmed eyes bespoke a mother's grief, a state of unraveling like a worn rug. Jemma's cheeks flared as she clutched Willie to her shoulder, while Lord Darington glowered at them over the top of his newspaper. He looked ancient today; the lines around his eyes were etched more ominously than Maria had ever seen them. Clearly Jason's absence was hitting home now, causing everyone here the same concern she'd been suffering alone in her room.

"Miss Palladino," her fiancé's father intoned as he eyed Rubio's flamboyant shirt. He stood then, remembering his manners. "May I please believe you've not come to join in this female hysteria? It's enough to make a man escape to a faraway island. Perhaps Jason had the right idea."

"Phillip! You've no call to behave so rudely!" his wife chided. She crossed the parlor to grasp each of them by the hand. "What have you learned, Mr. Palladino? Just your presence here brings me a feeling of optimism! Of hope!"

"I appreciate your confidence in my abilities, Lady Darington," he replied cordially. He made a show of kissing her knuckles. "And indeed, as I searched for signals from your Jason's spirit—his presence, anywhere—I have reason to believe he's aboard a ship bound for America. And that he was shanghaied."

"*Shanghaied?*" Lord Darington noisily lowered his newspaper to his lap. "Why would I even consider that, when the Yard has had no indication—"

"Ah, but London's finest can't be everywhere at once, even if they'd have us believe in their omnipotence. The long arm of the law won't reach out unless it has something to grab." Rubio cocked his head slightly, appealing to Dora's widened eyes, sensing she would give him the benefit of any doubt. "Even in this day and age, captains come up short of crewmen. It's not unheard of for an unscrupulous shipping magnate to employ indecent, illegal means to procure sailors for his ships."

"And my son's headed for America?" Jason's mother queried. "He should've been there by now! Why hasn't he *told* us about this, when he could telegraph from—doesn't he realize we're worried *sick* over his disappearance?"

Maria shifted. The expressions on their faces held a hint that perhaps Jason *had* fled, and that *she* was the reason. "It's possible he's hurt," she murmured. "Unable to respond when Rubio prods him from afar, searching for his energy."

Lord Darington still scowled. "He's an able-bodied seaman. Resourceful enough to get himself out of such a predicament—"

"Unless he's unconscious. Or dazed." Rubio turned to Jude then, reaching for his hand. "I came to see if I could establish clearer contact, with *your* help," he explained, "for the bond between twins often defies logic or any powers I possess. May I?"

"Certainly! I, for one, have no doubt my brother was abducted against his will." Jude joined hands with Rubio, all the while gazing at Maria. "Jason was deeply in love with his woman, and the pendant she wears speaks to her devotion, as well. Lest we Daringtons forget, Miss Palladino has dealt with more heartache and dejection than the rest of us combined. Yet she is *doing* something—using her resources—to bring Jason back to us."

Maria's heart swelled even though she dared not smile too widely: Dora and Jemma, while fascinated by her brother's allegations, realized this second son was demeaning their behavior. He'd no doubt pay for it, too, but for now Jude stood with his eyes closed, following Rubio's example.

The two men faced each other, deep in concentration, as the rest of the family watched. Her brother's breathing deepened and his eyelids quivered . . . his face tilted upward as though he searched the heavens—or that universe within reach of his mind—while remaining physically in front of them. Maria knew that if she spoke to him, Rubio wouldn't be aware of it.

After a few moments, Jude gasped. "Jason!" he whispered. "I fear he . . . has no idea of his situation. Shows no sign of recognizing me. No understanding of how to contact us—if indeed he . . . remembers he has a family at all."

"How can that be?" his mother wailed. "Surely he knows we've been worried sick—"

"Unless he was tossed aboard, or fell. Those who've been shanghaied are often given a potent drug so the captain can head for open waters before they wake up," Lord Darington remarked. His brow creased with concern. "If he got a good whack to his head, he could be cognizant but suffering from amnesia."

"Who *did* this to him?" Dora demanded. Her expression had changed from one of dramatic dejection to maternal purpose. "You should send the police to wherever Jason might have—"

The older Darington stood up. Silenced his wife with a withering glare. "Sending the law on a wild-goose chase does Jason no good whatsoever. However, I *shall* send telegrams to my partners on America's eastern seaboard, alerting them to this situation. Whatever vessel he's aboard—if indeed this scenario is accurate—should have reached its destination by now."

He studied Jude and then Rubio, weighing what to say next. When he focused on Maria, his harsh features softened slightly. "While I put little faith in performances given by the likes of Yosef Polinsky and your brother, Miss Palladino, I appreciate your rational approach—the fact that you brought this possibility to my attention," he said. "Forgive me for overlooking your distress during this ordeal. And please—consider the town house your home while we await word of Jason's condition."

Her heart pounded. "Thank you, Lord Darington! I—"

"It's the least I can do for a woman who doesn't yowl like a tormented cat." He smoothed the velvet lapels of his jacket as he glanced at his family. "I shall return after I've given my partners time to reply to my telegram—or when I'm damn good and ready. I expect to find order restored by then. Good day, Miss Palladino, and thank you," he added with a stiff nod. "With gratitude to your brother, too, of course."

Out the door he went, intent on his plans to locate his oldest son—and, most likely, to take the credit for finding Jason, too. Maria closed her eyes . . . focused on a fine, feisty vision of her fiancé in her mind's eye, while sending him her most fervent plea: *Please, Jason, never forget how much I love you! How badly I need you here with me! I miss you so!*

"Well, then! I suppose we've quelled Mumsy's thoughts about pining away in layers of black bombazine and crepe," Jemma said lightly. She grinned at Rubio, and then held out her albino ferret. "Would you like to say hello to Willie-boy? He *loves* to be stroked!"

Maria's brother gingerly touched the creature's head. Maria kept her hands clasped, smiling politely.

"Thank you for coming today," the young blonde remarked coyly. "I was *so* upset, fearing we'd forgo Lord Galsworthy's ball for Mum's sense of *decency*! Now I'm going to shop for exquisite fabric for a new gown! Something in crimson or pink! I feel like a woman pulled back from the edge of her grave!"

"And I shall join you, daughter! We have cause for hope, if not celebration yet." Gazing purposefully into Rubio's eyes, Dora rose on tiptoe to kiss his cheek. Then she glanced at Maria. "We're invited for tea at Meriweather Golding's tomorrow. We'd be pleased if you'd join us. I'm sure the hours pass slowly as you await word from Jason."

"Thank you, milady. I'll be happy to go along." Maria smiled demurely: behind his mother and his sister, Jude was trying to catch her eye. "Thank you again for assuring me a home until he returns to us."

"Yes, well—" Lady Darington's expression tightened, as if to say *at least you won't be living under OUR roof.*

Maria smiled again. She couldn't agree more.

Once mother and daughter strolled toward the stairway, gesticulating as they described the designs and fabrics of their new ball gowns, Jude stepped up. He bowed slightly, extending his hand to her brother. "What a relief you've brought us, with this word of my brother. Sanity's restored—until the next crisis arises!" he remarked quietly. Then he grasped Maria's hand, as well. "And if you need to return to your studio, Rubio, I shall be happy to escort Maria back to the town house. I have a wedding photograph to show her. Had I known you were coming, I'd have fetched it up from my darkroom."

Her brother's lips flickered knowingly. "I'm sure Maria will welcome the diversion—and your company. If I hear anything further, I'll let you know. And thank you for your assistance, Jude. It lent me a bit more credibility, where your father's concerned."

Rubio turned, and as his gaze locked with hers, Maria sensed he already knew what would happen next . . . could anticipate it even before the possibility twinkled like a star on her night's horizon. "Tread carefully, dear sister. Your welfare is my utmost concern."

12

"Where on God's earth are you taking me?" Maria whispered. Even with her hand firmly in Jude's, the dank coolness and the flickering shadows his candle cast in the winding stone stairway conjured up images of a tomb. Not the sort of place she'd imagined when Jude had spoken of her wedding portrait.

"My darkroom is my sanctum. My sanctuary," he explained as they reached yet another landing on the downward spiral. He stopped to face her, his eyes reflecting the small flame in the dimness of the cold stone walls. "Developing negatives requires absolute absence of daylight—which, of course, guarantees Jemma and Mum won't interrupt me. Despite her affection for that white *rodent*, my sister faints at the mere mention of mice. And spiders? The complete undoing of every female at Wildwood."

"Mice?" Maria murmured, trying not to look for them on the rough stone steps. "Spiders?"

Jude's chuckle reverberated eerily in the stairwell. "Never fear, sweet Maria. I mention such pests for the sake of my privacy, but I can't have them scurrying across my wet prints, nor do I want to deal with their droppings. The only thing in my darkroom you need concern yourself with is . . . the photographer. And his equipment."

Maria's chuckle got swallowed up in a kiss that teased her out of her fears. Why had she thought Jude would lead her anywhere frightening when he so loved to lead her astray? Jason's absence had forced them to remain apart these past weeks, and the caress of his eager lips ignited embers that had lain dormant too long. Her breath escaped in a sigh. She wound her arms around his neck and pressed herself against him.

He set the candle on a rough ledge. Jude moaned and ran his hands along her curves as though he'd forgotten how they felt. As he cupped her backside, Maria rose on her toes to unleash her need. He felt so warm and giving, so solid and satisfying, after calling up mere memories of Jason while she satisfied herself with that ivory dildo.

Jude released her lips yet held her close. "We should look at that portrait. It'll give you something specific to talk about, should your brother ask how you spent your time with me."

"He knows, you know."

Her lover blinked. "You didn't tell him—"

"Even if Rubio weren't a medium, he's got enough male instinct to figure things out." She tweaked his nose. "It's not like he's a paragon of virtue, either, so we keep each other's secrets. My brother might not entirely approve of our . . . three-legged arrangement, but he'll never reveal it to anyone."

Jude nodded doubtfully. "We'd best move along, anyway. Could be Mum and my nosy sister will figure things out, too, if they saw Rubio leave without you. You're going to love what you see!"

They reached the lower level at last, a dreary area where pieces of cast-out furniture loomed, draped in spooky sheets. Across the stone floor, Jude's candle revealed wooden partitions, and after they stepped through a doorway there he lit an oil lamp with a reflector. The enclosed den became immediately cheerier. Enameled basins were stacked neatly in one corner of his work area, which consisted of two large tables joined in the corner. An acidic smell made her wrinkle her nose, but his lemon verbena candle masked it.

"Now—prepare yourself, fair Maria," Jude murmured, pointing to an easel draped in a drop cloth. "While all three of the portraits I made show you to breathtaking advantage, this is my favorite. So I indulged my selfish whims and printed two enlargements of it. A gift to you, and to myself."

He gestured for her to remove the cloth, yet she hesitated. She and Rubio had come from a working-class family; had never sat for formal portraits. Most she'd seen appeared stilted and stiff, because the subjects had to remain still for such a long time. *What if I don't like it? He's obviously so eager to show me . . . so proud of his work . . .*

With a flick of her wrist she whipped away the cloth. Then she gasped. "Why, I resemble the Queen herself—when she was much younger, of course!"

"I was hoping you'd notice the resemblance, love. I've not looked at this portrait in natural light," he added with a boyish grin. "But I'm sure Mum and Jemma will wail that *they* have never been so breathtakingly . . . beautifully portrayed."

Maria stepped closer, running a finger along the plain yet elegant gilt frame he'd chosen. "It's—well, I've never seen anything like it! And this hint of color—"

"A light touch of gouache, to make your lips look so . . . kissable and lifelike," he whispered. "And to add dimension to your gown and hair that a mere photograph won't capture."

Maria swallowed hard. The portrait brought back all the anticipation—the bridal excitement—of those moments before they realized the wedding would be cancelled. "I wish Jason were here to—"

When her voice caught, Jude slipped his arm around her.

"And he *will* be, sweetheart! Soon! Father has by now sent out telegrams to all his American partners, thanks to you and Rubio. He remains sternly silent about the matter, but it's worn him thin. He detests feeling helpless."

"So do I. Thank you for understanding that—and for bringing me to see this, Jude. I . . . I wish it were *real*."

His eyebrow arched. "How do you mean, *real*? As surely as my arm holds your shoulders and my cock prods my pants, you are a living, breathing—"

"But that's a bridal portrait. And I came away from the church unmarried."

He pulled her close, so she could not look away from his insistent eyes . . . eyes that matched Jason's. "This dream shall someday come true, Maria. I can *feel* it! Among other things."

A snicker escaped her, and then she laughed out loud as the unladylike sound echoed around them. "You're incorrigible!"

"A man with a passion, my dear. A need for *you*." Jude pulled her into another ravenous kiss, which made her aware that even if, God forbid, she never saw Jason again, she was very much loved. Very much desired and cherished—even if Jude loved her in a different way.

But it was a way that thrilled her, wasn't it? What woman didn't adore a man who captured her so skillfully with his camera? And how could she not appreciate Jude's humor, his slower yet thorough way of inflaming her before he made love to her? His twin's tendencies toward rapid-fire, breathless lovemaking thrilled her because she loved Jason's little games: she was his willing victim every time he took her.

Right here, right now, though, Jude once again proved his unique power over her. His was the subtle, sensuous, sentimental soul . . . a belief that she deserved to be wooed and won, as proof of his affection for her. Maria felt his lithe body rubbing hers, and once again she succumbed to the forbidden thrill of making love to a man who passed as Jason but was not.

"Up you go, my little tart," he murmured as he lifted her to sit on his worktable. "I've a yen for honey and nectar, warm and pungent. Where might I find some?"

Maria's inner muscles clenched. His sly smile widened just inches in front of hers as his gaze swept her face—and loved what he saw there. "I know a place," she whispered. "It's dark and mysterious. Only the brave and the confident venture inside, for fear they'll never recover themselves after they enter those mystical gates."

"Show me the way with your hand." Jude slowly raised the hem of her skirt. "Am I on the right path, love? How shall I know when I arrive?"

Maria spread her thighs farther apart, pressing his palm at their moist juncture. "Just inside this seam . . . hidden behind a bush . . . God, how I love it when you rub my mound this way."

"I thought you might." Jude's voice was the softest whisper. His dark eyes shone in the candle's flickering light, and as he held her gaze, a single finger insinuated itself into the opening of her silk drawers. "Oh, Maria . . . so wet and willing . . . so sweet and warm. Your scent drives me absolutely insane."

Her head fell back as he inserted his long middle finger, circling in a hypnotic rhythm that made her gasp and need so much more. "Jude—Jude, please fill me with your cock and— it's been so fucking long since—"

"Ah, the lady prays a desperate prayer. But I shall make her wait, and . . ." Low laughter wrapped around her as he filled her with three fingers, to stroke her wet folds with maddening slowness. "I suspect my brother's bravado impresses you—has accustomed you to his aggression and speed. But I am not my brother, sweet Maria."

Her eyes flew open. And indeed she saw Jude's subtler charm: the catlike grin that said he thoroughly enjoyed the chase—the tease and lead-up—as much as the actual act of joining with her. "Do you spend your hours in this room dreaming

up ways to torment me, Jude? Did you make yourself a dupli-
cate of my portrait for those times when solitary satisfaction
must suffice?"

His eyes widened. "And what would you know of solitary
satisfaction? Between my brother and me, we leave you little
time to recuperate or grow needy again."

"You only whet my appetite for more. I'm insatiable, you
know." Maria nipped her lip, letting her hips wiggle with his
caress. "Did Jason ever tell you about the ivory dildo he brought
me from one of his trips? It's huge, Jude. Fills me so full, and
feels so . . . *solid* when I clench my puss around its loooong
thickness."

He swallowed hard. Fumbled with the buttons of his pants.
"And do you ease it in and out? Torture yourself with its ridges
and textures?" he whispered. "Or do you plunge and fuck
mindlessly, until—"

"Yes. Ohhhh yes."

He scooped himself out of his drawers as his pants slithered
down his legs. "And which way will you maneuver *me*, when I
become your love toy, your personal slave—"

"Enter the gates and find out." Maria gazed pointedly at his
erect cock, unrestrained and ready as he rubbed it in his palm.
"But first let me admire the photographer and his . . . equipment. What a picture you make, Jude. I could watch you all
day . . . could suggest that you fondle yourself while I hold my
hole open as your target. I bet you could splatter me from three
paces, like a magnificent fountain shooting cum from—" To
clarify her point, Maria slouched back against the wall and
reached between her legs. She tugged the soggy seam of her
drawers apart so she was fully visible to him, then held her inflamed folds open to reveal the little nub jutting above it.

"Jesus, woman, you excite me so much I can't think!" Jude
stepped closer, ready to plunge inside her. Yet he inserted only
his tip, and then stood very still, gawking at the length of his

cock as it bridged their quivering bodies. The springy hair at his root vibrated with his need as he tried to wait her out. Silently, he taunted her to be the one who lunged first.

The darkroom resonated with their unspoken challenges: his deeper breathing a counterpoint to her rapid panting; her feral scowl an invitation to yowl like a stray tom stalking a female in heat.

"Kiss me, Maria—"

"Take me, Jude, I—"

Words got lost in their sudden coming together. Hips angled and bucked, straining for the most solid contact before finding the familiar rhythm they'd established long, long ago. Jude grabbed Maria's ass to arch up against that spot deep within her—the sultry, sensitive place that always made her clutch him in desperate ecstasy. She held on, hard, oblivious to the table legs scraping the rough floor. All she knew was that she had to complete herself yet again in this sensuous man's embrace. He grew harder and more insistent, then convulsed to enter the mad, mindless frenzy of his climax.

"Yes, yes—*please*," she whimpered, racing toward that hard, sharp edge of delicious oblivion. With a final squeeze, her body became one unrelenting spasm. On and on she undulated, seeking the release and completion that would sate her body . . . her soul.

She went completely still then. Totally spent.

After countless heartbeats, Maria drifted back to her present reality. Knew she was still joined with Jude, caught up in his arms as he, too, let his breathing return to normal.

"For a moment, I was wishing Jason wouldn't come home," he confessed, his face buried in the soft fabric of her blouse. "That's selfish, of course. But there it is."

Maria opened her eyes. Gazed at the photograph . . . the portrait this skilled photographer had preserved for her, for Jason and Jude—and for the possibility that her wedding day might not be commemorated in any other way. "I understand," she replied with a hitch in her voice.

He sighed. "I didn't mean to upset you. Should've kept my mouth shut."

"No. We both miss him, for our own reasons. We can't deny the emotions his absence invokes, nor should we consider them inappropriate. We've come too far for that, Jude."

He nodded, and then eased himself out of her. Took a clean cloth from his table and gently wiped her before drying himself. Tugged the damp folds of her drawers together again, and then lowered her skirts. "I had intended to bring the portrait to the town house—"

"To avoid any repercussions from your family?"

"You know how ugly it gets when Mum and Sis act on their envy."

She nodded. Again studied the portrait on its easel as he helped her down from the table. "I think I look very much at home, enthroned as the queen of your darkroom, dear Jude. If I want to see it again, we'll have to find a reason to come down here, won't we?"

"As though I must *hunt* for a reason." Jude kissed her softly. Smiled ruefully. "Let's get you to the top of the stairs, and then I'll see that the way's clear. What a lovely surprise it's been, having you here—and moving forward in our quest to find Jason, of course. Shall we go?"

13

"Do come in, my dears! How lovely to see you—and you've brought Miss Palladino today!" Meriweather Golding grasped Lady Darington and Jemma by the hand as she flashed a spry smile at Maria. The old dear had to be nearing ninety, yet her fashionable cerise gown made her cheeks bloom; the two ringlets at each temple gave her a quaint but coy air. "We have a special surprise today! You'll never guess who's here to entertain us!"

Jude brought up the rear of their quartet, raising a sly eyebrow. Even as a widow, Mrs. Golding made the social columns regularly—because she served up either outstanding refreshments or the juiciest gossip in town. Maria smiled back at him, only vaguely intrigued. Everyone would ask them about Jason, which would upset Dora—which would in turn set off her daughter's temper or tears. Even an extraordinary entertainer would be challenged by such a double dose of drama.

"You ladies enjoy yourselves," he remarked. "I've brought plenty of reading material."

"Make yourself comfortable in the front parlor, dear Jude,"

their hostess said, gesturing toward the nearest room off the foyer. "I'll have Vera bring you a tea tray."

"Thank you, Mrs. Golding." He kissed her hand, lingering over her bejeweled fingers until she giggled. "I've never seen you look lovelier. These emeralds sparkle *almost* as brightly as your eyes."

Maria sighed as he entered the sunny front room. While it was best to get out among friends now and again, she was more in the mood to catch up on Miss Crimson's mail. At a surprised collective gasp from the adjacent music room, however, her ears perked up.

"Good afternoon, ladies! The radiance in this room, it dazzles me!"

As though she were a marionette whose strings had been jerked, Dora Darington swiveled her head. "Come along, Jemma!" she chirped. "We don't want to miss a moment of *this!*" As Dora steered her daughter quickly toward the doorway at the end of the hall, Mrs. Golding wore a catlike smile, as though she might burst with awaiting her guests' reactions to the afternoon's diversion.

"I believe I met some of you a few evenings past," the mystery man crooned, "and I wish to thank my kind hostess, Mrs. Golding, for bringing us together again. And—why, it's Dora! The lovely Lady Darington, whom I met at Lord Fenwick's! And this beauty beside you surely must be your—*sister*. Am I correct?"

Maria nearly walked into the two blondes, who had stopped in the doorway for the rolling pronouncement of their presence. And wasn't *this* a surprise? Yosef Polinsky stood beside the square grand piano, gazing happily at the roomful of women!

My God, he looks ready to devour Dora! Maria glanced at Mrs. Golding, who sparkled like a star as she stepped around the two Daringtons to take center stage.

"Didn't I *promise* you a most pleasant afternoon, ladies?" she cooed. Then she grinned girlishly at the foreigner. "Mr. Polinsky has graciously agreed to regale us with his magician's skills and his ability to read minds! And I can tell you, he's very, very good at *that!*"

Before their eyes, the little widow had dropped fifteen years. But it was Lady Darington's reaction that caught Maria's closer attention: Dora gazed directly at the man whose foreign accent had fascinated them last week, as though she and Polinsky were the only ones in the room. Her neck arched like a swan's as she widened her eyes coquettishly. "Mr. Polinsky," she murmured in a husky voice. "What a pleasure to see you again. May I present my daughter, Jemma?"

Jemma, thank God, had left Willie at home: she would have dropped the ferret, judging from her irritated expression when Polinsky had called her Dora's sister. Knowing an opportunity when she saw one, however, Jemma dipped in a graceful curtsy to the man in the tweed suit. As the magician stepped forward to take Miss Darington's hands, Maria pondered the little scene playing out before all these women. What was different about Yosef Polinsky today?

As he bowed over the flustered Jemma's hands, Maria realized some of his coarseness—the appearance of being fresh off the boat—had disappeared. The magician still spoke with an Eastern European accent, but his manner seemed more refined. Less provincial. More keenly attuned to the audience around him—

Because these women are here without their men.

Maria blinked. Oh, but Miss Crimson would love to report *this!* Without any of these cackling biddies knowing who'd written it!

"And—it's Miss Palladino, isn't it?" he continued. "Wearing such a lovely butterfly pendant in memory of her fiancé, lost at sea."

Around her, gazes sharpened. "And how would you know that, Mr. Polinsky?" she demanded in a strained voice.

The medium's mouth quirked. "I have contacted his spirit."

All in the room gasped, leaning in to catch this conversation. Dora grabbed her daughter's hand—and on second thought, reached for Maria's, too. "What have you learned about my son?" she asked breathlessly. "Nearly three weeks have passed since—since his disappearance. Do *not* toy with my emotions, Mr. Polinsky!"

The medium stepped closer, his gaze intent. "I would never *toy* with you, my dear. I feel the flutter of your heartbeat . . . the need for any word at all of your beloved Jason. And I can tell you he has gone ashore now, in America. And . . . how do I say this? Your son is involved in . . . nefarious affairs, I fear."

"Nefarious, Mr. Polinsky? How so?" Lady Darington stood ramrod straight. She allowed the medium to take her hand, yet refused to believe what he said. "My son is a most honorable, forthright—"

"Yes, of course," Polinsky demurred, "but he is not in his right mind, you see. And he is perhaps . . . operating under the orders of a superior."

"The captain who shanghaied him?" Maria stepped into this ring of emotional fire, suddenly eager to be heard—and to learn any tidbits this man would offer, even if her brother was the stronger, more trustworthy wayfarer in the spirit realm. "We've already surmised that he was taken hostage on the eve of our wedding, sir. Lord Darington, Dora's *husband,* has already contacted his shipping offices along the coast, and they will soon locate Jason."

"He eludes them."

The room suddenly felt airless. Maria detested being watched so closely by these women—spinsters and widows, mostly, in need of excitement. They followed every word Polinsky uttered as though he were an ancient oracle revealing mysteries and miracles. He appeared more polished today: his hair was carefully combed and his shirt collar stood stiff and white above his fresh serge suit.

"How do you know this, sir?" she demanded, sensing the two Daringtons were about to spin into a hissy fit. "Upon what authority have you—"

"The same omnipotent Spirit your brother calls upon."

Something was too smooth about this performance. Maria could not be a sheep in this man's flock: all the ladies around them appeared spellbound, clasping their hands in their laps as they leaned forward to follow every nuance of this bizarre exchange.

So she looked to Meriweather Golding for an escape. "I must apologize," Maria murmured. "It was not my intention to monopolize Mr. Polinsky's attention."

The little widow beamed beatifically at her special guest, and then gestured toward three chairs around a small table to her left. "Very well, then! I shall have Vera bring our tea and cakes, so we may enjoy Yosef's amazing repertoire of magical tricks!"

As Meriweather bustled from the music room, Maria noted how the chairs and small tables had been arranged so all the ladies faced the center of the floor, where Polinsky stood with his back toward the piano. "I shall now get acquainted with each of you on a more . . . intimate level—by reading your auras," he added quickly. "Very much the same as reading your souls. Your deepest needs and desires."

Eyes widened and lashes fluttered at his innuendo. Yosef was now their idol, and he played upon that power by strolling between them, to smile at each woman as he held her gaze. With his hands, he then followed the outlines of their heads and shoulders, about three inches away from touching them. No one dared speak, even to acknowledge his greeting, for fear of breaking the spell he wove. Mystery and anticipation filled the room. A palpable excitement simmered in each upturned face. Every woman present waited breathlessly for her turn.

Maria watched carefully, well aware of the techniques magicians and fraudulent mediums employed. Polinsky approached their table last, and on either side of her Dora and Jemma sat graceful and straight. Like baby birds eager to be fed, they perched on their chairs with their faces upturned. Their eyes widened in awe as his hands suggestively followed the lines of their bodies without making contact. Mother and daughter looked too awestruck to even *breathe* as this man held their gazes . . . wielded total control with his penetrating gaze and an expression that bespoke sexual superiority. Irresistible charisma.

To prove to him—to herself—that she would not be led astray by his staged behavior, Maria leaned back in her chair and pressed her lips into a thin, humorless line. She lifted an eyebrow, resisting the urge to slap the smug smile that made his square jaw and chin appear so powerfully male.

Polinsky's lips flickered and he moved on. Although he'd touched no one, she still suspected he was hoodwinking his audience: as soon as he turned from her, Maria's hand fluttered to the butterfly pendant. The cool texture of its pronged jewels gave her something real to hang onto as he continued to perform for his mesmerized guests.

For this *was* the realm of Franz Anton Mesmer, credited with controlling his patients by mentally reaching into their minds, following the cues of their bodily reactions to ascertain how best to direct them. She would *not* become this man's example because she was Rubio's sister! Nor would she allow speculation about Jason to divert her attention—and others'—by pursuing that subject further today.

"Again I shall say it," Polinsky stated in a stage whisper. "The beauty in this room dazzles me! Nothing I can say or do will eclipse it, so I shall be your humble manservant . . . a slave to your vibrations and light. Now—" With a sly grin he reached into his suit coat pocket. "To whom does this lovely piece belong?"

Every other woman in the room gasped as her hands flew to her neck. Maria bit back a grin: why did all of these gullible mice already dance to this pied piper's tune, even though the necklace could only belong—or even look familiar—to *one* of them?

Lady Martha MacPherson shot up from her seat with a bewildered cry. "My lord in heaven, how *did* you—my dear Chester gave me those opals! On the occasion of our twentieth anniversary! Mere months before he . . . passed from this world."

"And I congratulate you for making him the happiest man on earth during your life together," Polinsky replied in a sonorous voice. He concentrated on a spot just to the right of her plump, flushed face. "Did your Chester often wear the MacPherson tartan, either as a vest or a kilt?"

The other ladies at her table sucked in their breath, steadied her with their hands, as Martha looked ready to faint dead away. "Yes, sir, he did," she rasped. "How could you possibly know—"

"He's hovering above you, my dear. Smiling down on you from the spirit plane."

Every jaw dropped. A few reached for their hankies. Martha pivoted quickly, then gazed at the music room's ceiling. "Chester? Is it really you, my darling?" she bleated. "I've missed you *so!*"

"And he wants you to know he is happy and at peace. Watching over you." Polinsky's low, resonant voice filled the room. "He wants you to pursue your dreams now, Martha. To fulfill the . . . desires that burn deep within your soul."

Lady MacPherson's face flickered between deep pink and white. "How *dare* you presume that I—my heart shall *always* belong to Chester! We pledged our love eternally—"

Someone snickered: Chester MacPherson was notorious for

womanizing, while mollifying his wife with enviable clothing and jewels. She remained standing, still as a statue, while Polinsky reached around to fasten her opal necklace with a quick flick of his fingers.

He's had a lot of practice at that, Maria mused. He'd had plenty of chances to plumb the female psyche—among other areas, she surmised as she observed his polished, suave manner. Was it her imagination, or had his Russian accent disappeared?

"And your late husband shall indeed be with you forever, my dear," he intoned before stepping back to the piano. "We all live many lifetimes, coming and going with other souls we knew in previous incarnations," he stated in a mystical voice. "My mission, while I'm here among you, is to penetrate your resistance to those lessons . . . to help you grasp the unerring, cyclical nature of endings and new beginnings. Life and love, entwined through the ages as we perfect ourselves with each other's . . . assistance."

Penetrate. Grasp. And just what sort of *assistance* did this persuasive man have in mind? Maria saw various answers to that question shining in these ladies' eyes as they awaited his next demonstration. When Polinsky's gaze lingered just above Dora's plumed lavender hat, Lady Darington held herself more erect, subtly thrust her breasts toward him as her breathing made them rise and fall.

"And what do you see?" she demanded in a sinuous whisper. "I've watched many a medium perform, so—"

"Your full name is Pandora, after the goddess. Is it not?"

Maria thought she'd be sucked into a vacuum, the way every woman around her suddenly inhaled. If Polinsky was right, it was more than *she* had learned about Jason's mother during the months of her engagement. Even Jemma seemed surprised: her blue eyes widened and she shivered. "Mumsy! You never told me—"

"Hush! Mr. Polinsky is speaking."

The medium's nostrils flared. "You chose your name well as you were born into this lifetime, Lady Darington," he remarked in a low voice. "For if you opened your soul, as Pandora opened that box filled with wicked little intentions, you would set loose a *multitude* of secrets. But of course, I won't press you for those."

Not here, anyway. Maria nipped her lip. The man was a smooth operator, she'd give him that. And by alluding to incidents Dora had apparently hidden, along with her true name, Polinsky had left opportunity's door ajar as surely as the Greek goddess had flung open the lid to her box filled with the world's evil.

And where would that lead? Every woman in the room pondered this as Yosef Polinsky bowed to Lady Darington. Then he moved on to his next willing victim.

From one table to the next, this maddening magician circulated around the music room. Cups of tea, petits fours, and chocolate-covered biscuits were devoured without being tasted. Poor Vera did her best to refresh everyone's tea trays without disrupting the magician's performance. But it was doubtful any of the guests even noticed her: they were intent upon anticipating whom Polinsky would favor next, and what tasty secret he might reveal about her.

Maria sensed that she might be spared this hocus-pocus, since Yosef had whetted everyone's appetites with his predictions about Jason. And it was just as well: as though saving the best for his finale, Mr. Polinsky pulled a delicate bracelet from inside his dark gray suit coat, to let it dangle before them. A low "oooohhh!" echoed around the room when the gemstones caught the light and sprayed the opposite wall with rainbow stars.

"Diamonds!" one woman whispered.

"Whose can it be? I own nothing of the sort!" her tablemate replied.

Smiling suavely, the showman waited for silence. "I have been most pleased to entertain you today, ladies," he said with a courtly bow. "And I would be remiss if I did not repay our delightful hostess, Mrs. Golding, for her hospitality. Please, Meriweather—allow me to grace you with this small token of my . . . esteem."

Meriweather, was it? Maria sensed the rise of invisible antennae around the room as final sips of tea were taken. As Mrs. Golding fluttered toward him, the curls at her temples bobbed above her girlish grin. "Oh, you've no cause to tease me with such trinkets—"

"Ah, but I must! No *gentleman* would let such a favor go unpaid, my dear."

As he gently fastened the clasp around her wrist, Maria speculated about what was *not* being said during this touching scene. Yosef Polinsky's thick hair was streaked with a few silvery strands at his temples, but he had to be forty years younger than Meriweather Golding—

Who then rose on tiptoe to *kiss* him!

"Aunt Meriweather! Do tell!" Camille Bentley teased. Her twin chuckled, and together the two rounded, pregnant couturieres were the very expression of lusty love.

"Oh, I think actions have spoken far louder than words!" Martha MacPherson huffed as she stood to go. "This has been a most *interesting* afternoon!"

Mrs. Golding tucked her hand around Polinsky's bent elbow, flashing a triumphant smile. "It's my home, you know. And I'm certainly of an age to do whatever I please. I believe you're *jealous*, Martha!"

"What an *unseemly* idea, Meriweather! Highly unlikely." With that, the matronly woman bustled from the room, followed by the others' chuckles.

Maria, however, was observing Polinsky. The man looked devilishly delighted to be the cause of such a squabble . . . as though the notoriety he'd gained here today might take him farther than all the playbills he could've posted on the city streets: these other influential, *lonely* ladies would now vie for his presence as a guest in *their* homes, too.

What a crafty way to garner potential clients while not paying any rent! Sheer genius, that's what the man possessed, along with a persona that would entice any female he met. And while Maria hated to give Polinsky any further publicity, he was precisely the sort of act that would sell newspapers to those interested in Miss Crimson's dirt . . . and he had predicted things about Jason she could write about in her column without calling attention to herself or Rubio!

"Tell Jude we'll be ready in a moment," Lady Darington murmured. "I must first thank our hostess and bid this . . . *magician* good-bye."

"I think you've said quite enough, Mother. Let's go."

Dora blinked. Her son had come to fetch them, and he looked ready to spew venom. "Why are you acting so huffy?" she muttered. "And why are you telling *me* what to do, young man?"

Jude let out an impolite snort as he glanced at the ladies crowding around for a last grip of Mr. Polinsky's hand. "I heard every word that charlatan said—about Jason eluding the authorities, followed by that hogwash about auras and dead husbands speaking from the Beyond! This man is nothing but trouble—*Pandora*, is it?"

Lady Darington's expression turned catlike. "Does it surprise you that your mother keeps a secret or two? Every woman does, Jude. You'd be wise to remember that, should *you* ever start seeking a bride of your own." Her gaze flickered to Maria. "Would we care to speculate about *that* topic?"

"Jason's fiancée needs no more notoriety than his absence has already created for her!" Jude pointedly offered an elbow to his mother and the other to his sister. He had to nudge

Jemma with it, because she was gawking at the magician with a painfully obvious wistfulness: he had not expounded upon *her* aura! Nor would he bid her a special good-bye.

"At least Mr. Polinsky shed more light on your brother's whereabouts and condition. And never forget, dear second son, that should the heir apparent not return home, *you* must take on the responsibilities for the estates and the businesses, as well as for the Darington family and name." Dora's eyes took on a hard shine. "Your little hobbies would suffer if you had to *work*, would they not?"

14

_____

"Have you read this rubbish from Miss Crimson? Her vener-
ation of that fraud, Polinsky?" Jude shook his copy of the _In-
quirer_ at her. "I'd like to know _who_ among those ladies at Mrs.
Golding's writes this column! Or from whom Miss Crimson
received her information and such an—an overdone drawing of
him!"

Maria took the newspaper as she gestured toward the parlor,
hoping her expression didn't reveal too much. She glanced at
the column, considering her response to this man who knew
every inch of her body as well as what was on her mind . . .
most of the time. "That's the sketch from those playbills we
found outside Lord Fenwick's," she remarked. "Polinsky has
probably posted them all over London. And from the way Miss
Crimson presents these tidbits, she might've received the information from an informant. She couldn't possibly attend all the
events that provide fodder for her column. When would she
have time to _write_?"

She felt like a mother explaining Saint Nicholas to her young,
inquisitive child. She had purposely written her column as

though a reader had dished up such tasty gossip, right after Meriweather's tea. And as she wrote it, she'd wondered if she was doing her brother Rubio a disservice . . . yet it seemed a good way to flush out more information about Jason—and to keep Yosef Polinsky in the public eye, where everyone could see him.

"Jude, it's not like you to become so upset over everyday events," she ventured, glancing at him from the corner of her eye. "What bothers you about—"

"*Bother*s me?" he repeated archly. "It *bothers* me that this imposter is getting so much attention, when your brother Rubio is the superior medium! As if seeing spirits weren't enough, Polinsky was tricking the jewelry off those ladies!"

Maria considered this. "Rubio sees spirit images, as well. He doesn't tout himself as a magician, however—which, to me, covers such parlor tricks as making jewelry appear in his pocket. What *I* found amazing was how smoothly Polinsky did it! I was watching him with the intent to *catch* him at such shenanigans, and I couldn't."

"He's still a sham! And you'll not convince me that he knows anything of Jason, either." Jude exhaled, looking away in his anger. "He's just baiting you and playing upon Mum's sympathies! And he had the nerve to entice her into his web as well!"

Frowning, Maria placed her hand on his shoulder. "Why do you say that, Jude? He made every woman in the room feel special—and now every one of them wants him as her house-guest, too!"

With a disgusted sigh, he reached into his suit coat pocket and gave her a small envelope. "Here! Mum was scratching these out at her desk late last night. I don't know what it is, but Jemma acted as skittish as a new foal this morning, so *something* is afoot!"

Maria's pulse sped up: the small envelope contained a note

card embossed with the initials DD—a reminder that somehow Polinsky had known Lady Darington's initials should be PD instead. "It's an invitation to tea at Wildwood, at week's end. And Polinksy is billed as the guest of honor!"

"Sweet Jesus, does the excitement never end?"

Quentin appeared in the doorway then, bowing slightly. "Good morning, sir! Shall I bring the two of you any refreshment, milady? Perhaps a cup of chocolate, from the fresh supply Mrs. Booth has just acquired?"

"Excellent idea, Quentin! Something to soothe Jude's frazzled nerves."

"Frazzled? And yours are not?" Jude demanded. "I should think Miss Crimson's glowing account of Polinsky's trickery denigrates genuine mediums like your brother, as well!"

"Guilt by association?" Maria cocked her head slightly, again reading the invitation from Dora Darington. "Then it would seem your mother's tea provides you the perfect opportunity for calling him out, doesn't it? And if you want a *real* circus, have your mother invite Rubio, as well."

"Do you think he'd come?"

"Probably not." When Maria heard the eagerness in his voice, she wished she hadn't suggested this idea. "Rubio won't admit he has any competition. Nor does he dignify other mediums' challenges to produce apports, raps on the table, or other such *signs* to enthrall an audience. He stands on his integrity, and on the unwavering faith his clients have in him."

"Ah. Unwavering faith." Jude stuck his hands in his pockets and went to the window. "I suppose that's the real reason I feel so agitated by this whole affair. While it was rude of me to listen from the other room—or from right outside the music room door, when things sounded a bit too interesting—it was my mother's expression that sounded the warning bell."

"How so, dear Jude? Every woman in the room fell prey to Polinsky's charisma."

Jude smiled ruefully. "Yes, but those others weren't my *mother*. While she's a beautiful woman, admired by every man who meets her, I've never seen her *respond* like . . . like a young girl who's fallen head over heels. The way you gaze at Jason, when you think I don't notice."

Maria bit back a protest. It was inevitable, in a three-sided arrangement like theirs, that one man might feel slighted, or less loved.

But that wasn't the matter at hand, was it? Dora—Pandora—Darington had indeed appeared lovestruck, even at that first encounter with Polinsky at Lord Fenwick's. Was she hostessing this tea as another opportunity to bask in the magician's attention? Risking her husband's wrath for a few moments of intense eye contact . . . perhaps the chance to slip into one of Wildwood's secluded nooks for a more intimate rendezvous?

Given the chance, wouldn't most women behave that way? Or had her own brazen behavior with the twins blurred her definition of social acceptability?

"I'm sorry, Maria. I've been whining about my own concerns, forgetting that you bear a far heavier burden," he said with a sigh. "And in my haste to show you Miss Crimson's column, I've forgotten the item I came to deliver."

As the front door closed behind him, Quentin entered the parlor bearing a silver tray laden with fresh cakes and a fragrant pot of chocolate. He glanced outside, where Jude was reaching into the open carriage. "Is everything all right, Miss Palladino? Mr. Darington seems out of sorts today."

"He'll be fine." She flashed the butler a conspiratorial grin. "I think I've managed to misdirect him about the source of Miss Crimson's material—and we've received an invitation to a potentially *fascinating* afternoon at Wildwood."

"*We*, Miss Palladino?"

Maria poured two cups of the thick, sweet-smelling chocolate, grinning. "I'll need a driver, won't I? And from what I saw at Mrs. Golding's, Jemma will be in fine fettle . . . perhaps competing against her mother for Polinsky's favor. How might an enterprising man like yourself work this to his own advantage, Quentin?"

His sly smile made his sideburns curve rakishly. "Thank you for giving me time to consider the possibilities. To anticipate my . . . pursuit of Miss Darington's fancy." He glanced out the window and then resumed his more proper demeanor. "Your chocolate and cakes, Miss Palladino. Will there be anything else?"

"I think not, Quentin. Please thank Mrs. Booth for this lovely assortment of treats." She dismissed the butler with a proprietary nod as Jude entered the parlor, carrying a large, flat rectangular package. "And what might *this* be, Jude?"

He set the item on the hearth so it would lean against the mantel. "I thought it best to bring your portrait here, hoping you might enjoy it in the privacy of your room."

"And to prevent your mother and sister from seeing it?" Maria gauged his reaction as she tore at the brown paper wrapping.

"You heard Mum's remark about my little *hobbies*," he muttered. "And because she's invited her friends this weekend, I didn't want my gift to cause . . . undue discussion about your postponed wedding, Maria. Those gossips' tongues might chop your heart into mincemeat. And Lord only knows what tricks Polinsky might devise, were *he* to see this."

Maria fought a wicked giggle. She wouldn't intentionally create more conflict for Jude, in a family that insisted he was inferior to his twin, yet she loved to play the devil's advocate.

"Thank you again for this beautiful likeness." She sighed at the love light that shone in her eyes as she sat so proudly in the most exquisite gown she'd ever worn. The portrait was a testimony to the hopes and dreams she'd hung on Jason Darington, mere moments before she learned he'd disappeared. "I'll hang it in the front hall, Jude. Your father has declared this town house my home, so your portrait shall announce my position as its mistress! Just as it shall remind me of the man I am to marry . . . and the man who has portrayed me so lovingly as well."

Jude gaped. "You know how Mum will protest, when she comes to visit—"

"And must admit your photographic talent is more than a *little hobby*? That's how everyone else will see it, you know." Maria held his gaze and then approached the speaking tubes on the wall by the doorway. "Quentin! Will you please come to assist us with—"

"Yes, Miss Palladino?" As she'd suspected, the butler had been lingering in the alcove down the hall. He entered the parlor with a careful smile on his face, nodding at each of them.

"I've decided to replace that fox-and-hounds scene in the vestibule with—"

"What an *incredible* likeness! Even if I'd never met you, I'd say you were the most beautiful—the happiest—woman in the world." Quentin gazed at the photograph in utter awe. "And you created this portrait with your camera, Jude?"

"Well, yes, I—" He fought a grin, at a loss for a response. "With a wash of paint here and there, to render the likeness more like Maria herself, I—"

"It's nothing short of extraordinary, sir! Miss Palladino looks ready to *speak* to us!"

"See?" Maria grinned pointedly at the man who so closely resembled her Jason. And once again she wished her fiancé were *here*, as her husband. "You should never hide your light under that proverbial basket, Jude! High time you brought this out of your darkroom so I can display it with the honored placement it deserves!"

"Rightly so!" Quentin chimed in on his way out. "I shall

fetch the ladder and hang it at once, milady. That gilt frame and those lovely pastels will brighten the entire hall!"

Jude appeared flummoxed yet gratified. "Maria, please! You don't have to put this where everyone will—it was intended as a private gift to you—"

"Which, if your mother or Jemma stumbled upon it un-aware, would only confirm their suspicions about us." Now that they were alone, she gripped his shoulders, her heart over-flowing. "And if *you* won't stand up for your God-given gifts, Jude, it's up to me to trumpet your abilities. Your *worth*, to a family who doesn't appreciate you the way I do."

He let out his breath slowly, as though trying to believe what she'd said. "Thank you, my love," he murmured, and then quickly kissed her. "What would I do without you?"

Maria shrugged. "And what would I do without *you*? Now—it seems to me we should be looking toward your mother's tea and making our plans, don't you think? While Mr. Polinsky's presence agitates you, you've been given the perfect opportunity to foil him. On your own turf! What shall we *do* about that, Jude?"

15

Arrayed in one of the new day dresses from her trousseau, Maria paused beside the carriage in Wildwood's semicircular drive. "You're on your own, Quentin. Jemma and I have never been close, so I'll not cozy up to her and raise suspicions."

"Rightly so, Miss Palladino. I'm sure you'll have your own fish to fry, so to speak."

"Let's hope we don't all get burned today," she replied with a mirthless laugh. "Lady Darington and Jemma are sure to keep things . . . at a brisk boil. And there she stands, already lighting the fire."

Quentin followed her nod to where linen-draped tables were set about the side lawn and garden, beneath canopies. Lady Darington greeted her guests as they waited in line, while beside her Jemma waved Willie's paw and spoke to them in a childish—or was it a ferretish?—voice. The animal wore a little suit coat made from the green print faille of its mistress's new gown.

"I can't believe—tell me that's not Jason's sister behaving like a five-year-old!" Maria muttered.

Quentin chuckled. "Well, it's nice to see Miss Darington favors little . . . pets. I shall keep that in mind."

Maria nodded to another cluster of guests as they made their way toward the garden. "Yes, Willie made quite an *impression* when he got loose at the wedding," she whispered. "Ducked under some poor woman's skirts, judging from the screeches in the sanctuary. Do you suppose she'll . . . *come* today?"

Quentin laughed raucously and had to compose himself when Lady Darington glanced their way. "They say impressive willies have that effect on the ladies, yes. Shall I park the carriage and then escort you?"

"That would be best for both of us. Jemma will never guess it's *me* escorting *you*."

"I do admire the way you think, milady."

As she waited, Maria gazed at the imposing facade of Wildwood, with its white-pillared portico centered between wings that extended in either direction. In more carefree moments, she'd imagined herself the future mistress of this fabled estate— but would that day ever come? Dora would no doubt remark upon her dress, bought with Darington money for a honeymoon that hadn't happened. The willowy blonde looked stunning, in a shade of crimson taffeta that hinted at a woman of scarlet intent, as she nattered with her friends. But it was the conversation drifting her way on the breeze that gave Maria pause.

"—sister was just saying how very *unfortunate* it is that your Jason hasn't returned . . ."

"You must be *beside* yourself with worry, dear Dora! What if your son *never* comes home from—"

"We all have our crosses to bear, do we not?" Dora grasped the hands of Lady Martha MacPherson and old Mrs. Millingham, assuming an expression of stalwart nobility. "It was for this very reason I decided an alfresco tea—some uplifting company and entertainment—were in order! I shall go mad with *not knowing*, if I brood here alone!"

"Pardon my saying so, Miss Palladino, but I don't envy you today." Quentin stopped beside her to offer his arm. "These magpies can be so lugubrious—like the Queen herself, bedecked in perpetual black—when they dwell on Jason's disappearance. We'll return to town whenever you're ready."

"Thank you for understanding." Maria straightened her shoulders, mentally preparing herself. "Let's hope we both find happier distractions this afternoon."

"Hear, hear." The butler's smile waxed conspiratorial. "Care to wager upon whether *my* willy shall be waving before we go?"

"Quentin! You're incorrigible!"

"Made you laugh," he murmured. "As was my intent, before I set you loose as a lamb amongst these she-wolves."

Maria smiled her thanks at him as they approached Lady Darington. She concentrated on the perfect weather . . . the lovely green lawn, where white tablecloths and canopies billowed gracefully in the breeze . . . a long table laden with trays of crustless sandwiches and beautifully arranged confections. And beyond that, where hedges defined the rose garden, Jude was setting up a tripod. Maria was tempted to gaze at him until he felt her presence, but his mother had just taken her hand.

"Ah, Maria, such a lovely dress!" Dora spoke out for the benefit of her friends. "A *loyal* fiancée would save it for her honeymoon, as I intended when I bought you—"

"God in heaven, would you look at that—that shameless *hoyden*!"

At Martha MacPherson's outburst, all heads turned. Maria was grateful for whatever diversion would call attention away from *her*, and she was not disappointed: here came Meriweather Golding, prancing like a filly in a flounced gown of spring green, grasping Yosef Polinsky's elbow. She giggled at whatever he'd just said. Her plumed hat sat askew, which called attention to the loose tendrils of her snowy, upswept hair, and her legendary temple ringlets were mussed as well. The magician escorting her sported a double-breasted coat of navy blue over cuffed white trousers that set him apart from men who wore the same tweeds season after season. He lightly kissed Meriweather's upturned lips.

Then he turned his sparkling blue eyes upon Dora Darington . . . eyes that roamed over her lithe figure before he kissed the hand she offered him. "What a glorious day!" he rhapsodized. "*You* requested it, Pandora, and the heavens can't help but shine upon you. Thank you for inviting me—*us*—to share it!"

"The pleasure's all mine," Dora purred as she held the medium's hands a moment too long.

Maria stood absolutely still beside Quentin, mere inches from this telling scene that Jemma watched from the other side. Dora's daughter knew better than to wave her ferret's paw at Polinsky—or was she so incensed that the magician had rendered her *invisible* again, she could only gape?

"Yes, Dora, life is indeed a *pleasure* these days," Meriweather cooed. Then she tweaked Jemma's nose. "And you, missy, are too young to understand any of this!"

With an exasperated gasp, Jemma stalked across the lawn toward the tea table.

Maria smiled to herself. The drama was just beginning, and if she played her cards right, it would not center around *her!* "Mrs. Golding, how lovely to see you looking so—"

"Ecstatic? Rejuvenated?" the old dear twittered. "I see you've not wasted any time finding *company* yourself, Miss Palladino."

"May I present Quentin McCallum, Jason's butler and valet at the town house? He drove me here today," she replied pointedly. No sense in drawing Dora's attention away from her guest of honor: only a fool would rush in where Jemma feared to tread. "And if you'll excuse us, we'll refresh ourselves before Mr. Polinsky begins his *show.*"

Quentin, bless him, knew a cue when he heard it. They strolled toward the tea table, where her coconspirator snatched a few little cakes before excusing himself. Maria took her time choosing dainty sandwiches and thinking how she—or Miss Crimson—could best use what she heard and saw this afternoon. Even from across the lawn, among the other catty, curious guests, Maria felt the forces at work: Dora flirted freely, admiring Yosef's natty attire, while Meriweather doted on the medium from his other arm, oblivious to the other guests' stares.

Jude joined her then, bristling. "I swear to God if that huckster makes a fool of my mother—"

"Oh, every woman here can do that without Polinsky's help," Maria murmured. "I'll wager that in a few months' time, we'll be seeing more ladies with mussed hair and winter roses in their cheeks. All of them vying for the medium's unique ... magic."

"You think that fraud won't be exposed—or run out of London—by then?" Jude looked across the lawn, where Polinsky clasped the hands that reached for his as he riveted each victim with his fascinating eyes. "I've better things to do with such a fine afternoon than attend *tea* with Mother's friends. But it's my best way to see that nothing *unseemly* goes on between him and Mum."

Maria considered this. "After that first evening at Lord Fenwick's, your father has no idea of Dora's ... infatuation? Is it not *his* place to—"

"I'm the last one to remind Lord Darington of his *place!*" Jude pointed out with a mirthless laugh. He glanced at the chair he'd positioned among some glorious rosebushes. "Would you mind sitting for a photograph, so I may sight through my lens? I'm thinking these ladies might not be so gullible if I provide them a diversion."

Maria perched in the chair with a wry smile. It was a queenly piece: freshly painted white wicker with an intricate pattern of beads across its high rounded back. As she smoothed her skirts, she felt Jude gazing at her from beneath the camera's black cape. "Pardon my saying so, dear Jude, but you don't seem yourself today."

"You've never watched me protect my mother's reputation, have you?"

She winced at his shrill tone. "Why are you so upset? Because your mother bats her eyes at a handsome man? Have you never exchanged glances or provocative words with a fascinating stranger?" she quizzed him quietly. "And why do I detect *envy* every time you talk about Yosef Polinsky?"

The cloak behind the camera bobbed as he jerked his head. "*Envy?* Really, Maria! Why would I want to be like that Russian rake who uses his trickery—"

"His charisma?" she teased.

"—to befuddle poor old souls like Mrs. Golding? She doesn't even know he's fleecing her!" Jude declared vehemently. "Where's the sport in that?"

"Perhaps she doesn't care." Maria glanced toward the woman in question. "I've never seen her happier."

Jude extended his hand to one side, gripping the shutter bulb. "Hold absolutely still now, smiling . . . there you are, love. Absolutely beautiful. Three . . . two . . ."

She arched her spine and gave him her most flirtatious grin.

"One!" he called out as he caught the shot. "There! Perfect!"

Maria remained seated as he removed the glass negative and slipped it into a light-proof black bag before placing a fresh negative in the camera. Yosef Polinsky was already casting his spell, talking with the ladies at each table just loudly enough that the others followed his act rather than chatting among themselves.

"My dear Mrs. Grumbaugh," he crooned, reaching for the woman's plump hand. "I'm sensing . . . a rise in your pulse. A deep thrumming that has unsettled you of late, because you've become aware—"

"Aware that Meriweather has given up all pretense at modesty?" the widow in pink twittered.

The other ladies laughed like naughty debutantes and exchanged glances over their cups of tea.

The medium remained unruffled. "As though a fox has entered the henhouse?" he queried. He focused intently on Esther until she drew in her breath and held it. "My guide tells me those exquisite pearls at your ears were *not* a gift from your husband even though you received them . . . while he was alive. Am I correct?"

Every woman present sucked in her breath. Mrs. Grumbaugh flushed, but regained her presence of mind. "*You,* sir, would know about such things! And not because of any psychical abilities!" she blurted. "Am I *correct?*"

Nervous laughter flitted from canopy to canopy. The ladies leaned toward this fascinating exchange so as not to miss a word.

Polinsky's lips quirked. "You know that answer as well as I do. But I feel the vibrations from another among you—" He pivoted dramatically, to gaze at Lady MacPherson. "And *you,* milady, also covet the . . . *intimacy* implied by my becoming Mrs. Golding's houseguest. Do you not?"

When tea spewed from Martha's mouth, her two tablemates squealed and jumped backward. "How *dare* you insinuate—"

"It's time for my diversion," Jude murmured as he stepped

toward the guests. "Will you assist me, Maria? We'll have a cat-fight on our hands if we don't diffuse this ridiculous conversation!"

Indeed, the chatter was shrill around the tea tables, and it did *not* sound like genteel ladies discussing the next charity auction or meeting of the art guild. Esther Grumbaugh had cleared her plate and was scooting her chair back, so Maria approached her with a smile. "What a lovely pink dress, Mrs. Grumbaugh! Jude would like to commemorate his mother's garden party," she continued coyly, "and you look just like one of her roses!"

Suspicion curled her lips. "This is another part of that huckster magician's plan, isn't it?"

"Oh no, ma'am! It's Jude's idea—to better acquaint himself with his new camera!" she replied. "I just sat for a portrait, so I can attest to the—the *queenly* feeling of posing on such a pretty wicker throne!

Esther glanced toward the center of the rose garden, where Jude was seating Meriweather Golding. A catlike smile lit her chubby face. "Well, if *that* strumpet can sit as though she were the Queen, I shall have a picture made as well," she said with an eloquent sniff. "Mark my words! We'll look back on these mementos and be thankful when Yosef Polinsky has moved on! Finished making fools of us!"

As Maria walked with her toward the garden, she bit back a smile. Several of the other guests were now watching Jude fuss over Meriweather, even as the magician in their midst was pulling a bright red kerchief from his coat pocket—to unwrap a glistening pendant that was "magically" wrapped in it.

Dorothea Biddle squealed as her hand fluttered to her neck. "But how did you—without even *touching* me, you unhooked my necklace! My mother's favorite piece, I might add!"

"The hand is faster than the eye!" Polinsky replied smugly.

"He's a fast one, all right." Mrs. Grumbaugh studied Maria, her brow furrowed. "And you, my dear, might consider what that showman knows of Jason's situation as well! Didn't he come to town about the same time your man disappeared? Wouldn't that be a way to play upon Dora's emotions—pull her strings before he makes her son reappear? He'd be quite the hero *then*, would he not?"

Maria's eyes widened despite the widow's catty tone: it was an angle she hadn't considered. And it would explain how Polinsky sounded so certain Jason was on a ship bound for America, wouldn't it? But this was no time to approach Jude with such a radical idea: he had just slipped beneath his black cape and was instructing Mrs. Golding to tilt her head to one—

"Perfect!" he called out. "You'll treasure this likeness for years to come! I'll have a print ready for you by week's end."

"What a fine idea this was, Jude. Thank you for indulging your mother's old friends with a memento of her party." Meriweather gazed around the lawn until she spotted her houseguest beneath one of the far canopies. "And if Yosef sits for you, will you provide me a likeness of *him*, as well? Without letting on to him, of course. I'll gladly pay you for your trouble, Jude."

The surprise on Jude's face made Maria chuckle. Clearly, the younger Darington had never considered creating a sideline for himself with his camera, but if Meriweather Golding paid him, perhaps others would ante up as well. "The pleasure is all mine, I assure you!" he replied with a dapper grin. "And we've convinced Mrs. Grumbaugh to have her picture made as well!"

As the plump partridge positioned herself on the white wicker chair, she smiled at Meriweather's retreating figure. "Whatever she pays you for a likeness of Polinsky, I'll double it," the matron murmured. Then she quickly added, "Something new to throw darts at. I'm quite a competitive player, you know!"

As she exchanged a glance with Jude, Maria had to fight laughter. Who could've guessed this tea party would provide such entertainment? Not to mention income for Jude? It was better than thinking about Jason while at the town house, where the springs and floorboards creaked in such a provocative rhythm above her lonely room.

It occurred to her then that Jemma hadn't shown herself for nearly an hour. Nor had Quentin—not that their whereabouts were any of her business. Far more interesting to follow Polinsky's patter about spirit summonings during his séances, a topic his avid audience followed closely.

"Is there a chance we might *see* this spirit guide of yours?" Helena Farquar asked. She then engaged in a rapid-fire whispering match with Meriweather. "Of course!" she crowed. "If *Yosef* sat for a portrait, while concentrating on his spirits, something might show up on the print! Like it did in photographs of Eusapia Palladino when she performed for the Society of Psychical Research! Wouldn't *that* be something?!"

"Oh please, Mr. Polinsky!" someone else cried. "You really must summon your spirit guide, so we can see him! We mustn't interrupt your séances with the presence of a camera, of course. So *this* would be the perfect opportunity to verify his existence."

The magician didn't miss a beat: a knowing smile lit his features. "That's a fine idea! But please understand that in order to execute such a photograph—if indeed anything will manifest itself—Mr. Darington and I must retire to the house, where my spirit guide will feel more secure and will also be more visible. Outdoor light is much too bright."

"And while he and Jude are experimenting, we shall move into the parlor for cards," Lady Darington announced cheerily. "We'll enjoy our games without the breeze interrupting them."

Maria flashed Jude a secretive grin. Could this scenario have played out any better? It seemed as though Fate—or perhaps Polinsky's spirit guide—had written the script expressly for Jude: he now had the perfect opportunity to grill the medium.

And meanwhile, Lady Darington would be entertaining her guests indoors, like a proper wife and hostess, while Polinsky had to prove his powers. What a fascinating turn of events ... something Miss Crimson might have to write about in her next column.

"Maria, dear, you *must* be my partner at cards!" As Esther reached out with fingers like plump ivory sausages, her rings sparkled nearly as much as her little eyes. "You've a better memory for what's been played, you see. And meanwhile I want to hear all about your life since your wedding day—and what you've learned about Jason's disappearance. How vexing it must be, to live amongst his family without him at your side."

Maria blinked. Polinsky was approaching the wicker chair, while the other ladies called to her and Esther. There was no gracious way to escape playing cards in the parlor.

"Yes, Mrs. Grumbaugh, we're all living on pins and needles, wondering about my brother," Jude replied smoothly. "Thank you for engaging Maria in the afternoon's entertainment. My mother becomes ... preoccupied when she's seeing to details of her parties." His expression said what words could not: he was sending her inside with the ladies. Forfeiting any opportunity to be alone with her in favor of having time with Yosef Polinsky.

Maria disguised her sigh and clasped Mrs. Grumbaugh's hand. "Yes, thank you for your thoughtfulness," she murmured. "What would Jason's mother and I do without our friends?"

16

Before Jude could dismantle his camera, Polinsky held up his hand. "I've another idea, before we retire to your studio! I need a photographer to make my likeness for some new showbills! Meanwhile, might we also have a bit of . . . fun with these dear ladies?"

The showman who'd charmed jewelry from around his willing victims' necks now looked at him like a bosom friend; an enterprising man with a plan from which they both might benefit. Jude knew better than to ask the magician what he was *really* doing—much less to inquire where his heavy Russian accent had gone, for Yoseph Polinsky now sounded as well spoken as any educated Englishman. Smooth as the proverbial baby's bottom, too, as far as how he navigated the treacherous waters of these women's jealous streaks and emotions. "What did you have in mind, sir?"

Watching the last ladies enter the house, Polinsky grinned. He extended his arm across the top of the white wicker chair and then leaned into it, as though he were standing beside someone. "Wouldn't they love the surprise of seeing their portraits with *me*, as though we'd posed together? I must beg your absolute silence, of course—and I'd pay you whatever you wish!" he added quickly. "It just seems like a novel . . . harmless memento for them. *Heartbreaking*, the stories of their empty lives since their dear husbands passed on. They are requesting séances, but spirit contact is such a fleeting thing—if indeed their husbands' spirits cooperate."

Jude sensed he was about to be hoodwinked, as surely as this medium had waved his magic wand to ingratiate himself with Meriweather Golding. Yet something about the plan teased at him—and he certainly craved amusement, now that his brother was gone. "Such illusions would be a challenge to produce," he mused, "but I can manipulate the negatives . . . burn in the images you want when I make the prints."

Would he be sorry he'd agreed to this idea? Jude ducked beneath the black cape to gaze through his camera lens. Polinsky cut a fine figure in his natty dark jacket and white trousers. It was the man's face that demanded any observer's attention, however: the profile of his nose, and the way his riveting blue eyes shone on either side of it beneath thick, distinctive eyebrows, gave him a secretive look set off by a squared chin with an arresting cleft. His peppery hair had gone to salt at the temples—a look women supposedly found attractive. Especially women who were old enough to be Polinsky's mother, but didn't want to admit it.

YOUR mother isn't old enough to be his mother!

Jude shut out this distracting inner voice to adjust the camera's shutter. Something about this little deception felt good, if only because Polinsky believed he was calling the shots. "Nice smile now! And then hold it steady . . ." he encouraged as he held out the shutter bulb. "Imagine your . . . lady of the moment seated in that chair—yes, that's the look we want!"

He squeezed the bulb, sensing immediately that this picture

was precisely what Polinsky desired. "Perfect! I'll print these with Mrs. Golding in the chair, and Mrs. Grumbaugh, and—"

"Perhaps more of the ladies should sit for a portrait, so no one feels . . . left out later," Polinsky suggested furtively. "Meanwhile, I'd like a photograph of only my face, to print on my showbills for upcoming performances, and to advertise my services as a medium. I've been in London just a few short weeks, but it seems a promising place to conduct business."

Jude's stomach tightened. Would this presumptuous man use these trumped-up prints as gifts? Or to entice women to seek his services in the spiritual realm? Or—more interesting yet—would the bogus photos become bait so others would invite him to stay in their homes, as Mrs. Golding had? It only made sense that Polinsky plied a more lucrative trade among women who'd lost their men . . . which begged the question of what sort of *trade* he was actually in.

"Now—if you could move your camera closer, for a shot of my face alone," the magician suggested. He sat in the chair then, angling himself so the sunlight shone on half of his face, while the farther side remained shadowed.

Jude paused. This man was no stranger to the rules of good photography, nor to the sheer *presence* he exuded as he lifted his chin and gazed directly into the camera lens. He looked imperious and virile and—

Seductive. Omnipotent. Thank God he's not making eyes at Maria.

And why wasn't he? Maria Palladino was far and away the most arresting woman here today; a natural target for a shyster, too, because she'd endured a wedding gone awry and still had no idea where her fiancé was. Yet the man who sat before him, gazing through the camera lens as though to read Jude's thoughts, presumed to flirt with his mother—a well-married woman! It was time to broach that subject, while he and Polinsky were alone.

"Hold that expression," Jude instructed. For a moment he felt tempted to stand with the shutter bulb extended for long, long moments—making this visitor dance to *his* tune! But that would only alert the medium to other tricks he wanted to play while they had no witnesses. "All right . . . chin up just a bit—yes! Fabulous!" Jude exclaimed as he caught the shot.

He came out from under the cape then, bracing himself for a conversation about this man's feelings for his mother. "You know, Polinsky, I've got to wonder why you pursue my—"

"One more request!" The medium glanced toward the house. Stepped closer to Jude. Spoke in a lower voice. "You're set up to take those ladies' portraits, so rather than go inside—" Polinsky's gaze lingered on the back windows, as though to ascertain what each and every woman in the parlor might be doing. He then turned his back to the house, and damned if he didn't fumble with his fly buttons. "If you can be quick about it, I'd like a novelty shot—for calling cards of the randiest, dandiest sort! You see, I'm not the only one who fancies having his photograph made!"

Jude gaped. The man beside him had unfastened his trousers and reached inside them to scoop out—

"Quick, man! Before they come out to see what we're doing!" Polinsky rasped. "Get this picture!"

Too stunned to protest, Jude removed the camera from its tripod. He balanced it instead on the small table beside the wicker chair, then knelt to focus on his subject—and again his jaw dropped. While Polinsky wasn't a tall man, the cock jutting from between his legs was the biggest, thickest erection Jude had ever seen. No wonder Mrs. Golding looked so happy these days! This middle-aged medium was a *large*! And in the time it had taken Jude to reposition himself, Polinsky had slipped a jeweled ring over the head of his member and was stroking it into position at the root. It glimmered there with garnets and emeralds, like a Christmas gift that kept giving all year long: an invitation to experience extreme sexual hunger and then to satisfy it in a big way.

Jude swallowed hard. How must such an appendage *feel*, inside a woman? He hoped Maria never saw Polinsky's equipment, for she would surely find him and his twin lacking. "You must hold still," he insisted. "No hand movements! No shifting of your weight."

"Can you get it all in the picture?"

Jude bit back a retort: Polinsky's ego was every bit as oversized as his . . . pole. "I'll do my job and you do yours," he muttered. He squeezed the bulb, thinking how very sexual that simple act seemed in light of what he was photographing. "All right! We're finished."

Polinsky chuckled low in his throat. "No, Mr. Darington. We're just getting started."

And what did he mean by that? Holding the camera's sides, Jude straightened to his full height, aware of how his backside had been sticking out. This conversation—this whole scenario—suddenly smacked of something he wanted no part of. Before he thought carefully, he blurted, "While we're on the subject, I'll thank you to keep that thing away from my mother!"

The medium—the very *upstanding* medium—kept one hand on his member as he studied Jude with a guarded expression. "I think you'd better apologize! Or no—just stay the hell away from that subject altogether. Your mother's mature enough to do as she pleases, without her son's permission!"

"Tell that to my father!"

Polinsky smirked. "*I* don't need your permission, either, nor will I ask for it. Now—" He pulled up his pants and then fastened the buttons over the bulge in his fly. "If you'll have trouble maintaining a *professional confidentiality* about the business we're transacting, I'll pay you for those negatives this minute. And we'll be done with it."

There was no going back—and no denying he'd just gotten

caught in this quick-witted magician's web . . . sucked in with the charisma Maria had mentioned. No doubt Polinsky had waved the same devious wand of words to insinuate himself into Meriweather Golding's good graces. Which meant he was living in London as a perpetual *guest,* fawning his way into schemes and séances that would earn him a princely sum, at the expense of the dear old victims he swindled: lonely women who bloomed again in the sunshine of his sexual attention.

So why is he seducing your mother?

It was a question that would only land him in deeper trouble. And when Jude saw his sister coming around the side of the house, looking coyly over her shoulder, the chance to challenge Yosef Polinsky disappeared. "You'll have your prints by week's end," he said tersely. "I'll deliver them to Mrs. Golding's, along with an invoice."

Polinsky pulled a money clip from his pocket and peeled away several bills. "I believe in paying before services are rendered, Mr. Darington. I know you'll deliver superb photographs."

Jude stuffed the money into his jacket, following Jemma with his gaze. Her blond hair was tied back at the crown in a large ribbon that matched her green print dress, and with the rest of her curls spilling down over her shoulders she looked very sweet and girlish—until he realized she was leading some poor fool astray. But who was here, at this tea party?

"Hah! You see!" Polinsky murmured. "Even your little sister knows her power and how to use it. You could be marrying Maria Palladino, to become the envy of every man hereabouts, if you'd simply take what she's offering. Everyone but *you* realizes that!" With a chortle, the Russian smoothed his lapels. "I'm going inside now for a glass of punch. You'll have more sitters before the afternoon passes."

Jude nearly bit off his lip to restrain his anger. The nerve of that bastard, insinuating he should fill the vacancy Jason had left in Maria's life! As though neither he nor Maria saw anything *wrong* with that! Only an indecent—

Polinsky stopped at the back door to speak to someone before he went inside. When the magician's gaze wandered to where Jemma had perched on a bench at the far end of the garden, Jude sensed fate and advantageous timing had once again played into the magician's hands. He did *not* expect to see Quentin McCallum lingering on the stoop, exchanging gazes with his little sister, once Polinsky stepped inside.

And why was his brother's butler flirting with his sister?

And why wouldn't he? Everyone else is a bit old for him, aren't they?

Even that voice inside his head was playing devil's advocate, damn it! Jemma was clearly as engaged in this game of cat and mouse as Quentin, so it wasn't as though Jason's servant had acted out of turn—even though he'd overstepped the line separating employers and their staff.

Are you going to step in as your sister's social conscience, too? You didn't accomplish much when you acted on your mother's behalf.

Jude started toward Jemma, and then thought better of it. Why did he feel compelled to fix the problems women caused themselves? It was a fool's game, believing he could correct the missteps of every female who snapped up the bait men tossed them.

And when his sister stood up, trotted toward Quentin with open arms, and then *launched* herself at the butler, he had his answer. At least McCallum had the decency to look startled before he caught Jemma in the kiss she planted on his lips. When her laughter tinkled like a little bell on the breeze, Jude almost felt sorry for the slender fellow who'd just been ensnared: Quentin would bear the blame if Lord or Lady Darington learned of this indiscretion.

Indiscretion? It's a kiss, for chrissakes! Are you so desperate for affection you begrudge everyone around you?

There was no winning this inner war, just as there was no backing away from the job he'd taken as Polinsky's private photographer. *Or the photographer of Polinsky's privates.*

Sighing, Jude repositioned his camera atop its tripod. The trip-trap of dainty heels on the walk warned him a woman was coming, and he turned with a smile that felt pasted on. "Hello, Mrs. Farquar. Has the card game already broken up?"

"Oh my, no!" Helena replied with a roll of her eyes. "I'm such a poor player I've already eliminated myself, so I thought I'd beg the favor of a photograph—if you have the time, of course! It's been years since I had the inclination, or the occasion, to have my portrait made!"

Already he saw that shine in her eyes . . . the hopefulness of a girl standing at the toy store window. He didn't need to ask who'd put it there. "Of course," he said, gesturing toward the white wicker chair. "It's a privilege to capture your likeness in Mother's garden today. She'll be so pleased you wanted this memento of her party. Now: chin up . . . yes, with your shoulders back . . . like that . . ."

17

Maria rolled over, aware she was dreaming . . . drifting between wakefulness and not wanting the dream to end. She saw *eyes*. Eyes peering from beneath a pirate's bandanna, as though a man—was it Jason?—watched her from the window.

She hugged her pillow. It wasn't nearly time to get up, yet a tingling at the back of her neck suggested she was being watched. Her body tightened even as she tried not to move— just in case this sensation was *not* a dream! If the interloper thought she was awake, he might take advantage of her . . . might slip into her room and out of his clothes and then beneath the sheet she clung to . . . to discover she was naked. Waiting.

No, *longing*.

But for whom?

As the question floated like a cloud across her mind, Maria again tried to determine whom she saw beneath that rakish bandanna: the logical choice was Jason, since he so loved to don a pirate's props. Yet this man felt different. More predatory, because he was hiding his body from her mental view. And despite the warning bells that jangled her nerves as she lay absolutely still in the semidarkness, she wished the streetlight would illuminate his face rather than the shadowy furnishings of her room.

Maria! Come to me! I need you, my love!

She wanted that to be Jason's voice, yet this summons sounded out of rhythm and rhyme with the way he spoke to her. Did she dare answer back, even in the silence of her dream? She inhaled slowly, wavering again between wakefulness and falling more deeply into the dream.

I know you're awake, lovely lady. And I know you wait for me . . . naked and ravenous.

She swallowed. Her limbs stiffened from holding so still. But worse, she began to pulse lightly, all over her body—gooseflesh popping up—and felt a teasing tension between her legs. Exhaling between the sheets, Maria searched her mental image of the man again. His eyes danced with knowing she was aware of him, and he raised up enough that she could see his entire face: the squared jaw, made softer by a rough mustache and whiskered grin; the lean contour of his profile as he smiled at her.

I need you as badly as you need me, Maria. Open yourself! Let me in!

She nearly spasmed: what was it about this voice that made her do his bidding? He sounded so familiar, but how did he know she'd worn nothing to bed? Did he also know how the sheets teased at her skin? How the sound of her breathing belied her rising excitement? This was shameless—mindless—yet as her nipples rasped against the linens, Maria ached for the man who spoke so mysteriously, so intimately, to her. Was he casting a spell, or was she attracting his attentions somehow? Unwittingly inviting him to take control?

You're wet. I can smell your desire—your need, Maria.

A whimper escaped her. Damn him, why didn't he reveal himself?

You don't need to know who I am. But if it makes my presence more . . . permissable, then I can be whomever you choose, the low baritone continued. *But do choose, and soon, milady. Don't keep me waiting!*

How had her hand slipped between her knees? If this intruder knew she was nude, he knew what she was about to do to herself—

Oh yes, and I intend to watch. And then take my turn.

Maria twitched. Closed her eyes tighter, and gave in. As her fingers found her downy mound and then ventured into the slick crevice beneath it, she sighed into her pillow. The pirate— he was Jason, and yet he wasn't—stood behind her now, watching as the bedclothes shifted and whispered in the dimness. His pants hit the floor. He fumbled with his shirt buttons.

Randy little witch. I've got so much more for you than a slender finger. Here—

He curled his body around hers, lifted her upper leg, and entered her with a deep thrust. Her moan filled the room as he filled her, with a cock so long and thick she felt stretched to the limit. Yet deeper he plunged with each thrust, relentlessly claiming her as his own without her encouragement or permission. He wrapped his arms around her, held her captive and continued to seek his pleasure.

Maria . . . Maria . . .

"Yes," she murmured, appalled that she'd given herself to this unknown lover so freely, yet amazed at how he instinctively knew her body's wishes. Her hips writhed and the bed creaked in time with his thrusting, until the spark he'd ignited suddenly flared. Maria cried out, needing to thrash yet unable to break free from her imaginary lover's possessive arms. He bucked against her back, squeezing her tighter as his cock dove into her wet depths.

With a final gasp, he convulsed, taking her with him. A torrent of warmth filled her, and even as she feared he'd already gotten her with child, her body refused to release him. Maria curled inward and then thrust back against him in a final, wild implosion that drove her over the edge of a mindless chasm.

Again she drifted, not wanting the dream to end—for in a dream she could have Jason, or any man she wanted, whenever she needed release. As her body relaxed, her breathing took on the same rhythm as his. "Please," she pleaded, "you must tell me who you—"

"It's Quentin, milady. You're to meet Lady Darington and Jemma at the dressmaker's today, remember?"

Maria's eyes flew open as she clutched the coverlet around her body. The butler who leaned over her bed, wearing a furtive grin, was very real indeed. What had he seen? Or heard? Had Quentin tricked his way into her dream by donning Jason's pirate bandanna and eye patch from her nightstand drawer?

His expression said he knew exactly what she'd been doing. And he'd probably watched most of it.

"What are *you*—this is outrageous!" she wheezed. "Why isn't Mrs. Booth waking me—"

The butler's eyes remained fixed on hers. "She's indisposed."

And what on earth did *that* mean? Maria blinked away the remnants of her dream, yet her body still tingled in the most intimate places. Yes, she was wet. And the liquid oozing from between her legs felt like more than her own, as though a real lover had shot his seed.

"I thought it best to be sure you were awake, milady," the butler repeated. His gaze wandered along the curve of her hip. "You were having a rather . . . spectacular dream. Probably not something you'd want to explain to Mrs. Booth."

Her cheeks prickled with heat. The brazen bastard knew damn well what she'd been doing, yet he showed no sign of leaving so she could get out of bed. "Perhaps you're recalling

what you and Jemma did yesterday," she countered. "I *saw* the
way you kissed her in the garden at Wildwood—"

"Then you also know Jemma sprang at *me*, and not the
other way around." His tone sounded defensive, but then he
relaxed. "And yes, I got what I was hoping for. Thank you for
allowing me to escort you yesterday, milady. If I may be of assistance—"

"You may *leave* now, Quentin," she insisted. "There'll be
hell to pay if I keep Lady Darington waiting at LeChaud
Soeurs. And I do *not* require your help getting dressed, thank
you. If Jason finds out you've been coming to my room—"

The butler smiled knowingly, bowed, and then took his
leave.

Maria scratched her head. What was real, and what had happened only in her dream? The man in the pirate garb still toyed
with her senses: the musk in her bed was a blatant reminder of
how she'd spent the last several minutes. If only she knew with
whom.

"Jason, you've got to come home," she muttered as she
swung her legs over the edge of the bed. "Or you must at least
send word. I'm losing my mind without you—not to mention
all rational control of my body."

She listened. But her lover didn't reply.

"This gown looks so lovely, Miss Palladino. Perfect with
your dark hair and dusky coloring." Camille LeChaud Bentley
smiled as she smoothed the shoulder seam and then clipped a
stray thread. "Thank you for requesting a design that defies the
current mode. I so love a challenge, and together we've met it!"

As Maria gazed at her reflection in the shop's large cheval
mirror, she felt fully alive for the first time since her wedding
day. The aquamarine brocade shimmered seductively where it
dipped into the crevice between her breasts, leaving her shoulders and upper back exposed before draping suggestively over

her hips. Gone were the bustles and layers of lace that had once covered a woman's attributes: this gown revealed her best features and played up the colors of the butterfly pendant that rested at her collarbone.

And while she sensed Lady Darington's envy, and Jemma's irritation because *she* had not been singled out for the designer's praise, Maria refused to let these women irritate her today. Perhaps her morning's sexual satisfaction had invigorated her, or at least made her feel Jason's presence in a fleeting way. "Thank you, Camille. You've done a wonderful job, as always—"

"Yes, and we're so happy to *provide* such finery for Maria," Dora cut in, "even though the man she was to have danced with Saturday can't be present."

Maria sighed. Would these Darington women never let her forget she was beholden to them? "Yes, I'm grateful to you as well," she murmured. "You've been most generous, providing me a home and the means to enjoy a social life despite my . . . predicament."

"And such a shame that is, too!" Colette Bentley looked up from her ledger to smile compassionately at Maria. "Has there been no word at all, then? No response to Lord Darington's telegrams?"

"Nothing," Dora replied with a pathetic sniff. "It's as though the heir to the family name and estates sailed off the edge of the earth, to disappear without a trace."

"I'm so sorry, milady. Please accept our prayers for your son's return." Camille stood beside her twin, remarkably pretty in her advanced state of pregnancy. "I can't imagine surviving from one day to the next without my Heath."

"Nor I without Hadrian," Colette added, rubbing her extended belly. She fingered Maria's jeweled butterfly. "I hear our Aunt Meriweather has not enjoyed the same sort of luck in love, however. When she discovered some of her jewelry missing, she sent that charlatan Polinsky packing!"

"Oh *really!*" Jemma blurted. She turned at the mirror, admiring the way her new sky blue gown displayed her waist and hips to such advantage. "*That* tidbit should set her hen friends to cackling!"

"Jemma! We mustn't mock those who become the victims of trickery." As Lady Darington joined her daughter before the mirror, her preening took on a studied intensity: the scarlet gown was striped with black, symbolically declaring dismay over her missing son while dramatically displaying her sleek features.

"Indeed," Camille remarked sadly. "The poor dear was *so* happy to have a man in her life again. This whiff of scandal sets her off as a gullible old fool."

"Let's hope it serves as a warning to her friends," Maria remarked. "Everyone who meets Mr. Polinsky seems to fall under his spell."

"He recently conducted a séance at Esther Grumbaugh's home. And I hear Martha MacPherson has requested a personal consultation as well." Camille stepped behind Lady Darington for a final inspection of her gown. "Perhaps you'll hear more at the Galsworthy ball this weekend. By then Colette and I will be remaining at home, as our time draws near. You must keep us informed!"

Was it her imagination or had Dora held her breath during these revelations? Maria noted a rise in her color and a feline shine in her eyes . . . a turning of her head to hide a sly smile. "Oh, indeed we shall," Lady Darington replied. "Just as we shall spread the word about keeping one's jewelry—not to mention one's reputation—safely locked away. Desperation is such a despicable state. It drives us to do things, or to leave things undone, hoping to attract what we need in a . . . dark moment."

And what did Jason's mother mean by *that?* The creak in the floorboard above them reminded her that her brother lived in the apartment overhead, and Maria had the urge to discuss these newsworthy items about Polinksy with him. It would look too obvious, however, if she went upstairs while Jemma and her mother were present.

"Perhaps you should entrust your jewels to *me* then, Mumsy." Jemma flashed her mother a wicked little grin. "Mr. Polinsky never spares me so much as a glance, so I could flaunt your finery without any danger of him—"

"That's quite enough out of you for one day!" Dora turned, a signal to the Bentley twins that the fitting was finished. "You shall have my gems in good time, when I've no further use for them. And meanwhile, you must earn your own! Like the rest of us!"

18

"Here we are once again, arriving as each other's escorts," Maria said with a sigh. Even the sight of the magnificent Galsworthy home, with lights in every window and music drifting on the breeze, failed to raise her spirits. "You could've enjoyed this ball with someone more romantic—"

"How can you say that?" Rubio hugged her shoulders as he gazed at her. "You'll be the belle of the ball, and I'm pleased to be seen with one so lovely! I only wish Jason could be here to enjoy it with you."

"You could've come with—"

"But I didn't *want* to! Truth be told, I'm using you as a social shield," he confessed quietly. "A few of my clients have become . . . suggestive, of late. Insisting I have as much appeal and charisma as Yosef Polinksy—"

"Oh, you're *far* more appealing than he!"

"—so by doing the honorable thing, bringing you tonight, I'm also avoiding amorous, assertive ladies who might become . . . more trouble than they're worth." When her brother smiled, the ring in his nose winked at her. "Please don't take offense, Maria."

"How could I? You've always taken such good care of me, Rubio." Why was it that as she watched other guests in their finery, laughing as they entered Lord Galsworthy's home, she felt inexplicably sad? Not even her unique gown of palest aquamarine made her smile—not even when she caught the admiring glances of those walking by. "And here comes Jude, with the illustrious Miss Remington. What must Sarah be? At least ten years older than he! Gathering dust on the shelf because she refused so many eligible suitors, back when—"

"Shall I fetch you a saucer of milk, kitty? He's putting on a respectable show, same as we are." Rubio waved to the couple, so Maria did, too.

But her heart wasn't in it: had an evil spirit snatched it away and left a lump of coal in its place? Of *course* Jude had brought someone else! With his twin missing, all eyes were on the heir-in-waiting—and on *her*, the bride left unwed. So discretion was best.

Wasn't it?

Jude was such a caring, considerate lover . . .

Her brother's hand tightened on her bare shoulder. "You have reason to feel downhearted this evening, you know. A month ago today we were at the church, awaiting your Jason."

"A month? Some days it feels like a year."

"Change is in the air. Major change," the medium murmured as he steered her forward again. "While I'm not receiving any direct messages from Jason, my guides—and my instincts—inform me the sun's about to break through the clouds of your despair—"

Maria's eyebrows rose.

"—but this revelation will set another crisis into motion. Something involving . . . the Darington family."

"Doesn't everything? If no crisis presents itself, Jemma and

Dora create one." She put on a smile as they reached the main doors, where the evening's guests waited to be welcomed. It was a fine summer night, balmy with a light breeze that whispered in the manicured hedges. Maria recalled other balls last year, on Jason's arm, when she'd felt like dancing before the orchestra began to play. Yet Rubio had just hit upon something, hadn't he?

"I—I had a strange dream a few nights ago, and every night since," she murmured so no one else could hear. "It always involves a pirate—a lover coming to my bed. I want to believe it's Jason . . . yet in so many ways, it's not."

Rubio's eyes shone like hot coffee. "What does this pirate say? Or do?"

Maria focused on Lady Galsworthy when their hostess clasped her hands in greeting. "How lovely you look this evening!" she cooed. "That shade of blue accentuates your eyes."

Once a sought-after beauty, Rowena batted her thin lashes. "I've resurrected this poor old thing yet again," she said with a whimper in her voice. "Reginald claims it's his favorite, but he's so tight he squeaks when he walks. He'll like the looks of *you*, though, Maria! No word of Jason, I assume."

"No reply from Lord Darington's partners on the American coast, nor any clue to his whereabouts." She held her smile steady, as it would be her best ally tonight. Again.

"Except, of course, what Mr. Polinsky and your brother share with us from their spirit realms." When Rowena gazed knowingly at Rubio, Maria got the distinct impression she might be one of those potentially troublesome clients he'd mentioned.

Her brother bowed over her wrinkled hand to kiss one of her rings. "I'm confident Jason will turn up," he declared, loudly enough that guests turned their heads to listen. "I predict he is not only alive but . . . thriving. The Darington heir was never one to shrink like a violet or bemoan whatever hand

Fate has dealt him. And he has Maria waiting for him! What more could any man want?"

Maria caught Jude's gaze from the ballroom doorway, where he stood with Sarah Remington's hand tucked in his elbow. When she held his attention to share the hope Rubio's prediction kindled, he winked at her behind Sarah's back.

"Well, *some* men want to ingratiate themselves with well-heeled women," their hostess continued in a quivering voice. "And they're coming up short when they open their jewelry boxes—which is why I'm *so* relieved the man in question declined our invitation! And so pleased *you* are here, Mr. Palladino." Rowena fluttered like a fan as she gazed up into Rubio's eyes.

"Rowe! For God's sake, the guests are lined up outside!" Lord Galsworthy called from the top of the stairs. "Save your stargazing for when Palladino can earn a little something from your nattering!"

Their hostess withered. "So lovely to see you," she murmured before smiling at the couple behind them.

Rubio guided Maria upstairs then, so they could exchange pleasantries as the small orchestra on the dais tuned their instruments. Maria recognized most of those who socialized in this circle: she'd written of their soirees in her column . . . which seemed her best survival tactic for an evening of questions that had no answers. An evening when the man she wanted to dance with was nowhere to be found.

As always, she made a mental note of the colors and fabrics the ladies wore, not to mention which gentlemen circulated the ballroom with their wives at the evening's beginning and which ones slipped away—and with whom—during the course of the ball. Was it no coincidence that the wives who never wore the same gowns twice, who regally displayed their stunning gemstones, were married to the sly foxes who provided the same gifts for secret lovers?

She considered this as she chatted with peacocks of an echelon she might never attain. As Jason Darington's wife, she would eventually find acceptance among most of these couples—although it would take a grandchild or two to convince Dora she had much worth. But now, as an unattached female, Maria felt like a loose end waiting to be tied.

". . . and they say he lasted only two days at Esther's, before she caught him rifling through her bedroom safe!"

"No! Is he that intelligent? Or does his spirit guide tell him the combinations to locks, too?"

Girlish laughter rose above the strains of a Strauss waltz as Maria eavesdropped on the conversation behind her, at the punch bowl. Helena Farquar strolled up to make it a trio of twittering birds. "No doubt he'll be heading out on the proverbial rail, tarred and feathered, if he continues such blatant behavior!" she chirped. "Why, I hear he had the most *revolting* calling cards printed! With a picture of his—his—"

"Why, Helena, I've never seen *you* blush, dear!"

"And he was wearing a jeweled ring on it! Can you *imagine*?" Helena finished breathlessly.

"I'd have to see it to believe it. But for all we know, he made up his name to go with that bulge in his trousers. Pole-insky."

Maria nearly spewed punch as the ladies laughed aloud. This newest voice in the mix belonged to none other than Dora Darington . . . the Pandora so fond of letting secrets out of the box. The woman Yosef Polinsky singled out of a crowd with his penetrating eyes.

Dora's younger son waltzed by then, and as he guided Miss Remington in a tight turn he gazed directly at *her*. Had Jude taken the photograph his mother and her friends were gossiping about? It seemed the epitome of arrogance for a man to want a likeness of his cock, but what did it say about Jude for making it? He couldn't have just stumbled across Polinsky while his pants were down . . . with his camera at the right height . . .

"And what might *you* be contemplating, Maria? That's the wickedest grin I've ever seen, young lady!"

Maria gripped her punch cup to keep from dropping it. Phillip, Lord Darington, stood before her, expecting an answer—although she sensed a rare glint of amusement in those direct gray eyes. But how could she reply that his wife had been discussing another man's *pole?* The ladies behind her moved away from the table, no doubt because Darington's daunting height and disposition tended to quell any merriment. "I—you must excuse me for overhearing some gossip, milord," she stammered. "It's hard to avoid at gatherings like these."

A grin flickered across his face, gone almost as soon as she saw it. While Jason's father had always been cordial—and he *had* allowed her to remain in the town house indefinitely—she had often wondered how his sons had turned out so . . . easy to get along with. So accommodating and compassionate. She straightened under Darington's scrutiny, uncertain whether his lingering gaze meant he liked her new gown, or he was lost in his own thoughts and no longer really saw her.

"Had I met you thirty years ago, my life would be drastically different," he murmured.

What a startling remark! Had she heard it correctly? Maria's mouth opened but she didn't dare remind him that thirty years ago, she hadn't been born. No, a man whose gaze smoldered, tinged with such aloof arrogance, wasn't thinking about age.

He's hiding behind his arrogance. With a wife like Pandora—

"Will you dance with me, Maria?" he asked with another of those lightning-strike smiles. "Damn shame that the most fetching woman in the room has nothing better to distract her than catty tongues."

When he extended his hand, she set her cup on the table and

followed Lord Darington to the dance floor. The orchestra struck up Beethoven's "Minuet in G," and he smiled defiantly. "May I have the honor of a *waltz*?" he insisted. "Much more suited to enjoying the way that gown becomes you, Miss Palladino."

"Thank you, milord. I—yes, I much prefer the waltz myself." Why was he paying her such close attention? Was it pity, because her man was absent?

Not likely. Lord Darington felt sorry for no one.

Was he *interested* in her, then? In a way she'd not considered before . . . a way he'd not shown even at home, those times she'd been in his company with Jason? As he swung her easily into the three-quarter rhythm, Maria felt the gazes from around the Galsworthys' ballroom: while the other dancers followed the pattern of honors and step formations for the minuet, she and her not-quite father-in-law blithely twirled face-to-face.

And Phillip Darington looked as delighted as she'd ever seen him. The lines around his eyes and mouth relaxed as he ignored whatever disapproval or speculation this waltz might provoke. "Mrs. Booth tells me your bridal portrait now graces the hall," he said in a voice that reverberated beneath the music. "I shall come and admire it soon."

She took the opportunity he'd just supplied. "You knew Jude made that likeness before the wedding, didn't you? He's an avid—and very able—photographer."

"Yes, he is. But it's the subject that leaves one unable to look away—or to catch his breath."

This was getting awkward! Maria concentrated on the succession of twirls he led her through, almost as though he didn't want her to *think* too much about what he said of his sons. "You flatter me, Lord—"

"No, my dear, for once I'm enjoying a topic of conversation that brings me great pleasure." He pulled her closer to execute the next steps, which swayed forward and back before he again led her into a trio of turns. "I haven't danced like this in years. Thank you for indulging me, Maria."

"You're welcome, milord. I—"

"Lord Darington! Phillip, Lord Darington, where are you, sir?"

All turned at the urgent tone of the Galsworthys' butler as he searched the crowd. "Far side of the orchestra!" someone called out. "Dancing with Miss Palladino, he is!"

Maria's partner stood taller, pulling her protectively against his body. The music came to a disjointed halt as each musician followed this development. The ballroom became silent.

"Begging your pardon, milord," Cleaver puffed as he trotted toward them. "The courier insisted this message was of utmost importance! A telegram, it is!"

Phillip smiled apologetically at her. As he accepted the envelope he glanced impatiently about the room. "No need to stop the party on *my* account!" he announced. "Has my family not endured enough speculation, without you following my every raised eyebrow? Play on, I say!"

The guests looked quizzically at each other as the lead violinist flipped his music to another song. When Phillip Darington placed his hand on her back to guide her off the dance floor, Maria felt the thrum of his anticipation—along with the steely reserve that made him *wait* until dancers moved around the floor again and the other guests pretended not to watch him so closely.

"I'll leave you to your reading," Maria suggested, but his hand tightened on her shoulder.

"If this requires an immediate reply, I shall trust you to help me compose it. I left my spectacles at home."

Nodding, Maria remained beside him. Who knew the all-powerful Lord Darington required assistance for his correspondence? But then, his valet would've assisted him had this missive been delivered to Wildwood. Only bit players, writing under assumed names, penned their own messages.

"Damn it to hell, could that telegrapher have written a more contrary hand?" he muttered, thrusting the message in front of her.

Maria skimmed the small, tight penmanship, her pulse lurching into a gallop. If this message were true—if its author weren't demanding a ransom payment, then it could only mean—

"Well?" the man beside her growled. "You're not getting this excited over an invoice from the fish market!"

Maria gulped air, not sure whether to laugh or cry. "He's a *pirate*!" she crowed. "Jason's alive and well—and he's the captain of a ship! He's been plundering the Darington fleet along the coast of North America, sir!"

19

Lord Darington's face froze. "That's the most ridiculous thing I've ever heard. Pirates disappeared from the high seas more than a century ago."

Maria couldn't pull her eyes from the tiny, embellished printing—not only to be sure she'd read the message correctly, but because her heart suddenly had wings! The last time she'd been with Jason, pillage and plunder were foremost on his mind. Could anything serious have befallen him, if he recalled his love for playing the swashbuckler?

Although the musicians forged doggedly ahead in their song, everyone else had stopped to stare at them. She longed to read the telegram aloud, at the top of her voice, so all could share this wonderful news: Jason was alive! Jason was *alive!*

Not only alive but thriving. The Darington heir was never one to shrink like a violet or bemoan whatever hand Fate had dealt him.

Her heart rose into her throat. Rubio had predicted this when they arrived, and here it was, come to pass! And as though he sensed she might need him, her brother was making his way through the crowd. "What did you say, sweetheart? What's the news about your Jason?"

"Yes! Yes, we must all hear this!" Dora clapped her hands for silence. "Please, Maria! Keep reading!"

Maria gripped the telegram, caught in the crossfire of Lord and Lady Darington's gazes . . . the center of attention because she'd blurted out the news her heart had yearned for.

Jason's father cleared his throat. "As we can't unring the bell, my dear," he murmured tersely, "you might as well keep reading, so we all hear it firsthand. Start at the beginning, if you please."

She nodded. Even though Lord Darington seemed glad this message had arrived, she might have slipped a rung or two on his ladder of acceptability—

But she'd never been a social climber, had she? Jason Darington had sought *her* out and courted her, for she would never have presumed herself his equal.

Oh no, you much prefer being beneath him . . . between him and the mattress . . .

She cleared her throat. Jude now flanked his mother, thank God, in case Dora staged one of her dramas. With the Darington family and Rubio forming a shield between her and the rest of the guests, Maria felt more secure. She also felt Jemma's glare from across the dance floor: her long-lost brother had taken center stage without even being present. She'd have to find another way to get attention . . . another audience with whom she could hold court.

"This is from the office of Darington Shipping in Charleston, South Carolina—"

"The American headquarters, yes. Please go on," Phillip muttered impatiently.

"—and it reads 'Greetings, Lord Darington, from your shipyards on the southeastern coast of—"

"I know where they are! Get to the point, for God's sake!"

She glanced up at the intense eyes that focused on her. "Yes, milord . . . it says 'a man closely resembling Jason Darington has taken command of the *Sea Witch*, and, after rallying the crew to mutiny against its captain, Terrence Dunner, he has assumed the name of Johnny Conn. To date he has plundered three of our ships as they left port for—' "

"What in bloody hell is that boy thinking? For chrissakes—"

"Phillip! If you'd stop interrupting, we'd hear the message!" Dora stepped forward to snatch the paper from Maria's hand, but her husband grabbed her by both shoulders. "And what the hell are *you* thinking?" she cried. "Unhand me, damn it! This is my son we're hearing about!"

"Mother! Father! *Really!*" Jude muttered. "Is this any way to behave in the Galsworthys' ballroom, with everyone looking on?"

Lord Darington glared at his younger son. "Never forget which side your bread's buttered on, Jude, nor the fact that your brother holds the knife! Maria, you shall continue with the pertinent details. *Now.*"

Maria held the telegram tightly to keep it from rattling. Phillip's face alternated between the colors of rare beefsteak and boiled potatoes, and in these few minutes he'd become more agitated than she'd ever seen him. She nodded and returned to the message. " 'It seems Johnny Conn and his brigands have attacked other ships, as well, evading port authorities. It is believed he has hidden lucrative cargoes of sugar, cacao, and other valuables in caches all along the eastern seaboard—"

"Christ Almighty! Have I not paid them enough in tariffs and bribes to—" Lord Darington raked his wavy hair with both hands, looking frantic. "How difficult can it be to follow a rogue ship and capture its crew—"

"If they believe this Johnny Conn to be your *son*, Lord Darington," Rubio said in a low voice, "the authorities have held their fire. And Jason has taken every advantage of it."

"We believe he was shanghaied, remember?" Jude watched his father struggle for control, so he chose his words warily. "And often when that occurs, sailors are thrown or dropped onto the ship from trap doors in tavern floors—Amelia Beddow's brothel, no doubt—and they can suffer blows to the head."

"Which could explain why, when I locate Jason with my senses and my spirit guides, he does not respond." Maria's brother slipped an arm around her shoulder, his dark eyes wide with concern. "If Jason believes he is the pirate Johnny Conn, then he has no idea he's attacking his own ships!"

A gasp went up around them. Even as Maria pieced together this puzzling picture of her beloved and his adventures, she couldn't help thinking how *exciting* Miss Crimson's next column might be! Jude reached around her then, to tug another folded page from the envelope. "What else have they sent us, Maria?"

"And why was I not informed of this earlier?" Phillip rasped. His voice sounded strangled as he tugged at his shirt collar. "This is ridiculous! I pay my partners and the coastal patrol to—utter *nonsense*, that—"

"Hush, Phillip!" Dora focused intently on her younger son as he unfolded the remaining page. "Jason has never disappointed us. He must have a very good *reason* for looting Darington ships—and I suspect some of your seamen have behaved just as corruptly when they might profit from it. Without informing *you!*"

But no one was listening to Lady Darington. The room sucked in a collective breath as Jude unfolded a large WANTED poster: Johnny Conn leered proudly at them, wearing a pirate's bandanna and a gold hoop in one ear. He'd grown a longer mustache, which curved wickedly around his lips and down past his chin.

"Sweet Jesus," Maria whispered. She covered her mouth,

but it was to hide a smile. *He looks so rugged and virile . . . so damn handsome and indestructible! Just like the last time we made love!*

Jude's eyes widened, yet he appeared skeptical. "If the navy and the authorities can't catch him, who took this photograph? Unless Jason's—"

"So cocky and confident, he's circulating the poster himself, to rub the navy's nose in it. May I?" Rubio took the WANTED poster, to look deeply into the pirate's eyes . . . to venture into the depths of Conn's soul by connecting to it on a more ethereal plane.

A gasp made them all look at Lord Darington. His eyes had grown wide at the sight of the pirate wanted by the law, but he was struggling to remain focused. Pale as a fish's belly, he was. Getting goggle-eyed, as though he couldn't breathe.

Rubio grabbed his shoulders. "Doctor! I say, is anyone here a physician?"

The other guests looked at each other but no one stepped forward. Phillip wheezed, clutching his chest, and had Maria's brother not steadied him he would've crumpled to the floor. Maria sensed Jason's father felt such shock and dismay, he'd lost control of his muscular functions. As Rubio lowered him to the floor with Jude's help, the steely-haired man began to flop and flounder.

"Phillip! Phillip, for God's sake, stop it! You're upsetting everyone!" As Lady Darington raised her foot, presumably to nudge some sense into her husband, Lord Darington's eyes opened. He focused on his wife with such a venomous scowl that she drew back with a terrified whimper. When his hand clamped around her ankle, Dora screamed and began to kick at him.

Lord Darington then opened his mouth, as though to renounce her, but an ominous gurgling sound came out instead. His eyes rolled back and his body went slack.

"Doctor! Surely there's a doctor in this crowd!" Maria cried as she knelt to loosen his shirt collar.

"Doctor, my arse! Get him off me! He's crushing my foot!" Lady Darington's voice rose to a piercing shrillness and she didn't stop hollering profanities until Rubio pried Phillip's large hand from her ankle. "My God, what a beast!" she cried. "And here, in front of all the Galsworthys' guests!"

"Let's get you home, Mum," Jude murmured tersely, while his sister skirted the scene. As Jemma rushed from the ballroom, her wail rose up the stairway behind her.

Maria's heart thudded. She slapped the sides of his face, but Lord Darington didn't respond. The man who, moments ago, had been dancing with her and then railing about his absent son's misdeeds, now appeared—

"He's gone." With a sigh, Rubio rose from the floor. His eyes looked as large as chocolate pies and his mane of chestnut hair waved as though an unseen breeze riffled it. "His soul has passed from his body, like a whisper."

"But I—I was only doing as he told me—" Maria covered her mouth with a trembling hand. "I've never seen him so upset—"

"Nor so critical of his firstborn. His . . . heir." Jude backed away from a truth he didn't want to acknowledge, even as he wrapped an arm around his mother's slender shoulders. "Mum, what are we to do about—"

"Do?" Dora wheezed. "Why are you asking *me,* when obviously your brother and his pirate cohorts have shocked your father so badly he tried to—to—pull me down with him!"

Rubio supported Lady Darington from the other side. "I'm so sorry, dear lady," he murmured. "No one could've anticipated this revelation about Jason, not to mention its effect on your husband. We must get you back to Wildwood, and someone will see to Lord Darington's proper . . . disposition."

"I'll take her," Jude said, tightening his hold on his mother's shoulders. "Come along, Mum. We've caused enough excitement for one evening."

As they turned, Lord and Lady Galsworthy were immediately behind them. Their host gestured at the orchestra. "You lads, proceed downstairs and Cleaver shall pay you. The rest of you—" He waved his hand to encompass his wide-eyed, silent guests. "Out of respect for this sudden tragedy, we ask you to vacate the premises immediately. No need for good-byes or social niceties. Lady Darington, you and your family may remain as long as you care to, and I shall send someone for an undertaker."

"You can't mean—Lord Darington has really *died?*" Rowena Galsworthy gawked around Maria, gasping when she saw displeasure that distorted the nobleman's face. "Oh my God, come along, Dora dear! We must get you away from such a—a malevolent presence! Saints be with us all!"

The guests parted to allow them an unobstructed path. As Maria fell in behind Rubio and Jude, who guided Dora Darington between them, a sense of separation—of distancing herself from the reality of this blow—wrapped around her heart like a dense, dark blanket. All around her, anxious faces bespoke shock and sympathy. It felt wrong to leave Lord Darington lying lifeless on the dance floor, yet what could she do but follow the others? Maria snatched the offending telegram and WANTED poster from the floor, and then hurried to catch up with Jude and her brother.

Jemma sat hunched inside the carriage, as though she might faint or vomit. Dora seated herself beside her daughter and then stared straight ahead. Not wanting to be the one Lady Darington's empty—or accusing—gaze fell upon, Maria crowded in beside her.

"I'll follow you to Wildwood," Rubio said as he looked in at them. "Perhaps I can be of assistance."

As a perplexed Pearson closed the carriage door, Maria

sensed they were beyond any help even the most well-meaning medium could provide. Across from them, Jude stared stoically out a window. Jemma's pathetic sobs echoed inside the otherwise silent coach. Dora sat ramrod straight, her gaze fixed on a point of the vehicle's upholstered ceiling, inches above her second son's head.

And where do I fit in now? Maria fretted. Should she go to the town house and pack, because her benefactor had passed on? When Lady Darington came out of her shock, she would surely blame the one who'd read the message that sent Phillip into his fatal fit. Her beautiful brocaded gown suddenly felt restrictive. She reminded herself to *breathe* and not panic . . . to remain a few steps ahead of the shock that had already silenced her three fellow passengers.

What would Miss Crimson do?

Ah, therein could be found a solution. At the first lurch of the carriage, Maria braced herself physically and emotionally for what might lie ahead. To collect her thoughts, she composed and revised the opening paragraph of her next column, yet her current reality distracted her.

Jason . . . Jason, what have you done? And what am I to do, as a result of it?

20

———————————

"I don't suppose you want to hear what Miss Crimson reported in today's *Inquirer*?" Jude sat across from his mother, reading the newspaper by a single dim bulb in the dark parlor because Dora had ordered all the curtains drawn. He sounded tired, but mostly dulled from the deep mourning his mother had declared throughout the house.

Maria sat on the opposite end of the settee from him, hearing the bait in his voice: Jude was using Miss Crimson to get a reaction—anything—from the woman who'd sat absolutely still, for hours on end, since she'd come home from the Galsworthy ball. Maria's gaze wandered over Dora's ebony dress and the dark veil she'd not taken off since the mourning warehouse had delivered them yesterday. Phillip's funeral couldn't come soon enough.

How could she endure another day of this endless emptiness? These hours of suspended animation with only the ticking of the mantel clock to assure her Time itself hadn't died. Thank God she'd written that column when she'd returned to the town house for the darkest gowns in her wardrobe—which

Lady Darington had scowled at because, after all, the dresses had been intended for her trousseau.

The resounding silence drove Jude to read further. "It says here that Rubio Palladino is partly responsible for locating Jason, and Miss Crimson thanks those readers who sent the information that was so helpful."

Dora flinched.

"And what do you think of *this*?" he queried, keeping the newspaper between his face and the woman who seemed to ignore him. "Miss Crimson describes the onlookers as 'shocked' and 'aghast' at the fit Lord Darington pitched, until they realized he had expired in their midst."

"Why should I give a flying fig?" Dora's lips barely moved and her emotional state was hard to gauge behind the dark veil. "My husband, lord of this manor, and my son—the light of my life—are both lost to me. My life is . . . over. Why should I go on?"

"Someday the sun will shine again for you, Dora." Maria glanced over to where poor Jemma sat by herself, bored to tears yet aware the gloom wouldn't soon disperse. Trapped by her mother's sense of propriety. "Jemma will find someone to love, and the wedding arrangements will brighten your—"

"Oh, for Chrissakes, Jude, you might as well read the damn column to me! This is no time to be teasing your poor, grieving mother."

Maria didn't know whether to laugh or cry. These were the first lifelike words Dora had uttered, yet once she began to pick apart Miss Crimson's column, the fur would fly.

Flashing her a subdued grin, Jude folded his *Inquirer* so he could hold it closer to his face in the dim light. " 'Well, Dear Readers, at the Galsworthy ball it was truly the best of times and the worst of times,' " he began in a spirited voice. " 'Lord and Lady Darington received word from his lordship's American shipping partners that their beloved son, Jason, has been plundering the family's own ships while posing as a pirate from days of old. The news sent Lord Darington into a fit of—' "

"I swear to God I'll rip that woman's head off when I find out who the hell she is!" Dora sat forward, sweeping the veil back from her face to glower at them. Because she wore no kohl or rouge, she looked ten years older than she had at the party. "No sense of decency or civility in our time of trial! Kicking poor Phillip when he was down!"

"Like you tried to, Mumsy?" Jemma breathed. "I've never been so humiliated in my life as when you started wailing that he had a death grip on your—"

"Enough of your insolence, missy! Go to your room."

More relieved than upset, the impertinent blonde strode past them with Willie cradled at her shoulder.

Again Jude ventured a grin, but Maria knew better than to respond. Dora seemed to be emerging from her shock so it was no time to flirt with him. At least he'd broken the icy silence. "Perhaps now's not the time," she began hesitantly, "but if we were to go in search of Jason—bring him *home* to familiar surroundings—perhaps he'd regain himself—"

"What an absurd idea! How could *we* capture him if the authorities cannot?"

Maria shrugged, restraining her excitement. She had to propose this idea very carefully, or it would appear she suggested it only for her own needy reasons. Visions of that hoop earring and Johnny Conn's devilish mustache goaded her on. "But if Jason were here—restored to his right mind—*he* could silence Miss Crimson! As the new Lord Darington, he would not *tolerate* the way his family name and reputation—"

"Begging your pardon for the intrusion, Lady Darington, but you have a caller." Thomas the butler peered into the dim parlor to be sure he was addressing the correct female.

Dora waved him away. "I've told you I do *not* wish to be disturbed until several days after his lordship's service tomorrow—"

"Yes, milady. And when I mentioned that, the gentleman asked that I give you this."

Was that a grin flickering at the manservant's lips? He and Lord Darington were cut from the same bolt of stiff, starchy cloth, so it was difficult to tell if the old fellow had any sense of humor. Yet when Dora's eyebrows flew up and a little cry escaped her, Thomas stifled a fit of rude laughter.

"Arthur Thomas! How dare you insult me with such a—"

The butler cleared his throat loudly. "Yes, milady. He said you'd say that."

Lady Darington's expression changed like a kaleidoscope as Jude watched his mother's reactions over the top of his newspaper. When Dora noticed their attention, she slipped the card into her skirt pocket. Then she smoothed the black lace veil into place again, tilting her small hat at a slightly jauntier angle. "You may admit him, then—but only because Maria and my son are present to maintain proper decorum."

"Yes, milady. I shall tell him."

When the butler stepped from the room, Dora's neck arched. Even through the veil, her eyes burned more brightly. "Not one word from either of you!" she warned. "You have no defense for your own questionable behavior, and therefore no cross to crucify me upon—unless you plan to hang on either side of me. Do I make myself clear?"

"Perfectly, Mother," Jude murmured—but then he stiffened.

Yosef Polinsky stood in the doorway. He entered the dark parlor and then paused to let his eyes adjust. With his hands clasped before him and his hair smoothed back from his face, he looked the perfect gentleman. And indeed, as she considered it, Maria wondered why Lady Darington felt so . . . compromised by the medium's condolence call. In the coming weeks she could expect several of her friends to stop by Wildwood— *And isn't it INTERESTING that Polinsky is the first?*

Jude folded his paper with crisp precision, announcing his irritation with each noisy crackle of the pages. "Mr. Polinsky. What brings you here, sir? Can you not see that my mother—"

"Please accept my sincerest sympathies at the passing of your father, Jude. It must have come as quite a shock to see him enjoying himself one moment, and then lying, expired, on the ballroom floor the next." The medium stepped forward with his hand extended, which demanded that Jude stand to accept his condolences.

"Thank you," he muttered.

"And do I understand correctly that his passing resulted from news about your brother—and your fiancé, Miss Palladino?" Again this guest spoke with utmost concern as he approached Maria, bowing before her.

She offered her hand and he took it. His eyes were riveted on hers in the dimness, with the intensity her brother employed to plumb the depths of a client's heart and soul. Because she was observing him, embraced by the warmth of his hands and eyes that sparkled even in the shadows, Maria returned his direct gaze with one of her own. She'd done this to Rubio since they'd been children.

"Yes, Mr. Polinsky, it was with mixed emotions we learned of Jason's escapades," she replied. "His father, Lord Darington, was understandably flummoxed when his American partners admitted they'd lost some ships to the pirate Johnny Conn, whom Jason pretends to be. But then, you no doubt got your information from Miss Crimson's column."

Polinsky dropped his gaze first, perhaps sensing she was toying with him. "I remain amazed—somewhat appalled—that a society columnist relays more vital information about the case than we've received from Scotland Yard. How frustrating that must be for all of you."

Maria held her expression steady as he released her hand. Was he telling her he *knew* of her secret life as Miss Crimson?

"Oh, pish! As though we take stock in *that* woman's gossip and lies!" Dora perched on the edge of her chair, watching the medium work the room and tempering her remarks as though Polinsky was saving the best for last; making her wait while he gave lip service to the minor players, whom he would dismiss when he focused on *her*.

But she had settled herself, much like a cat preening when sunlight beams through a window: Dora held her shoulders back, displaying her breasts despite the harsh black dress that buttoned primly at her neck. And when Yosef turned in her direction, her body seemed to lighten: the heaviness of her presence disappeared, now that she had a different audience. Maria found this fascinating even though Jude remained standing, to witness every exchange and nuance between the medium and his mother.

"I could not help but overhear, as I awaited permission to express my sorrow, the suggestion that someone should . . . pursue your son, to bring him home." Polinsky took Dora's hands and lightly rubbed her knuckles with his thumbs. "I was going to suggest that very idea today, if you were capable of discussing it! My spirit guides tell me that while Jason is unaware of the ironic twist of his fate—which has led him to plundering Darington ships—his childlike soul is enjoying the adventure so much he might never come to his senses. Why should he, if he continues to elude the port authorities? On the other hand—"

Polinsky's dramatic intake of breath . . . his drawn-out pause that begged to be filled with his answers, had all three of them leaning forward to follow his every suggestion.

"Yes, Mr. Polinsky?" Dora whispered. "Be very careful what

you say to me. The foundation of my life has been knocked away, and—like a house left teetering on a chasm after an earthquake—I might drop into the valley of the shadow at any moment. You must assure me, Yosef, that you'll never lead me astray for your own nefarious purposes."

The medium straightened slightly. "The fact that you use the word 'nefarious' in the same sentence with my name distresses me, Pandora. Why do you doubt my intentions? My integrity?"

His wounded tone made Maria bite back laughter. Lady Darington could play the wilting widow to perfection, but she was in no mood to be duped by a sweet-talker. Would Polinsky play along with her?

"I have heard more than once this past week, Yosef, that your former... *hostesses* are missing some jewelry. These women aren't flighty or losing their minds, either."

Jude's expression was priceless as he watched his mother back the magician into a conversational corner. Maria, too, wondered how the illustrious charmer would talk his way out of this one.

Yet Polinsky gently placed Dora's hands back on her lap. "Just as you become outraged when you read what Miss Crimson writes about your family," he said in a guarded voice, "I must deal with women—or clients, who are mostly women— who become distraught when they believe others attain 'inner circle' status before they do. Or perhaps they believe they'll *lose* that status. And indeed, this concept of an inner circle is based on hearsay and faulty logic."

Polinsky turned slightly, to include Maria and Jude in this conversation. "Much as I hate to say it about the dear ladies I've met here, I suspect *envy*, that green-eyed monster, is at the root of these disappointing stories. If I stooped to stealing jewelry, Pandora, how would I ever face myself in the mirror?" he queried softly. "And before you reply, ask yourself if *you* have ever repeated dirty little lies—or even created them—in those moments you felt betrayed or abandoned, or just disappointed in someone you admire. Someone you might possibly . . . wish for."

Dora sniffed indignantly. But there was no doubt she was framing her reply as she turned her head . . . which presented Polinsky with her haughty profile beneath her veil.

Maria knew a dodge when she heard one. But like the Artful Dodger in the Dickens story, the medium had twisted Dora's insinuation into an invisible noose around her own slender neck.

"You compliment yourself, Mr. Polinsky. Or perhaps you are delusional," Jude's mother answered crisply. "I am recently bereaved, a woman who grieves the loss of her husband and possibly her firstborn as well. I do not *wish* for anyone! I pray for the return of my son, so he might take over his father's estates and title."

Lady Darington stood then, facing the medium. Even though her face remained veiled, her voice brooked no argument. "And why should I settle for *envy*, when vengeance is so much more effective? It's time for you to go."

Maria's jaw dropped. Had Dora really dismissed the man with whom she'd so eagerly flirted before? And what on earth did she mean: *why should I settle for envy, when vengeance is so much more effective?* It sounded like something Miss Crimson might say. She should write it down so she wouldn't forget it!

The medium remained silent. He bowed and left the parlor.

Lady Darington watched after him, silent as well. Then she retrieved his calling card from her skirt pocket, to gaze at it as though no one else were in the room.

Maria would've given her week's pay from the *Inquirer* to see Dora's face without that damn veil! Or to see that calling card. For long, awkward moments she and Jude awaited what his mother might proclaim next.

Finally, she put the card in her pocket again. "I shall retire to my chambers now, and I refuse to be disturbed until I emerge tomorrow, ready for the funeral proceedings. Good afternoon."

"Yes, Mum. Good afternoon," Jude mumbled.

"Rest well," Maria added, not knowing what else to say. In the twinkling of an eye, Dora Darington had changed from a martyred mother to the mistress of her own script again. And while it wasn't strange that Yosef Polinsky had delivered Dora from her misery, Maria would *never* have anticipated the medium's dismissal. "What do you suppose was on that calling card?" she mused aloud. "I've never seen a piece of paper bring about such a change in attitude!"

Jude smiled wryly, not quite meeting her eyes. "They say a picture is worth a thousand words. I suspect Polinsky chooses them well."

21

"Ashes to ashes and dust to dust," the vicar droned as he gazed into the grave now filled with Lord Darington's casket. "We commend the spirit of Phillip, Lord Darington, into Thy care, O God . . ."

Maria's weary mind wandered. From beneath her veil she observed those around her: Jude, on her right, looking downcast and very concerned about his possible role as the Darington heir. The crook of his arm tightened around her hand, and she squeezed back.

On her left, Dora stood with stoic dispassion, a rose between her gloved fingers. She was a column of uninterrupted black, from her smart new hat with its longer veil to the tips of her stylish new pumps: the widow now in the public eye among the many friends who'd gathered at the cemetery.

Jemma stood to her mother's left, mewling miserably. She'd been forced to leave her ferret at home, so her hands flitted from adjusting her veil to smoothing her gown of black bombazine. The dress, cut closer to her hips and legs, made her look dangerously alluring. Maria sensed these funereal details frustrated the youngest Darington, who was unaccustomed to enduring ordeals not of her own creation.

Father Stoutham cleared his throat pointedly, and Maria refocused on the funeral. Lady Darington stepped forward, dangerously close to the gaping grave, to drop her rose on her husband's casket. Then she lifted her chin; planted her hands on her daughter's trembling shoulders to urge her to follow the script. Sniffling loudly, Jemma half-threw her rose rather than look down into the hole that held her father. Jude then stepped forward with Maria, and they, too, paid their final respects. Thank God it was all going according to plan. . . .

Yet when she saw how Rubio scanned the crowd, scowling, Maria sensed something would soon change that. The vicar pronounced his benediction. The somber crowd parted for the family's return to the carriage behind the hearse, a magnificent black vehicle drawn by plumed ebony horses. Maria nodded at the murmured condolences as they walked the path between the tombstones, spotting Lord and Lady Galsworthy, Lord Fenwick, Lady MacPherson, and Mrs. Grumbaugh among the mourners.

Dora had announced her need for total privacy—no condolence callers—so as Maria approached the hearse, the rest of this endless day loomed before her. She was itching to write a column—anything to occupy her mind with the *living*—but proper decorum and respect for Lady Darington demanded that she remain at Wildwood until evening, when Rubio was to escort her back to the town house. The undertaker asked for a word with Dora and Jude, so Maria stepped into the black carriage first.

From the far end of the seat, Yosef Polinsky put his finger to his lips.

Maria was too startled to speak. What was this man trying to prove? She knew the answer to that, of course: he was positioning himself to fill the empty spot in Dora Darington's life. But how flagrantly could he flaunt his desires in a funeral carriage and still be considered a gentleman? Was she condoning whatever trick Polinsky had up his stylish sleeve, if she sat down without questioning his intentions? When Jude saw the magician, he would protest long and loudly.

But Dora entered the carriage ahead of her son. And at the sight of Yosef, her sigh camouflaged laughter and she promptly sat down beside him. "So!" she cooed. "You have come to beg my forgiveness for your impertinence yesterday?"

Jude stopped halfway inside the carriage. "What the hell's going on *here?* My mother has requested a day of solitude and seclusion—"

"You may sit beside Maria and keep your mouth shut, Jude." Dora gestured impatiently for Jemma to step inside. "Obviously, God has brought this man to us, knowing our . . . deep need for guidance in our time of crisis. And if Mr. Polinsky can summon your father's spirit, ask him how to bring your brother Jason home, I should think you'd be grateful for his assistance. Your sister has always wished to attend a séance, so here's her chance."

Maria sat back, stunned. Had this scenario and the séance been secretly arranged beforehand? Or were Dora and Yosef cleverly playing upon each other's conversational cards now that the medium had showed up unannounced? The more she watched the two of them together, the more she sensed an unseen force was indeed at work—and it had nothing to do with the spiritual realm. It was lust, plain and simple.

The carriage seat wheezed as Jude landed beside her. His expression remained ominous as he studied the couple across from them. Jemma blinked, looking unsettled yet fascinated.

The undertaker peered in before closing the door, and then his eyes bugged. "Begging your pardon, Lady Darington, but I heard raised voices and—I understood you were to be driven home—"

"All is well, Mr. Cromley. You and your driver may proceed with our plan. I shall pay you immediately—and generously—for the way you have so kindly assisted us in our time of bereavement." Even from behind her dense black veil, there was no mistaking Dora's intent or her presence of mind.

The portly man nodded, understanding his role in this little drama. The carriage door closed with a solid *whump*, and moments later they were rolling down the road toward Wildwood.

Rolling toward what? The silence had so many different shades of meaning between the five of them, Maria couldn't guess what might happen next. Revelation? Or the total rearrangement of everything proper and habitual; the things that kept their lives on track, day in and day out?

"Yes, Pandora, this table shall be perfect. Quite appropriate that Lord Darington, rest his soul, sat in this cozy parlor as he read his newspapers." Yosef Polinsky gazed around the darkened room, nodding as he spoke. "We shall close the door to prevent intrusion. Once the spirits have replied to our summons, we want no chance of interruption."

Despite the way she watched this medium for hints of fraud—he was a magician skilled in sleight of hand, after all—Maria found her pulse pounding. She'd grown up in a house inhabited by spirits, and she'd been a sitter at séances her brother conducted, yet this event felt fortuitous: it seemed as right a time as any for contacting Phillip Darington's spirit or for attempting to reach Jason. She would protest if Polinsky employed any unusual or unseemly methods, aware that *anything* might happen if the spirits of her fiancé or his father actually responded to them.

"You shall sit here beside me, my dear lady, along with your son and daughter," Yosef said as he pulled out the chair nearest the end he would occupy. "And you, Miss Palladino, shall take the seat on my left. Does anyone have questions before we

begin? I must insist that everyone sit at this table of his own vo-
lition, believing in the power of the spirits we invoke. If you
doubt this process or my abilities, speak now! Negativity produces chaos. Results of which are irreversible."

"May I hold Willie?" Jemma asked in a bleating voice. "If I
keep him in his cage—"

"Absolutely not!" Jude snapped.

"Jemma, dear, that's a silly idea. Your ferret will distract—"

"Animals are far more sensitive to the presence of spirits
than we are," Polinsky intoned as he lit an oil lamp in the table's
center. "But I must concur with your brother and mother, Miss
Jemma, for if you're holding Willie you can't join hands with
the rest of us. The energy to summon spirits comes from the vibrations and continuous electrical impulses we pass around our
circle."

Jemma didn't reply. Instead, she observed the seating arrangement as the others settled into their chairs: she would face Polinsky from the opposite end of the oval, while a space gaped
between her and Maria. "How am I supposed to clasp hands
with Jude and Maria, when I can't reach? And shouldn't we
have another sitter to make the number even? Five is such a
lopsided—"

"Ah, *five*! The number of conflict and tension and change."
Polinsky stood behind his chair, a teacher surveying his small
class. His eyes lingered on Dora. She had removed her hat and
veil, when the medium had hinted that spirits preferred to communicate with sitters who appeared open and inviting. "If you
prefer, milady, you may invite a trusted servant to sit with us,
or perhaps—"

The clatter of the brass doorknocker made them all jump,
and then listen as the butler opened the front door. Had Polinsky contrived for a sitter of his own choosing to join them?
Maria watched his expression, his striking male profile as he,
too, awaited any message from this visitor before proceeding.

The conversation at the door was muffled, yet Maria sensed an intense energy, the presence of someone—

"Rubio!" she blurted when his familiar tread passed the parlor. "Rubio, come in and—"

The door opened and her brother appraised the situation with one swift glance. While his black cape looked elegant enough for the funeral he'd just attended, its lining of red and purple paisley print made him appear more of a magician than Polinsky. "Well! It would seem I'm just in time to round out your séance table!" he quipped. "A stroke of good fortune, indeed."

Maria felt a surge of relief when he pulled up a chair between her and Jemma. His foxlike grin hinted his appearance was anything but coincidental. "We were about to summon the late Lord Darington's spirit," she murmured. "To ask about Jason's whereabouts—"

"So we can pursue him," Dora insisted. "We *must* bring him home now, and hope a return to these familiar surroundings will restore his memory."

"And because it's pretty damn embarrassing that he's plundering our ships," Jude added wryly.

At the end of the table, Jemma beamed as she reached for Rubio's hand. "And with the *two* of you mediums here, working together, how can we fail?"

As Maria watched the conversational ball bounce around the table, she held her protest in check. It had been *her* idea to go after Jason, when they'd received the telegram that provoked Phillip's dramatic passing! Finally, with all the major players gathered at this table, Dora seemed eager to proceed— or at least eager for Yosef Polinsky to prove himself, now that Rubio had appeared.

"Let's get started, then!" Rubio reached for Maria's hand and then Jemma's, while the others completed the ring around the table. Polinsky sat down, appearing darkly powerful in the shadowy parlor; a man who intended to lead them to the answers they sought, if only to outperform his competitor.

When Yosef gripped her hand, Maria jerked: a jolt of awareness passed from Polinsky's palm on her right, through her body like an electrical shock, to shoot out through her hand and into her brother's. Rubio swiveled his head to gawk at her—and then at the other medium—before returning a similar surge of power.

"Gentlemen, please!" Maria gasped. "We must decide who will lead and who will follow, before I become your human sacrifice! Use your power to attract the spirit assistance we need, not to play childish games!"

The ring in Rubio's nose twinkled like Gypsy fire. "Excellent point. Since this séance was your idea, Polinsky, I shall act as a conduit rather than a source. But should your efforts fail, I'm not above showing you how it's done!"

Yosef sneered, his eyes a-glitter. "With all due respect to our hostess, we shall set aside our differences—our mutual animosity—to seek the spiritual guidance Pandora has requested. Shall we close our eyes to concentrate?"

The parlor rang with an anticipatory silence. The measured tick of the mantel clock marked the passing moments, until the man at the head of the table inhaled deeply. "We beseech you, spirit guides, to act on our behalf," he began in a reverent voice. "We seek the former Lord Darington, known to us as Phillip and Father . . . and we ask that you, my guides, channel your information and encouragement through me."

Polinsky's words resonated in the quiet room. Through one slitted eyelid, Maria observed the others: Dora with her ethereal, uplifted face; Jude, who concentrated his thoughts despite the way Jemma fidgeted on his other side. Was it her imagination or did the room's temperature plummet and then rise again? The flame in the oil lamp flickered once . . . twice, even though nothing stirred the air around them.

Jemma flinched. "Ouch! Who *pinched* me?" She looked accusingly around the table. "Mr. Polinsky, if that's *you*, sending your rude thoughts my way, you can stop it right now!"

The magician's smile looked wolfish and . . . domineering. "I didn't do a thing, my dear. It's all in your mind."

Maria considered this. Would Yosef claim that everything that happened—or didn't—was only in their minds? Or that the séance didn't progress because they hadn't properly harnessed their thoughts? When a current of air brushed her cheek, she looked to see if Rubio was playing tricks with the energy around them. He appeared, however, to be minding his own business . . . which, because his eyes were closed in apparent meditation, might mean he was conjuring up ghosts of his own. Would his guides compete with the spirits Yosef Polinsky had called upon?

"I feel something," Dora murmured, awestruck. "A current, a pulsing of air around my shoulders, as if—"

"As if your dear, departed husband were wrapping his arms around you?" Polinksy smiled indulgently at the woman beside him.

She smirked. "Phillip rarely touched me. He wasn't a demonstrative man—"

"Well, someone is touching *me*!" Jemma blurted. "As though a cat were twining between my legs under the table! Is that *you*, Willie?" The young woman reached with her feet and then broke the circle of hands to peer beneath the table, but her ferret wasn't there.

"We are indeed in the presence of spirits. They've come to introduce you to the spiritual plane before we delve into deeper communication," Rubio intoned. Still he sat with his eyes closed, his empty palm inviting Jemma to complete the circle again. "It requires great effort for a spirit to manifest its presence. We should be grateful that all who hover around us bring peace and the benefits of their influence."

Dora chortled curtly. "Well, I would expect nothing different, since—"

"Never assume that all spirits are friendly, or that they have our best interests in mind," Rubio cut in pointedly. "There are those who would mislead us. Those who would frighten us, so we would leave them be, in their otherworldly realms."

"And what about Father? Which group is *he* in?" Jemma's voice sounded high and childlike. Her blue eyes shimmered with unshed tears. "He—he was not an overtly affectionate man, as Mummy said, but he wasn't mean or hateful, either. At least not to *me.*"

"And when I summon him, you will realize that his nature remains unchanged." Polinsky glared at Rubio before looking to his left and his right, addressing Maria and then Dora. "Shall we continue?"

Across the table, Jude appeared doubtful about this whole scenario. But he closed his eyes and held the hands of his mother and sister again.

The parlor echoed with their silence . . . the different sounds of their breathing as they waited . . . for what? Again Maria sensed an unseen hand that stroked her shoulder, but she remained quiet. Was it Phillip Darington, resuming the suggestive patter they'd engaged in before the courier's telegram made him ill?

"I ask you now, my guides, to invite Lord Darington into our midst. And through him, we might resolve this conflict with Jason, to bring him home."

Again they waited, until Dora let out a long sigh. "Yes, I feel his presence—or at least the presence of someone very much like Lord Darington," she breathed. Again she turned her face upward, entreating the mystical presence. "How shall we bring Jason home? How will we capture him when the port authorities have been unable to find him?"

Maria wanted to blurt out *her* opinion as though she'd heard it from above, to move these proceedings along. But she refrained. It was best to align herself with Rubio, to cooperate with Polinsky's spirit guides.

Across from her, Jude sat bolt upright. "Yes! Yes, Father, I agree! We must sail to America at once—to work with the port authorities and capture Johnny Conn before he does anything truly detrimental. Or gets himself shot."

Dora and Jemma sucked in their breath. Jude's voice sounded eerily detached, as though he were merely the mouthpiece for whichever spirit had spoken.

"And what do *you* think, Maria?" Rubio queried softly. "Jason is your fiancé, after all."

She opened her eyes, slightly dazed from her prolonged concentration. Her brother's earnest expression urged her to speak up, but it was Jude's changing face that sent a surge of sexual heat through her body: he opened his eyes to stare at her as though he had assumed the persona of his brother. Or was it Johnny Conn the pirate who now undressed her with his lustful gaze? The change of atmosphere felt so sudden—so direct—she squirmed in her chair. "I—my God, it's as though Lord Darington's here with us! He's entered Jude's body to address us himself!"

"Phillip?" Dora asked doubtfully.

"No, it's Jason—the new Lord Darington! Coming through as Johnny Conn! Jude's eyes—the sensations I feel—tell me this is exactly what's happened!" Maria focused on Jude then, daring him to concur with her assessment . . . or to play along, as if he was initiating a game so things would go his way.

"I've heard yer cry in the night, sweet Maria, and I've come for ye." Jude's lips moved in an exaggerated way, as though he himself were not forming the words, while the voice sounded far more imperious than his own. "Ye say ye're intent on bringin' me back, yet here ye all sit on yer arses, mournin' a man ye scarcely paid any heed while he was alive!"

Dora sniffed indignantly. "I beg your pardon! Phillip was the center of his family—"

"A fine thing ta say, milady. Another matter entirely, now that ye're entertainin' the likes of that huckster beside ye!"

Jemma giggled nervously. Maria gazed from one medium to the other: was it possible for Rubio to create this little diversion, speaking through Jude to discredit Polinsky?

"I'll thank you to remember whose home you're in!" Dora spouted, although she clutched Yosef's hand more securely. "Whoever you are, be gone if you can't speak politely of Jude and Jemma's—and Jason's—father!"

"Says *you*!" the voice replied in a swaggering tone. "Every one of ya at this table is keepin' secrets—"

"And what's *your* secret, Conn?" Rubio demanded. His voice was low and calm, as though he were accustomed to conversing with unseen entities. "Why are you attacking Darington ships? Where are you hiding your booty?"

"Maybe ye should find out fer yerself—if ye've the balls to make the trip!" he challenged. Jude's face shifted into a leer that looked out of place, yet deadly serious, as he eyed each of them. "I want no part of yer whinin' to the port authorities—crooked in their own right—if ye get to America and I don't leap out at ye with all the answers! Take a chance!" he exclaimed with a nasty laugh. "Send Maria after me, and maybe I'll take yer bait! Maybe . . . she'll not return to ye."

Jude shuddered and then shook his head to clear it. He gazed around the table as though he were disoriented, perhaps wondering why they were all here, holding hands. "What happened? Did I doze off, or—I've gotten so little sleep these past few nights, I—"

"We're sailing as soon as possible." Maria stood up, releasing their hands. The challenge pronounced by an unseen pirate had stirred *hope* within her, along with desires too long dormant. "You heard him yourselves, and you know it wasn't Jude talking," she insisted. "I for one know better than to let any more time pass before we take action."

"But we buried Phillip—your father!—just this afternoon," Dora reminded them in a wavering voice. "It will be seen as disrespect for his memory if we so hastily—"

"How long do you intend to wait, Mum?" Jude rose as well, a new purpose ringing in his words. "And who says you'll be going along? Mourn if you must, but I'm sailing to America to bring my brother—now Lord Darington himself—home."

22

As she sat facing Rubio and Jude in the carriage, Maria felt alive and purposeful again. "Rubio, be honest! Were you playing games with Polinsky? Creating the transformation we saw in Jude with your own power?"

Her brother swept his long hair back from his face, smiling. In his dashing black cape with its purple and red lining, he could have been a stage magician coming away from a very successful performance. "Does it matter?" he teased. "Did you not feel the presence of spirits in that room?"

"Well, to be honest . . . I've never been as attuned to such things as you are—not until I watched Jude's face and voice change so dramatically, anyway." Maria thought back to what she'd witnessed at the séance table. "I'm not sure Dora really felt anything, either."

"I believe she was *trying* to feel an invisible presence, if only to please Polinsky," Rubio agreed. "Nevertheless, we heard Johnny Conn's challenge and you did the right thing, insisting we sail as soon as possible. Conn's not the type to wait for us. He has bigger fish to fry."

"Other ships to plunder," Maria mused. "And other adventures to launch when he tires of this one." She smiled at Jude, whose suggestive expression teased at her. "Did you *feel* the changes that came over you? It happened so quickly—"

"I have no idea what I did or said. It was as though I'd dozed off, yet when I came to myself again, I knew decisions had been made—and that everyone at the table had witnessed something astonishing." He focused on her as though he was still getting his bearings. "I shall go to Father's headquarters on the harbor and have a ship outfitted for the voyage. But if you and I sail to America, that leaves Mum and Jemma without a man to watch over them—"

Rubio snickered. "Oh, I doubt your mother shall be alone."

"—yet I can't insist that she go along. I don't know that she's ever left dry land," he mused aloud. "And if Mum comes, my sister would. Do we want them both retching for the entire voyage? Or should they remain here to tend to the social details of Father's passing?"

Maria nodded, following him with one part of her mind while her thoughts raced. She'd never left dry land, either, but of *course* she was going to find Johnny Conn! What woman could resist that lilting voice and the pirate behind it? It was all the proof she needed, hearing him speak through Jude: how else would that spirit know to name her specifically?

But what would happen to Miss Crimson's column while she was away? Would anyone connect her absence in the *Inquirer* with Miss Palladino's voyage to bring the new Lord Darington home? Maria gazed out the window, unseeing . . . careful not to betray her concerns to the men seated across from her. Should she hint of a holiday abroad in her next column? Inform the editor she might be away for several weeks?

"Are you getting out, dear sister? Or shall we remain in the carriage the rest of the day?"

Rubio's voice startled her out of her woolgathering. And

here came Quentin to open the carriage door . . . Quentin, the butler who knew the secrets she must now keep more zealously than ever.

"And how is everyone, now that Lord Darington has been laid to rest?" he inquired graciously. "My condolences to you, sir, as you mourn the passing of your father and wonder about the whereabouts of your twin—"

"Thank you, Quentin, but we have no time for tears. Jason's spirit has instructed us to sail to America! Immediately!"

"And I'll be going along, because he—alias Johnny Conn, the pirate—asked specifically that I come as *bait*." As Jude helped her from the carriage, a bold new sensation made Maria look more closely at him. Was he himself again or still under the influence of that boastful buccaneer he'd channeled at the séance?

The butler chuckled slyly. "What man could resist such temptation? Doesn't surprise me that milord stated his case that way, Miss Palladino, after the things he told me before you were to be married—all of them respectful and glowing with praise, of course," he added quickly.

Maria blinked. What sort of cat and mouse was Quentin McCallum playing, that he spoke in such a cavalier tone? As Jude tucked her hand around his elbow, his expression bespoke an urgency, a purpose he wasn't yet revealing, although his instruction to the butler brooked no doubts.

"McCallum, I'm counting on you to keep the town house— and Mrs. Booth—under control, the way Jason intended when he hired you. Mother's in no condition to manage a second household—and, as we all know, Father handled the finances." He smiled purposefully at the servant. "I'm sure we'll all be glad to have Jason home again, as Lord Darington, because *he* will see to such everyday details as your . . . pay."

Quentin's single raised eyebrow spoke volumes. "I wish you and Miss Palladino Godspeed and all the help you need to fetch him back! I'll remain loyally at my post no matter how long that might require."

"Thank you, Quentin. My brother depended on you, and I'm pleased his trust was not misplaced." Jude paused inside the town house doorway. After a moment's thought, he addressed Rubio, who'd entered behind them. "Perhaps you've not considered it, but *your* presence on the voyage would be immensely helpful, Palladino. My brother revealed himself today because of *your* influence rather than any power Polinsky wielded."

"Jason knows *I'm* not making a play for his mother." Rubio allowed the butler to remove his cape. "And while your invitation suggests an adventure like I haven't enjoyed in years, I have many upcoming appointments with clients to—oh my. What a wonderful likeness of Maria!"

Her brother stepped farther into the foyer to gaze at the portrait that hung above the mahogany table: in the light from the lamp, Maria's voluminous wedding dress glowed warmly and the roses Jude had so skillfully tinted in her cheeks gave her an ethereal, angelic air. Her brother turned to look at her and then at the likeness again. "My compliments, Jude! You've truly outdone yourself. No doubt whatsoever about who's the queen of *this* house!"

Maria's cheeks tingled. While her brother often complimented her, the portrait had apparently stirred something he'd never noticed. "And thank you to Quentin for getting it hung," she remarked. "I second Jude's suggestion that he be entrusted with the running of this household in our absence. Mrs. Booth and I have both relied upon him to . . . carry on as only a younger man is able."

As soon as the words left her mouth she realized how improper they sounded. The three men around her smiled indulgently. "Might I suggest you change into something less . . . funereal, dear Maria?" her brother said. "And McCallum, if you'd request some refreshment, I'll wait in the parlor. If I meditate upon sailing to America to find Jason, perhaps I'll receive an answer by the time you come downstairs, dear sister."

"Excellent!" Jude loosened his tie. "Perhaps wearing Jason's clothing will help me with our discussion, as well. I need all the assistance he can give me." He gestured for Maria to precede him up the stairway.

As she ascended, she felt his gaze on her backside, heard his breathing accelerate more than climbing the stairs required. His reason for changing clothes made perfect sense: who wanted to wear black as they planned a voyage? Yet Maria sensed an ulterior motive—

Jude pinned her against the wall as they stepped beyond the first landing. "I don't know how you do it, minx," he murmured as he reached up her skirts. "Ever since Father's service, I've wanted to yank down your—"

She gasped as her opera drawers landed around her ankles.

"—and bury myself inside your hot, wet cunt."

The words struck like lightning, words spoken the way Jason would've said them—made more dangerous because their voices echoed in the stairwell. "Jude, really!" she whispered, pointing frantically toward the first floor. "What if Mrs.—?"

"Yes, really! And quickly! Quentin and your brother know damn well why I wanted to change clothes, so let's not keep them waiting." His eyes glowed in the dimness of the upstairs hall as he helped her step out of her drawers. "If this isn't what you want, you'd better speak up, Maria. I've had to be so *fucking* patient since Jason disappeared, because Mother's watched me like a hawk! Do you know how badly I *need* you, Maria?"

Had his words goaded her? Or was it the desperation with which he spoke them? Jude had always been the more sensitive, lingering lover, yet this risky opportunity made her pulse race. The day before her wedding, when she'd bedded both brothers, seemed like a distant dream . . . she'd spent so many nights alone in this house where other bedsprings creaked and other lovers met each other's needs. . . .

When Jude sent her black veiled hat sailing up the stairs ahead of them, her heart soared with it. Too long she'd gone without this sort of play. "In here!" she whispered, motioning toward the bathroom. "Jason's bedroom is directly above the parlor and mine's above the dining room, so—"

Jude steered her ahead of him, into the little room where he'd wooed her on the eve of her ill-fated wedding. Instinctively they moved, latching both bedroom doors and then tossing towels to the floor to muffle their movements. With a wicked grin, Maria twisted the sink spigots, so the water gurgled in the drain. "Here's to a few moments of clean living," she quipped. "How shall we do this?"

Her lover glanced at the bathtub, the water closet, and then the large cabinet where linens were stored. "Off with your dress!" he whispered. "No more of this awful black garb, when pale pink skin becomes you so much better."

"Off with your clothes, too! We came upstairs to change, after all." Maria quickly unbuttoned the fitted gown of black bombazine, watching as Jude's somber suit coat and trousers landed on hooks beside the door. He'd shrugged out of his white shirt and was peeling down his union suit by the time she stepped out of her dress: the flush in his cheeks matched the heat she felt in her own face . . . the illicit excitement of sating each other's hunger while her brother awaited them made her throb all over. She widened her eyes, asking what came next.

Jude gazed avidly at her: she was clad only in her black stockings, pumps, and a fancy corset from her trousseau. "Up you go," he murmured as he lifted her to sit on the linen cabinet. "Why haven't we thought of this before? This is precisely the right height—"

Maria spread her bare thighs and tipped back in his embrace.

Her pulse pounded so loudly she wondered if anyone down-stairs could hear it.

He stepped in and stopped with the tip of his cock in posi-tion. "Damn, but you're lovely, woman. And such a sport about it, too, that I—"

She pulled him into a kiss that made them both squirm. Their impassioned sighs mingled with the gurgling of the water as they rubbed their bodies together. The rasp of his coarse hair against her silk corset only inflamed her more, and his skin felt like warm velvet as he wrapped his arms tightly around her. His cock teased at her curls, prodding her mound while denying her that surge of entry she sought. Despite the need for speed, Maria allowed herself to exhilarate in Jude's affection—and in his brazen way of expressing it.

"Maybe it wouldn't be such a bad thing if we *didn't* find Jason," Jude murmured.

"But we will," she assured him between kisses, "and the three of us will continue as lovers. But right now it's *you* I need, Jude. I'm so wet I might slip off the cabinet—"

She stifled her gasp against his bare shoulder as he plunged inside her, tipping her back to find the best angle. Biting his lip and clenching his eyes shut, Jude concentrated on stroking her with his cock. Maria clutched his shoulders to suspend her body so the cabinet wouldn't bump and creak. He felt needy, this man who'd claimed her so quickly. Jude rode her faster, stiffening with the intensity of holding back, of remaining quiet as he thrust and then eased away . . . thrust and then—

"I want to feel you squirt, hot and hard," she muttered near his ear. "Want you to spasm deep inside me, like a dog rutting a bitch in heat—clutching and fucking—knowing she won't let go of his red-hot cock until he's satisfied her. And then—"

"Jesus God, Maria!" Jude held her hard against his body as he rocked relentlessly, caught in the throes of an orgasm that triggered her own.

Maria ground her hips against his, inhaling hard to keep from screaming, flying on the verge of absolute madness until his low gasps subsided. Together they caught their breath, careful not to knock against the cabinet.

"We'd better dress—"

"By now they're wondering where we are and—"

"Begging your pardon, Miss Palladino. Would you like lemon cakes with your tea, or the fresh jelly tarts I baked this morning?"

Maria gaped at Jude as his grip tightened around her. She pried herself from his arms to turn off the water. "Yes! Both!" she exclaimed toward her bedroom. "Thank you for asking, Mrs. Booth."

Was that a sly chuckle coming from the other side of the door? "And do you suppose Mr. Darington would enjoy fresh strawberries with clotted cream?"

As Jude opened his mouth, Maria clapped her hand over it. "Yes, please! Strawberries would be *lovely!*"

"The least I can do, considering all the shock and sadness of these past few days."

Why didn't the damn housekeeper leave her to that shock and sadness, then? Step away from the door and go downstairs?

As if you don't know! How will you face her, knowing she'll remark about—

"Mr. Darington, sir, shall I find you a fresh shirt and trousers from Jason's armoire while you're washing up?" Quentin spoke from Jason's room, and as she and Jude scrambled for the same washcloth, Maria swore the butler was laughing. In cohoots with Mrs. Booth, no doubt—and, for all they knew, the two servants had been listening at the bathroom doors for several minutes. Jude covered his own mouth this time, nodding at the door where the housekeeper might still be hovering.

"Thank you, Quentin," Maria replied with exaggerated patience. "I'm sure he'll choose something when he returns. Gentleman that he is, he's allowed me to freshen myself first."

Again they heard no footsteps or movement. What if they unhooked the doors and came face-to-face with those two foxes, who seemed determined to catch them at a game they themselves knew well?

And what does that matter? Didn't Rubio just declare you the queen of this house?

Maria inhaled, bolstering her nerve. "If you would be so kind, Quentin," she continued in a honeyed voice, "would you go downstairs and inform Mrs. Booth that my brother Rubio prefers chocolate to tea? It sharpens his focus when he listens to his spirit guides."

"All right, I shall, milady. Will there be anything else?"

Maria rolled her eyes. Was there no end to this butler's brazenness? "*No,* I think not! Tell Rubio I'll be with him in two shakes of my tail!"

"An image we'll all enjoy, I'm sure. As you wish, milady."

At least this time they heard the butler moving toward the main door of Jason's room—or was that a ruse? Even if she emerged first, to dress, would the servants hover in the hall to confirm Jude's presence in her private quarters? What a nuisance, to be so closely watched! She was tempted to send them on holiday, except Jude had already told the butler to be in charge while he sailed to America.

Maria pressed a precautionary finger to her lips. Jude nodded, reaching for his clothes. Quickly she wiped between her damp thighs with the washcloth, and then unhooked the door. When she peered into her room, she saw only the sunny yellow walls and the furnishings . . . no sign of Mrs. Booth or her accomplice. She selected a dress of apple green taffeta—a gown with a pink flounced overskirt and bodice ruffles that always lifted her spirits—and then checked her mirror. It was too late to recoif her hair, so she hastily repinned a few loose tendrils.

Then she tapped on the bathroom. "Coast looks clear," she whispered.

"I'll be down momentarily, love. You were wonderful!"

Maria glowed all the way down the stairs. She might have taken an unladylike ride, seated on the long, glossy banister, had she not seen Quentin awaiting her in the vestibule. He held a silver tea tray with a plate of cakes and tarts, and the bone china cups Mrs. Booth preferred for these afternoon refreshments. "Thank you, Quentin, but I requested a pot of chocolate for—"

"And Mrs. Booth'll be along with it shortly," he replied in a tight voice. He glanced around them and then fixed her gaze with his dark eyes. "Might I inquire what shall happen to Miss Crimson's column, if you leave London in search of your Lord Darington?"

Leave it to this busybody to ask about that! Maria studied his face for any ulterior motives, and then checked to see that no one else could hear them. "Why do you ask? Why is it a concern of yours if—"

"Your readers will fear the worst, Miss Crimson!" he breathed. "If you don't report on His Lordship's funeral, and the séance Mr. Polinsky conducted at Lady Darington's request—"

"Only *two* of the events I intend to write up, when I get a moment," she whispered brusquely. "And why wouldn't Miss Crimson go on holiday now and again? Everyone else does!"

"For *weeks*? Without any assurance of her return?"

"I won't become Johnny Conn's hostage—although it sounds much the same as living *here*, where I'm constantly spied upon!" She caught herself and lowered her voice. "I'll inform my editor I shall be writing from afar, sending my posts to him by way of the transatlantic cable—"

"At the risk of someone else intercepting them? Perhaps

using them to discredit Miss Crimson while you can do nothing to prevent it?"

Maria straightened to her full height, trying to capture the thoughts that spun so wildly in her mind. "What are you after, McCallum? If you're wasting my time to catch Jude when he—"

"*I* could write your columns while you're away, Miss Palladino!" Quentin's slender face lit up with unabashed glee. "I've read *every one* of your pieces, committed the best ones to memory from sheer admiration and rereading! So why shouldn't I become your—your ghost writer?"

Her jaw dropped. Again she peered around the vestibule to be sure Mrs. Booth wasn't coming with the tea and chocolate—and an ear for such an incriminating secret. "Where on earth did you get *that* idea?" she rasped. "But more important, what will give you entrée to the social affairs and parties Miss Crimson frequents? I pride myself on *never* reporting what I've not seen and heard firsthand!"

"Didn't I figure out your identity, your delivery method, before you were even slightly aware?" Quentin lowered his face to within inches of hers. "To whom else can you entrust your responsibility for the truth? Your *reputation* as a journalistic visionary?"

"That's the most outrageous—"

"But confess! My proposition's the answer—the one method of preserving all you've accomplished with your writing." The young butler popped a lemon petit four into her mouth when she tried to protest. "I could send you the gossip from my forays, by way of the cable, and then deliver your written posts to the *Inquirer*. But your career—your audience—will be the furthest thing from your mind as you search for Jason, even if such a strategy could remain timely. Week-old gossip is about as relevant, as fascinating, as rubbish left to rot on the curbs!"

Maria couldn't believe what she was hearing. This opportunistic butler believed he could share her social favor, her *glory*, by writing under her name! As though readers wouldn't know the difference in reports written from a man's viewpoint, after trusting Miss Crimson to deliver the dirt in her inimitable way these past few years! It sounded like a subtle form of blackmail, the way this young swain had so thoroughly considered the angles of her absence and then positioned himself to—

Footsteps on the stairs made them step away from each other.

"We'll talk later!" Maria muttered. She strode toward the parlor, pausing to assess the room from the doorway: her brother stood in profile to her, looking out the window. His faraway expression bespoke a trancelike state he invoked to receive information from his spirit guides . . . or to convince others he was lost in his own thoughts rather than delving into theirs.

Rubio knew she was Miss Crimson. Just as he knew both Jude and Jason Darington were her lovers. But with Jude descending the stairs behind her, it was no time to trot out the secrets they each kept, because what might Mrs. Booth reveal to Lady Darington after their ship set sail? If Jason's mother learned of her role as the gossip columnist, Maria would lose far more than her reputation as a writer: the pirate she brought home might not marry her, at his mother's insistence. And *then* where would she be? Especially without Phillip Darington to defend her.

Lost and alone . . . with no one to blame but myself.

"Your tea, Miss Palladino. And the chocolate you requested for your brother." Mrs. Booth gave a stiff curtsy from the opposite arched entryway to the parlor. A sly light glimmered in her eyes as Jude entered the room. "You two must surely be . . . *exhausted,* after the trials and tribulations of this fateful day. One can only guess what might *change* now that Phillip, Lord Darington, has passed on, with the heir to his title nowhere to be found."

"And we shall correct that situation by week's end, Mrs. Booth." Jude strode to the housekeeper to take the tray. "We no longer require your services today, so why don't you and Quentin enjoy some time off? Miss Palladino, her brother, and I have a great deal to discuss about fetching Lord Darington home, and we will *not* be interrupted—or spied upon. *Thank you.*"

The old woman pursed her lips, but Jude's purposeful gaze kept her silent. Indeed, he waited for both servants' footfalls to fade down the hall before he turned toward Maria and her brother again. "High time my brother returned, if only to discipline his domestics!" He set the tray on the table with an unceremonious clatter of the pots. "Far too presumptuous they've become, trapping us in the bathroom and then pretending each didn't know what the other was doing! I would dismiss them, except we'll rely upon them while we're gone. Mum couldn't stomach interviewing new ones in her present state. Father always did that."

Rubio sat on the edge of the settee to pour his chocolate. "Are you concerned about her welfare while we're away? I could recommend a physician, or a companion from—"

"Hah! You hit the nail squarely on the head when you implied she'd be *entertaining* in our absence. It's best I won't be around to watch that."

The medium's lips flickered. "And how convenient, that you and my sister shall be free to do the same while aboard the ship, eh? Almost like a . . . honeymoon without the nuptials."

Maria perched beside her brother to serve the tea, aware that both men in this room were acting oddly. When had Jude ever taken command of household matters? And when had Rubio dared to imply her love life seemed dubious? As though *he* didn't bed numerous ladies, be they friends of the Queen or the fetching blond seamstress who lived in the apartment across the hall from his! As she handed Jude his cup, it chattered on the saucer like teeth on a cold day.

Both men eyed her suspiciously. She glared impertinently at them and then jammed an entire jelly tart into her mouth.

"Maria appears agitated—about something other than her voyage to meet Johnny Conn." Rubio glanced sideways over the rim of his cup. "All the more reason I should accompany her to find her beloved."

"So you're going with us! Hallelujah!" Jude stuck out his hand exuberantly. "Your presence—your powers—shall be an enormous boon as we locate Jason!"

Rubio grinned and grasped his hand. "Partners, then! Too long I've worked without time away to rejuvenate my spirit, and the fresh sea air—not to mention the company of my dear sister—shall be tonic for my soul."

Why was it she'd just heard a *click* in her mind? Like the closing of metal handcuffs? Why was it every man here suddenly had designs on her? Quentin wanted to assume her secret identity and the notoriety that came with writing her column. Rubio saw himself as her keeper, the guardian of her reputation. And Jude would never get beyond being the *second* brother, would he? So he coveted her company and planned to make the most of it while his mother wasn't watching.

The gold ring in Rubio's nose winked in the light from the parlor window. Just for a moment, Maria imagined the hoop earring a certain pirate wore . . . the lascivious grin that lit his face when he let her play "bait" after they found his hideout.

She gulped her steaming tea and chose another jelly tart. Far as she was concerned, that ship bound for America couldn't sail soon enough.

23

"Ahoy there, Darington! We sails in fifteen minutes! All aboard what's goin' aboard, sir!" The uniformed captain waved his hand above his head as he smiled down at them from the rail. He smoked a curved pipe and sported a white beard like Santa's, so Maria liked him immediately. A stalwart, barrel-chested fellow named Moses MacLeod inspired trust and confidence, didn't he?

As the breeze from the harbor whipped around her, Maria's heart soared. While Jude had said the *Fortune's Opportunity* was the oldest cargo steamer of the Darington fleet, to her it looked like an opportunity for fortune, indeed—a fortune that had nothing to do with the booty Johnny Conn had stashed away. Her dreams of Jason, every night since the séance, had felt so vivid, so *real:* she was touching him, kissing him, taking him into her body and soul, only to awaken alone in her bed . . . trembling and wet. At last, her lonely nights would come to an end!

As a stevedore clumped up the gangplank balancing one of her trunks on his shoulders, Jude smiled. "Shall we go, sweet

Maria? It's the moment we've been waiting for. Soon Jason will be with us again!"

"Whether he wants to or not!" Rubio chimed in beside them. He shielded his eyes from the bright morning sun, a grin lighting his exotic features. "I'm teasing, of course. I predict that once he lays eyes on Maria, the ship will sail us home in record time, powered by his excitement."

He offered her an arm, as did Jude, and the three of them ascended to the deck of the ship. And what a glorious view! From the rail, Maria could see the flags and smokestacks of ships from around the world, bobbing on water that sparkled with diamonds. Beyond that, the ocean beckoned. Sea birds squawked, dipping and gliding on the currents.

She imagined herself as one of those birds, free and flowing in a fresh direction. While it was fine to be the queen of Jason Darington's town house, she much preferred this unfettered feeling of boundless possibility. Not only would this voyage take her to the man she loved, it gave her time to contemplate her future . . . to consider letting Miss Crimson die a quiet literary death in her absence. She would miss the thrill of reading her columns in the *Inquirer*, yes, but perhaps that secret career had served its purpose. Far more important to be the wife Jason, Lord Darington, would cherish forever—the woman he'd have no reason to doubt or forsake. Once they were married, firmly ensconced in their new home, she'd have no need for the income, anyway. And once their babies started coming, such a subversive sideline would seem highly inappropriate!

Maria inhaled deeply, aware of Jude standing beside her, lost in his own thoughts. She glanced surreptitiously at him, relishing the close resemblance he bore—at least physically—to his twin. Was it her imagination, or did he *behave* more like Jason as well? Was he a different man since he'd channeled his brother's spirit at the séance?

She leaned against the rail so she could converse more easily, because at this height the wind competed with her words. "Penny for your thoughts, dear—"

"What in God's name is *Mum* doing here? And that charlatan Polinsky?" he snapped. "And Jemma! Oh, for chrissakes—"

Maria stared toward the pier as Jude hurried away. The sailors were in position to hoist up the gangplank, yet one raised arm had distracted them from their orders: Yosef Polinsky held them in sway with his charismatic smile as he urged Dora Darington and her daughter ahead of him. Jemma, clutching Willie to her shoulder, beamed at the burly stevedores as her pumps tapped a pretty tattoo on the gangplank. Her mother appeared regal in a traveling suit of deep plum trimmed in black: not a *merry* widow, perhaps, but a woman whose stylish hat gave her a purposeful, well-to-do air. Even though the crew had no idea who she was, Lady Darington exuded an élan no sailor would argue with.

And she looks so smug about it, too. As though she had this card hidden up her pretty sleeve all along, and Polinsky is playing it. Maria gawked between the rails as Jude confronted their unexpected guests, but all she caught were their voices.

"What is *this*? Coming aboard at the last possible moment? You know damn well—"

"That's no way to address your mother, Darington! She has every right to search out her son—"

"Did you think I could remain in that empty house while you and Maria went galavanting across—"

"Willie! Willie—oh *no*, Willie! Come back here!"

Maria sighed. She had been so ready for this escape, this mission for making her dreams come true.

As Rubio approached, his expression remained serene . . . as though he'd been far away in his thoughts while walking the deck. When he heard those voices below, however, one eyebrow arched. "So the three-ring circus has arrived after all? Why am I not surprised?"

Maria was going to quiz him about how much he knew, but a white bullet-shaped blur shot past their legs.

"After him!" Jemma screamed, gesticulating wildly at the sailors around her. "You really *must* catch my Willie! Poor little fellow's never been on a ship before, and—well, what if he jumps overboard?"

"We should be so lucky," Rubio muttered.

"No, it would only make things worse," Maria replied with a roll of her eyes. "She would spend the rest of the trip weeping and wailing, inconsolable. Not to mention intolerable."

Her brother gazed steadily at her, while crewmen thundered past in pursuit of Jemma's ferret. When he ran a finger along her butterfly pendant, her heart hammered beneath it. "Prepare yourself," he said in a low voice. "Much will be revealed about many on board this ship. Indeed, we shall learn more about members of Jason's family than about his adventures since he was shanghaied. What you *do* with that information will chart the course for the rest of your life, my lovely sister."

"And what do you mean by that?" Perhaps it was the lurch of the ship away from the pier that set her off balance. She fondled the butterfly pendant for luck. "What *would* I do with any compromising information, out on the ocean, miles from anyone I know?"

"Miss Crimson would think of something."

"Miss Crimson is on hiatus." She crossed her arms, looking directly into his bottomless brown eyes . . . wondering if he saw through her ruse. "Her days are numbered, you know. She hopes to become so involved in wedded bliss and motherhood, she won't even *miss* her eavesdropping and journalistic pot-stirring."

Rubio's smile suggested he knew better. Which meant she should *not* hint about Quentin's offer to write her society column. Maria hadn't gotten the chance to talk with him alone this week: Mrs. Booth had hovered constantly as they packed for her trip. So while she hadn't encouraged the butler to take up Miss Crimson's pen, she hadn't forbidden him, either.

Her brother's clouded expression suggested he had bigger secrets in mind, however ... revelations imparted by his spirit guides even as the chaos continued around them. Willie was no doubt terrified by so many strange men chasing him in their heavy boots, so when the ferret squirmed through a hole in the grating and disappeared below deck, a loud cry went up.

"Enough! Return to your posts!" Captain MacLeod commanded above the ruckus. He turned to the Darington women with a grim smile; removed his pipe to emphasize his point. "Beggin' your pardon, Miss Darington," he said in a strained voice, "but your wee beastie is *your* concern, while the sailin' of this ship is what I hired these sailors to do. Our rule aboard the *Fortune's Opportunity* is 'every man to his own work.' Do I make my meanin' clear?"

Wide-eyed, the young blonde nodded. Jemma's forlorn expression appealed to the burly men's sympathies, however, just as her youthful sweetness and female form held their attention. But they returned to their duties without further comment.

"Here's your chance, Polinsky!" Rubio flashed the other medium a daredevil grin. "Use your intuitive powers to find Miss Jemma's pet! Think of the favor you'll gain, not only from the captain but from your lady friend, as well!"

"Rubio, honestly!" Maria blurted. "Why pour oil on the fire—"

"I wouldn't dream of it, dear sister." With his gaze still fixed on the trio that stood partway across the deck, Rubio raised his voice again. "If I were you, I'd start in the galley, sir. Before the cook puts ferret stew on tonight's dinner menu."

As Jemma's hands flew over her mouth, Dora pulled her daughter closer. "That will be all from *you*, Mr. Palladino! Jemma has endured enough, losing her brother and her father, and now being uprooted to come on this voyage—"

Rubio shrugged, making the folds of his brocaded cape ripple richly. "Check the kitchen, I tell you. Start with the stew pots." And with that, he strolled off toward the bow of the ship.

Maria sighed. They'd not even lost sight of land, and the confrontations had begun.

"Would you look at that *shameless* display!" Jude glared through an old spyglass he'd found in his nightstand, and then handed it to Maria. "Father not even cold, and that shyster's leading Mum down the primrose path."

As she looked through the porthole, at the couple sequestered in an alcove where lifeboats and coiled ropes were stacked, Maria smiled wryly. "With all due respect, your mother's leading as much as following. She looks quite fetching in that red dress. Younger and more carefree than I've ever seen her."

"And what are they doing now? *Kissing*, for God's sake?"

She snickered as Jude snatched the spyglass. "Not much different from what *you* were doing, moments ago. Curiosity not only killed the cat, as you recall, but it's cost you the last few moments of your own enjoyment. I must get dressed now, so we're not seen coming from your cabin together."

Maria slipped into yesterday's clothing, eyeing the man at the window. Jude seemed possessed—obsessed—with the interplay between the two mediums, and between Polinsky and his mother. "For some women, it's difficult to navigate life's ebb and flow without a partner," she remarked. "Dora's still youthful and attractive, the widow of a wealthy man. She'll use her wiles to attract another love, even if her flame for Polinsky burns out, you know. She's made that way."

Jude's disgusted grunt was her cue to leave.

The morning fog made her exit from his cabin less obvious. Her own quarters were four doors down, along a narrow walkway: she passed Rubio's room and heard his soft snores . . .

Jemma slept silently in the larger cabin she shared with her mother . . . Polinsky's was unoccupied. She entered her tiny space, only as wide as the length of her narrow bed, and poured water from her pitcher into the washbowl.

Last night after dinner, the Darington women had loudly protested the absence of modern facilities, but they'd been met by the mute stares of the male crew. The *Fortune's Opportunity* was a cargo steamship, so no one had claimed this voyage would be luxurious—nor had they expected Dora and Jemma to come along. It hadn't helped that Rubio's prediction about finding Willie in a stockpot proved correct. Tensions only increased as the two mediums sat across the dinner table from each other, as though they had to constantly watch each other and prove their own powers.

As she emerged from her room in a fresh gown of simple coral serge, with a light shawl around her shoulders, Maria wondered if the entire trip would be marked by strife. The only two enjoying themselves were Yosef and Dora, and as she peered in the direction of the lifeboats, Maria envied the bliss on Lady Darington's face: Polinsky was pressing her against the wall, his knee between hers, pouring himself into a passionate kiss.

She and Jason had kissed that way so many times . . . stealing affection at every opportunity, away from prying eyes. Maria stepped behind a post to watch them. Would she feel these same urges when she was Dora's age? Would she still inspire a man's excitement? Still crave the intimate give-and-take between lovers, after years of marriage?

When Polinsky pulled away from the lingering kiss with his eyes closed, Maria felt a wave of need. The men who met this magician distrusted him, but women . . . none were immune, were they? She walked resolutely toward the stairway, then eased herself to the deck below.

"No need to sneak around, Maria. I've known of your presence all along."

She turned at the bottom of the stairs to find Polinsky watching her, his arms crossed as he leaned against the rail. The replies that came to mind would only confirm that she'd been spying—from Jude's room—so she remained silent.

So did he. The sea breeze toyed with Yosef's silver-streaked hair, but his expression remained inscrutable, as though carved in marble.

Dear God, he is attractive . . . even if he's probing my thoughts with his mind. His presence was so unsettling, Maria was glad she'd had experience with Rubio's quirks and powers. Where was Dora? Why did it suddenly feel as though she herself and this master magician were the only ones on board, enveloped in the morning's mist?

Yosef's gaze lowered, to linger on the butterfly pendant. "Made by one brother as a gift from the other," he murmured. "Be careful, Miss Palladino. Your infidelities will bring consequences."

"Eh-everything does," she pointed out, wishing she sounded more confident. What right did he have to judge her? Or to speak as though she were guilty of more than *one* infidelity—which, given her mutual agreement with the twins, had never been considered a breach of trust! Someone really should bring this imperious wizard down a peg or two.

He turned then, leaving her to simmer in resentment. Maria tugged her shawl around her shoulders and strode toward the bow of the ship, hoping to find her brother: he loved to ruminate near water, for it refreshed his soul. The rail along the ship's front was unoccupied, however, so Maria gazed out over the ocean alone. Mesmerized by the swirling water as the ship moved through it . . . hidden away in the dense haze of early morning, she yearned for the serenity—or the excitement— she'd envisioned for her first ocean voyage. Yet the presence of

Dora, Jemma, and Yosef Polinsky guaranteed she would feel only more anxious as the hours passed and they approached the shores of America.

How long before they'd see land? What would she say to Jason when she first laid eyes on him? What if he didn't know her—and didn't want to?

Maria felt claustrophobic in the fog, so she started down the stairs to the private dining area Captain MacLeod had set aside for them: since cargo ships rarely carried passengers, guest amenities were limited. Before she reached the bottom of the steps she heard voices ringing in the small room.

"—nothing but a silver-tongued devil, leading my mother astray! Manipulating her in her time of grief and vulnerability!" Jude spouted. "And *your* behavior, Mum, is nothing short of appalling! Letting this man *handle* you—"

"That'll be enough of your judgmental *mouth!*" Dora replied tartly. "Young, impressionable ears are present."

Maria paused. Once again Jude's uncharacteristic wrath surprised her: while he'd received his share of criticism from his parents, who favored his brother, he'd never been one to fight back. But that, too, had changed since Jason had spoken through him at the séance. She entered the small room cautiously, wishing she didn't have to walk to the far side of the crowded table. All eyes followed her as she took her seat between Jemma and Rubio, who frowned in the chair at the end.

Dora's expression grew more catlike. "And now that all the apppropriate parties are present," she remarked archly, "I will warn you again, son: don't point any fingers or cast any proverbial stones! More than once I kept your father from finding out about your *dubious* three-way arrangement with Jason and Miss Palladino! More than once I saved you from being banished from the estate altogether—for that's what Lord Darington would've done, had he learned of your illicit activities!"

She turned to address Maria then, a she-dragon ready to

shoot flames. "And *you*, missy, would *never* have enjoyed the favor Phillip bestowed upon you—much less the town house, after Jason was abducted—had he known of your duplicitous nature! I find this whole sordid affair disgusting! Disgraceful!"

Her accusations rang in the small room as the group sat before plates of cold, rubbery eggs and bread left from last night's dinner. Not that Maria felt inclined to eat: Lady Darington's glare left no doubt of her intention to win this battle. Her expression softened slightly, however, when she glanced at Polinsky: he sat beside her, ready to jump into the fray like a snarling dog if she wanted him to. Jude appeared stunned. Maria's brother straightened in his chair and took her hand.

On her other side, Jemma sat wide-eyed: she was indeed hearing of matters not generally discussed in front of young ladies. And she was certainly old enough to understand Lady Darington's accusations about the triangular love knot Maria had tied with Jason and Jude. When she gawked openly, Maria kept a straight face and returned her gaze. The young blonde blinked and looked down at her untouched breakfast.

Should she respond to Dora's scathing remark? Or would she only dig a deeper pit? As the moments of silence crept by, the little room felt so airless . . . Maria wanted to blurt out a rebuttal, or excuses, or *anything* to relieve the rising tension—

Which would play right into Lady Darington's hand, wouldn't it? Nearly anything she said would incriminate her. And it was one of Rubio's favorite tricks, remaining silent so a client would talk.

So Maria kept her facial expression noncommittal. Let her gaze wander to each of the others at the crowded table, determined not to knuckle under to Dora's accusations. When Jemma's fork clattered to her plate, everyone jumped.

"Mumsy, I—" The girl was at a loss without her ferret to fondle, so she bungled ahead. "Mumsy, you've never talked about Daddy—about how you fell in love, or the party you had at your wedding. Or why you married him in the first place. You've scarcely referred to him since the funeral, and I—I would like to hear about those things. *Sometime,* anyway."

Again the little room got quiet, but with a different tension this time: Lady Darington's mask of control crumpled—if only for a moment—before she found a reply, as though her daughter had stumbled upon a very touchy subject.

"My marriage to Phillip, Lord Darington, was not what it seemed," she stated quietly. "Without elaborating about . . . unseemly details, I will say that while this voyage is an effort to reclaim my son, it's also a declaration of my independence. I remained a steadfast wife until death did us part, but I refuse to follow society's code of mourning for a man who married me for reasons . . . other than love."

Dora stood then, visibly shaken. "I pray that you, dear daughter, will never endure the trials I have survived for the sake of raising my children . . . to best advantage. Please excuse me, I—"

As Lady Darington rushed from the room, a sob escaped her. Jude and Jemma appeared flummoxed by what their mother had revealed, yet both rose to follow her. Polinsky stood up, as well, taking each of them by the arm.

"Allow your mother some time alone," he suggested in a surprisingly compassionate voice. "She has repressed some very strong emotions since your father's passing, so you wouldn't see how helpless and vulnerable she feels right now— so you wouldn't worry about her . . . mental state." The medium glanced at Rubio, to check for any challenge in his eyes. Then he looked at Jude. "How much longer before we reach America?"

"Another day or so, I think. Why do you ask?" Jude removed the magician's hand from his arm. "This may sound cold, but I've witnessed Mum's little exit scenes a hundred times—usually when she was trying to get her way and Father wasn't budging. If you're instructing us to leave her be, then the same goes for *you*, Polinsky!"

"I have no intention of intruding upon her—"

"After what I saw this morning, your *intention* looks quite self-serving!"

"Oh, this is all my fault!" Jemma began to cry noisily. "I shouldn't have asked such a personal question in front of— well, why would Mumsy answer it in front of you men? You don't understand *anything!*"

"But you're right, Jemma." With a puzzled sigh, Jude opened his arms and his little sister threw herself into his embrace. "She's never spoken of her marriage, and you'd think she would've recalled fond memories of her own wedding when we were preparing for Jason and Maria's. I, too, have been curious about her feelings for Father . . . because she's never displayed any."

While she was pleased to see Jude comforting his younger sister, Maria felt awkward watching them discuss their parents' relationship. She excused herself to go outside, where the morning sun had burned away the fog. The sea breeze lifted her spirits, yet she wondered if she'd have to remain holed up in her room to avoid further confrontations. It *was* an emotional time for Dora Darington: she understood that. But she suspected Jude was right. His mother had staged a little scene when Jemma's questions sent the conversation in an unexpected direction.

She heard voices behind her on the deck, saw Jemma strolling, carrying Willie in a birdcage one of the sailors had found in the hold. The young woman had no more than paused at the railing before two deckhands greeted her with eager grins—just what any girl needed to feel better, wasn't it? Maria gazed ahead of the *Fortune's Opportunity*, wishing land would appear because it meant she'd be closer to finding Jason . . . closer to feeling better than she had for weeks.

But all she saw was endless blue-gray water, in every direction.

"For you, dear sister."

Maria smelled something wonderfully warm and sweet—and then snatched a thick slice of fresh bread, redolent with cinnamon and currants, from her brother's hand. "Where did you find *this?*" she asked before taking a huge, unladylike bite.

Rubio chuckled, chewing on his own slice. "Pays to make friends with the cook. I'm the one who rid his kitchen of that ferret, after all."

"Thank you. I didn't realize how hungry I was while all that . . . finger-pointing was going on." Sighing with sheer enjoyment, she bit into the fresh bread again. "I can't tell you how glad I'll be to reach port. I just want to find Jason and go home to my happily ever after. Is that too much to ask?"

He smiled ruefully. "You have every right to ask for that happiness—and to *expect* it, from what I can sense. But in the meantime, do you recall how I predicted several secrets would be revealed before this voyage concluded?"

Maria sighed. "And my . . . arrangement with Jason and Jude is just the first?"

"We've only just begun. Brace yourself for rough waters ahead, Maria."

24

"What are we to do, Jude? Will your mother watch us every moment now? Even after we find Jason?" Maria sighed as they strolled along the sunny deck, wishing she felt as lovely as the morning that made sun diamonds sparkle on the sea. Captain MacLeod had said they'd catch their first glimpse of American shores this afternoon, and it couldn't come soon enough: tensions aboard the ship escalated with every conversation.

"What *can* she do?" he replied quietly. "Without us, she'll never find her beloved firstborn son—*if* he lets us locate him. I've wondered if his pirate impersonation is a game, an escape route so he won't have to return home and deal with Mum." Jude smiled sadly. "But then, I can't imagine him forfeiting *you*. He'd come home to you even if Wildwood and the title weren't to be his."

"And how would Jason know his father has died, if he's eluded Darington Shipping's partners? And the law?"

Jude nodded, ducking as though to steal a kiss. But he jerked away. "That's a logical way to look at it. And we're being looked at, as well."

Yosef Polinsky stood at the rail ahead of them, gazing out over the endless ocean—or had he anticipated the two of them walking past him? Maria had learned long ago not to assume anything impossible for those with connections to the spirit world, those who possessed the second sight.

The medium's smile seemed speculative as he looked at them. "We'll spot land any time now. My spirit guide has informed me your brother is cutting his capers near the port of Charleston, so I shall instruct the captain accordingly. And might I add"—as he smiled at Maria—"that the moment he sees you, Miss Palladino, will be the moment we'll have him in tow. I feel Jason's spirit yearning for affection! Calling out to someone he's been missing but can't quite name."

Maria's stomach fluttered, yet she did not reply. If she believed what this clairvoyant said, would she betray her brother and *his* guides?

Polinsky tilted his head slightly, imploring her with a smile. His gaze smoldered with blue-eyed fire. "When you accompany Pandora and me—"

"My sister will be with *me*, Polinsky." Rubio spoke from behind them. Maria hadn't heard her brother approach but his hands closed firmly around her shoulders. "Not only are you mistaken about Jason's whereabouts, I don't trust my sister in your company. I don't like the way you've been eyeing her unusual pendant."

Polinksy stiffened. "Are you implying—"

"No, I'm saying outright that the rumors flying about London are true. Meriweather Golding and her friends are too embarrassed to go to the police, after they welcomed you into their homes, but *you* were the scoundrel who absconded with their jewelry."

"Now see here, Palladino! It's one thing to challenge another medium about his predictions, but you're calling me a thief—"

"Calling a spade a spade."

"—without any proof to back you up! And I resent that!" Polinsky glanced behind them and then smoothed the lapels of his navy blue suit coat. "Out of respect for Jude's mother, I suggest we take this conversation elsewhere—"

"Why? Mum's presence might shine just the light we need!" Jude smiled at his approaching mother and held out his hands to her. But Dora ignored him.

"And what might *this* flock of birds be pecking at?" she asked cheerfully. "Captain MacLeod has told me we'll be going ashore before the sun sets, and I for one can't wait to feel solid ground under my feet again."

"Yes, it has been a trip of . . . shifting emotions and shifty characters," Rubio remarked. His hair blew around his face like chestnut flames while his dark eyes burned with his convictions. "Do you recall, Lady Darington, the stories ladies whispered at Lord Galsworthy's ball? Of gems that had disappeared?"

Dora's eyebrows rose. "I heard that Meriweather Golding lost track of some emeralds her husband had given her, but Dorothea Biddle speculated that she'd sold them years ago, when she'd learned they were an appeasement after Mr. Golding took a mistress. I doubt the poor dear recalls *what* she did with them."

"Nevertheless, Mum, you should consider yourself warned," Jude replied cautiously. "Palladino believes your new *friend* here made off with them!"

Dora looked askance at Rubio and then at Maria. "We're known by the company we keep, are we not?"

"And Rubio's also saying Jason's not around Charleston, as Polinsky believes, but instead he's—"

"Who will you listen to, Pandora?" the older medium interrupted. "Palladino resents me because I have eclipsed his reign as London's favored seer! This is his envy talking!"

"We'll see about that, won't we?" Rubio jeered. "The proof is in the predictions!"

"Gentlemen, please!" Maria shrugged out of her brother's grasp, glaring at both of them. "We've had nothing but conflict for this entire voyage! Captain MacLeod is the man to settle this!"

Off she stalked, her mind a-whirl with the need for peace . . . the need to be with Jason again. While it was lovely to hear Yosef Polinsky's romantic sentiments, he had other motives for insisting she accompany him and Lady Darington when they went ashore.

The ship rolled and she grabbed a support post to keep her feet. Some of the crewmen mopped puddles on the deck while others painted a section of rail: they smiled at her as she passed, but she saw none of the officers who might escort her to the captain. Perhaps if she went up to the wheelhouse. . . .

Maria halted on the first landing and clapped her hand over her mouth. Here indeed was one of the young officers who'd taken charge when Willie had escaped—a handsome swain with midnight hair and broad, strong shoulders. Eric O'Keefe, if she recalled correctly. But this time O'Keefe had captured Jemma Darington—or she had tempted him with her coy gazes? The couple had ducked into a shadowy nook, and as they kissed their sighs reminded Maria of what she'd been missing. Anyone could see these two had kissed many times before, the way they angled their mouths and noses in unison . . . the way his hand cupped the swell of her breast and she pressed herself into his palm.

It was rude to stand here gawking at them, yet Maria watched every nuance, spellbound, until she recalled her mission. Better to separate these lovebirds before Jude or Lady Darington discovered them, wasn't it? And because she'd caught them, perhaps O'Keefe would be more inclined to take her to the captain, as a bid for her silence.

But first she observed the tender yet commanding way Eric held Jemma's neck, to assert his power . . . to tilt her lips so he could deepen the kiss, leading her into the next phase of this amorous dance. Jemma's hand slipped lower, as though it knew exactly where her pursuer would become her prey.

Eric hunched when the devious blonde gripped his cock through his trousers. "Yes, yes . . ." he murmured, incoherent with need. "Turn him loose and give him release! Here, use my handkerchief to catch—"

But Jemma pulled away with a sly smile. She'd deftly unfastened his fly, to fondle his erection out of his trousers. "If I sit on the stairs—take you in my mouth—my skirt won't become rumpled."

"My God, girl, if someone walks up here—"

"We'll make it fast and furious. No one will know!"

Maria pressed against the wall to remain out of sight. While she wanted to get Eric's attention, perhaps this wasn't the best time. . . .

Within a heartbeat, Jemma sat down and leaned forward to suck him. O'Keefe gripped her slender shoulders as she grasped his hips and drove her mouth up and down the solid column of his cock. Aside from being a wicked, titillating sight to behold, it was a startling revelation: Miss Darington was not the innocent she pretended to be! Had she acquired such sexual skill with Quentin, the butler? Or was she more accomplished— more brazen—than her mother and brothers assumed?

Her blond hair shimmied with the rhythm of her thrusts as her full lips squeezed and released. Up and down she went, with urgent accuracy. Concentrating fully, with her eyes closed, Jemma looked more focused than Maria had ever seen her; more sophisticated than her childish behavior suggested when she plied what she wanted from her family. As Maria watched, her own heat flickered. Her body trembled with unmet needs, driven to an extreme by this illicit spying! If anyone came down from the level above, she would appear as decadent as the lovers she watched.

It didn't stop her, though. The ache between her legs intensified when Eric grimaced: he was beyond caring if anyone caught them. Maria squeezed her inner muscles to quiet the intense throbbing there, yet when O'Keefe let out a desperate groan she, too, needed the relief he sought.

Maria stuck her hands in her skirt pockets. Her fingertips found the open seam of her drawers . . . then the warm, fleshy folds that needed fondling while she tightened her inner muscles. One more glance at O'Keefe's cock, now red and ready to burst forth, had her rocking in place, rubbing frantically. When the ebony-haired officer gasped and his hips danced crazily, she surged to her own release. Her spasms were so intense she fell against the wall, biting back a loud, lovely groan. She rested there a moment, her eyes closed so the inner tingling would last.

I am lewd and crude, she thought. Yet she felt not one bit of remorse or shame. What harm had she done, after all? Her exertions had released a great deal of the tension created by the two sparring mediums—

"Miss Palladino, have you fallen ill?"

Maria's eyes flew open. Eric O'Keefe stood before her on the stairs, his eyes a-glimmer. Other than the heightened color in his cheeks, he looked completely recovered—and so genuinely concerned about her that she was momentarily speechless.

How long had she been leaning against the wall with her eyes closed and her hands in her pockets? And what sort of expression had he seen on her face? "I—my stomach took a turn when the ship rolled a few moments ago," she stammered. "But I'm fine, honestly!"

"Yes, we all felt the force of a sudden wave," Jemma remarked as she peered around him. "As though an underwater explosion had rocked the ship."

Maria straightened. This was no time to point a finger at this amorous couple, when they might have guessed the real reason for her odd position. "Mr. O'Keefe, I'd like to ask the captain about our destination, and I don't know where to find him." She smiled. Even though Miss Darington stood behind him, it felt nice to have a relative stranger looking so raptly at her.

"I would be pleased to escort you, Miss Palladino. Captain MacLeod will soon be steering us into the harbor, so we should

be on our way—*if* you're certain you can climb these steep
stairs."

And what if she couldn't? Would this dashing young officer
carry her up to the captain? Now *there* was a fantasy!

"Oh, I'm fine. Truly." She took the hand O'Keefe offered,
and stepped up to his level on the landing. "I was pausing to be
sure the dizziness had passed. No point in retching on the captain, is there?"

Up they went, past Jemma, until they reached the enclosed
wheelhouse, where the ship's navigation took place. O'Keefe
turned, squeezing her hand in the crook of his arm. "Shall we
exchange favors?" he murmured. "I saw you while Miss Darington was . . . working her magic. It was your ecstatic expression that sent me over the brink, so I'm sure you understand
my need for confidentiality. A lovely lady like yourself under-
stands the difficulties—the deprivation we seamen face when
we sail for months on end. Yet now we transport a cargo so
much more attractive than textiles or spices or furnishings."

Maria smiled. He sounded desperate enough to do anything
she wanted. "My brother shared the most fabulous cinnamon-
flavored bread with currants—the tastiest food we've eaten on
board," she suggested wistfully. "I don't suppose you could
find me a—"

"We all crave one form of sweetness or another, do we not?"
O'Keefe bowed slightly before pounding on the wheelhouse
door. "I'll request a fresh loaf and bring it to your cabin as soon
as it comes from the oven."

Maria smiled triumphantly. "I think we *have* indulged each
other's need for something soft and sweet. Thank you so much,
sir."

"The pleasure is all mine."

"And how might *I* please ye, Miss Palladino? I trust that my
chief officer has performed to yer satisfaction?"

Maria bit back a laugh. Had this bearded, barrel-shaped man

overheard their exchange? Could he, too, be convinced to do her bidding? "I'm sure you've heard our two mediums sparring over where we should search for Jason, the new Lord Darington? Where do *you* propose we dock and—"

"As the Darington partners're headquartered in Charleston, South Carolina, we's been instructed to meet with 'em before we—"

"But Rubio Palladino, London's foremost seer, tells me Jason is hiding farther north! He's been in contact with Johnny Conn, the pirate who—"

"Mr. Palladino's yer brother, is he not?" His tone expressed what his words did not. Moses MacLeod gestured for her to precede him into the noisy wheelhouse. "Lemme be the first to welcome ya to America, dearie. Because the shore ye see ahead is much more real, more tangible than a pirate who might or might not exist."

Maria scowled. "Surely you've seen the WANTED poster! And heard how Johnny Conn has attacked Darington ships and then buried the booty—"

"Hearsay, Miss Palladino. Pirates wearin' bandannas and earrings disappeared shortly after Edward Teach, the notorious Blackbeard, was brought down. Which was nearly two centuries ago." He smiled indulgently, stroking his white beard. "While I understand the romance of such legendary scoundrels— their appeal to the ladies—I have me orders. I'll not be pursuin' a pirate who might exist only in yer pretty imagination."

"Even if he's Phillip, Lord Darington's son? Surely you know Lady Darington came along expressly to find her oldest—"

"With all due respect fer the lady in her grief—which seems as fleetin' as this pirate fella, Johnny Conn—I'll be followin' orders issued by real, rational men." The captain clasped his hands behind his back, smiling beneficently at her. "Good day, Miss Palladino."

25

Real, rational men. What the hell do THEY know?

Maria gripped the rail, gazing toward the harbor in Charleston, where—from this distance—the stevedores resembled busy ants. Within the hour they would disembark, and then find lodging and organize their search for Jason.

With each passing moment, her apprehension grew. If they obeyed orders from Darington Shipping partners, who'd been unable to apprehend Johnny Conn, would they be sent home without a chance to follow Rubio's instincts? Or had Yosef Polinsky persuaded Captain MacLeod—either with his powers or a cash advance—that Charleston was Jason's hiding place?

"Your brother and I have been talking." Jude paused beside her, gazing around the bustling harbor as Captain MacLeod expertly steered the *Fortune's Opportunity* toward an empty slip. "No doubt in my mind Rubio's instincts are right. His triumphant expression as he connected with Jason's spirit moments ago cannot be denied!"

"Where does Rubio think we'll find him?" Maria's pulse sped up desite her misgivings. "The captain waved me off as an insignificant *female* with a vivid imagination when I insisted we sail farther north."

Jude's smile suggested he adored imaginative females, and that he'd love to bed one when they found a hotel room. "The captain has no idea about the forces at work in our favor, sweet Maria," he said in a husky voice. "I say we play along—get our rooms, and then I'll meet with Father's partners to plan our strategy. But meanwhile, you and Rubio might explore . . . other options."

"Such as?" Maria braced herself as the ship came within inches of the pier. Crewmen were tossing ropes to the steve-dores on the dock, while others prepared to lower the gang-plank—for their first steps into America! She couldn't suppress a grin, despite the captain's uncooperative attitude. "Where did Rubio say Jason was?"

"Hiding out among the islands of the Outer Banks, along the North Carolina shore—just like the swashbucklers of old." Jude smiled with pride, and perhaps envy. "The shallow inlets and miles of uninhabited shoreline allow him to plunder a ship and then dart into hiding. We suspect he has his booty stashed in various locations."

"And my brother thinks he can find these caches? And out-fox Johnny Conn?"

"I'd bet the estate on it! After all," he added in a more sub-dued voice, "the estate won't be the same without Jason as its earl. Mum won't let us forget that, either."

Below, the gangplank landed with a loud *thunk*. The air around them had stilled, and a dense heat had replaced the ocean breeze they'd enjoyed for days. "All ashore what's goin' ashore!" a sailor sang out.

Already Yosef Polinsky stood with Lady Darington on his arm, as though to make a grand entrance. Jemma waited behind them, peering at the muscular longshoremen from beneath her lacy parasol. She carried Willie in his birdcage, now adorned with ribbons that matched her pretty amber gown. Dora had donned a traveling suit of bittersweet silk with a stylish feathered hat. The trio looked downright regal as the medium popped a top hat jauntily onto his head and led the two ladies off the ship.

"And who might that be?" Maria pointed to a handful of men in suits who seemed extremely interested in the *Fortune's Opportunity*. "We're not the only ship to arrive—"

"Father's partners, I'm betting. Shall we introduce ourselves and get this process started?" Jude offered his arm. "May I take you along as my talisman? Your presence will encourage me before I begin my negotiations. And how can they deny Jason's beautiful fiancée anything she wishes?"

"It would be my privilege, Jude." Maria flashed him a confident grin. "Despite the way you doubt your abilities, I believe we'll find your brother—and that *you* will lead the way!"

"I could kiss you for saying that. But too many eyes are upon us."

He stepped toward the gangplank then, his hand upon hers. Something made her glance back, to find Rubio watching them from the doorway of his cabin. But why wasn't he coming ashore with everyone else? Maria almost waved, but thought better of it: her brother almost always behaved as though he *knew* things. Because he did.

Ahead of them, the men in dark suits circled Polinsky and Lady Darington, bobbing their heads like polite crows as introductions were made. Then one gentleman, the tallest of the lot, glanced at Maria and Jude as they approached. His monocle flashed in the sun as he squinted to see them more clearly. He reached into his pocket and unfolded a paper, oblivious to the chatter of his partners.

"I say! I say! Is that not the Jason Darington we're chasing down?" He pointed excitedly, waving the paper as he looked around the pier. "Police! Police—arrest this man! He's a thief and a scoundrel! It's that blasted Johnny Conn, the pirate!"

A whistle trilled loudly and, from several directions at once, uniformed officers rushed toward them. Maria froze, clutching Jude's arm. Was this really happening, or was her overactive imagination at work? "Wait! You've got the wrong man!" she cried. "This is Jude—"

"Grab him, MacTavish! Cuff him quick, before—"

"Might'a knowed he'd sail in on a Darington ship!"

"And disguised as a regular gentleman, too—the bugger!"

"What in God's name are you doing?" Jude demanded, but he was already surrounded by policemen intent on his capture. "I am *not* Jason Darington—"

"Oh, call yourself whatever you like! You're the image of the man in the WANTED poster, without the bandanna and earring!" the officer with the handcuffs declared.

Maria was lifted by a pair of beefy hands and set down a few feet away from the fracas around Jude. "Beggin' your pardon, miss, but you'd ought not be seen with the likes of this one!" the uniformed lawman said.

"You've got it all wrong! He's the *twin* of the man you seek!" she protested. "Jude has come to help you *capture* Jason Darington! Jason's now *Lord* Darington, and we must take him home to London!"

"Oh, he'll not be leaving anytime soon, miss! Not on *my* shift!" The man with the monocle had rushed over to supervise the policemen: he appeared ecstatic when Jude stood surrounded by blue uniforms with his hands cuffed in front of him. "Justice prevails! You'll be answering to my partners—and to the judge!—for the ships you've destroyed and the cargo you've stolen!"

Jude tried to shove away from all those officers holding him hostage, but he was outnumbered. "I have your telegrams in my pocket! *I* am the Jude Darington who *requested* this meeting so we could apprehend my brother—"

"We'll not be falling for *that* trick again!" A shorter partner approached Jude, looking ready to spit at him. "You might have telegrams in your pocket, but I'll wager they're fakes and forgeries, like before!"

It was all happening so fast, yet it felt like a nightmare from which she couldn't awaken. Maria saw the bittersweet feathers on Lady Darington's hat trembling as she rushed into the fray, joined by Jemma, who squealed and gesticulated with her parasol. Polinsky stepped in, too, raising his arms for silence. "Gentlemen!" he declared in his rolling baritone. "Gentlemen, you indeed have the wrong man! Please—listen to me!"

The policemen stopped nattering, as did the partners of Darington Shipping. They watched the medium warily, as though they doubted *his* motives, too.

"Did I not just introduce you to Lady Darington, wife of the late Phillip, Lord Darington, the head of your shipping empire?" Polinsky looked urgently at each man, sensing he didn't have much time. "Lady Darington is the mother of the man you seek, here to find her lost son! We believe Jason Darington was shanghaied from London weeks ago! And that he has since been out of his head—"

"Who do you take us for? Imbeciles and idiots?" another of the partners exclaimed. "Three ships we've lost to this man! And he's obviously hoodwinked *you*, or you'd not be taking his side! Away to jail with him!"

Maria gaped. Dora and Jemma sidestepped to avoid being knocked aside by the policemen who held Jude captive. Polinsky followed them, his tone more strident.

"This is an outrage! An obvious miscarriage of justice, and I demand my right to be—"

The monocled man turned to sneer at him. "You are on American soil now, sir. And as you've been aiding and abetting this *criminal,* I don't believe this is Lord Darington's widow—don't believe a word you've said! Tell it to the judge!"

"This can't be happening!" Dora muttered. Then she, too, trotted after the quick-stepping posse. "Jude, dear—we *will* find a lawyer! Or Captain MacLeod! And we *will* have you freed immediately, son!"

Captain MacLeod! Maria pivoted and ran back to the ship. How had this coming ashore gone so wrong, so fast? She must find that man who resembled Saint Nicholas and hope his goodwill—or his reason—would convince these misinformed managers of their identities. These men had probably never met Lady Darington or Jemma, but were they not aware of Lord Darington's two identical sons, who would succeed him in his shipping business? Up the gangplank she scurried, frantically looking for that round man in the bushy white beard.

But the *Fortune's Opportunity* appeared abandoned. Not a sailor was to be seen.

A sob escaped her. She stood staring down the long rail, at a loss for what to do, as the harbor breeze blew tendrils of hair around her face. Their adventure could *not* end this way!

"The captain and crew went ashore while you and Jude were making your introductions, sister." Rubio leaned on the rail outside his room, just as he had before she and Jude met with that unspeakable mess on the pier.

"What the hell's going on here?" Maria demanded. "If you *knew* those policemen were waiting to pounce on Jude—"

"I knew nothing of the sort. Although I sensed Captain MacLeod was withholding information, just as he was holding his temper after dealing with Dora, Jemma, and Polinsky during our voyage."

Inhaling to quiet her pulse, Maria gazed up at him. "Is that why he insisted we dock in Charleston? Because he knew the partners here were out for blood?" she asked. "Maybe MacLeod betrayed us . . . sent telegrams ahead, saying we had Jason aboard, without his Johnny Conn attire."

Rubio shrugged. By the time he joined her on the main deck, Maria had plopped on a wooden bench, flummoxed. Were things always this chaotic in America? So damn confrontational? Those men in the dark suits had barely acknowledged Lady Darington, much less the loss of her husband—the owner of the enterprise that kept them all employed! And they hadn't given *her* a second glance, except to bodily move her out of the way! How *rude!*

Her brother sat down beside her and patted her hand. His smile had that faraway look. "No matter how it may appear on the surface, Maria, things are working out quite nicely!"

"*Nicely?* Is that what you call it when those overbearing, underhanded *blackbirds* have stuck Jude in jail?"

Rubio chuckled. "He'll keep them occupied and out of *our* way while we go after the real Jason Darington. I know where he is. I just have to figure out how to get us there."

Something about his playful tone irritated her . . . yet she'd seldom known her brother to be wrong. "What sort of trip are we talking about? I can't say I'm eager to go ashore again, among those irrational—"

"Bear with me, sister. I sense the solution to our problem will soon come to us. Perhaps in uniform."

Maria frowned. Her brother was in one of his moods, perhaps letting his mind shift as he sent out vibrations to his guides. And if the captain and his crew had disembarked for shore leave, she and Rubio might be sitting here for days! What kind of a solution was that?

She heard a measured tread on the steel steps . . . saw a man's head rise up from the hold below. And damned if he wasn't wearing a uniform! "It's O'Keefe!" she blurted.

"You know him, I take it?"

And how did she answer *that* question? *Very carefully, hoping Jemma's lover plays along . . . perhaps repays the favor we discussed earlier.* "He took me to see Captain MacLeod when you and Polinsky were sparring over our destination. I . . . found him and Jemma together."

"Excellent! His smile reinforces the idea that you know too much, and he's beholden to you." Rubio helped her up from the bench, snickering. "See there? We're in the right places at the right times! Accidents and coincidence play no part in the turning of the Universal wheel."

"Mr. and Miss Palladino!" O'Keefe extended his hand to Rubio as he closed the gap between them. He smiled brightly at Maria. "I thought you'd be ashore, assisting Mr. Darington with his mission."

"Lord Darington's partners handcuffed Jude and hauled him off to jail! They claimed he was Johnny Conn, the pirate who's been attacking our own ships!" Maria exclaimed.

Eric O'Keefe's expression was priceless. "After their exchange of telegrams—both with Jude and the captain? How very odd."

"But it gives us the opportunity we need," Rubio interjected. He spoke in an urgent tone and focused intently on the chief officer's eyes. "If *you,* sir, could sail us north along the coast, into the islands of the Outer Banks, you may take credit for the capture of Johnny Conn!"

Maria's jaw dropped, and so did O'Keefe's. "You have no idea—I would need the captain's permission—"

"Why? You would be sailing a Darington ship on its original mission," the medium insisted in a low, penetrating voice. "I know precisely where to go, sir. We'd be away no more than a day or two."

O'Keefe's ebony hair was the only thing that moved in the breeze. Was he stunned speechless by Rubio's relentless gaze?

Or was he pondering his options? "Mr. Palladino, sir, if the captain returns to find the *Fortune's Opportunity* missing—"

"We can be back in this slip before they miss us. But we must act *now*!"

"I—it would require charts and crewmen to safely navigate—"

"You'll need neither, if you'll trust me to guide you, Officer O'Keefe."

Maria followed this exchange with clenched hands. Why did Rubio believe he could take charge of this steamship? And return it before anyone knew it was missing?

O'Keefe blinked but he didn't drop his gaze. Perhaps he couldn't, caught up in Rubio's trancelike spell. "It's my responsibility to see that—"

"And what can anyone do if the ship pulls away? Chase after us?" her brother queried softly. "I doubt that happens. MacLeod knows you stayed aboard, does he not?"

The chief officer nodded, still doubtful.

"And you *are* his chief officer. In command, in the event your captain cannot sail."

Again O'Keefe nodded. He licked his lips, wanting to comply but still hesitant.

"With any luck at all, we shall return with Johnny Conn *and* the booty he stole," Rubio continued exuberantly. "Will Captain MacLeod or the Darington partners be angry that you took such an initiative? I'm thinking you'll be up for a promotion very soon, sir!"

"You . . . you make a very enticing point, Palladino."

"Of course I do," Rubio replied with a soft laugh. "And *enticing* will be our method for bringing Jason back, when Maria shows herself at his hideout. Have you ever seen tastier bait?"

Eric exhaled as though someone had punched his stomach. "I'd best not reply to that, sir," he remarked as he eyed Maria. "But again, you make a valid point."

"So what are we waiting for? Maria and I will assist with whatever you need, Officer. Your wish is our command as we take you to Johnny Conn's hideaway." Rubio glanced behind him. "Shall we pull up the gangplank and be off? The sooner we find the lost Lord Darington, the sooner you claim your reward."

26

As the *Fortune's Opportunity* slipped away from the pier in the Charleston harbor, Maria's pulse pounded. Her brother—who knew *nothing* about navigating a steamship—had convinced Eric O'Keefe to follow his sketchy plan for finding Jason! With only a whisper of suggestion, in that voice that had made thousands *believe*, Rubio had commandeered a steamship for their private mission.

"How did you *do* that?" she murmured as the ship's bow swung slowly around to point them toward open water.

Rubio chuckled smugly. "Why do you still doubt my powers of suggestion, sister? Did I lie to O'Keefe? Or put him in a compromising position?"

"Well, *that* remains to be seen!" She looked back, to search the pier for men the size of clothespins waving their arms or calling after them. But it seemed her brother had gotten away with another caper.

"O ye of little faith," he quipped. "O'Keefe was having thoughts about *you* as surely as he was listening to me. I had a sudden vision of him ... has he *exposed* himself to you, Maria?"

She nearly choked on a laugh as the incident flashed in her mind. "He was with Jemma, as I told you. I just happened to be ... standing nearby when she coaxed him out of his pants."

"And now he adores you like a puppy, for remaining silent to his superior officer. Tell me again that this was coincidence, rather than a fortuitous playing-out of events." When he grinned, the gold ring in his nose sparkled like his dark eyes. He was damn proud of himself for accomplishing this mission—especially since he was once again proving Yosef Polinsky wrong.

Maria couldn't be peeved at him. He hadn't earned his reputation as the star medium for Queen Victoria's court by blathering nonsense at his clients; the proof *was* in his predictions. And he was rarely wrong.

A smile warmed her face like the setting sun, the first true happiness she'd felt since they'd left London with unexpected guests. "Thank you, little brother," she murmured. "Now, let's hope Jason cooperates with your vision of our happy ending."

In the moments before dawn, Maria rubbed her eyes and gazed at the muted fuchsia sheen on the water around them. The *Fortune's Opportunity* had sailed through the night, and Maria felt sorry for poor O'Keefe: with only two other sailors he'd found snoozing in their berths, he'd kept the steamer on the course Rubio had suggested. Now the three of them occupied the wheelhouse, where the table was covered with maps of the tiny islands comprising the Outer Banks chain that followed the coastline of North Carolina.

"See there? It's the Cape Lookout Light Station." The officer raked his dark hair back from a face that looked exhausted yet resolute. "If you're sure Jason's on Ocracoke, we'll steer in closer as the light increases. That harbor's a devil to get in and out of: captains are advised to hire local pilots or avoid it altogether."

"Lifeboats." Rubio gazed at the black-and-white checkered lighthouse tower ahead of them, his hands still on the wheel. He'd been steering by instinct and his guides, those times O'Keefe needed to tend other functions on the ship, and his keen delight shone on his face. "Just as Jason fancies Ocracoke because it was Blackbeard's haunt, we can use his pirate's sense of adventure to our advantage."

Maria's inner muscles clenched: oh, but that name "Blackbeard" was a reminder of a body part she held near and dear—and longed to hold again! "He loved to play swashbuckler even before he was shanghaied," she mused aloud. "What are you thinking?"

Her brother shrugged, covering his rising excitement. "Why not anchor the *Fortune's Opportunity* in plain sight, to catch his attention? Whet his appetite for another attack? Meanwhile, if we slip over to the island in lifeboats before daylight, we might catch him off guard."

O'Keefe tapped the map with his pencil. "It sounds better than running aground. If we're playing this game, we might as well keep the *sport* in it rather than becoming a sure target. Have you a feel for where Conn might be?"

Rubio motioned for O'Keefe to take the wheel. "Let me get some fresh air. See what I see. Meanwhile, Maria, I want you to put on your most provocative clothing. Less of it rather than more. Pirates don't fancy modest women."

His raised eyebrow made her laugh even as tingles of anticipation danced up her spine. "You think I don't know what catches Jason's attention?" she countered. "This is the moment—the role—I've prepared myself for since we decided to sail."

As she went to her cabin, Maria felt a surge of exhilaration: today she would see Jason! And touch him again! And feel his strong arms around her, as she'd dreamed of so many nights since his abduction. Would he recognize her? Would he still *want* her, even if he didn't remember who she was?

What if he never regained himself? Would this entire journey be for naught?

She couldn't allow the *thought* of such a possibility. She rummaged through her trunk to find the lovely unmentionables from her trousseau: a black camisole that tied in the front, made of sheerest French lace, and a matching garter belt to hold up silk stockings—all part of the ensemble she'd planned to wear during their honeymoon. Maria slipped the stockings over her legs, savoring the whisper of the silk ... the way the black lace patterned her calf in such a wicked way. She left off her corset and wore only the strapless camisole, pulling its black laces so the filmy fabric fit like a second skin and her breasts bulged until they nearly spilled over.

Her tiny cabin had no mirror, so she yanked the crimson skirt and its matching jacket from her trunk and scurried to the room Dora and Jemma shared. The shaving mirror on their washstand was barely adequate but Maria saw enough to suck in her breath.

She looked like a whore.

The camisole's black lace peeked up where the red jacket's neckline plunged to the single button ... a garment easily removed—or ripped off—when Jason saw her unfettered breasts beneath it. Without a chemise, the skirt clung to her legs when she walked, so unladylike as to present the *perfect* picture to Jason Darington. Her upswept hair had loosened during her night of keeping watch on the deck, and she left it messy: the dark tendrils hanging haphazardly around her face added to the wanton expression shining in her eyes.

The bejeweled butterfly pendant rested at her collarbone, in plain sight above the lace camisole. It was an emotional straw she clutched: she hoped to jog Jason's memory with every pos-

sible reminder of the life they'd enjoyed before he was shanghaied.

Was she pretty enough? Provocative enough? Her body
thrummed with the visions running through her mind . . . Jason
grabbing for her, ravenous and randy . . .

As Maria stepped out of the cabin, she noticed that the dull
rumble of the steam engines had stopped, and the ship no
longer moved through the water. O'Keefe and his sailors
manned the winch that lowered the anchor, while on the bridge
Rubio assessed the island directly ahead of them.

She imagined the flamboyant Blackbeard in his frock coat,
with his many braids sticking out beneath his tricorn hat—
smoldering, to scare away any who would deter him. Her next
thought brought Jason's own Blackbeard to mind, tall and
thick and crimson, throbbing to be inside her . . . mightier than
any pirate's sword, in its way. Maria shivered with an urgent
inner need. She took the old spyglass from Jude's room and
then descended the stairs to the deck.

Eric O'Keefe flushed and grabbed himself. His two assis-
tants gaped openly at her—proof to her wayward heart that she
possessed the power to seduce Jason Darington, or Johnny
Conn, or any man who crossed her path.

"I—I'm ready, gentlemen," she said as Rubio joined them.

"I've done been there and gone," one of the sailors groaned,
while O'Keefe put on his best attempt at a businesslike expression.

"I daresay, Miss Palladino, that if Johnny Conn doesn't
come rushing out to ravish you, he's a blind man."

"And I should surely *love* ta take 'is place," the second sailor
asserted. "With all due respect, o' course."

"*Respect* isn't what my sister's trying to attract. Obviously."
Rubio teased at a tendril dangling at her temple, his expression
a mixture of admiration and wariness. "Can you do this alone,
Maria? Or shall I shadow you from a distance? We can't predict

Jason's reaction, in his present state, and I will never forgive myself if I've put you at risk."

Maria's grin flickered. "If I'm taken hostage—hauled off as a pirate's prisoner—it's an improvement over living in that town house without Jason, isn't it?"

"It leaves Jude and his mother in an untenable position, if Lord Darington can't carry out the duties of his title . . . the responsibilities Jude seems reluctant to assume."

"That's Jude's problem, isn't it?"

The words rushed out and took Maria by surprise. Yet life with a pirate sounded much more fascinating—and more satisfying—than dealing with Dora and Jemma Darington if she returned to London without the man she loved. And, despite her deep feelings for Jude, her relationship with the Darington twins was much more enjoyable when they were both enjoying *her*. Jude, the family artiste, would never be happy overseeing the family's affairs. He would become peevish and tiresome faster than she cared to think about. "What's our plan, then, gentlemen?"

Eric O'Keefe raised his binoculars to survey Ocracoke Island, its harbor and the huddle of houses beyond that. "I like your brother's idea of using a lifeboat. He and I shall row you to shore on the far side of the island—"

"That's where I sense the presence of an abandoned shack. Abandoned, but not unoccupied." Rubio's voice sounded distant, connected to an unseen source. "Johnny Conn has remained at large this long by not attracting attention to himself. By using the hills, trees, and caves to best advantage."

"And in the meantime," O'Keefe continued, "Rubio and I shall remain at the ready with ropes and a pistol—"

"You'd *shoot* him?" Maria's stomach lurched. "The idea is to bring him back alive!"

"But under our control. We need proof, for the Darington Shipping partners, that we have indeed rid the American coastline of this marauder," the chief officer pointed out. "Jason will also be Jude's ticket out of jail. And if the Darington heir is to take over when you return, he must be bodily present even if he never . . . regains a true sense of himself. English law allows no *assumptions* of an heir's death, you know."

"Which would place Wildwood and the other Darington properties in limbo, because Jude won't assume the title unless his twin is deceased. And that's the *last* thing we want, of course." Rubio squeezed her shoulder. "All of this frightening talk aside, however, I sense we're on our way to a successful venture! Shall we go?"

Maria waited for O'Keefe to swing himself over the edge of the ship, to the narrow iron ladder, so he could assist her into the lifeboat that bobbed below. She was glad she'd left her extraneous garments behind: petticoats and shifts might have caught on the ladder's edges or wrapped around her ankles as she stepped into the unsteady vessel, with Rubio close behind her.

As the two men rowed, she studied Ocracoke through Jude's spyglass. The activity in the harbor, with its bobbing boats and flagged masts, gave way to a more undeveloped side where trees and underbrush had taken over. The rugged sand beach looked desolate in the pale morning light. Not a place for a lady in fine shoes.

"Are we getting closer?" O'Keefe removed his uniform jacket and rolled his shirtsleeves to his elbows. He kept his gaze trained on the landscape—except when he stole glances at her.

Maria sensed a totally different reaction than this man had experienced with Jemma, even at the height of the pleasure she'd given him. That gratified her, even if she didn't intend to do anything about his randy inclinations.

"The sensations are . . . muted, at best." Rubio let his oars rest as he closed his eyes and faced the rising sun. "Perhaps our pirate is away from his hideout. Or asleep. I get no sense of

Jason's energy, even though my guides tell me we're on the right path."

Silence then, except for the lapping of the water as they dipped their oars. Maria strained forward, determined to find the man she loved. Their efforts on Jason's behalf would not be in vain! The spyglass made her squint, and its ancient lens rendered everything smudgy and indistinct, and yet—

"Wait! Is that a shanty?" she whispered. "On the other side of those trees?"

Her brother and Eric stopped rowing. Rubio inhaled deeply, his eyes closed. "I think—yes! *Someone* is there, although a deep stupor veils the signals an active spirit might emit."

The medium opened his eyes, returning to his present time and space. Then Rubio grinned: he never allowed limitations or obstacles to block him when he was close to a goal. "Might as well go ashore and see if Conn sniffs the bait—with great appreciation for *being* our bait, Maria."

Her heartbeat throbbed in her ears. It was her turn to win the day, to convince Jason Darington to follow her into the lifeboat, back to the *Fortune's Opportunity*—and then to London. As the little vessel rode a wave to the beach, Maria reminded herself what was at stake. The Darington heir should assume his rightful title, of course, just as he should see to his mother's and sister's welfares in the wake of his father's passing. But those things paled compared to the huge hole in her life—her heart—that only Jason could fill. Jude might *look* like his brother, but the imitation was never as good as the original, was it?

"Good luck and Godspeed, Miss Palladino." Eric O'Keefe offered his hand from beside the beached boat.

"We're with you all the way. You'll never leave my sight, dear sister."

Nodding, Maria gazed at these two men one last time. They believed in her. They acknowledged that she could accomplish what they could not. She faced the wooded area then, contemplating her strategy: Jason had been her lover for years, but who knew what his memory and mental state were like? *Better to play for keeps, devil be damned,* she mused. *He'll never fall for it any other way.*

Maria took two faltering steps in the deep, loose sand and fell flat on her face.

"Maria! Are you all right?"

"Perhaps we should go along to—"

"Stop it! Leave me be!" Her face flushed the color of her suit as she struggled to her feet. Not even away from the lifeboat, and already she'd floundered! Sand had filled her pumps and crept down her cleavage, and her upswept hair felt so loose it might come unpinned at any moment. Why would the dashing Jason Darington—or the swaggering Johnny Conn—even look at such an incompetent, sand-matted woman who'd sprawled on the beach when there was nothing to fall over?

Because she's a damsel in distress. What man can resist such a helpless, vulnerable creature?

Maria blinked. Perhaps appearing confident and in control wasn't her best ploy.

With a naughty chuckle, she tore open her new jacket, trying not to care that its mother-of-pearl button flew askew, to be washed away by a wave. She speared her fingers into her hair and mussed it more. Kicked off her pretty pumps and tossed them back to the perplexed pair of guardians who watched her warily. Afraid for her sanity, no doubt.

But what good was sanity? If she didn't take Jason home with her, unhappiness would eventually lead her down the lonely road to dementia anyway. A laugh escaped her as she wiggled her toes in the wet sand. Then she lifted her skirt, focused on the shanty, and slogged awkwardly toward it. "Ahoy, there!" she cried in a husky voice. "Anybody home?"

She negotiated a few more yards of the beach. A pair of

sandpipers eyed her, snatched at a morsel worth sparring over, and then skittered farther down the beach.

"Anybody here?" she repeated more urgently. "I—I've washed ashore! Lost my way! Help me, please! *Anyone?*"

Was that the clinking of bottles she heard? The sorry little shack had glass left in only one of its windows, and the wooden steps leading to its weathered door sagged to one side. If Johnny Conn had plundered three laden ships, why would he be holed up in such a dilapidated place? Maria stopped a short distance from the shack's entrance and glanced over her shoulder.

Rubio, O'Keefe, and the little boat had vanished. She was on her own.

If her brother had mistaken the vibrations from this place, what did it matter if she hollered? If Jason wasn't here—

What if someone else is? Some shiftless vagrant you've awakened with your noisy approach? By now he's had time to grab his gun and—

A shot rang out. Maria screamed.

"Halt in yer tracks! Who goes there?" A scuffling noise came through the gaping windows, along with a cantankerous amount of cursing.

This wasn't how she'd planned it. Should she turn and run?

"Answer me, damn it! I knows yer out there, and I knows yer up to no good!" The shack's tenant fired a second time and the remaining pane of glass shattered. He swore some more, and then two forearms poked out of the empty window frame on the far side of the door.

Such ragged, dirty shirtsleeves should have warned her what she was up against, but it was the pistol dangling from one hand that held her attention.

"Drop yer gun, fer chrissakes!" she cried, mimicking his thick, antiquated speech. "If ye've not got a spot o' rum fer me parched throat, then ta hell with ye, man! Plenty o' other places fer a lady the likes o' me to find what she needs!"

"*Lady,* are ye? Then wot the hell're ye doin' *here?*" With a final effort, the owner of that whiskey voice hoisted himself up to the window casement. He stared at her with eyes that seemed to spin, even from this distance.

Maria's hand flitted to her chest, and then to the jeweled butterfly. The vagrant who gaped at her sported no jaunty pirate's bandanna. His untrimmed hair and dirty shirt weren't much to go on, either. Yet she studied him, hoping . . . "Jason?" she demanded. "Jason Darington, of the Wildwood estate near London?"

A rude chortle escaped him. He leered at her as he tipped a bottle to his lips. "Ye must be drunker'n *me,* wench, if ye're believin' I be anything but the dregs o' society. But I got a mighty sword pokin' outta me pants! Wanna see 'im, girlie-o?"

She fought a snicker. Edged closer, hoping for a better look at his bearded face. "Johnny Conn, then? The pirate what's got the law cursin' yer bloody name?"

His bottle slipped from his hand as he gawked at her. "Who're *you* to be sayin' that?" he demanded in a hoarse voice. "Johnny Conn's a *legend*—nothin' more'n the thin air he comes and goes from."

Ah. So she'd struck a sore spot. But she reveled in the thundering of her pulse—in her heart's recognition of the man camouflaged by the grime and his liquor. "I's heard Conn has a way with the ladies," she teased, standing more erect to thrust out her bosom. "But yer not him, obviously. The pirate I'm seekin' has the reputation of a dandy, not a man who lives with the pigs. Ye'll not be gettin' none of *my* favors, boyo."

She pivoted in the sand, nearly tripping over the silk skirt that clung to her legs. Would he fall for the line she'd cast? Would he come out of that shack—or sink back into his bottle? And why was he in such a state? She'd imagined the cocky, flamboyant pirate who'd posed for that WANTED poster, not the has-been who now belched from the window.

"Stop, or I'll shoot ye!" he bellowed. "State yer business here!"

Maria paused, her back to him. Surely Rubio and O'Keefe could hear what he was saying and assess if she were in real danger. But she saw no one in the thicket of trees . . . no sign of the lifeboat. Nothing on the beach except forked branches of driftwood and gulls searching for food. She turned slowly, hoping the right words came. "I'd hoped to meet the illustrious Johnny Conn," she replied in a brazen voice, "on account of how me . . . puss is hungerin' fer a mighty sword to fill 'er. I could make a man of ye, boyo, but yer not my type. Too nancy by half."

"Nancy?" he shot back. He lumbered to the doorway, holding on for support as he squinted at her. "*Nancy,* ye say? Show me yer tits—if yer woman enough! Make it worth me while, damn it!"

Now *that* was the sort of thing Johnny Conn—or Jason— would say! Maria inhaled to control the pounding of her heart. It was too late to back out of this randy cat and mouse. But she had to play for keeps. "Drop yer pistol and I'll give ye a peek!" she countered. "If there's a damn bullet hole in one of 'em, they won't be a matched set fer the next fella! And ye can't grab me arse if yer holdin' a gun, now, can ye?"

He took a hesitant step forward, gawking as though recognition might dawn. His chest heaved with exertion—or was it need?—and as he spat, still studying her, he tossed the pistol aside. "Hell with it," he muttered. "If the law sent ye to set me up, ye'll be worth the trouble. Ain't seen titties like that fer many a blue moon. Jesus, woman!"

She had him where she wanted him—or at least on his way. Maria shrugged out of the jacket, exaggerating her motions so her loose breasts jiggled at him in their black lace casing. "Like wot ya see?" she taunted as she shook them. "Now—gimme a peek at that sword yer braggin' on. Matter of fact, git outta all yer clothes, boyo. Yer gonna take a bath afore y'even git yer hands on these two darlin's."

When she grabbed her breasts from either side and squeezed them together, her prey moaned and swore in the same breath. Hastily he peeled away his dirty shirt, and as he dropped his pants, Maria turned away. She swayed across the beach . . . unfastened her skirt and let it flutter to the sand . . . flashed her bare bottom and silk-stockinged legs at him as she approached the ocean.

His ragged breathing accelerated behind her . . . he gasped as he followed her into the chilly waves. When they were knee deep, Maria untied the camisole's laces, then gripped the two sides of it—

"Turn yerself around and stand still, damn it! If I grab 'em, I'm a goner."

Maria's heart flew into her throat. Jason had teased and tormented her that way, playing rough-and-tumble pirate! Were Rubio and Eric O'Keefe still watching? They were about to get an eyeful, but she was beyond caring . . . even if, when she got a closer look, this man was *not* Jason.

And what'll you do then? If you expose yourself, you can't apologize for mistaking his identity! You're in it up to your . . . hot little puss now.

Maria turned slowly, and then yanked the two halves of the camisole. Her pursuer's eyes nearly bugged from their sockets—and yes, his erection swung high and hard between his muscular thighs. She knew that body! Eyes closed or open, daylight or dark, she'd recognize Jason Darington—and here he was! In the flesh! Wanting her so badly his hands curled as though he were kneading the soft breasts he'd always worshipped. It was the answer to her prayers!

Not that religion was on either of their minds.

Maria stood stock still while the waves lapped at her knees. Her nipples pointed at him like persistent little fingers as she stood like a wanton, in her black garter belt and lace stockings, with her camisole flapping in the breeze. He gazed hungrily at her, his chest rising and falling rapidly with his desire. Did he recognize her? Or did he just want to?

Do you think he really cares? He's a man! And he's got a very big itch to scratch.

It was an alluring itch, too. Thick and randy, his cock gazed at her with its tiny eye. A droplet of juice dripped off its end. "Jason?" Maria breathed. "You and Blackbeard—do you remember me at all?"

He frowned. Studied her again, now that she'd dropped her coarse, accented speech. "I don't know what yer talkin' about, lass, but I wants what I sees. I'll beg ye fer it, but ye'd better not be teasin' me or we'll both be sorry."

He shook his head as though to clear it. Still gazing at her breasts and thighs, Jason stepped into the oncoming wave to let it wash over him. He rubbed his face and body all over, both to sober himself and to be clean enough to deserve her. And when the cold water ebbed Jason stood before her, dripping wet and still so erect she had difficulty not grabbing his familiar, magnificent cock.

"Oh, I'm not teasing," she rasped. "You might not know me, but I guarantee I could *never* forget the likes of *you*, Lord Darington!"

He backed away warily. "Darington. Man by that name owns a shippin' company, headquartered in Charleston—"

"He's your father! And—and he has recently passed on, Jason," she blurted. This was *not* the way she'd planned to restore his memory, but what else could she say? "I'm sorry to inform you this way, but *you* are now his heir! And your twin brother, Jude—"

"Ye think I *care* about such nonsense?" he demanded

brusquely. "All I want is to plunge between yer legs and fuck the livin' daylights outta ye, lass! And then I'll want to do it again! So why're we standin' here like we don't know what comes next?"

She stepped toward him. "My name's Maria—"

"Is it, now? And ye think I give a flyin' fig about—"

He was on her then: threw his arms around her as though she might be a figment of his inebriated imagination, might float away if he didn't hold her so tightly. Or *was* he drunk? His lips certainly knew their way around hers. As he ground himself against her, his breath came in short gasps with each intense kiss, until he settled in for a very long one. He tasted of rum and fermented fruit, a heady combination that made her suck his tongue into her mouth and hang on.

As the surf surged around them they kissed hard, as though they were opponents rather than lovers. Jason's erection poked her thigh as he grabbed her ass and rubbed his chest against her breasts. "Let me in," he muttered. "Damn it, wench, I won't wait no longer!"

He trotted her beyond the waves and together they landed on the wet, packed sand. Jason grappled to be on top and Maria opened herself, reveling in the way he took what he wanted without apology or question. "Ride me, then!" she challenged. "You're the one who claims he can fuck the living daylights out of—oh! Oh God, Jason—Jason!"

He plunged deep inside her and she spread wider to accommodate him, to glory in the reunion of their bodies and souls. Her hips bucked upward as he straddled her, drilling her with a piston that got hotter and harder with each entry. "I—don't know—who ye are or how ye think ye know me," he rasped as he drew closer to climax, "but I'll not be fergettin' this fuck anytime soon. Jesus, woman—yer squeezin' the jizz outta me—"

On impulse, Maria shoved him up and to one side. It was

her turn to mount this wild pirate and hang on until they both collapsed, quivering, in the sand. Her effort caught Jason by surprise—

And so did the driftwood log.

She saw what was about to happen but couldn't stop in time. When his head hit the petrified tree trunk with a sharp *thwack*, he cried out—yet it only fanned his flames! "Wicked wench! Tryin' to knock me outta me misery, are ye?" he panted. "I'm gonna shoot you fulla my—"

"Jason! I can't wait—can't stop—" Her hips spasmed crazily, driven by the clenching of her inner muscles. Her back arched as she drove them faster, more frantically, toward sweet release. The first shot of his wetness made her scream and lose all pretense of control.

Together they rolled and tussled until all their spasms were spent. Maria collapsed on him, aware only of his animal strength—the body she'd longed for—as the waves lapped around their legs. They caught their breath, neither of them letting go.

Had she done a foolish thing? She'd been in such a mad rush to couple—to control him—she hadn't noticed the log until it was too late. What if he became totally lost now? Unable to recall *anything* about his previous privileged life? Maria lay with her face on his chest, inhaling the salty scent of man and sea . . . praying her adventure hadn't come to an end before she reclaimed the Jason she loved.

"Christ," he muttered. "I'll have one helluva goose egg, but it'll be worth it. Maybe you knocked some sense into me."

Maria held her breath. His heavy accent had disappeared. But what did that mean, really? She raised up on her arms to study his face, to see if his eyes were rolling, out of focus.

Jason looked steadily at her. His hand went to her damp, bedraggled hair, and then drifted alongside her face to rest on the butterfly pendant. She longed to remind him where it came from, yet sensed she should let him reason it out.

"A distinctive piece like this doesn't belong on a trollop."
He gazed warily at her.

"I . . . I was playing along, to see if you remembered me. I'm
not a shipwrecked whore, Jason. I'm your fiancée, Maria Palladino." She longed to pour out more of their story, but the
look on his face stopped her.

He rubbed the sore spot on his head. "What if I have no reason to believe that?"

NOW what'll you say? Maria gazed into golden-brown
eyes, glad to see they'd stopped spinning. But if he didn't recall—

"After all," he continued quickly, "why would a beautiful
woman like you seek out a low roller like me? If you had any
idea what I've done—"

"But I do, Jason! When Rubio located your spirit—when
we saw the WANTED poster with your picture and got the
telegram about the Darington ships you've plundered—"

"Damn. So the law *did* send you." Jason's eyes lost their
light. He looked away. "I thought you were a dream come true.
A woman who could rescue me with her love, just like in the
fairy tale where the princess kissed the frog."

Maria's heart stilled. Her damp hair blew wildly around her
face while her wanton black lace clung to her, along with wet
sand. She felt like the aftermath of a storm at sea, yet he'd called
her beautiful! If Johnny Conn wanted a fairy-tale ending and
the princess to go with it, all was not lost—if only she could
make him remember who he really was!

"No, Jason! Your brother Jude and I came after you, to
bring you home to England!" she insisted. "Home to Wildwood, because the estate and your father's title are now *yours.*
You're an earl! Your name is Jason, Lord Darington!"

He gently shifted her so he could roll into a sitting position.
"Then who the hell is Johnny Conn? And if I'm not Conn,
who's been looting those ships you mentioned?"

Maria blinked. Somewhere in those questions they'd find the seed to his defense, but for now it meant he was sobering, thinking and talking like a rational man, even if his memory wasn't intact. She racked her brain for more conversational connections. "Do you have any sense of . . . *missing* something—someone—important? Identical twins share a strong bond—"

"I'm a twin?"

"Your brother's name is Jude. He looks exactly like you, but *I* can distinguish between you, even . . . even in the dark." She cleared her throat, wondering how explicit to be about their three-way arrangement. "While you are a leader and an adventurer, Jude creates beautiful photographs and—and he made this butterfly pendant!" she exclaimed, holding it up. "You gave it to me on the day before our wedding, and then you were shanghaied! We believe you hit your head when you fell onto that despicable captain's ship, probably from a whorehouse on the London waterfront."

Jason looked away quickly. He seemed troubled, but as he tried so hard to *think*, he could only sigh forlornly. "I want to believe you, but . . . how do I know you're not leading me down some primrose path? To jail, perhaps, if I really did plunder those ships!"

"*Jude* is in jail!" she crowed. "Because the Darington Shipping partners thought he was *you!*"

His expression shifted. "So if the coastal authorities think they've caught me . . . you and I could remain on this island together? Forever? And no one would come after us?"

Maria's heart rushed into her throat. It wasn't a good time to mention that Rubio and Chief Officer O'Keefe lurked in a lifeboat nearby. "What a lovely fairy tale that would make," she agreed in a dreamlike voice. "I *would* stay here with you forever, Jason. I love you, and I've missed you so badly . . . rolling about in that town house like a dried pea in a shoe box—except for Quentin and Mrs. Booth, of course." She glanced over to see if her words had any effect, but his bearded face still showed no signs of recognition.

Jason was studying *her*, too. His lush lips twitched. His gaze followed the sway of her bare breasts and the flare of hips partly clad in black lace. Maybe there was a better way than words to reach inside him and coax his memory to return.

"You're having wicked thoughts. And I like them."

She laughed, a burst of mirth that made her breasts shimmy and awoke the needs she'd buried deep inside when this man had been taken from her. What could it hurt to seduce him again? If one coupling had brought him this far out of his drunken stupor . . .

27

Maria rose from the beach to stand before him. She brushed sand from her thighs, slowly, to provoke him as he gawked at the slender black garters that still, miraculously, held up her stockings. Flicking her fingers through the dark curls between her legs, she watched his reaction. "Sand gets in the damndest places—"

"Let me help." He reached for her, his eyes shining playfully.

But she stepped beyond his reach. "Humor me," she said in a low, insistent voice. She glanced back at the ramshackle house, allowing ideas to roost like homing pigeons. "I want you to take me again, Jason—like the last time you made love to me before you left the town house for your bachelor party."

He sighed. "But I don't remember . . . I'm sorry. That hurts you, and it's not my intent."

Her heart went out to him. He was trying so valiantly; had sobered completely and become a gentleman again, despite his unkempt hair and beard. "You're not so far off the mark! You blindfolded me and bound my wrists to your bedpost, Jason. And then you leaned me forward—"

"And ravished you from behind? I can do that again!"

"—while you talked in the same pirate's accent you were using moments ago!" Her voice rose with excitement as his body reacted to this suggestion. It was a marvelous sight, that his cock hardened again so soon after he'd pleasured her. "I keep a thick, wicked dildo in my night table—"

"*You* have one of those? Naughty girl!"

"You gave it to me, remember?" Maria watched his eyes, but then continued with her original idea. "Last time you were with me, you and Blackbeard—"

"How'd *he* get in the picture?" Jason stood, gazing around the beach and the horizon as though searching for the pirate and his ship. Then he focused on her with a sigh. "Are you sure you're not making this up? Blackbeard hasn't haunted this island for centuries."

"What could it hurt to return to that love scene with me?" Maria started toward the shack, praying this idea didn't explode in her face. She reminded herself of her mission: to make him remember who he was, at best, and at the very least to get him aboard the ship for their return to Charleston. "I enjoyed playing your prisoner, Jason," she hinted. "Perhaps the slapping of our skin . . . the way you tormented me with that blindfold, and then fastened the butterfly necklace on me afterward. Repeating those actions might knock something loose in your mind."

"Sounds better than banging my head on a log," he agreed. He walked beside her with long, sure strides, eager to carry out her plan.

"I'm sorry about that, Jason. I got too rough and careless—"

"Never that!" He flashed her a grin that brought back so many fond memories, she nearly cried for wanting him—wanting the real Jason to emerge again. To love her again. "I prefer a woman who loves to play. None of those prissy princess types for me!"

A sly smile overtook her face. As they approached the shanty door, her mind raced. "Prove it, pirate!" she teased. "I'll not be your princess *or* your prisoner until you *make* me give in to the demands of that monstrous cock!"

"Aaaargh! Yer askin' fer it now, girlie-o!"

Maria ran, laughing so hard it was no contest. But what did that matter? She had no traction in the loose sand, and no real reason to evade him anyway. It was enough to be *playing* with her man again, chasing around the beach wearing the scantiest of—

When Jason caught the loose edge of her camisole, the lace gave way with a wicked whisper. He whirled her around. Ravished her with a lewd gaze, his eyes afire as he roughly cupped her breasts. "Where'd ye get such flimsy clothes that—"

"Your mother and sister chose them! For my trousseau!"

"—any man can rip 'em off ye?" He let out a piratical laugh. "Yer not foolin' me fer a minute! Yer a tramp and a trollop, and ye'll be disciplined fer yer wicked ways!" With a yank, Jason deftly removed one of the ribbon laces from her camisole. He whipped it around her wrists before she could wiggle free—not that she tried—and then led her to a sapling beside the shack.

"Please, sir!" she pleaded in a melodramatic voice. "I promise I'll behave like a lady, if only you'll—"

"And wot the hell would I do with a *lady?*" He fastened her to the tree's slender trunk with the other lace, then tested the knot's tightness. "In this rugged outpost, a woman's gotta have *grit* to get by—unless, o' course, she bares her ass at her man's every whim!"

Maria could hardly talk for giggling. "And didn't I do that fer ye just an hour ago? On account o' yer bein' such a nancy-boy I had to show ye how it's done?"

"Ye'll not be callin' me names, missy. I can see there's no

hope fer yer wicked soul save to *spank* yer pretty arse—like so!"

Whap! His palm landed on the fleshiest part of her backside.

She cried out in protest, yet this sounded so familiar! Jason had reverted to the script they'd often used before he disappeared! "Oh! Oooooh!" she wailed pathetically.

"Do ye repent of yer lewd and lascivious ways, girlie-o?"

There it was again: a hint of good times past, shared in his bedroom. Maria did her best to control her excitement as she played their little game. "Nay! I'll never repent fer the likes o' *you*, Darington! Yer a pirate, and nothin' good can come of ye!"

Smack! Smack! His hand met her backside as his laughter mingled with hers.

"Apologize, I say! Or ye can assume the position and take whatever punishment I force upon ye!" he replied gruffly. "Yer obviously too high toned fer yer own good, wearin' the likes of them stockin's—teasin' every man in sight with yer naked white thighs!"

"Hah! You love my thighs! Don't deny it, boyo!"

"There's no help for ye, then! Plunder and pillage it is!" he crowed. "Open up—I'm comin' in!"

Maria bent lower and shook her backside at him.

"Spread yerself! Give me sword enough room to plunge in and—"

Together they cried out as Jason entered her, filling her full of his relentless erection. Maria felt delirious at both ends: her mind reeled with all the similarities of this little skirmish, while from behind she was being pillaged with the finest sword of all. What else could she do to coax his memory back? He was *so close* to being the Jason Darington she'd gone to the altar for. Already so close to ecstasy, she writhed faster to catch up to him.

"Dammit, woman, yer gobblin' me up!" he muttered hoarsely.

"How'm I s'posed to make ye pay fer bein' such a wicked wanton, if ye get me so fired up I can't—I can't hold back!"

With a grunt, he rutted like a crazed dog, grasped her hips to center himself. Her breasts jiggled lewdly and Maria thought he might jar *her* memory out of kilter.

And it felt glorious, didn't it? To have a man—*this* man—so crazed for the feel of her, the ecstasy only she could deliver. Hell, even if he never came to himself, she'd found him and she would never let him go. Maria gripped him tightly with her inner muscles, allowing the rest of her body to move loosely with his.

"Jesus . . . Jesus . . ." The strained groan told her it was mere moments until—

"Holy mother of God! *Maria!* Mariiiii-ahhhhh!"

Maria stifled a sob of joy as she gave in to the all-consuming ache he'd inspired. She curled in on herself and grabbed the tree, allowing the waves of delicious tension to claim her once again. Because Jason had claimed her! He *knew!* He knew *her!*

His corded arms encircled her heaving rib cage. They leaned against the tree trunk, straining to breathe, to regain full consciousness . . . to find the words that expressed what had just happened. Jason nuzzled her bare shoulder, kissing her skin so lightly a butterfly could have been lighting. "What have you done to me, woman?" he whispered. "It was as though a wall crumbled, a wall I'd been dancing behind—trying to climb—for, well I don't even know how long!"

"Weeks," she murmured. "Endless weeks of empty days and nights gone unfulfilled."

"And suddenly I . . . I was inside *you*, Maria." He sounded incredulous, yet overjoyed. "And at that moment I was *home*. Where I belonged, instead of hiding out on this island, evading those who pursued me. I—I'm not even sure who they were or why they were chasing me."

She wanted to swipe at tears, but her hands were still fastened to the tree. "Who am I, again?" she asked, testing him. No sense in letting her hopes soar if this moment didn't last.

"Maria," he replied prayerfully. "Maria Palladino. *My* Maria Palladino, thank God."

She nodded, too moved to speak.

"I don't know how you found me—"

"Rubio did."

"—and there's time for hearing the whole story," he continued breathlessly, "but I need your assurance, Maria. I need to see your face—your beautiful brown eyes—as we discuss it." He reached along the length of her arms to untie her wrists, rather than give up his hold on her. When he straightened to his full height, to turn her gently, Jason looked like a changed man.

"You're back," she whispered. "Oh, thank God, you're *back!*"

He rested his forehead against hers. A moment of utter, absolute understanding passed between them as the world around them went still.

Jason broke the reverent connection with a sigh. "Tell me you'll love me, no matter what I must confess to," he pleaded. "While I'm aware of some details, parts of the story—pieces of the puzzle—elude me still."

"It's all right," she said, taking his face between her hands. "We do have time, and between the three of us—you, me, and Rubio—we'll fill in all the blanks. What matters most is that you've come back to yourself, and that I love you. We can complete our mission and take you home."

"Yes. Home." His eyes closed as he smiled blissfully. "I've missed you so badly, sweet Maria. Yet all I could do was lie awake nights, unable to put an image of you with an indescribable *need* I couldn't name. Will you forgive me if things come to light that—"

He stiffened. Wrapped his arms more tightly around her, with one hand protectively at the back of her head.

"Jason? Are you all right?" she whimpered. He was nearly smothering her as he held her against his chest and bare body.

"Don't move, love. There's a man crossing the beach. He's pointing a pistol at us."

Maria peered beneath Jason's arm. Saw the familiar uniform and hoped this was another instance of the fortuitous timing Rubio often spoke of. "Officer O'Keefe! Eric!" she called out. "This is *not* the time for target practice! Everything's fine! Really, it is!"

O'Keefe stopped a short distance away, holding the gun steady. "It was one thing to watch you cavorting on the beach, Miss Palladino. But when this man tied your wrists and took you prisoner, I thought the tides might have turned—"

"It's our little game!" she replied brightly. Then she flushed: she was standing against Jason's naked body, wearing only stockings and a black lace garter belt, revealing a very intimate part of her romantic relationship to this relative stranger. "Honestly, sir, Jason is regaining his memory! It's the way we'd hoped things would go!"

The arms around her tightened when she tried to face O'Keefe. "So you *did* come with the law?" Jason muttered. "If this is some underhanded ploy to—"

"No, Jason! This man, Chief Officer O'Keefe, is the reason we could sail to Ocracoke to find you. Captain MacLeod refused to—oh, it's rather complicated!"

"And considering the way he's looking at you—*gawking* at you, Maria—I *will* require an explanation!" Jason exclaimed. "Who *is* this man?"

She closed her eyes, exasperated. Why were men sometimes so lackadaisical about details, yet so damn dense and insistent at others? Not five minutes had passed since Jason recalled who she was, and he was already in a jealous snit! "If you'll let me step inside—and if you'll fetch my clothes from the beach," she said in a strained voice, "we'll have our proper introductions so the truth can come to light."

"Here, sister. I've been trailing you, to be sure all went well." Rubio stepped from behind the little shanty with her scarlet skirt and jacket folded over his arm. "We men shall set things straight while you make yourself presentable. Then— just as I'd predicted!—we can start back to Charleston."

She'd known her younger brother all his life, yet it wasn't easy to look him in the eye as he handed over her clothing. It was one thing to be naked with Jason; another thing entirely to feel so *exposed,* knowing Rubio and Eric O'Keefe had witnessed both bouts of their lovemaking. Now they watched her breasts sway between the parted halves of her lace camisole . . . saw the way her black garter belt framed the dark vee of hair between her bare thighs.

"You had it right," she said, partly to placate Rubio and partly to return his thoughts to the business at hand. "I'll leave the formalities to you, brother dearest, since you know both of these men." Into the shack she hurried, ducking beyond the windows so she could dress in relative privacy.

Outside, Rubio grilled her fiancé. "It's good to see you again, Jason. Good to hear you and my sister have rediscovered each other—"

"But why are you holed up in such poverty and desolation?" O'Keefe demanded. "You've stolen enough cargo from three Darington ships, and probably others, to be living quite handsomely."

"And why should I tell *you* that?"

Maria winced as she stepped into her skirt. They sounded like dogs circling with their teeth bared, and a confrontation would erupt if she didn't prevent it. Without the laces that held her camisole together, there was nothing to do but hold her buttonless jacket over her breasts until she returned to her cabin on the steamship. Her hair felt like a rat's nest, beyond repair, so she stepped back out into the afternoon sunlight.

"You don't appreciate such questions, Jason, for they suggest we don't trust you," she remarked softly, "but I, too, wondered why you've landed in such a . . . dismal setting. And if we can *return* the cargo you plundered, the partners in Charleston are less likely to toss you in jail with your brother."

Jason blinked. He stepped into his pants—an awkward task with two watchdogs looking on—and then scowled. "I have a twin, you say? Oh, wait—" He grimaced, as if forcing his mind to travel backward for such details. "Jude! We look so much alike that you, dear Maria, are among the few who can distinguish us."

"There! See—he's coming back!" She smiled pointedly at Jason's interrogators and then took her fiancé's hand. "When we got off the steamer in Charleston, your father's partners seized Jude, thinking he was the pirate in the WANTED poster! The police hauled him to jail, so your mother and Polinsky were to search out a lawyer to—"

"Polinsky? Do I know this fellow?"

Maria glanced at her brother and O'Keefe, wondering how much to reveal: would Jason's memory withstand so *much* startling information at once? "He . . . Yosef Polinsky is a magician and a medium, a different sort entirely from Rubio, and he came along to help us find you," she hedged.

Jason nodded doubtfully. "So Jude is in jail because *I* have plundered ships, like a pirate from the days of yore?"

Rubio smiled as he handed Jason a folded paper. "Johnny Conn has led the authorities on quite a chase," he remarked. "In fact, it was this WANTED poster, along with a telegram from the Darington Shipping partners, that upset your father so . . . so terribly, that I'm sorry to inform you of his demise. You have my deepest sympathy, Jason."

The medium paused to let this information sink in; to watch

the shock play upon Jason's features as Maria wrapped her arms around him. "This makes *you* the new Lord Darington," she continued in a low, earnest voice, "which means you must stop plundering ships and eluding the authorities, so you can go home to manage the estate for your mother."

Jason's mouth fell open and then shut again. He stared at the poster as though the character looking back at him were a complete mystery. "My God, I . . . I had no idea. So how did I come to be in America? Acting like a pirate?"

"You were shanghaied, we believe. From your bachelor party, the night before you were to marry Maria."

Jason's hand fluttered to the back of his head. Then he gazed at Maria in horror. "This explains my terrible headaches . . . and now I recall a captain whose cruelty inspired a mutiny, and I—I took charge!" he exclaimed as the recollections returned. "I commandeered the *Sea Witch*, and the others elected me their captain!"

"Not surprising," Maria said with a grin. "But where are they now?"

He cleared his throat ruefully. "Some of them, like me, were on board against their will and elected to return home. Others wanted no part of my . . . pirate escapades once the port authorities came after us. So I guess I'm the last man standing, as far as proud, stalwart swashbucklers are concerned."

"And a fine swashbuckler you are, too," Maria murmured.

"Wily enough that I didn't *attack* those ships you say I plundered." He gestured beyond the beach to the open ocean. "The Outer Banks have seen many a shipwreck over the centuries because of their dangerous shoals and tricky inlets. I merely teased those crews into chasing me into the shallows, so their ships ran aground."

O'Keefe's eyes widened. "So you didn't engage them in battle? Or otherwise seek to destroy Darington Shipping property?" he asked in a thoughtful voice. "If you can prove that, I shall report it to the company partners. Perhaps get the charges against you waived, if you'll go before the magistrate or whatever else the men in Charleston ask of you."

"I can do that. As long as—" He gripped Maria's hand, looking lost in thought again. "As long as you promise me, Maria, that such revelations won't dissuade you from marrying me. Does this mean you went to the church, preparing for the wedding and . . ."

"You were nowhere to be found," she affirmed quietly. "Your father and Jude searched for you, interrogated your friends. But even Scotland Yard had no idea where you'd disappeared to."

Jason let out a slow, sad sigh. "I am *so sorry.* That was *never* my intent, sweet Maria. I cannot imagine the shame you've endured. Not to mention Mother's reaction." He fingered the jeweled butterfly then, as if it made more of his memory return. "If you have doubts about my love, my intentions, I'll remain here as an outcast rather than ruin your chances . . . to marry a man more deserving of you."

His contrite tone made her heart beat painfully hard. "Who says I'd be ruined?" she shot back. "If your father's partners are too pigheaded to—"

"My partners now? This is all so much to take in," he murmured.

"—believe your story and Officer O'Keefe's report, then to hell with them!" Maria blurted.

Rubio laughed. "And there you have it! Sentiments expressed as only my dear sister knows how!" He grinned at Eric O'Keefe. "Shall we inspect those ships? I can't wait to see the look on Polinsky's face—and to rub those partners' beaky noses in it—when we reveal what we've found here."

28

The devastation of three proud ships was a painful sight, even to Maria, as she studied the wreckage from the rail of the *Fortune's Opportunity*. The grounded Darington vessels lay on their sides like corpses, with smokestacks, pilothouses, and other parts sticking dejectedly out of the waves. Rubio steered the steamer well to the east of the treacherous shoals in Cape Hattaras, Pea Island, and the Drum Inlet, so O'Keefe could discuss the incidents with Jason.

"Tell me this, Darington," the chief officer mused aloud. He peered through his binoculars as though he couldn't believe what he was seeing. "How is it these ships ran afoul of the sandbars and shoals, when their captains were familiar with these obstacles?"

"I have no idea what they were thinking, sir. Once I raised my colors and sailed within spitting distance, they were in it for the sport. And I won."

Maria chuckled. "After word of the first shipwreck, I'll wager the subsequent engagements were more to even the score—or so those captains could have the honor of capturing the illustrious Johnny Conn."

"I know *I* considered it a contest," Jason replied with a grin. "And they were so easily led into it!"

"And where was the captain of the *Sea Witch*? The man who shanghaied you?"

Jason gazed at the wreckage as he thought back. "When we mutinied, we put him off on an uninhabited island to fend for himself. Dunner, his name was . . . had a cruel streak a mile wide," he recalled with a scowl. "Nobody talked of it for fear of his vengeance, but we'd heard more than one sailor crying out for mercy during a flogging. We didn't have as many men complete the voyage as started it."

Eric O'Keefe lowered his binoculars, considering this. "So, did you stash the Darington cargo, as we've been led to believe? Or have you already bootlegged it—"

"Do I look like a man living in the lap of luxury, sir?" Jason smiled wryly as he swiped his unkempt hair back from his face. "I unloaded the cacao, sugar, and other items before the sea could ruin them. My *booty* is safely stored in caves along the coast."

"Because?" O'Keefe's imperious tone left no doubt he intended to ask the pertinent questions even if they caused Jason pain.

Jason shrugged. "I had lapses when I wasn't sure where I was or what I had done. But I sensed I couldn't sell such valuables without getting caught. So my stashes are intact."

"Which explains why you look like . . . well, something the cat dragged in." Maria sighed, yet she felt hopeful: anyone, even those crows in their black suits, would see that Jason couldn't be blamed for the shipwrecks, and that he'd rescued the cargo rather than making any profit from it. "Did any crewmen die from those captains' foolishness? Because they thought they could outwit Johnny Conn?" she queried.

"I haven't found any bodies floating. Those sailors probably scrambled ashore and found their way back to Charleston."

"We'll soon find out." Officer O'Keefe laid aside his binoculars. "Thank you for steering, Palladino. I'll take the wheel now, while the three of you freshen up for our return to Charleston. Welcome aboard, Lord Darington. It'll be my privilege to escort you to your shipping headquarters and witness to your true behavior."

"As we near the harbor, let us not forget that our mission is to rescue Jude and restore order in your shipping offices, Lord Darington." Rubio spoke quietly, in that mystical way he had. "When you encounter situations that seem . . . questionable, or different from the way you remember them, allow us to fill you in on what you missed while you were away."

Maria sensed her brother referred to Jason's mother and Yosef Polinsky, but it wasn't her place to raise the lid of Pandora's box of surprises. It was enough to be sitting at the table beside Jason, Lord Darington, who had bathed and shaved his scraggly beard. After she trimmed his hair, he'd dressed in one of Jude's suits. He looked so good, had felt so good sharing her bed in the night, she didn't care what else might happen. Order had been restored in *her* world, and her prayers had been answered.

"It still feels odd, to learn I'm now the earl, entrusted with Wildwood and my mother's welfare," he murmured. "While Father and I were not particularly close, I never thought he might *die* anytime soon."

"I'm sorry, Jason." Maria scooted her chair closer to his. "Do you have questions my brother might help you with? A tarot reading might provide insight you need about these events or why they're happening."

"Indeed, I was in touch with your spirit after you disappeared." Rubio slipped a small organza bag from his pocket.

Dressed in a deep green velvet jacket with a collarless silk shirt, he resembled an eccentric nobleman—until the ring in his nose glimmered. "You weren't aware I sought you out at those times, but I was glad to find you alive. Responding in the best way you could."

Jason shook his head, still puzzled over his weeks as a pirate. "And had you not found me, Rubio, who knows how long I might have languished in that shack. The captains who pursued me assumed I lived as a reckless adventurer, but it was a lost, lonely existence most days." He patted Maria's hand and flashed her a grateful smile. "I—I knew important details were missing, but I had no way of learning what they were. Can you tell me what I should know, before we dock in Charleston? Perhaps point up any hidden agendas or obstacles I might encounter?"

"Excellent question." Rubio passed him the thick deck of cards. "As you mix the cards on the tabletop, concentrate on what you've asked me. When you've stacked them the way you want them, choose seven."

Jason focused on the cards' ornate design as he swirled them around. He stacked them and then tapped the edge of the deck on the table. When he'd placed seven cards facedown in a row, he glanced at Rubio. "Did I do that right? I've never had a tarot reading, so I could be—"

"There's no wrong way, milord. Let's see how the cards have answered you." Rubio moved to the chair on Jason's other side to turn the cards faceup. "I prefer to arrange them in a way that points us toward a positive direction and *opportunity*. The tarot doesn't forecast doom and gloom, nor do the cards predict what will happen. They show us circumstances and possibilities so we can interpret them according to our unique situations."

"Ah." Jason studied the cards, tapping at the center one. "So this skeleton with his scythe—number thirteen—doesn't foreshadow death and destruction? I don't much like the looks of him, after all I've been through."

Rubio placed that card at arm's length in front of them. "The Death card is not about physical demise or the Grim Reaper crooking his bony finger at you," he assured Jason. "But it speaks to an *ending*—a necessary part of a new beginning. You can't start fresh if remnants of the old, decaying past are in your way, so this card signifies a clean sweep. Highly appropriate, now that you are the new Lord Darington, don't you think?"

Jason's smile seemed reserved. "Thirteen has never been my favorite number."

"In ancient times it was reserved for priests and sages, those who possessed special wisdom. Superstition has colored our perception over the centuries." He quickly rearranged the cards so that two were beneath the Death card, and three beneath those, with a single card centered at the bottom. "This is a Tree of Life spread, for it resembles an evergreen. It allows us to exercise our free will, rather than falling victim to circumstances we feel uneasy about."

They sat in silence as Rubio concentrated on the cards. "What do you see here, brother?" Maria murmured. She was no stranger to interpreting the tarot, but she let her sibling guide the reading. "If Jason begins afresh now that his memory is restored, what can he expect?"

"I see those two ladies beneath the Death card and sense . . ." Jason fingered the card on the left. "They are both queens. And each seems to be looking at *me*, as though demanding my complete attention. My exclusive loyalty."

"An astute observation!" Rubio chuckled. "Care to hazard a guess as to their identity? Court cards sometimes stand for specific people—or, in the case of queens, they concern emotional control rather than the more physical power represented by the kings."

Jason's glance made butterflies flutter in Maria's stomach. "This woman seems more ... open and giving than the one with the sword in her hand."

"The Queen of Cups is about love and creativity, whereas the Queen of Swords is about reason and logic," Rubio replied. "I sometimes refer to her as the Bitch of Swords because her tongue can cut as sharply as the weapon she holds like a scepter. Even if you don't care to designate which queen is whom—"

"This is Maria. And this is Mother." Jason cleared his throat, as though searching for words that wouldn't get him into trouble. "While they will both seek to rule my world, each in her own way, if they come to cross purposes, we'll all suffer. I knew this when I announced my betrothal to your sister, Palladino."

Rubio nodded as though he kept a deep secret; something he foresaw but couldn't yet share. "Circumstances have changed, milord. These ladies' competition may result in revelations— perhaps revenge—that surpass even *my* vision."

Maria raised her eyebrows. The last thing she wanted was anything that threatened her future with Jason. She silently resolved that Miss Crimson would fade into literary oblivion—if the columnist hadn't already been dismissed for abandoning her post. "And what do you make of the man in the chariot?" she asked, mostly to steer this conversation away from herself. "He usually signifies victory, does he not?"

"Indeed."

"But the cards on either side of him show a club in one hand and a sword in the other," Jason ventured with a grin. "Does this mean I'll need *weapons* to control those two queens?"

"You'll feel that way at times!" Rubio laughed with him, while Maria rolled her eyes. Why did men believe clubs and swords affected a woman's way of thinking? Much less her behavior?

"Tradition says it's the hand of God holding that Ace of Wands and the Ace of Swords, and aces signify new directions.

New ideas," her brother continued in a more serious tone. "But it's up to us to *accept* those for the gift they are, and put them to best use."

"I like that bottom card. Much more promising, with that couple dancing in the sunshine." Jason kissed Maria's hand. "Even when I didn't know it was *you* I was missing, my love, I longed for the day when the sun would shine in my life again. When I felt my purpose again."

"And The Sun is a fine forecast for anyone's future," Rubio agreed. "Any way you arrange these, milord, you chose cards that predict fortuitous results—even if those two queens will insist on their way. But when haven't they?"

"Excellent point, Palladino. Thank you for bolstering my confidence as we approach Charleston." Jason stood and shook the medium's hand. "While I don't believe Jude has caused much trouble in jail, who *knows* what Mother might've stirred up? It would be just like her to reorganize Father's business, or to demand my brother's release from the governor. Let's hope we arrive before she's done more damage than we can repair."

29

"Jude! How on earth did *you* get here?" Lady Darington sputtered. "I've talked myself blue in the face for two days, informing these *obstinate* partners that you are *not* the pirate who pillaged three Darington ships!"

Jason stood in his father's American office—or in the partners' sanctum, anyway—and merely smiled. It was a telling moment: his own mother didn't know which twin he was. It was precisely the point he'd hoped to make by entering alone, and a devilish inspiration told him to see what else transpired before he revealed his true identity. "Good morning, Mum. How lovely you look in that shade of scarlet."

When his mother exhaled in exasperation, the red feather in her hat fluttered. "Have you heard *nothing* I've said? These men still believe you raided your own ships! Cannot get it through their thick skulls that you just crossed the Atlantic to *find* your brother! To *cooperate* with them!"

Jason glanced quickly around the room, which was much larger and more nicely appointed than his father's dockside London headquarters. The four men in black looked better suited to the clergy or the classroom than to running a shipping enterprise. And who was the man beside Mother? His blue eyes widened as he sidestepped slightly. Jemma sat behind one of the massive desks, spinning in the chair, bored with this entire situation.

A telling moment, indeed.

"Cooperation is precisely what's required in this . . . tricky predicament," he replied. "The future of this Charleston office—of our entire shipping enterprise—rides on what transpires here."

One of the men put a monocle to his eye and came forward, squinting. "How the deuce *did* you get out of jail? I instructed Sergeant MacTavish that you should remain incarcerated until we had absolute *proof* you were not Johnny Conn!"

Again Jason smiled, biting back a laugh. "I'm sorry, sir, it's been years since we've met. Jason, Lord Darington, at your service."

"And you bloody well ought to *know* that I'm Theodore Dreyfus, the director of your Charleston—" He adjusted his eyepiece and began to wheeze. "What did you just say? Who the hell *are* you?"

Jason smiled, for this scenario was unfolding just as Maria, Rubio, and O'Keefe had predicted. "Jason, Lord Darington, at your service," he repeated. "And how long have you been with us, Mr. Dreyfus?"

The older man coughed. "That seems of no concern, when something smells *fishy*—" Dreyfus turned to the other partners, appealing for their assistance. "Did you hear what he said? And do you believe it? Explanations are definitely in order before anyone threatens the future of Darington Shipping—"

"Jason! Jason, it *is* you!" His sister bolted from the chair, her arms outstretched.

He closed his eyes and hiked her off the floor in a hug.

Jemma squealed, as she'd always done, and the familiarity of this exchange gave him the confidence to proceed. His sister seemed so oblivious most of the time, yet she'd caught on first. As Jason bussed her temple, he glanced at his mother and the four men in their dark suits, letting his gaze linger on Dreyfus. Father had described the old coot perfectly: he'd been invited into the partnership more for financial backing than his managerial skills.

A door behind them closed quietly: the steely-haired man who'd stood beside his mother had made his exit. Another telling moment, was it? He would save that for later. Jason hugged his sister again. "It's good to see you, sweetheart. I—"

"You are in *deep* trouble with Maria for leaving her at the altar!" she blurted. "And things have only gone downhill since then! Why, Father—"

"Jemma! Let's remember where we are and what we're doing!" Their mother watched them closely, her expression guarded. "You know how your brothers love to switch places, to fool you. We've more important matters than airing the family's . . . dirty linens right now."

Well, his mother's tongue hadn't lost its edge in his absence: the Bitch of Swords was charging forth in her effort to control every situation. And by the looks on the men's faces, she'd worn out her welcome and they tolerated her only because she was Father's widow. He released his sister and turned toward the front door. "Maria! O'Keefe!" he called out. "It's time to come in!"

All eyes turned toward those he'd invited: his beautiful fiancée, the chief officer of the *Fortune's Opportunity*, and another burly, uniformed man he hadn't met. He reached out and Maria grasped his hand.

"Captain MacLeod caught up to us at the pier!" she said. "Captain, may I present Jason, Lord Darington—the man we've just retrieved from Ocracoke Island. Jason, this is Captain Moses MacLeod, who brought us to America."

"This is the gentleman who justified my taking the ship without your permission, Captain," O'Keefe clarified. "When you hear our entire story, you'll agree we were right to follow Palladino's guidance."

The chief officer then addressed the dour quartet of partners. Was that a sparkle in his eye when he smiled at Jemma? "Johnny Conn, the pirate you've been pursuing, is only a figment of your imaginations! He existed mostly on that WANTED poster you circulated," O'Keefe declared. "After thorough examination of the wreckage in the Outer Banks, I must report that it was pilot error—outright foolishness of our crewmen!— that lost us those three ships, rather than the shenanigans of a man posing as a pirate."

Dreyfus and the others scowled at each other. "What sort of imbeciles and idiots do you take us for—"

"Oh, pish! You're the same imbeciles and idiots who hauled Jude to jail without listening to *me!*" Lady Darington spouted. She still stared at Jason as though she didn't believe what was happening, but she also followed his lead, knowing which side her bread was buttered on. "So! If you're Jason, where's Jude?"

"One must assume he's still in jail, Mother." Jason tucked Maria's hand in the crook of his elbow. It felt good to hang on to the one solid rock of his existence, here among these men who'd jumped to such an erroneous conclusion. "I came here first, and I've made my point. If *you,* my own dear mother, didn't know which twin stood before you a few moments ago, I rest my case: my brother is being held by mistake."

His gaze encompassed the four partners and the captain, who vaguely resembled the charioteer on Palladino's cards, driving him on to victory. "I suggest you dispatch a cargo steamer to recover every last crate of cacao, sugar, and coffee beans from the three wrecked ships—items I stashed in caves before the water ruined them. I see no reason for anyone to be detained, or tried before the magistrate. Is that how *you* see it, Captain MacLeod?"

The man in the white beard had followed this conversation closely. He took his curved pipe from his mouth, nodding. "I have more than once entrusted my life to Officer O'Keefe," he affirmed. "And after this report of the situation in the Outer Banks, we should be questioning those pilots involved in destroying three Darington ships, rather than detaining the new Lord Darington, owner of our enterprise, and his twin brother."

"Thank you, Captain." Jason gripped the man's hand and shook it. "Your decisive actions have earned you a promotion and a raise in pay. And as your man, O'Keefe, has proven invaluable in this investigation—reporting firsthand and confirming my assertions about how those ships came to be destroyed—I am promoting him into partnership." He gazed pointedly at the men in the dark suits. "I value the service of seasoned officers who've come up through the ranks of this company, and I trust their opinions. Any objections, gentlemen?"

Dreyfus and his three cronies seemed to shrink a size as they looked at each other. "I—we bow to your opinion and your judgment, Lord Darington," the old goat finally said.

"Good. You'll be seeing a lot more of me than you did of my father. He'd be greatly disappointed about your performance in this matter." Jason stood tall and straight, facing them all down even as he felt like an impostor, a man assuming duties for which he wasn't prepared. Yet it felt right, what he'd just done. And Maria's bright smile was all the confirmation he needed. "Shall we fetch Jude from jail, then? He's served his purpose there, I believe."

"Exactly what I've been saying all along!" his mother clucked. She motioned for Jemma to walk beside her. "Thank you, son—Lord Darington, indeed—for stepping in to remedy this disgraceful, disgusting farce. We've not a moment more to waste!"

As they entered the small, smelly building that housed the jail, Jason's confidence soared. It might be the place where they detained seamen who'd downed too many pints and the whores who serviced them, but here he would establish himself in the minds of his father's partners, give them a foretaste of their future. What he'd seen of Dreyfus and the other magpies didn't impress him. Gone were the days when these figure-heads could make decisions from across the sea without closer supervision and increased accountability.

The man behind the messy desk bristled to attention as they entered. When he saw the suits and uniforms, he quickly stashed a copy of *The Pearl* in his desk drawer. "What's the meaning of this? Have I not been informed of something important, Theodore, that you bring these people into my—"

"Take us to the man you've been watching so carefully, MacTavish," Dreyfus said with a raise of his eyebrow. "It seems we've had a . . . misunderstanding about his identity."

The police sergeant frowned—and then gaped at Jason. "How the hell did *you* get out?" His face flushed as he implored the rest of them to believe him. "I swear to God I haven't left my post, not once in these past two days—"

"Save it," Dreyfus warned. "We've more important fish to fry."

The sergeant glowered but motioned them down a hallway. When Jason caught sight of his twin, he felt a weight lifted—a bond reconnected—and again he realized how oblivious he'd been after he'd gotten shanghaied. "I say, it must be the pirate, Johnny Conn!" he teased as he extended his hands between the cell's bars. "What a pleasure it is to meet you at last, sir! I've heard so much about your escapades!"

"Jason! You damn—Jesus, but it's good to see you!" As Jude gripped his hands, joy and relief radiated from his face.

"Holy mother of God," MacTavish muttered. "Wouldn't believe it if I weren't seeing it with my own eyes."

Jason turned, to nail the sergeant with his gaze. "So tell me, officer—which of us *is* the notorious Johnny Conn? If your life depended on it, could you choose?"

MacTavish smirked. "Don't get smart with me! Just because you look enough like—"

"May I introduce Jason, Lord Darington," Dreyfus interrupted with a purposeful gaze. "Which means, now that Phillip has passed, we're dealing with the heir and new owner of Darington Shipping. Do I make myself clear?"

The policeman looked unimpressed, but he kept his mouth shut.

"Or could it be that *I* am Jason, Lord Darington?" Jude demanded in a voice that matched his twin's. "And if I am, imagine what the magistrate will say if you take me—or both of us!—to trial for plundering three ships."

"A crime that has been proven false," Captain MacLeod added triumphantly. "While you and Dreyfus sat as snug as bugs in a rug, thinking you'd restored order along the coast, my chief officer actually *investigated* those shipwrecks. We shall interrogate the captains and pilots of those vessels," he added, studying the reactions of the four suited partners. "But in the meantime, we owe the Darington family our apologies for this grievous miscarriage of justice. *Do we not?*"

The hallway rang with silence. Jason couldn't quit grinning at his twin, who looked a little frazzled but pretty damn fine, all the same.

"Unlock the cell," Dreyfus muttered. "I've had my fill of this two-sided tomfoolery, trying to distinguish between twins after—"

"Then I'll be pleased to dissolve your partnership, sir." Jason remained calm. It felt absolutely right to sever such a stuffy old autocrat whose blindness went far beyond what he couldn't see with that silly monocle. "My father's attorney will attend to it as I review the estate with him. We're on the cusp of a new century, and it's time for *change*. A fresh viewpoint."

Without another word, MacTavish swung open the barred door. Jude smiled tiredly at Jason and Maria. "We've got a lot to catch up on, brother," he murmured as he preceded them down the hall. "Be ready for some surprises. We'll need a huge broom for all the clean sweeps we need to make—and I, for one, am damn glad you're here to make them!"

"All right . . . tell me about this man who's kissing Mother."

Jason lowered the spyglass, scowling. The afternoon had been a total triumph, springing his twin from jail, dispatching a cargo ship to fetch the crates from his caches, and then boarding the *Fortune's Opportunity* for the voyage home. It had given him a particular thrill to announce his homecoming, as the new Lord Darington, in a telegram to Quentin, so he and Mrs. Booth would know when to expect them.

Now, however, his pulse pounded. His gut told him there was far more to this flirtation than his mother taking comfort after his father's passing.

Jude cleared his throat. "That's one of the surprises I mentioned. And you should—"

"Be aware that your mother knows about *us*, too," Maria remarked. "As in, the *three* of us."

"And how the hell did *that* happen?" Jason frowned at them, but then put the spyglass to his eye again. "She didn't learn it from *me*, because I've been the soul of discretion since before we became engaged."

"She's a mother. She knows things," Maria said with a sigh.

"Eyes in the back of her head. Or maybe Jemma's been tattling," Jude remarked sourly. "You know how she turns that damn ferret loose, just to follow him places she isn't supposed to go. Not that she ever needed an excuse for being nosy."

Jason shook his head. "What I've seen surpasses my tolerance for—" He looked away. Couldn't watch that steely-haired stranger devouring his mother against a secluded wall of the steamer, in a kiss that would've made him grab Maria, were it any other passionate couple he'd spied upon. "How long was I gone? Hell, I'm not even sure what day it is, much less—"

"Years, it seems." Maria smiled sadly. "In reality, we should've been married for two months, as of today."

"I have a lot to make up for, sweetheart," he murmured. "But right now, I believe this bastard is an opportunist, taking advantage of our mother's grief and vulnerability before Father is even cold in—"

"Oh, she glowed like a candle at Christmas the first time she met Polinsky. And Father was there with her." Jude, perhaps to add fuel to the flames, plucked the spyglass from Jason's hand. "Yosef Polinsky has appeared in various homes to conduct séances and perform magical tricks, most of which involve making ladies' jewelry disappear, as a jest."

"And then in actuality, we hear," Maria continued. "Mrs. Golding reported some gems missing after she invited Polinsky to be her . . . houseguest."

"You can't be serious! She's eighty if she's a day!" Jason snatched the spyglass from his brother for another look at the man in question. "This fellow can't be *that* desperate. If he weren't somewhat attractive, I'd think—my God, now he's fondling her, with his knee between her—that's it! This has to stop, *now!*"

"No! Wait!" Maria grabbed him from one side and Jude from the other. "If you confront them, you'll exacerbate the venom she'll spew at *you!*"

"Exacerbate?" he demanded. "Let me think. The root word

there is *ass,* and I'm about to kick that fellow's to Kingdom Come!"

Jude tightened his grip. "Polinsky uses his charisma on all the ladies—"

"Charisma? Like I call mine Blackbeard and yours is named Longfellow?"

Maria snickered in spite of their unpleasant exchange. "He's a medium, like my brother. Uses his power to mesmerize women . . . and then ingratiate himself. When Mrs. Golding threw him out, Martha MacPherson was waiting in the wings to welcome him."

"He'll know you plan to rip into him even before formal introductions are made. You can't fool these fellows with psychical powers, Jason." Jude stood taller, listening to something. "There's the bell, announcing dinner. An occasion not to be missed, in that ugly, crowded room. Polinsky and Rubio have been snarling at each other the entire trip, and Mum has been her usual bossy self—only more so, because she's seducing a new lover—"

"And Jemma is witnessing this?" he demanded. "That alone is reason for me, as the head of the family, to reprimand their brazen behavior. And Mother barely into mourning, too."

"She refuses to weep and wail over your father's passing," Maria remarked quietly. "Has informed us she didn't marry Phillip for love, and that she'll put on no false airs about her feelings for him."

Jason's mind reeled. How had so many things gone awry since his abduction and his father's death? And why did he suspect this charmer, Yosef Polinsky, was behind most of them? He set the spyglass on the windowsill. "Shall we go down to dinner? See who gets chewed and who does the chewing?"

30

Maria held her breath as footsteps approached. The tiny dining room had become even more airless while they waited five . . . ten . . . fifteen minutes for Lady Darington and Yosef Polinsky. Jemma fidgeted; made a face at the bowl of cabbage that swam in grease and the platter of unidentifiable meat beside it. Rubio and the twins glanced repeatedly at their watches.

"This is inexcusable!" Jason muttered. "When I get my hands on—"

"Shhh! They're coming!" Maria braced herself for the accusations that would spew like steam from a teakettle. Her brother's predictions still rang in her mind, about revelations and revenge, and she sensed they might come true sooner rather than later.

Lady Darington paused in the doorway, looking serenely poised in a fresh gown of robin's-egg blue. Her smile hid secrets . . . strategies intended to get her what she wanted. "Good evening, children—and Miss Palladino and Rubio, of course. Jason, may I present Mr. Yosef Polinsky, whose spirit guides helped us search for you these past—"

"Yes, Mother, we've *seen* what Polinsky is searching for, when he kissed you behind the lifeboats." Jason stood to establish his superior height—and his mood. "I find your behavior repugnant, in light of how little time has passed since Father died. This *charismatic* opportunist is taking advantage of your unsettled emotions and—"

"Let's call a spade a spade, Darington." The silver-haired medium stepped around Dora, his gaze afire. "Your mother and I are adults, mature enough to know an extraordinary bond existed even before we'd met. Out of respect for her *unsettled* emotions, you can keep your presumptuous opinions and accusations to yourself!"

"Not when my sister is present, I won't! And not when the two of you so lewdly *paw* each other, in plain sight!" Jason raked his hair back from a face flushed with disgust. "As the head of this family, I should take you down to the hold and chain you to the ring in the wall—the spot reserved for prisoners and those who might endanger others on board!"

"*Do* it!" Polinsky challenged. "Chain me wherever you think I belong! I guarantee you, I'll be no less a part of your mother's life!"

"Let's go, then!"

"Jason!" Maria struggled to rise from her tightly tucked chair. "Please don't incite any more ill will than—"

"No, no, Miss Palladino. I insist that your fiancé follow through on his foolish threat," the middle-aged medium replied in a calm voice. "He shall prove his point—just as I shall prove him impotent against my powers. The sooner the better, I say!"

When the two men left, their taut retorts drifted back to the little nook where everyone else sat crammed around the table. Everyone but Dora, who stood behind her chair with a scowl fixed on her face. "We need to discuss a few basic premises," she said sourly. "But I shall wait for Jason to return, so I need not repeat them."

The room became unbearably warm as Lady Darington eyed each of them in turn. Jude looked cautiously at Maria, masking his expression with the confusion and curiosity they all felt. Jemma tapped her fork tines against her plate.

"Enough of that racket, damn it!" her brother finally rasped.

Jemma's face curdled. "Mummy—Mummy, I'm not feeling well! I'm going up to the room with Willie—"

"You'll remain right where you are! What I am about to say affects you as much as it does your brothers." Dora's sour expression mirrored Jemma's. "High time, daughter dearest, that you act your age, is it not? From what I've seen of your . . . *relations* with Chief Officer O'Keefe and with Quentin, we should find you a suitable husband before your reputation ruins our chances for that."

Jemma turned deathly pale. She focused on her empty dinner plate, as though she wanted to disappear into its network of tiny cracks.

Only Rubio seemed unfazed by Dora's mood or by the time Jason took to return. He sat with his hands clasped in his lap, his eyes nearly closed, swaying slightly as though he'd entered a trance state.

Maria hoped he was gleaning powerful, worthwhile information to deal with whatever Dora was about to drop on their heads. Jason's mother looked none too comfortable, despite the way she'd taken control of this room, this voyage home. When she gripped the back of her chair, Maria noticed she no longer wore the gold wedding band Phillip had given her. In its place rested a sizable chunk of aquamarine, which matched her gown. The ring's asymmetrical design differed distinctly from her other jewelry.

Maria composed herself when she heard quick, purposeful footfalls approaching. And then she prayed that whatever happened during this family gathering, she would still return home to marry Jason. Pandora looked formidable enough to make those sweeping changes her brother had described during Jason's tarot reading. Revelation and revenge might not cover it, the way she was seething.

"You needn't have waited." Jason gestured toward the food as he took his seat. "I was securing Polinsky to that iron ring in the hold with a double chain because—"

"Oh, for God's sake, Jason!" his mother muttered.

"—he *goaded* me into doing it!" her son continued with a pointed glare. "You couldn't have chosen a more pompous, arrogant asshole for a companion, Mother! Are you happy now?"

Dora's lips twisted. "Matter of fact, my dearest children, it is indeed time to talk of my *happiness.* Now that you're the head of the family, Jason, I can reveal the realities of my marriage to Phillip so you'll know who you are. And whose."

Maria's throat went dry. Jason widened his eyes at his twin as possible meanings of his mother's announcement sank in.

"What on earth do you mean, Mummy?" Jemma whined. "If we're not going to *eat* this repulsive food, may we please hold this discussion elsewhere? I'm going to absolutely *retch* if I continue to inhale—"

"Enough out of you!" Dora's knuckles turned white even as she smiled, as though she were about to grace them with a revelation far more delicious than the congealed meat on that platter. "Perhaps, as you grew up, you noticed your father and I were not particularly . . . affectionate."

"Mum, it was never our place to say—"

"Silence! Must you torment me in my moment of truth?" Dora shot her younger son a look that withered any inclination for him to speak again. "There's no easy way—no pretty, polite way—to explain the details, so I'll just blurt them out. Your father didn't marry for love, nor did he acquire any such feelings for me in our thirty-two years under the same roof. He was a nobleman in need of an heir, and I was . . . the tarnished daughter of a prominent family, seeking refuge and respectability. It was a match made in hell."

Maria glanced nervously around the table. The twins and Jemma sat tensely, ready to spring from their seats, yet they appeared too stunned to move. Rubio remained somewhat distanced. Why hadn't Lady Darington excused him from this potentially damning discussion? Why on earth would a wife of thirty-two years say such uncomplimentary things to her children about their father—even if she'd been so unhappy? Why not bury her feelings with Phillip and move on—as she obviously had, by taking up with Polinsky?

"And it went downhill from there," Dora continued in a whisper. "Can you imagine the irony of marrying a dashing, wealthy nobleman who desires an heir, only to learn he's been rendered impotent by the *pox?*"

Jason and Jude exchanged a guarded look. "Mother, if this is a subject best confessed to the vicar or laid to rest—"

"Cowards!" she cried. "I'm doing you an enormous favor, telling you Phillip was not your father! Perhaps this will free you from whatever disappointment or disagreement you found with him, for he was as frigid and unlovable with you as he was with me!"

She inhaled noisily to keep from crying. This time no one interrupted: they all felt too uncomfortable to even shift in the hard wooden chairs.

"Had he been slightly agreeable or accommodating, considering how I spent the prime of my life keeping his reprehensible secrets, I might have at least respected him," she continued in a wavering voice. "As it was, I bedded his two best friends— with his consent—to disguise his condition, and to find occasional satisfaction for my . . . sexual hunger. I might be your mother, but I *do* have needs!" she blurted. "I refuse to mourn the man who never loved me! And I will no longer deny myself the physical delights I have done without for so long."

Was this one of Dora's dramas, scripted to cast her in a more auspicious light? Or to divert their attention from matters she did *not* want to discuss? Maria glanced at her brother. Rubio's face remained serene as he looked directly at Lady Darington . . . which suggested her recitation had rung true for him.

"Please let me add that the joy of raising you three children was the only thing that made my marriage to such a boorish, peevish nobleman bearable," she said softly. "Most of the time."

Most of the time, her children had made the marriage bearable? Or most of the time it was a joy to raise them? Maria didn't address this difference aloud: she still wondered why *she* had been included in this discussion, along with her brother. If Dora had asked for her support or encouragement, woman to woman, she wouldn't have proposed Yosef Polinsky as the antidote to Lady Darington's loneliness.

"Well, then," Jemma mused in a high, childlike voice. "If Daddy was not my father, who was?"

"And how does this affect Wildwood? And Darington Shipping?" Jason queried carefully. "While I'm sorry your marriage was unfulfilling, Mother, I cannot believe Father groomed me to assume his estate—his business concerns—only to let me drop off the edge when he died."

"He couldn't let that happen, don't you see? His friends were never to know of his infirmity. He covered it well, as he did everything else." Dora shifted her weight and sighed heavily. "It's all spelled out in his will and the other legal agreements in his files. We'll dig them out when we return home. It is such a *relief* that we found you, Jason, and that you've returned to your right mind. I couldn't have dealt with the *messiness* of—"

"All's well that ends well, milady. And despite this valley of the shadow you wander in, I assure you the best is yet to be." Rubio stood, slowly, so he wouldn't knock the table into anyone. His gaze remained on Dora as he squeezed behind Maria and Jason to slip a reassuring arm around her shoulders. In his turquoise shirt emblazoned with stars and crescent moons, he looked like a wizard ready to impart his wisdom, yet his youthful face glowed with vitality . . . and with a *knowing*.

Maria prepared herself: she *knew* that expression. All had not yet been revealed. And none of them were home free, as far as remaining unscathed for their own little secrets.

Dora looked deeply relieved. "Thank you, Rubio," she murmured. "I truly appreciate your assistance as we searched for my Jason. Forgive me if I've seemed rude or ungrateful."

"Forgive *me* if I fueled the flames of confrontation when Polinsky challenged my predictions." He gazed at Dora until she looked up at him . . . succumbed to his bottomless brown eyes. "Shall we finish what you started? Answer that most indelicate of questions, which is foremost on your children's minds? Please correct me if I'm wrong, or if I speak out of turn."

Lady Darington nodded slowly, entranced.

"I sense Lord Fenwick sired your fine twin sons . . ." He waited until Dora's dreamlike smile confirmed this. "And was it not Lord Galsworthy who gave you Jemma?"

Lady Darington blinked when he released her from his powerful gaze. "You truly amaze me with your powers of perception, Mr. Palladino. No wonder the Queen and her court adore you."

"Thank you, milady. And if I might venture one more prediction—"

"Reginald *Galsworthy*? That old *toad* is my—Mumsy, how *could* you?" With a sob, Jemma grabbed Willie's cage and looked for the easiest way past the backs of their chairs. "My God! You pointed the finger at *my* relations, when you bedded *two* old goats who—"

"Once again, Jemma, you jump to your childish conclusions." Dora blocked her daughter's exit; turned sideways to face Jemma with her arms crossed. "As part of the bargain with those upstanding *gentlemen*, I secured *your* future, young lady, as well as Jude's! In exchange for my favors, I insisted Galsworthy pass his estate to you upon his death—bypassing his new bride, Rowena—just as Lord Fenwick agreed that Jude, the second son, would inherit his estate after I bore his twins! I chose childless men of means for this very reason! I prostituted myself to get this in writing, all tidy and legal. For *you!*"

Jemma glared at her mother. "Just move, damn it," she blubbered, "before I retch all over your—what a *wretched* way to learn about these things! Jesus!"

Rubio stepped aside. Maria looked away, embarrassed . . . empathizing with Jemma's shock and disgust while noting her mother's cool, calculated air. Jude and Jason gazed at each other across the table, in that way twins shared information. When Dora moved, her daughter rushed toward the stairs, bawling. Poor Willie's birdcage banged against each metal step.

The room's silence became stifling again.

Rubio cleared his throat. He moved to Lady Darington's side once more, this time taking hold of her left hand to admire the stunning aquamarine ring. When he touched it with an inquisitive fingertip, his eyebrows flickered. "More revelations will be forthcoming. Just as your Mr. Polinsky is," he murmured. "Be very careful, milady. Things are not as they seem."

Maria held her breath. Oh, how she itched to take up Miss Crimson's pen and report on what she'd witnessed these past few minutes! News would soon leak out about who had sired the Daringtons' children, for Jemma couldn't keep such a secret. And certainly, when Lord Galsworthy and Lord Fenwick died, the passing of their estates to Jude and Jemma would confirm the gossip Miss Darington stirred up as she sought the sympathy of her friends. No doubt Phillip's affliction would come to light, as well. And where would this leave Rowena Galsworthy?

And what had Rubio learned when he'd fingered Dora's

ring? Maria sensed he'd offered the lady his consolations partly so he could *touch* her . . . to ascertain what she wasn't telling outright. Then—just as he'd predicted—a triumphant knock at the door made them all look up.

Yosef Polinsky stood there, grinning proudly. Sprung padlocks dangled from the two lengths of chain with which Jason had bound him.

Jason rose so suddenly his chair hit the wall. "What the hell are *you* doing here?"

"Proving my point—and my power," the medium replied slyly. "As an admirer of the imminent Harry Houdini, I've perfected my abilities to escape any form of bondage. Thank you for indulging me, Lord Darington."

"Yosef! How wonderful you are! And how amazing!" Dora beamed, and then opened her arms to welcome him.

Rubio resumed his seat. Polinsky entered with a grand air of accomplishment, to wrap Dora in his arms and noisily kiss her cheek. "You have explained things to your children, I gather? They'll require time to understand the implications of all you've shared with them."

The magician turned to them then, his handsome face imperiously composed. "Like it or not, your mother and I are in love," he announced. "You need to see her in a different light now, for you are adults and she has desires you fully understand—if you will put yourselves in her place. I assure you I will take good care of her. And I have no intention of intruding upon *your* lives, so long as you allow Lady Darington a chance to live hers."

Maria didn't dare breathe. Beside her, Rubio fought a foxlike grin. Seconds ticked by.

The twins stood up simultaneously. "I've seen enough for one day," Jason muttered.

"Hear, hear," his brother replied. "A lot to chew on, indeed."

31

"Welcome home, Lord Darington! It's *so* good to see you, sir!" Quentin McCallum pumped Jason's hand as they came off the gangplank at the London pier. "And you, too, Miss Palladino! You must be feeling feisty and fine, now that you've found your man and brought him around again!"

Feisty and fine. After these past two days of strained conversations and Jemma's outbursts aboard the *Fortune's Opportunity*, Maria was ready to feel feisty and fine! Matter of fact, it sounded like something Miss Crimson would say! She *yearned* for a copy of the *Inquirer*, to see how the columnist had fared—what she'd posted—these past several days.

As the stevedores hauled their trunks toward the waiting carriage, a movement caught her eye. "Maria! Dora!" a halting voice cried. "Jude—and Jason! Jason, Lord Darington, home at last!"

"Mrs. Golding, how nice to see you!" Maria rushed forward to embrace the little woman, who might faint from her excitement. "What brings you here? How did you know we'd be—"

"Why, Miss Crimson's column yesterday spilled over with

the good news! We've all been *so* concerned about you Daringtons!" she nattered. "I've had Vera prepare you a light supper, knowing how tired you'd be!"

"Well, isn't that the sweetest idea?" Maria turned to see if the others had heard the old dear's invitation: Meriweather looked smaller and more fragile, yet her eyes sparkled in her rouged, withered face . . . and she would show Maria that column, to catch her up on the latest news! "Did you hear that, Dora? Mrs. Golding has prepared supper for us!"

Lady Darington frowned as she took the last steps down the gangplank on the arm of her firstborn. "After this exhausting trip, I couldn't think of going anywhere but—"

"What a lovely thing for you to do!" Jason crouched slightly to clasp the dowager's hands. "The food on our voyage left much to be desired, and you always served the lightest, freshest scones, and—well, I'll be there! Won't the rest of you join us?"

"You, too, Mr. Palladino!" Meriweather said with a grin. "I can't wait to hear your stories, about how you located Jason and saved the day!"

Jemma sighed loudly and rolled her eyes. Jude glanced around them, and then took his mother's arm. "I'll be there, as well, Mrs. Golding. What a thoughtful gesture."

"I wouldn't miss it!" Maria chimed in.

Their old friend nodded excitedly—and then she sobered: Yosef Polinsky was coming down the gangplank, chatting with the captain and O'Keefe. He stopped to give her a courtly bow. "You're a sight for sore eyes, Meriweather. How nice to see you."

"And you, sir." Her lips tightened into a thin, colorless line before she added, "My invitation to supper includes you, as well, Mr. Polinsky."

"You are too kind," he replied.

Well, wasn't *this* interesting? Maria settled into a carriage with Rubio and the twins, leaving Jemma to ride with her mother, the butler, and the magician. "Can you believe it?" she rasped. "Not that long ago—before she gave him the boot—Meriweather and Polinsky were as giddy as young lovers."

"So sickeningly sweet on each other, it turned my stomach," Jude recalled.

"And she said Miss Crimson announced your return yesterday, Jason. All of London is celebrating—just as I am!" Maria hoped her exuberance covered her concern: had Quentin McCallum been writing the column in her place? Or had the editor kept the gossip flowing so his paper would sell? She couldn't wait to get her hands on Meriweather's copy of the *Inquirer*.

"Damn! You mean it's all over the papers that I've come home? I'd hoped to settle Father's legal matters before..." Jason frowned out the carriage window. "How the hell did London's biggest tattletale know when I'd arrive? The only word I sent was addressed to Quentin."

"And how could he keep such good news to himself? Quite possibly, the telegrapher who deciphered your message spread the word, as well," Rubio replied without missing a beat. He leaned forward, gesturing toward Maria. "Your bride was beside herself, you know. We were *all* worried sick about you, milord."

"That's no reason to post it in that damn scandal sheet—"

"But Miss Crimson helped us find you!" Jude chimed in. "Father and I searched the pier, at the recommendation of your chums from the bachelor party, but Scotland Yard was baffled. Had Miss Crimson not begged her readers for information, when she wrote her column on the wedding—"

"Jesus! Don't tell me the entire city believes I stood up my bride!" Jason's face became the same shade of red as the leather upholstery. "If I find out who pens this vicious drivel—"

"Please, Lord Darington, let's show a bit of sympathy for your bride! With hundreds of guests in the church, awaiting your arrival, your disappearance was by no means a secret."

Rubio fixed his gaze on Jason, while Maria sat very still. This discussion—her fiancé's heated opinions—didn't bode well for Miss Crimson's continued career. She had to corner Quentin before Jason collared him. . . .

"And let's not forget, dear brother," Jude said quietly, "that while Johnny Conn lured ships into the shoals with his pirate shenanigans, *we* were dealing with your abduction *and* Father's passing. Feeling quite flummoxed in the wake of our double tragedy."

Jason gazed at his twin for several seconds. He exhaled loudly and took Maria's hand. "Please excuse my outburst, love," he murmured. "All these revelations about Father not being my father—among other things I've had to accept these past few days—have skewed my perspective. I didn't mean to offend or upset you, dear Maria."

"It's all right," she murmured. Her heart still fluttered like a frightened bird's. "We've all been on edge. No one could've anticipated your mother's confessions, not to mention Polinsky's declaration of love, or your father's . . . condition. I had no idea he was ill. He and I danced and had a pleasant chat just moments before he collapsed."

"To the unassuming eye, Phillip appeared normal," Rubio mused as he nodded in agreement. "Not unusual for a man's sudden death to bring unexpected secrets to light."

They rode quietly the rest of the way to Mrs. Golding's, lost in their private thoughts. Thank God Rubio had diverted the conversation, and Jude had joined in without knowing he'd covered her little secret! Maria reminded herself what a joy it was to be seated beside the love of her life again, holding his hand . . . even though he detested what she did for an income. She had to believe Miss Crimson could take her literary leave without Jason being the wiser. What a delicious secret it would be, to remain a mystery to the entire population of London, after her years of enjoying such public anonymity!

As the carriage pulled up in front of the brownstone, Rubio's surreptitious wink put her in a better mood to enjoy Meriweather's surprise supper. Once they entered her home, however, the *real* surprise jumped out! From behind the settees and the grand piano, nearly a dozen friends sprang up, crying, "Welcome home, Lord Darington!" Their chorus turned into chaos as everyone greeted the guest of honor, the lost son come home again. As Meriweather stood in the doorway of her music room, she giggled like a schoolgirl.

"You sly cat!" Maria spoke beneath the cacophony. "This is quite a party you put together for Jason's arrival. Did you say you read of it in Miss Crimson's column?"

"Why yes, dear! And I've saved all those copies of the *Inquirer*, knowing you wouldn't want to miss a single thing that happened in your absence!" She pointed to a stack of newspapers on the hall credenza. "I'm so happy you and Jason convinced the others to come! What would I have done with all this food?"

Maria's fingers itched to open those issues containing her column. She now had the perfect excuse to read them when she returned to the town house—or even during the carriage ride home! So for now, she should pay attention to who had attended this gathering, perhaps as fodder for her final column. She accepted congratulations from Martha MacPherson and Esther Grumbaugh before Colette and Camille Bentley caught her up in a double hug. Her journalistic eye wandered around the noisy rooms: she greeted Lord and Lady Galsworthy and Lord Fenwick . . . an interesting twist, because Meriweather didn't know of their covert ties to Dora Darington and her children.

Did she?

As Sarah Remington made her way through the crowd toward Jude, Maria was struck by how much she knew about some of these guests—and what she might *not* know. After all, who would have guessed Phillip might have succumbed to the pox, had a heart attack not claimed him first? Who knew Dora had married him to veil her questionable reputation?

And what of Rubio's allusions to things not being what they seemed? As Maria watched Yosef Polinsky nod and grasp hands, gazing into the ladies' eyes as though he saw all the way through to their souls, Dora made her separate rounds. How did she feel about Polinsky so affectionately *handling* these women, now that he'd proclaimed his love for *her*? Would the couple announce their intentions today, while so many of their friends were here? Many ladies whispered behind their hands, about the widow Darington dressed in silk the color of buttery sunshine: reason enough for gossip among these pillars of propriety. Society kept its secrets—or divulged them—in ways even Miss Crimson had no way of foretelling.

So Maria relaxed. She smiled at this gathering of family and friends who, beneath their aristocratic manners and heirloom jewelry, might conceal a veritable *hotbed* of scandals a common columnist like herself could only speculate about. Perhaps people of the Daringtons' ilk could better *afford* secret lives . . . one more facet of privileged living to which she must adjust. Her activities as London's most quoted, most mysterious gossipmonger probably *paled* compared to what these guests had done.

"Please, everyone!" Meriweather spoke above the clamor. "Fill your plates at the buffet! Vera has prepared a wonderful supper!"

Maria noticed Jemma then, wringing her pink gloves as she stood in a nook behind Meriweather's piano. Poor girl. With her mother's lover present, as well as Jude's new admirer—not to mention the two "old goats" who'd fathered the three of them—she resembled a mouse cowering in a cabinet. Jason still regaled his well-wishers with his adventures, so everyone she usually talked with was occupied. Jemma knew better than to pitch a pity fit in someone else's home, so she was stuck. Too bad Quentin had returned to the town house.

Maria picked up a plate and smiled at the bewildered blonde. "May I join you, Jemma? While this surprise party was a splendid idea, I'm tired and I really don't wish to make polite conversation with anyone."

Jemma's blue eyes widened. Was that amazement on her face, or sheer gratitude? "Yes, I'd like that," she murmured. "Knowing what I now know, I can't make *any* kind of conversation with . . . certain parties."

"I can't imagine how awkward it must feel, to cogitate about your father, by blood, only to be confronted with him the moment you got here. Life is sometimes more a thicket of thorns than a rose garden, isn't it?"

Her tremulous smile touched Maria. They chose food from chafing dishes filled with roasted squab and sliced beef in gravy, seasoned root vegetables, and a large compote of stewed fruits that glistened like wet jewels. The sweets on the far end of the sideboard tempted her, but there wasn't enough room on her plate—and still Vera carried out steaming pans of food. What a relief that most of the older guests sat at the long dining room table while the twins, Sarah, and Rubio chose chairs in the adjacent parlor where she and Jemma sat.

"Quite a gathering," Rubio remarked. "Much nicer than returning to my apartment alone."

As though you would be, Maria mused. Alice, the blond seamstress across the hall, had probably missed him.

"And so much nicer to join you ladies in here than to act *polite* in Polinsky's presence. A cross between a peacock and a bantam rooster, is he not?" When Rubio imitated the way the other medium raked his hair back from his temples, Jemma laughed out loud.

But then the mystical man sat straighter . . . tuned in to voices they couldn't hear. "He's going to be sorry he took the bait," Rubio murmured, as though no one sat around him. "It might well be his undoing."

Maria smiled at Jemma and shrugged.

When they returned to the buffet to consider dessert, however, Yosef Polinsky was working his way around the long table. He flirted shamelessly with the ladies, entertained the guests with his account of searching for Jason while he performed tricks with the table service.

"Which hand holds your salt cellar, Mrs. Grumbaugh?" he queried playfully. "I bet you know! You've watched very closely."

The chubby woman tapped his left hand. When he opened it, a loud gasp flew around the table: a delicate bracelet of emeralds and sapphires dangled between his fingers.

"My stars, Mr. Polinsky!" Esther protested. "How did you *do* that? I had no idea—"

"The hand is faster than the eye," the magician quipped. "But I'll repeat the trick, while you observe again. I am passing your salt cellar between my fists—"

"Don't fall for that old shell game, Esther!" Across the table, Martha MacPherson scowled and stood up. "And why are *you* acting so amazed? Yosef gave *me* that bracelet weeks ago, when—"

"I beg your pardon, but you're dead wrong!" Esther Grumbaugh smacked the table and then stood up so suddenly she nearly bumped heads with Polinsky. "My first husband, Leopold, gave me this pretty little piece after the birth of our daughter, Maggie!" To emphasize her point, she fastened the bracelet around her wrist and then shook it at the matron across the table.

Maria took Jemma by the shoulder to stop the girl from venturing across the room toward the desserts. As those around the table glanced quizzically at one another, they straightened, spoiling for a catfight.

"What do you say to *that*, Mr. Polinsky?" Lady MacPherson's cheeks flamed with indignation. "After you *left* me—to pursue your next biddable chicken—I had time to ponder your pretty lies. And low and behold, I discovered that some of the boxes in my jewelry chest were *empty*! So one has to wonder—"

"Well, there's no wondering about *this*!" At the other end of the table, Rowena Galsworthy dug through her reticule and then flashed a calling card. "*Not* that I've seen this pole myself, but we all know who'd be arrogant enough—*cocky* enough—to wear a jeweled ring around his *thing!*"

Her husband Reginald nearly choked. "*Really*, Rowe! This is not a proper topic—"

"As if anything about Polinsky is *proper*!" Colette Bentley, too, produced a calling card with the magician's bejeweled member on it. "And how many of us received these special mementos of Lady Darington's tea?"

Every woman at the table fiddled in her reticule, to hold up a small photograph of herself in a wicker chair, with Polinsky's arm slung behind her as he grinned gleefully at the camera. The room rang with chatter as they compared the photographs, while their men exchanged suspicious scowls.

Wasn't it interesting that while these ladies berated the magician in their midst, they all carried his photograph? Maria made a note to mention that in a future column . . . but when she saw Yosef edging toward the door, she strode over to detain him.

"Yes, Maria! We'll not be letting that wily fox out of the henhouse just yet!" Meriweather Golding trip-trapped daintily across the parquet floor, her mission written all over her care-worn face. "I wish I could say I'd cleverly arranged this moment of truth, but you, my friends, have saved me the effort—the humiliation—of confronting Mr. Polinsky myself!" She stopped in front of him, her fist on her hip. "If you're returning jewelry to Esther, I'd like mine back, too!"

"So would I!"

"And would I!"

The magician didn't miss a beat. "Ladies, I'm flabbergasted that you think I'd sink so low as to—"

"Lower than a snake's belly! That's how you've behaved, and how I felt after you *deceived* me!" their hostess cried. "I blamed it on a memory gone faulty with age, but you took me for a fool and I proved you right. Will you return what you've stolen, or shall I summon the police?"

Trapped between Maria and Mrs. Golding, with a roomful of witnesses, Polinsky held up his hands as though he'd walked into an invisible wall . . . or had been placed under arrest already. "I assure you I shall restore what is yours, dear ladies. If you'll list what is missing, I shall return to my room for—"

"Do you *have* a room, sir? Or are you a *guest* of yet another unsuspecting hostess?" Rubio demanded from the doorway. His mane of glossy brown hair rendered his face godlike as he awaited the magician's answer. "When I suspected your duplicity—your *thievery*, Polinsky—I went to the Yard, where I discovered a *string* of complaints from across the Continent. Heartbroken women who reported jewelry missing after you performed in their towns. Using three different names."

As Rubio stepped forward, he narrowed his piercing eyes. "You're not even Russian, are you, Joseph Pohl? And you didn't intend to unpack your trunks after we docked today, did you?" he demanded. "Instead, you planned to leave London before a scene like this one exposed you for the shyster you are!"

The room rang with silence. To a woman, they all appeared stricken. A whimper escaped Dora Darington.

Maria felt genuinely sorry for Jason's mother: even the feather on her jaunty yellow hat drooped with her dejection. While the other ladies appeared indignant yet vindicated, Lady Darington tried very hard not to betray her devastation. Behind Rubio, Jason and Jude appeared in the doorway: their taut expressions conveyed their disgust at the story they'd over-heard.

"I ought to run you up a flagpole and hang you for what you've done," Jason muttered. "I see no recourse but to escort you to jail—"

"I'll take him. You have other matters to attend to, Lord Darington." Rubio surveyed those at the table. "I'm sure Galsworthy and Fenwick will assist me."

"Thank you, sir." Jason sighed tiredly. "And thank you, Mrs. Golding, for this lovely homecoming surprise. However, our family has endured much distress these past few weeks, so we'll be leaving now. Mother?"

As the two gentlemen rose to assist Rubio, and Jason went around the table for Dora, Meriweather Golding held up her hand for silence. She looked at Polinsky as though she might cry.

"I'm sorry it came to this, Yosef," she said in a halting voice. Then she smiled bravely and dabbed at her eyes. "It was a small price to pay, losing jewelry my late husband gave me each time he took a new mistress. While you were here—while you en-tranced me with your voice and your passion—I felt young and attractive again. *Alive* and in love! I shall never regret that."

All in the room were departing, but they stopped to look at their hostess. Martha MacPherson clapped her reticule shut. "There's that, all right. You burned me good, Mr. Polinsky, but those missing gems held no shine compared to *your* jewels! You made me feel devastatingly beautiful when we were—"

"There won't be another lover like Yosef Polinsky. Might as well live out the rest of my days in a convent." Esther Grum-baugh sighed over her photograph and then slipped it into the pocket of her flowing skirt.

Maria yearned to hear more midnight confessions; to pon-der the magic this chameleon worked with that wand pictured on his business cards. Miss Crimson's mind was spinning out phrases that would shock and delight her readers, even if Polinsky was the only character she named in this drama.

Jason, however, took his mother firmly by the shoulders. "Again, my thanks to all of you for your concern while I was absent and indisposed," he said as he steered Dora toward the door. Then in a lower voice he added, "None of this mewling sentimentality for *you*, Mother! He's a thief and a huckster, no matter how you slice it. Justice has been served, and we shall return home to sort all this out."

32

"I will tolerate *no* further displays of your protection!" Dora spouted when the carriage door closed behind them. "I don't care if you *are* my son, Lord Darington! *No* one tells me how to feel or whom to love."

Jude and his brother gaped at their mother. Maria stayed out of this squabble, and she hoped Jemma, on the opposite carriage seat beside her mother, had the sense to remain quiet, too.

Pandora Darington, who looked every inch the mythological goddess, sat ramrod straight with her wrists crossed atop her parasol handle. "As I told you before, I fulfilled my obligations by providing each of you an estate. Any *normal* mother would have been happy that her firstborn received the entire package, but *I* loved my children equally! I sacrificed my dignity—the best years of my life—to compensate for your father's disinterest!"

Maria glanced out the carriage window, pondering what Jason's mother did *not* say. By all appearances, she'd recovered from her loveless marriage—but then, Dora didn't hold society's measuring stick up to her own experience and settle for it. And Maria admired that.

"We're all exhausted, Mother," Jason muttered. "We have never questioned your love or sense of maternal duty. But I cannot allow you to become yet another doormat for Polinsky! I distrusted him the moment I saw him—"

"Precisely my point! You wouldn't like *any* man I fancied!" Dora then glared at Jude, who sat silently beside her. "And *you* couldn't care less who I'm in bed with as long as it doesn't interfere with your amusing pursuits—not that you're any more honorable than I! Masquerade with Sarah Remington all you want, but you haven't the decency—the integrity—to stop sneaking around with Maria! Do the three of you intend to share the same bed after the wedding?"

"For God's sake, Mum—"

"I should inform the vicar of this situation," Dora continued in a rush. "If only to ensure the Darington heirs' bloodline remains pure—"

"What the hell does *that* mean?" Jason spouted. "If Jude and I are both of Galsworthy spawn, we've been living under an assumed name all our—oh, this is a fine mess, Mother! Quite the spider you've been, weaving such a web of deceit!"

He grabbed Maria's hand. She felt his pulse racing; sensed the tension in his muscles as he struggled to control his emotions. "We'll sort this out at the town house," he announced in a dangerously quiet voice. "I can't discuss your sexual escapades in my father's home—even if he did know what was going on."

As she glanced at the stack of newspapers by her feet, Maria cringed. All she wanted to do after the revelations at Meriweather's party—not to mention the emotional roller coaster of the voyage to America—was hole up in her room, undisturbed, to read Miss Crimson's columns. If any of these Daringtons learned the truth about her . . .

Or would the fact that the *Inquirer*'s gossipmonger had continued writing while she was in America prove she was *not* Miss Crimson?

Maria shifted, clutching that straw. Once inside the town house, Mrs. Booth's excitement waylaid their previous conversation: the old housekeeper wanted every detail of how they'd located Jason, what he'd done while he believed himself a pirate. . . . Maria slipped away from the parlor on the pretext of freshening up before they resumed their family discussion.

Quentin grabbed her in the vestibule. With a finger on his lips, he steered her to the alcove beneath the service stairway at the back of the house, where he stored his tools. From a wooden crate that had once held tins of peaches, he pulled a fat burlap bag. "Mail for Miss Crimson!" he whispered. "I kept your column alive, milady, but I fear I've botched the job! Insulted the wrong society types."

Maria's heart raced. "How do you mean, insulted the wrong—"

"Here—these two notes came from the *Inquirer*'s editor, insisting Miss Crimson either apologize to her readers for—for misrepresenting the Queen and her court, or—"

"You made mincemeat of the *Queen*? How on God's earth—" Maria clapped her hand over her mouth and then glanced behind them, through the kitchen and into the dining room. She slipped the letter from its envelope, to skim her editor's familiar handwriting.

Dear Miss Crimson, I regret to inform you that several of our most influential and generous sponsors insist I curtail your column unless—

A whimper escaped her. She unfolded the other missive, dated yesterday.

Dear Miss Crimson, Because you don't seem yourself of late, I have placated readers and sponsors alike by temporarily sus-

pending your column. I'm hoping you will apologize in print and beg forgiveness—

"Or I will be taken to court on charges of libelous— *Quentin!*" She glared at the slender butler, heat prickling her face. "After I suggested you *not* be my ghostwriter, how could you insult my readers to the point—you assured me you'd read every column Miss Crimson wrote! And yet in just two weeks, you've gotten me fired unless—"

A gasp made them look up. There stood Jemma, clutching Willie to her shoulder as she gawked at them. "Oh my stars!" she breathed. "*You,* Maria, are—Mumsy! Mumsy!" she cried as she trotted down the hallway. "You'll never *believe* it! Maria is Miss Crimson! *Maria* is that foul-mouthed society snitch you want to rip limb from limb!"

The blood drained from Maria's face. She went cold and began to quiver; knew she had some very tall explaining to do, yet couldn't move from the spot where Jason's butler had stored this bag of incriminating letters.

And that's where Jason found her: still rooted to the floor of the butler's closet. Her fiancé seemed very tall and strong and formidable and . . . yes, ready to dismember her. "Is it true, what Jemma said?" he demanded. "I don't believe half the fanciful stuff she spouts, but I must hear this from *you,* Maria. I'm tired. And frankly, I've heard all the outrageous stories I can handle for one day."

Maria prayed for the floor to open up and swallow her. Her future with Jason, Lord Darington had just come to a crossroads: a painful, humiliating end, if she didn't find the right words, right now. His tawny eyes bored into hers, begging her to refute his sister.

But she could only stand there alongside Quentin, swallowing rapidly. Struggling to breathe. "I never wrote a word that discredited you or—or your family!" she stammered. "It was all in your mother's interpretation—"

"And *you* have penned this hideous column from its inception? Since before I knew you?" His anguished expression implored her to correct him—to *lie,* if need be, so he could set his mind to rest and get on with other matters at hand.

But she couldn't do it. Didn't have an alibi ready—and damn it, now that this huge cat was out of the bag, Maria couldn't bear the thought of covering every secretive walk into town after dark . . . watching her back and forever concealing the writing she had always loved, once she married this man. If people read her columns carefully, they knew her scandalous humor gave all of London something interesting to talk about! But she reported only what she herself had seen and heard. She had *never* embellished or falsified her stories.

And she would not start now.

"Yes, I am Miss Crimson," she confessed. "Except that while I was away, finding you—"

"I am to blame for this entire episode," Quentin confessed dolefully. "Miss Palladino, I am profusely sorry for the mess I've made. And Jason—Lord Darington, sir—I shall pack my belongings right now and—"

"Nonsense." Jason glanced at the bulging burlap bag and then at his manservant. "You are excused to assist Mrs. Booth in the kitchen. She insists on serving the family tea and tarts none of us wants to eat. Meanwhile, I have matters to discuss with Mar—Miss Palladino."

Her throat closed over a protest. Miss Palladino, was it?

Maria resigned herself to the ugliness that would be hurled by those who waited in the parlor. If this weren't such a hideously painful moment, when her future hung by an unraveling thread, she could congratulate herself for giving these Daringtons a diversion from their family feud. But she must face the music . . . even if it were a funeral dirge for her career as a columnist. Hadn't she sensed this moment would come? Hadn't Rubio hinted at this in his predictions before the wedding? *Joy juxtaposed with excruciating pain . . . deception, yet revelation.*

But Rubio was off dealing with his own demons. She must face hers, too.

They sat in the parlor, staring as she entered a step ahead of Jason: Jemma, Jude, and Dora. Judge, jury, and executioner. Pandora Darington rose and pointed a finger, resembling the Grim Reaper despite her sunshine yellow dress. "*You!*" She bit off the word as though it tasted foul. "A traitor in our midst! Hiding your true identity from us all this time! And to think you almost married my son!"

Maria stood stoically, her hands clasped in front of her. Jason left her then, to face her from behind the settee where his family sat. Never in her life had she felt so alone.

"What? Not a word of explanation or apology?" Dora demanded. "Not even a weak excuse to defend all the scandalous accusations and *lies* you've published about us?"

She opened her mouth to speak, but Lady Darington wasn't finished.

"Oh, this is *rich!* Left to your own secretive devices, while living under our roof, you deceived us and shamed us in print! But when brought to account, you've nothing to say?"

"How did *you* get to be Miss Crimson?" Jemma blurted. She shrugged incredulously. "I mean, of all the fine ladies who *could* have been—"

"You make a worthwhile point, Miss Darington." Maria's blood finally reached a full boil as she looked at the princess of this family. "Might I remind you that I was not raised in the lap of luxury? Lord knows you and your mother never miss an opportunity to remind me I'm trash!" she cried. "But when I came to this country with my brother, shortly after we'd been orphaned in Italy, I had no one else to turn to! No one making secret *deals* to ensure I inherited an estate!"

She paused, but she'd gone too far to stop. It was time to

state her case and let the chips fall where they may, wasn't it? "Rubio has made his mark as London's foremost medium and visionary, while I've employed my gifts for observing and reporting—yes, while hiding beneath Miss Crimson's cloak of anonymity. *Why?*" she demanded, her arms outstretched. "Because I needed an *income!* I refused to depend upon Rubio, and have supported myself for nearly five years now! Frankly, I think he and I have done rather well for two penniless foreigners!"

Their faces registered disbelief. Quentin entered the hushed room with a tray of petits fours, tea cakes, and tarts. He set it on the table between the two sides of this confrontation. "Not to overstep my bounds," he said in a low voice, "but if you've ever *read* Miss Crimson's column with an open, objective mind, you'd know she has not demeaned your family—or anyone else's. She simply tells London's social story as it *is.*"

"Out!" Dora exclaimed with a curt wave. "The day I require advice from the *help* will be a dire time indeed!"

The butler bowed. Was that a furtive look he and Jemma exchanged as he left the parlor? Maria snatched at any sign of happiness, for she'd dug herself into a pit with no foreseeable means of getting out.

Jude, however, scooted forward to choose two little iced cakes. He popped them into his mouth, his expression speculative. "While this revelation comes as a shock," he said quietly, "haven't we always known Maria Palladino possessed a certain élan . . . an irrepressible sparkle we envied? For her to remain anonymous as a columnist all these years, while she gained entrée into London's most elite circles—"

"She was only invited because she was Miss Crimson!" Jemma piped up. She, too, snatched a tea cake and jammed it into her mouth before sharing the last morsel of it with Willie.

"But who *knew* she was writing that column? My point *is,*" Jude continued in a more excited voice, "that Maria has far more talent and ability and—and *pluck*—than we give her credit for! And she has achieved this distinction on her own, without any connections at Court or help from well-heeled friends."

"But why did she write under cover? And use the peerage for target practice?" Jason protested. His scowl predicted how he'd look in fifty years if he allowed sour grapes to turn to vinegar in his soul.

"Who wants to read about common, everyday people? Certainly not anyone who would pay for a paper!" she shot back. Her fiancé's attitude startled her . . . and now he and his twin were talking as though she weren't in the room. Perhaps it was best to discover his true feelings before she married Jason Darington: becoming an earl hadn't improved his disposition, had it? "Let's not forget that Miss Crimson put out a plea for information, which Rubio then connected to his visions, or we'd have had *no* idea where you'd disappeared—"

"Where *did* you go that night?" Jude turned to address his brother, distracted by missing links that had never been reconnected. "Miss Amelia told your chums her driver took you home! At least they admitted where you'd been! But when Father and I went to the whorehouse—"

"Jude, really!" his mother sputtered. "Must you be so crude? Ladies are present."

In light of what Dora had revealed about her marriage, Maria bit back a retort. The parlor got quiet as the twins and Jemma also considered their mother's remark.

Mrs. Booth entered the parlor then, with a teapot and their cups. "Have you ever *read* Miss Crimson's column, Lord Darington?" she asked crisply. "I find her observations about the aristocracy to be quite astute—and she plays no favorites! She did indeed solicit help for locating *you*. And didn't she shine the spotlight on that Russian medium, Yosef Polinsky? I hear he's made quite a splash amongst lonely ladies of the upper crust."

The Daringtons gaped at the housekeeper as though they might strangle her, while Mrs. Booth took her leave, unaware of the splash *she* had just made. Jason came around the settee to snatch two cherry tarts. "Since when has our help presumed to question our personal affairs? I must consider hiring new—"

"She has no way of knowing about Mum's connection to Polinsky. Or that he was taken to jail," his twin pointed out.

"And you may *stifle* your judgments about Yosef! He's the victim of circumstance and yes, a clutch of lonely old ladies, each of whom fancies herself his lover." Dora's eyes flashed at her sons before she, too, took a tea cake. "He loves *me*, you know. I knew he was my destiny the moment we met."

And how could anyone respond to *that?* Maria once again realized that she stood alone, outside the Darington social circle—and outside this cutting conversation. But if Jason remained so unforgiving, while his mother defended a thief yet condemned *her* for earning an honest living . . . what was the point of remaining here, an outcast in this home? She might as well—

"Do you call it love, Mumsy, just because Mr. Polinsky kissed you on the ship when no other ladies were available?" Jemma's voice had a self-righteous whine to it. "Then why did everyone but *you* have her photograph taken with him at the tea?"

Dora looked stunned. She raised her hand to slap her daughter and then drew it back. "And where *did* those photographs come from, Jude?" she demanded archly. "If that was your idea of a humorous prank, having Yosef pose with . . ."

Maria slipped from the parlor unobserved. Considering how few belongings she had, it wouldn't take her long to pack.

33

Jason saw her leave but remained beside the settee, where his mother and brother bickered. After gobbling another cherry tart and two petits fours, he realized how much he'd missed decent food while he was out of his house, out of his head. And he realized how many things had gone awry while he was gone.

Or was *he* the one who'd veered off course? Was *he* the lone wolf—the rogue pirate—who believed everything should be where he'd left it, and no one should've changed while he was away? True enough, his mother had revealed some eye-popping information these past two days . . . but cast in that perspective, was it really such a crime that Maria had earned her living as London's most notorious gossip?

"I did what Polinsky requested, Mum. And mostly, I took those photographs to keep an eye on him!" his brother replied.

"I do *not* need you to watch over me, Jude! Or to—"

"Mumsy, tell me! Did Polinsky steal that amethyst choker I told you *I* wanted?"

Jason slipped behind his squabbling family and into the vestibule. God, but they squawked like a flock of magpies!

How had Maria tolerated so much contention—not to mention the *drama*—after the wedding was canceled, and while they were confined to the ship?

And yet when he'd cornered her about being Miss Crimson, she'd looked him square in the eye and admitted her double identity. None of Jemma's whining, or his mother's repositioning of the facts, or Jude's looking like a whipped dog. Maria had gazed up at him with those limpid brown eyes, imploring him to understand her side of the story.

And he'd rebuked her.

And, truth be told, he had *not* read any of Miss Crimson's columns. He'd listened when Jude or Jemma regaled him with the columnist's piercing insights into people he knew, but had considered himself above such inconsequential sensationalism.

Yet Maria Palladino was a *writer.* While everyone protested when she shoveled up the dirt on their family, who didn't secretly hope Miss Crimson would attend their next gala? It was a feather in anyone's cap when this mystery columnist singled them out for notice! Not only had Maria concealed her identity for these past years, she'd submitted her material right under his and Jude's noses. And they'd never guessed! And she'd supported herself with her writing! He thought very hard, but he didn't know of one other woman who'd paid her way in the world, dependent upon no one.

Not even you, boyo. She survived your absence, and she could still earn her living if you left her. Who are you fooling if you think Maria NEEDS you?

Jason headed for the staircase but something stopped him: in place of the traditional foxhunt painting above the credenza, he saw the most glorious portrait of Maria . . . waiting to be his bride. Jude had done an extraordinary job of capturing her coquettish smile and her glowing Italian complexion and the splendor of her ivory gown. The jeweled butterfly he'd given her shimmered around her graceful neck—a defiant refusal to wear the traditional pearls—but it was Maria Palladino herself who radiated such love and exquisite beauty. She gazed right at him, her brown eyes aglow with the anticipation—the joy—of becoming his wife. God, how he wished he would've been at the church that day!

And why had he gone missing? Last he remembered, he'd staggered into Amelia Beddow's brothel with his friends . . . must've succumbed to a drink she'd drugged . . . fell through a trap door with a frightened cry, and then landed in a heap on the deck of a waiting ship. That was how captains shanghaied crewmen: an ugly practice, and a fate he'd never dreamed would befall *him*.

He couldn't even recall if he'd sampled the madam's charms before he dropped. But as he gazed at this portrait of the woman he'd left standing at the altar, Jason felt like the lowest, most irresponsible—most reprehensible—kind of toad.

Was there a chance the fair princess would kiss him and turn him into her prince again?

He sighed and gazed up the stairway.

The doorbell chimed and before its sonorous tone had died, Quentin opened the door. "Well! A fine day it is, Mr. Palladino," he said pleasantly. "And good day to you, as well, Mr. Polinsky. Do come in."

Polinsky? What the hell was he doing out of jail? Jason nearly ducked into the kitchen to avoid them, but they'd already spotted him.

"We meet again," he observed in as even a tone as he could manage. Polinsky—or whatever his real name was—carried a wooden chest under one arm and, despite the way those biddies had pecked at him at Meriweather's, he looked unruffled. Undaunted by the accusations hurled at him before he'd gone to jail.

"We have reached an accord regarding Mr. Polinsky's *acquisition* of jewelry while he performs his magic," Rubio said with widened brown eyes . . . sensitive, soulful eyes like Maria's. "I hope you won't object if he's come to outline his plan for reparations."

What could it mean that Palladino, sun and moon apart from Polinsky in personality, asked this favor in his opponent's behalf? Jason suddenly felt so world weary, he didn't want to think about it. "Take your chances," he warned, nodding toward the nearest doorway. "We've had a lot of news to digest since the party."

"I—please excuse me for the uproar I have caused," the blue-eyed magician implored. "I cannot imagine how *unimpressed* you must be, as Pandora's oldest son."

Jason suppressed a smile. This fellow exuded a sense of derring-do and style most men would envy—if Polinsky wasn't seducing their mothers! "I don't have the last word, you know. Lady Darington is in the parlor."

He started up the stairway before they could detain him. Even when he hadn't been gazing at it, the portrait of Maria had watched him . . . worked on him from the inside out. It occurred to him that her sparkling smile, her playfulness, her refusal to be intimidated by a lewd, unshaven pirate, had awakened something in him even before he'd hit his head on that driftwood log.

True enough, she'd undone that lacy black camisole and her large, lovely breasts would've excited *any* man—but she'd crossed the ocean to find *him*. God love him, the sight of her skirt fluttering down her legs as she stumbled across the sand had whetted his sexual hunger, and he'd have followed her halfway across the planet to sate his appetite. His *need*.

Did that make him an animal? Or did he know before he surfaced from his mental oblivion that this was the woman he was destined to love? He paused at the top of the stairs. The door to Maria's room was ajar, enough that he could peer inside.

She was packing.

His heart slammed against his rib cage. Maria found it so intolerable here that she was leaving him without a word. Folding her clothes into her trunk without begging for another chance, the way Polinsky was. No hysterics. No hissy fits. Maria was moving out of his home, out of his life, because it seemed the practical, prudent thing for her to do.

And what did that say about *him?* Jason thought again of that glowing bridal portrait in the vestibule and he wanted to cry. What could he do to restore Maria Palladino's faith in him? How could he again become the man who made her radiate such love and anticipation and joy?

Jason stepped into his bedroom to catch his breath; to formulate loving, compelling phrases that would convince her to stay. Something on the nightstand caught his eye and he picked it up . . . the jeweled butterfly pendant. He closed his eyes against hot tears and clutched the piece so hard its prongs dug into his palm.

She didn't want his wedding gift, a piece she could sell for a pretty price. Or she could've returned it to Jude. He, at least, sounded supportive of Miss Crimson and the talent Maria had brought to her role as London's mystery columnist.

Jude won't waste a minute. When he sees Maria leaving, he'll claim her for himself. He'll know the right words, the right tone . . . those sensitive, sensual, sentimental things a woman wants to hear.

And when had *he* ever waxed sensitive or sentimental? Hell, he forged ahead like a steamship into battle, taking his pleasure—and taking it for granted that because Maria made those provocative noises, she, too, was caught up in the throes of his passion. When had he ever shown her tenderness, or wooed her with poetry, or—

Was that the closing of her door? How would she lug that

impossibly awkward trunk down the stairs? Jason surged
through the bathroom to catch her before she—

But she'd locked the door. From her room.

"Damn it, no!" He slapped the wood before he realized that
was the sort of stupidity that had gotten him into this mess.
"Maria, please! Open the door, darling! I—I need to beg your
forgiveness and apologize for all the—"

The door swung open and there she stood, wide-eyed.
Clutching her chemise to her chest, because she'd been . . .
changing her clothes. And she was . . . otherwise naked.

"God Almighty, woman," he breathed. "Why do you lead
me into such temptation when I'm trying to behave like a gentleman?"

Her neck constricted as she swallowed. "Jason?"

He almost gushed some sort of flowery nonsense, but
stopped short. That voice . . . it was coming to him . . .

"Are you all right?" she asked quietly. "You look like you've
seen a ghost."

"Your voice," he said in a strangled whisper. "It was the one
I heard calling my name while I was out of my head. I had no
idea why, or who you were. But that was *you* calling out to
me—"

"I prayed for you . . . talked to you. I missed you, Jason."

He squeezed his eyes shut. How did this woman so effort-
lessly disarm him? "I know that now. I'm not sure how you
and Rubio reached me, but the two of you kept me from going
beyond the point of no return," he murmured. "When I felt
helpless and lost, thwarted by Captain Dunner's malicious
tricks, you encouraged me! In my dreams! So I led the mutiny!
I—"

Jason halted. These were not the deeds of a brave, worthy
mate for the woman who stood before him . . . nearly naked.
God love him, as she clutched her filmy chemise to her chest,
her nipples beckoned him from either side of it. Yet her face

was a Madonna's, so devout and devoted. "I wrecked three Darington ships," he finished with a sigh. "And once again it was you and your brother who believed in me. Gave me the logic and words I needed, so O'Keefe would speak in my defense."

Still Maria watched him. What did she see? A man worth staying for? Or one who'd given her every good reason to leave?

"Maria," he rasped, his heart racing ahead of rational thought. "If I asked you again, this minute, would you still marry me?"

Maria's pulse thrummed and her heart sang to its beat, yet she faltered. If *no* came out too quickly, it was all over. She saw it written on Jason's weary face, along with that desperate hope that made him hold his breath, awaiting her answer.

God Almighty, he thought. *What have I done now? She's not answering me . . . Jude might as well waltz up here and claim her—*

"If you say yes," he blundered on, "I want you to stop—to stop being with Jude. As his lover. I don't intend to share you with anyone. Not anymore."

She clutched her chemise, aware that it was no disguise for her true feelings. Her nipples jutted out and her whole body tensed: he'd proposed to her again. But what was he asking?

Jason sighed. "After the way I spoke so harshly about Miss Crimson, I have no right to make demands—if you'll have me back. But I feel very strongly about this. I want you to be *my* wife. All mine."

Her heart thudded, but it was a steady, determined beat she had marched to all her life. It was the drum that propelled her forward, beyond doubts and failures and confrontations like the one she'd endured downstairs.

"And what about Miss Crimson?" Her voice sounded low

and clear. She stood straighter, aware of her power to make him crow—or crawl. "While you were gone, I considered letting her fade away, so I would have nothing to hide from you. But I've changed my mind."

His eyebrows lurched. His hand shot up, but stopped short of caressing her face. "Changed your mind about what?" he rasped.

"I *love* writing her column! I love the delicious invisibility of it!" she declared. "And I will stand on what I said before: I have *never* knowingly misrepresented what my subjects said or did. But if you—and your family—cannot accept me for who I am, then I don't belong here. *Do* I?"

The fingertip she pressed to his chest pierced his heart. "I—I can't answer for Mother—"

"Yes, you can, Lord Darington." She smiled bravely up at him, pushing her luck . . . pushing her finger in a gentle circle around his beating heart, hoping one word didn't shove him off the edge. "You will insist upon my continued anonymity, now that they know I'm Miss Crimson. And you will inform them that you support my choice to continue writing. I can forsake Jude, although he will be deeply disappointed, but I will not forsake myself. Agreed?"

Jason got swallowed up in her gaze. Felt the shift of focus and strength, as though the scales now tipped in her favor. "You'll no longer need the income, if you marry—"

"Money has nothing to do with it! Sometimes your family's money feels like a cumbersome load—although I understand why you must assume your father's title and become the man of this family." She smiled resolutely. "Lord knows you don't need *me* for that. You'd have a smoother row to hoe if Maria Palladino weren't a constant reminder to your mother of how you *lowered* yourself to—"

"*I* never said that!"

"Then be the man who's *proud* of my accomplishments!"

she challenged. "Be the husband who loves me more than his mother or his title—and who will inform his twin of the change in our arrangement! The Jason Darington *I* love would do that!"

Damn. She had indeed turned the tables. Would he be more the man if he insisted on his own way? And what would he gain if Maria lost her spirit? The career she'd come to love?

Look at her face and find your answer. She's made up her mind.

Jason cleared his throat. "What makes you so sure the *Inquirer* editor will have you back? It sounds like Quentin cooked your goose."

The solution to that quandary popped into her mind so fast, Maria grinned proudly. "He won't want Miss Crimson taking her audience to the *National Advocate*, will he? I might even demand a raise in pay if I stay!"

"As well you should!" He laughed in spite of the tension her single, circling finger caused him, the misery she inflicted with her flirtatious intelligence. "Your column helped locate me and announced my return, after all. It should be apparent to that editor how many strings you pull, how you remain aware of noteworthy situations yet remain invisible. Uninfluenced by those who would *pay* you to present their stories in a more favorable light, perhaps."

Maria considered this. She stopped drawing the circle and pressed her palm to Jason's solid chest. When his heartbeat assumed the light, steady rhythm of her own, she smiled. "You could be my partner, Jason. Your political clout and business associations could open a whole new avenue of social awareness that goes far beyond the soirees and teas Miss Crimson usually covers!"

Her excitement grabbed him—and then *she* did. Maria's hand closed around his balls and her gaze didn't waver. "But we must not reveal this to *anyone!*" she insisted. "Before Quentin stumbled upon my secret identity, Rubio was the only one who knew how I earned my rent—but then, my brother has other-worldly powers at his disposal."

"You think *I* can't transport you to another world, Maria?"

She sucked in her breath. Her bottomless brown eyes drank him in, and it was much more than the way he had hardened in her hand: he had played her game and then turned the tables. To make his point, he cupped her breasts, gazing relentlessly into her eyes. Demanding an answer.

"Make it worth my while to love only you, Jason. Prove that I'll no longer miss the man I can't have."

In one swift movement, he swept her into his arms. He tossed her onto her bed, and then yanked open the drawer of her nightstand. "If I have to bind you to the bed . . . fuck you to Kingdom Come," he rasped, "you will *never* be tempted to ball my brother again! You won't have the strength! Or the opportunity!" He deftly thrust her arms above her head and then wrapped the silk straps around her wrists. Seconds later she was tied to the bedpost.

Maria squirmed, resisting him. "What if one man's not enough? What if—what if I want you *and* Johnny Conn?"

"The pirate?" In the blink of his tawny eyes the transformation took place. "It's the discipline o' the ship yer wantin', is it? The way all who calls me *captain* must *obey* me every whim and demand?"

"Says *who?*" she countered saucily. "You might be in command of your ship, Conn, but *I*—Miss Crimson!—set the course for London's morning! Thousands reach for their newspapers to hang on my every word!"

"Well, goody fer *you!* Hang on *this!*" He stepped out of his pants and then sprang to the mattress to straddle her. "Wot ye see is wot ye get, missy! Can a mere writer like yerself handle all of it?"

Maria snickered. His long, lovely cock pointed at her as he unbuttoned his shirt. Gone were all signs that Jason had doubts—or would let his family interfere in their marriage. And who needed Lady Daringon or her other children? She had a man in her bed who was ready to play the game she loved best. And he'd called her a writer! "My pen is mightier than your sword, sir!" she quipped.

"Har! My tongue'll have you singin' a different hymn, missy!" Jason pivoted to plant his face between her legs, which he'd spread with his hands. At the first moist, warm probe of his tongue, Maria cried out. She writhed so hard the bed scraped the floor. Fueled by her response, the pirate rocked on his knees to give his licking more energy—and to kick up a suggestive racket that made them both laugh.

Maria couldn't hold still. With her hands bound, her only recourse was to squirm and kick and buck, so Jason complied by delving deeper inside her with his thrusting tongue. His muscled backside flexed, inches in front of her face, and his bobbing balls and cock made her strain to catch them in her mouth. "Damn you, Conn! Let me play, too!"

"Aarrgh! It's *me* wot's callin' the shots now, wicked wench," he growled from between her legs. "Ye'll just have to suffer! Or beg fer mercy!"

"I'm finished begging!" she rasped as he plunged into her slit again. "I'm demanding! I'm ordering you to plunder and pillage, pirate. Miss Crimson has her pick of dozens of—oh, Jesus! *Jason!*"

He'd slipped a finger, then two, into her aching hole while he tickled her clit with the tip of his tongue. Maria nearly flew to the ceiling, the sensations felt so intense. She writhed, mindless, beneath his relentless teasing, until her body bucked of its own accord. "Oh . . . oh! Please, Jason, don't—"

"Is that the sound o' beggin' I hear?"

"—don't you dare stop!" she finished hoarsely. "Turn around and finish me the way you want to, Conn! If you make me come now, I'll not be offering any consolation prizes."

"Har! Yer a prize if ye think I'm fallin' fer *that* weak-kneed excuse!" One last time he wiggled his tongue in her slit and then licked it from end to end, ever so lightly, to drive her insane. He so loved it when she lost control . . . even though Maria Palladino would always know exactly how to pull his strings. And he could live with that—if she would live with him.

She was panting for it now, nearly convulsing. Jason knew her sweet body so intimately, he lithely switched his position. "Look at me when I'm fuckin' ye," he commanded in a guttural voice. "I wanna watch yer eyes pop outta yer head when Blackbeard takes ye prisoner. It's my name yer gonna be screamin' fer the rest o' yer days, wench. Savvy?"

Maria gawked at him, too far gone to protest. Her hips arched to capture the prize he dangled just above them—a fine, feisty sight from this angle, too. "Dip your pen in my well, sir, or there'll be no ink to sign that marriage certificate. And *then* you'll miss me! *Savvy?*"

"Aarghhhhh! Ye drive a hard bargain, wench."

"You drive a pretty hard"—Maria locked her legs around his hips—"bargain yourself, Lord Darington."

Jason inhaled fiercely. His eyes devoured her and his breath came in accelerating gasps. With his chestnut hair flying wildly around his ears and his lips glistening with her dew, he looked so randy, so ready. He smelled of her sex and his own male need. Maria knew she'd agree to anything if he'd look at her this way for the rest of her life.

"Take me, Jason," she whispered desperately. "I never wanted to leave, you know."

With a grimace of victory he lost himself inside her. So warm and wet and tight she was, he nearly climaxed with his first thrust. Many times he'd played with Maria this way, but this time his hunger went far beyond her bed and body: he wanted her mind and soul now, too. He eased into a quick but controlled rhythm, rocking high and hard against her. "Get ready."

"Eyes wide," she countered, matching her thrusts to his. "We're entering into this bargain looking straight at each other. No one else."

"Just the four of us," he grunted. "You and me, Crimson and Conn."

He convulsed and Maria sucked air to keep from screaming. She reveled in the power and beauty of the man who was making her his woman, on her terms. Then she surrendered to the spasms that quaked inside her. "You and me," she rasped. "Crimson and Conn."

34

"Mother. Everyone," Jason said with a nod to all at the dining room table. "Maria and I have come to terms. We will set a new wedding date when—"

"Terms?" Lady Darington arched an eyebrow. "We left the parlor, fearing the bed would come through the ceiling. Which tells me you gave in to your animal urges and let her lead you by the—"

"Something other than his nose," Jude said under his breath. Rubio choked on a laugh while Jemma rolled her eyes and crossed her arms. Seated beside Dora, Yosef Polinsky watched them closely. Perhaps savoring his own secret.

Jason held her hand in the crook of his arm, smiling confidently at her. "Maria has agreed to be my wife—again," he said with a fleeting glance at his brother. "And she will cleave to me, forsaking all others, as we will vow before God and everyone at the ceremony."

"What a novel idea! Jude is so happy for you—aren't you, son?" Lady Darington rose from her chair with a sly smile. "Now, if you'll excuse us, Yosef and I have notes to write.

We're going to Wildwood where we won't be disturbed by lewd noises."

The steely-haired medium nodded to them, picked up the small wooden chest, and escorted Pandora from the room. Their whispers and sly laughter floated behind them, and then the dining room went silent. All that remained on the tea tray were crumbs and their dirty cups.

"My best wishes to both of you," Rubio finally offered. He stood to kiss Maria and shake Jason's hand. "Order is restored. All's well that's ending well, as I'd predicted. And we have a bit of news ourselves."

Maria observed each of them carefully: Jemma cradled Willie on her shoulder, lost in her bitter thoughts; Jude stood, stuffing his hands in his pockets, concealing the dejection she'd expected. Her heart went out to him, but it belonged completely to Jason now. In time, she hoped to convince Jude he deserved a woman who could give herself to him completely, but he'd endured all he could handle for one day.

"I might as well be going," he murmured.

"One other point to make, now that Polinsky's gone." Jason smiled. "Quentin and Mrs. Booth? You might as well join us, as this concerns you, too."

The two servants came from behind the folding Chinese screen that concealed the entry to the kitchen. "My congratulations to you," the housekeeper chirped. "Not that any of us are surprised."

"Not at all," the young butler agreed. "But I'm still sorry I made a mess of—"

Jason held up his hand. "Miss Crimson and I have put our heads together—"

Jemma groaned dramatically.

"—and we agree she is to pursue her career—*anonymously*, as before," Jason insisted. "We have even discussed broadening her—"

"There's a baby? *That* was quick!" Mrs. Booth quipped.

"—horizons to cover other segments of society with her razor wit, and to publish serializations of novels," Jason announced proudly. "Her column in the *Inquirer* is only the beginning! Miss Crimson has much bigger fish to fry!"

"Is *that* what I smell?" Jemma remarked. When she saw Quentin was gazing at her, however, she straightened her shoulders and thrust out her small breasts.

"Better and better, as I predicted," Rubio said with a nod. "And you two should know that Dora and Yosef have come to terms, as well. He has asked her to help him write apologies and return the various pieces of jewelry he kept as mementos from his . . . previous conquests. Dora will then have the pleasure of setting fire to his address book."

"I suggested she allow a cooling-off period," Jude remarked with a resigned laugh. "But you know how Mum responds when others tell her what to do."

"She does what she damn well wants to," Jemma replied tartly. "I swear to God if I have to remain in that house, with so much kissing and giggling and squealing, I'll absolutely vomit on them!"

Quentin, who had sidled nearer to her—probably to peer down her cleavage—looked suddenly stricken. "Perhaps the answer is to go elsewhere, Miss Darington," he suggested quietly. "I'm sure your mother and Polinsky would prefer it."

Jemma considered this, then flashed him a coquettish grin. "And would *you* prefer it, Quentin? I've always valued the advice of . . . older, more experienced men."

"Saints preserve us, " Mrs. Booth muttered. As she spun around to return to the kitchen, the young butler bowed.

"I'm here to serve, Miss Darington."

When Quentin, too, retired from the dining room, Rubio chuckled. He stretched like a languid cat, making the moon-and-stars print of his shirt shimmer in the light from the chandelier. "It's so gratifying when my predictions come to pass—right, dear sister? Sexual ecstasy and joy, juxtaposed with excruciating pain. Deception, yet revelation," he mused fondly. "A journey into the unknown for all of us. And once the unknown becomes the known, we begin afresh."

The medium slung his arm around Jude. "Would you care to stop by my apartment above the Bentleys' dress shop? You and Jemma can stay the night there—but meanwhile, the new moon's calling me to pop a cork and consider my next journey. And perhaps yours, my friend."

Rubio waved good-bye to Jason and blew Maria a kiss. When he grinned at Jemma, beckoning her with his eyes, the gold ring in his nose glimmered like a promise. "There's a pub down the way, where artists and writers and dancers go to tip a pint. A fine, feisty crowd—and several of them are women! I think you'll . . ."

Maria laughed softly as the front door closed behind the three of them. "Well, milord, that leaves just you and me here at the town house—"

"Home. Where we belong." Jason reached into his pocket and pulled out the jeweled pendant. He fastened its clasp behind her neck, and then gently positioned the butterfly above her collarbone. "Just the four of us. You and me—"

"With Crimson and Conn," Maria whispered. "Sounds like the perfect blend of fantasy and reality, doesn't it?"

Jason kissed her, and she had all the answer she'd ever need.